ALL ON THE LINE

A Denver BANDITS NOVEL

LO EVERETT

Lo Everett

https://loeverettbooks.my.canva.site/

FOREWORD

Lo, I'm always going to be blown away by your creativity, determination, and ability to function on no sleep. I assume no sleep based on how hard you work as a mom, career woman, and now author. And how fast you read the entire ACOTAR series (I'll never get over that). I'm forever grateful for your friendship, snark, and love of adventure (fuck the Porkies, though). This book is a tribute to your love of spice and our friend group's shenanigans, and I laughed throughout its entirety. I love where this journey is taking you; it is just the beginning.

Katie Hernke

Lo's very first reader and the one who told me to do the damn thing.

DEDICATION

To the hype women who make us believe anything is possible.
You are the real heroines. Without you, dreams don't come true.
Especially Katie, Nyk, Kendl, and Anna. Love you all!

"Anything is possible when you have the right people there to support you." — **Misty Copeland**

CHAPTER 1

HENDRIX

BANG. BANG. BANG.

The wall behind the bed rattles, waking me from my pregame nap. I rub my hands down my face scratching the coarse hair on my jaw as the noise reverberates through the wall again. Groaning out loud, I roll over to my back. These wake-up calls have become an almost daily occurrence. They're throwing my whole routine off. And as a professional athlete, I rely on a strict routine to help keep me healthy and sane. This is the third time it has woken me up from a pregame nap this week alone. *Fucking enough already.*

My skin is prickling with the anxiety of knowing I'm dealing with another interruption to my gameday schedule. My patience is fading fast. This apartment was supposed to be my oasis away from the stadium, but the noises coming from next door are getting old.

I looked at dozens of places before finding this one. I was thrilled when the realtor called with the listing boasting about the floor-to-ceiling windows overlooking the Rockies. She excitedly prattled on about the location and natural lighting. It was perfect for me, spacious enough for when my family is in town, and an easy walk to the stadium. All things that were important to me. Some of my teammates have pretty extravagant places, but that's never been my style.

The photos she sent lived up to the hype, so I cut my workout short and made an offer on the spot. It was exactly what I was looking for on paper, but the listing didn't include a warning about the lack of insulation between the neighboring apartment.

Reaching my arm out, I tug the spare pillow over my head and check the watch on my other wrist. Two o'clock. I groan into the pillow. I need to be at the stadium in less than two hours for batting practice before our home opener tonight. As if the pressure of performing on a new team isn't enough, now my neighbor's very healthy sex life is fucking with my routine.

I use my arm to secure the pillow over my ear, pulling it tight with my bicep to drown out the sound. Readjusting the covers with my other hand, I settle back into bed to try and fall back asleep. I focus on breathing. My thoughts shift to Nana and what she would say if she witnessed my tantrum to this afternoon's intrusion on my nap.

I'm not judging my neighbor's sex life, but it's a huge inconvenience to be woken when she decides she's in the mood midafternoon. Internally I laugh, albeit slightly bitter, at the lecture I would get from my grandmother if I passed judgment on someone for their sexuality.

My mother, barely an adult then, dropped us, leaving my grandmother to raise two kids under the age of two. Nana is one of the most sex-positive people I've ever met. She never shied away from uncomfortable conversations with me or my sister. My grandmother also ensured that regardless of our gender, the expectations were the same. Her attitudes toward sex and gender impacted who I'm as an adult and how I treat women.

My anger isn't based on my neighbor's body count or kinks. I'd just really love to be able to sleep. I'm not sure if this girl works nights or if the need just hits midday. Maybe it's my schedule that's the problem. As a baseball player, I'm home during the day. With the travel my job requires and the physical demands of playing at the highest level, I need to stick to a set plan on game days. Wake up, eat, run, lift, nap, pack my bag for the game, eat, practice, and play. It's served me well over the years, and right now, my nap is not happening.

The pillow muffles the noises coming from next door, where my mystery neighbor is exuberantly going at it. It's not enough to drown out the moaning from the other side of the wall.

And what the hell is that — meowing?

Is she purring like a cat? *Hmmm — not something I'm into — but good for her.*

The bed bounces off the wall in quick succession again. I slide my back up the headboard and let the covers pool around my hips. The sounds coming through the wall grow louder and more urgent.

My arm reaches across to the nightstand where I started keeping noise-canceling headphones since I moved in a month ago. Just as I'm about to slip the headphones on, I hear my neighbor cry out. Her voice breathy and ethereal, "Yes... Yes, you big bad tomcat. I love it when you touch me like that. Your fur is so soft when you rub against me." She groans loudly. "Right there. Oh fuck, I — I'm coming. *Purrrrr.*"

Even my open-minded Nana would have a hard time keeping a straight face for that one. The back of my fist comes up to stifle a laugh, remembering that if I can hear her, chances are high that she can hear me too.

Should it alarm me that I found her voice so enticing, given the context?

Even through the wall, I can tell it's got a sultry quality to it. She sounds like one of my sister's audiobooks. Her voice is slightly deep and smooth in a way that makes it undeniably sexy. Rubbing my eye with the heel of my hand and forcing my shoulders to relax against the headboard, I sigh, resigning myself to being awake.

I recheck my watch, and I only have twenty-five minutes left before I need to eat and get ready to leave for the stadium. I pull the leather strap free of its buckle and rub my thumb over the worn inscription on the back, "Believe in the beauty of your dreams. Love you the most. — Nana."

I can still picture the tears shining in her pale blue eyes and her hand trembling as she handed me the small box wrapped in black paper. Her voice shook as she fought through the emotion clogging her throat, telling me how proud she was on my graduation day. We both knew the odds were against me from the moment my mom realized she was pregnant. Had they left me with any other guardian, the outcome would not have been the same. My grandmother went above and beyond to show us unconditional love. There was no doubt that she wanted us, regardless of how she became our sole parent.

Refastening my watch as I push off the bed, and shuffle across the cool wood floors to the Denver Bandits duffle bag. It's packed on the armchair by the window with my clothes for the evening folded neatly next to it. Grabbing a pair of black joggers from the chair, I push my feet into them more aggressively than necessary.

Frustrated that my routine is thrown off, I pull them roughly up my legs, letting them rest low on my hips. I comb through my hair with my fingers and head to the kitchen to grab a prepared meal from the fridge.

I'm so cranky from my unexpected wake-up call that I don't even wait for my meal to cool after I pull it from the microwave and play hot potato with it before dropping it on the kitchen island. Lesson learned, I manage to eat without searing my tastebuds off, and go through the rest of my routine before heading out the door to meet my teammate, Cruz.

It's still brisk even though the sun is shining, making it look like a much warmer day. I'm learning that spring in Denver can be deceiving that way. I opted for a pair of slim-fit black jeans with a forest-green Henley and a black leather jacket. Comfortable enough for the walk and just warm enough to chase away the chill in the air. As the elevator doors slide open and I step inside, my phone buzzes in the pocket of my jeans.

CRUZ:
Outside. Should I wait or walk?

HENDRIX:

Incoming. We can walk together. I need coffee. Didn't get a full nap.

CRUZ:

The neighbor at it again?

HENDRIX:

You know it. This time she was a cat or pretending to be with a cat. Who knows. It was a new experience for me.

CRUZ:

File that under shit I never thought my teammates would text me.

I slide the phone back into the front pocket of my jeans and adjust the duffle bag on my shoulder. The elevator doors open to the sleek lobby, and I make my way to meet Cruz. Marv, the security guard for our building, sits at the desk. I give him a nod and smile. It's not his fault my neighbor has noisy midday sex.

"What you got for me today, Marv?"

"Milwaukee Bucks by six over the Knicks," Marv states, the corner of his lips twitching up while his weathered face remains stoic.

Pausing, I playfully clutch my heart. "Why you gotta do me dirty? Making me bet against my team." The corners of his lips rise into a full smile now as he brushes some invisible lint off his black suit. There's a teasing gleam in his eyes. He's clearly playing the game with me. "What's the wager?"

"One of Miss Lilah's *Orange-you-Glad* scones."

"This one hurts. I'm not even sure I'll be able to enjoy a scone if it's soaked in the salt of my own tears from a Knick's loss that I bet on." Shaking my head, I push through the doors and look over my shoulder toward the security desk. "You're on, Marv."

"Hit one out of there tonight, Hen." he states with a wave. "I'll be watching."

I duck in a quick nod as I join Cruz on the busy downtown sidewalk. It's midafternoon, but the sidewalk is full of people in a hurry and dressed for the workday. Most of them are probably rushing to meetings or back to the office after a late lunch. We get a few curious looks, but no one stops us as we head toward the stadium.

"Coffee?" Cruz questions without taking his eyes off the phone in his hand.

"Sure, we have time," I remark checking the time. "Cold brew, please."

Cruz's fingers move along his keyboard texting his friend Lilah, the owner of Buns and Roses. He pockets his phone, glancing over at me with a sly smile lighting up his dark brown eyes.

"So, we are cheering for the Bucks today?"

"Absolutely not," I scoff. "I'd buy Marv a thousand scones before I'd stoop that low."

Cruz is a step ahead of me and reaches out to open the door to Buns and Roses, the coffee shop down the street. The scent of coffee and baked goods are heavy in the air. From what Cruz has told me, Lilah built this place from the ground up. The whole place seems to radiate her personality and taste.

Everything from the textured white-and-black tile on the wall to the trinkets and plants that line the floating wood shelves. The centerpiece is a retro jukebox that plays music selected by customers.

"Two cold brews coming right up," Lilah croons. Aerosmith plays in the background as she comes through the open archway from the back of the shop. A strand of blonde hair falls loose from the messy bun as she shimmies her way around the counter.

"Are my two favorite ballers going to kick the season off with a win tonight?" she questions looking up at Cruz through her eyelashes. Her lips quirk up just enough to convey the teasing in her tone.

Reaching out to grab his coffee with one hand, Cruz brushes off some flour that's clinging to her black vintage Denver Bandits shirt, letting his hand linger longer than needed. Her shirt is cut into a crop top, exposing a sliver of skin above her leggings with the apron folded down and cinched around her hips.

"That's the plan. Hen here has to hit one out of the park for Marv," Cruz offers, taking my cold brew from Lilah and passing it to me.

"Thanks, Lilah. If we win tonight, we will have to stop and order the same drink before every home game." I raise the cup for my first taste and savor the subtle sweetness of vanilla. "Damn, this is good. There are worse superstitions."

"I suppose." She nods as the door chimes, and Lilah's blue eyes shift behind us.

"Are you sure you're ready for that?" I question, catching sight of the woman approaching in the reflection of a coffee machine behind Lilah. "That's an awful lot of time to spend with this guy." I joke, my attention is glued to the redhead's reflection, but Lilah's focus shifts back to Cruz and me.

Lilah quirks a brow and lifts her fist to rest under her chin and elbows propped on the worn butcher block countertops. She pretends to ponder and her head tilts to the side as she sighs. "That would be a lot to ask of anyone."

"*Delilah*, I thought we were friends." Cruz teases using her full name.

Giggles fill the air as Lilah comes around the counter and wraps her arms around Cruz's waist. The other woman gives Cruz a side hug joining the conversation.

"Don't go getting all grumbly. You know how much Lilah loves having you around," the redhead says pointing her thumb at Lilah, whose cheeks are tinged pink. "Someday I'll knock you off that best friend pedestal and take your spot,"

I shift my body and prop my hip on the front counter, content to watch the show. Cruz has his arm draped around the shoulder of the most stunning woman I've ever seen.

Her long coppery red hair is twisted into two loose braids that disappear behind her slender shoulders. She has brilliant green eyes framed by thick lashes with freckles dancing across her cheekbones and nose. I'm almost stunned speechless until I hear Cruz's voice pulling my attention back to him.

"Poppy, this is Hendrix James. The guys on the team call him Hen. He was just traded to Denver from Los Angeles in the offseason," he explains removing his arm so she can step forward to wrap Lilah in a hug.

Poppy gives me a warm smile over her friend's shoulder. Her eyes twinkle like there's no place she would rather be than here with Lilah.

"Nice to meet you, Hen." Poppy beams. Her arms fall to her sides causing her wide-neck shirt to slip down to reveal a tattooed shoulder. My gaze traces her shoulder up to the lace bra strap resting along the gentle slope of her neck and back to her eyes.

"I stopped in to feed the babies," she explains, turning back toward Lilah.

"*The babies*?" I wonder aloud, running my hand along the stubble on my jaw.

My gaze darts between the three of them. Like there's a secret love child somewhere in the coffee shop that no one has told me about. I'm always jumping to the worst possible conclusion. It's a side effect of my trust being repeatedly broken from an early age.

"Yep," Poppy exclaims, popping the P and pointing toward the shelves behind the counter lined with plants. "Plant babies."

I'm not a plant guy in the sense that most people who love plants appreciate all things horticulture. I only love my plants because the sentiment behind them. When I was called up to the majors, my nana started bringing me a plant with every visit. My attachment to them has nothing to do with clean air or a green thumb and everything to do with the woman who raised me.

"You know where the watering can is, get to work, my little plant whisperer." Lilah laughs as Poppy heads around the counter.

I've had beautiful women throw themselves at me and my teammates in some unique and crazy ways. Of all the things I've seen, Poppy bending over to grab the watering can from the bottom cupboard might be the one that causes my heart to stop.

Her tight, worn black jeans mold to her body, showcasing the curve of her ass and hips until they stop right above her ankles. The look is casual and laidback when paired with her purple Chuck Taylors, braids, and a white off-the-shoulder shirt. As she leans forward to grab the can, her shirt slips up an inch, revealing a peek of skin hinting at how her curves narrow in at her waist. She is one hundred percent my type. I have to look away before I end up with a semi from the spectacular view in front of me.

"Ready, Cruz?" I ask checking the time as a distraction.

Looking up from the quiet conversation he's having with Lilah, he nods and pulls her in for a quick hug before laying a quick kiss on the top of her head. "Are you coming after you close up?" he asks before letting her go.

"Of course, I wouldn't miss it. This totally average looking, kind of okayish player gifted me a pair of tickets." Lilah's voice is dancing with mirth as she gives Cruz a hard time like it's her job.

"*Okayish? Average looking?* Careful, Lilah, you might hurt my delicate man-feelings." Cruz shoots her a sly smile as he follows me through the coffee shop.

"I was being generous," Lilah throws the barb right back.

"Take an Uber so you aren't walking alone." Cruz's brows furrow suddenly more serious. Lilah nods in return as we push through the door.

"Hey, Baller!" Lilah calls out. "Prove me wrong and earn your spot as my favorite Bandit tonight."

Cruz smirks back at her and waves as we step outside to finish our walk to the stadium.

"Are you sure you and Lilah are just friends?" I question, looking over my cup at my friend. "You've never crossed that line?"

"No. We haven't," he says clipped, his coffee free hand comes up to tug on his neck.

"You want to."

"*Wanted to*. We were both going through some things when we met, and the timing was off. She was the first person outside the team I connected with when I moved here. Jarrett had just passed away, and she was the brightest spot in my day. Baseball kept me moving forward, but she made the sun shine again." He doesn't elaborate and pulls his hat down focusing his attention forward. I don't believe for a second that he isn't still interested but I take his cue let the conversation drop.

I push my wet hair back off my forehead and emerge from the shower. My towel secured tightly around my waist, I walk through the steam and post-game chatter of the locker room.

I reach my locker to grab my phone, checking my messages I see several notifications.

NANA:

So proud of you, Hendrix. That homer in the 3rd inning really turned it around. And that catch in the 9th... You almost gave this old lady a coronary. Still on for our call?

HENDRIX:

Wouldn't miss it for the world... and you're not that old.

NANA:

I ain't no spring chicken.

"Hey, Hen. Are you heading to Draft?" Dean, our first baseman asks. A bunch of the guys are heading to a local bar to celebrate our first win of the season. And what a win it was, Dean hit a walk-off home run to beat our divisional rivals.

"Sure, man. I have to make a quick call and I'll meet you guys there." He pats my shoulder as he walks past.

I check the locker room, looking for a clear training room or office I can duck into. When I find Dean over my shoulder, he's fussing with his hair in the mirror attached to his locker door styling it so it's just the way he likes it.

"We have a few tables they rope off in the back. See you there," Dean says, swinging his locker door closed.

Making my way across the locker room to the empty trainers' office, I pull my shirt over my still damp hair and secure my watch on my wrist. Scanning the small space for a place to sit, I perch on the edge of the training table and hit the contact for my grandma.

"Hey, Henny," she greets me as she answers.

"Hey, Nana. How's your night going?"

"It would be better if you turned on FaceTime."

"I'm in the locker room. I'm not sure my teammates would appreciate that."

She huffs. "I know. Why do you think I asked? I was hoping to catch sight of a baseball butt... maybe more..." She's as mischievous as always, her voice light and right on the edge of laughter as she talks to me.

I glance around the locker room, which is mostly cleared out. There's nothing to see in my background besides a black brick wall with posters of the human musculoskeletal form behind me, so I switch the call over to FaceTime.

"That isn't the anatomy I was hoping to see," she grumbles, her lips pulling down into a brief frown before shifting her attention from the posters behind me back to my face.

Her clear blue eyes light up when they connect with mine. "You wouldn't want to flip that camera around for me, would you? As much as I love seeing your face, even us old ladies can appreciate the male specimen at its peak... so gimme a peek?"

"Are you trying to get me in trouble?"

"No, no. Me? Never, I'm a perfect angel." She laughs, knowing she's the dirtiest bird in her retirement community. "I suppose I could deal with looking into those baby blues instead."

She's never let me off easy, thriving on busting my balls while simultaneously making sure I know I'm loved and wanted.

"An angel with the mind of a teenage boy," I tease, using the window as a mirror to comb through my hair with my fingers.

"Are you primping while you talk to me?" Her eyebrow raises in question. "Do you have plans with the team tonight? Or —"

I cut her off before she can start meddling in my nonexistent love life. The woman is a saint for stepping in when my mom checked out on the parenting gig, but that doesn't give her an all-access pass to be nosy.

"I'm meeting some of the guys at a bar down the street from the stadium for some food. Are you going to bingo tonight?"

"Of course. It's ladies' night, and Anderson RSVP'd on Facebook. Last time I sat next to him, I got lucky." A coy smile passes over her face, then she gives me a teasing wink. Sharing is not caring in this case.

I run my hand down my face and look at her through my fingers. "I'm just going to let myself believe you are talking about your bingo winnings."

"Whatever helps you sleep at night, dear. Have fun. You know I will."

"Just try not to have too much fun and be safe. Text me when you are tucked in."

"Always. Love you, Henny. You played really well tonight. I'm proud of you." She fluffs her sleek silver hair and brings her signature hot pink lipstick up to line her lips.

"Love you too, Nana. You look beautiful. Knock them dead."

"I like my men alive and kicking — and that's too real a possibility at my age. Don't jinx me." She laughs, puckering her lips together and appraising herself in the camera before ending the call.

The hostess at Draft points me to the back corner, where I see several of my teammates huddled around high-top tables and a small corner bar that has a dedicated bartender. Weaving my way through the crowd of fans coming from the game, I pull my hat low hoping that I can make it to the back without getting swarmed. When I feel a tug on my arm, I prepare myself with a smile for the fan that I'm sure is looking for a selfie or autograph.

I glance back, and I'm pleased that Lilah is the fan in question.

"Hey, Lilah. Did you walk over with Cruz?" I ask, pulling her to my side for a quick squeeze.

"Poppy and I used the family pass he gave us and waited for him after the game. He insisted we walk over together," she explains, brushing her long blonde ponytail over her shoulder as we make our way through the crowd.

I nod, not the least bit surprised. Lilah brings out Cruz's protective side. I still haven't figured out if that's a side effect from losing Jarrett or something directly related to the woman at my side.

"It's like the man can't fathom that I navigated this city for years on my own before he showed up."

"He just wants to make sure you're safe, Lilah. You're special to him. And after his brother — his people are just really important to him. You're one of his people." Cruz and I haven't known each other for long, but we learned a lot about each other as roommates during spring training. He's quickly become a good friend.

She nods. Sadness and maybe longing flash in her eyes but disappears just as quickly when she covers it with a big smile and points to where Poppy and Cruz are sitting.

As I lead Lilah toward the back, I see Cruz and Poppy tucked into the corner of the bar. She throws her head back laughing, her puffy pink lips slightly parted. Silky red braids stick out from under her Bandits hat and trail down her back. She looks just as gorgeous as she did this morning — not overdone with makeup or dressed to kill. Poppy doesn't need all that glitz and glamour to look sexy as hell. Her personality exudes fun and confidence. It draws me right in — wanting to get closer and know more.

"What's the story there?" I ask Lilah, nodding toward where they sit.

"Poppy?" she says confusion crossing her face. "Like Poppy and Cruz? Or..."

"You and Poppy, how'd you meet?" Relief crosses her face like the idea of Poppy and Cruz distresses her.

"We bonded over coffee and dirty jokes."

"This I need to hear. My nana tells the dirtiest jokes." Stepping up to the bar, I push my sleeves up a few inches and rest my forearms on the cement bar top and signal the server with my other hand.

"The first time Poppy stopped in for coffee, she caught me with swollen eyes from crying over a breakup. She told me a joke to cheer me up," Lilah explains, glancing across the bar at her friend. A smile tilts her lips. "What's the difference between an 'oooh' and an 'aaah'?"

"Hmmm... not sure, what is it?"

"About three inches." A laugh rumbles from my chest. Lilah waits for me to gather myself before continuing. "A penis joke started it all. She stopped in every day for the next two weeks with a new joke to cheer me up and check in on me." Her smile turns from playful to sweet.

"Sounds like she's one of the good ones," I muse as the bartender approaches asking for our order and then handing off our beers.

"The best. Between her and Cruz, they made sure to get me out of my funk. I'm not sure my heart would've fully healed without their friendship."

I can see that with Cruz. When one of the guys is having a rough game, he's the first one to hype them back up. Being traded to a new team is disruptive. Finding your groove with your teammates and building a new friend group can be a challenge. I really lucked out with my trade. Cruz and I bonded, and my friendship with him means there's a good group of people like Lilah to keep me grounded. That was missing with my last team, so I'm thankful to have found it here.

We make our way past several teammates stopping briefly to say hello and move to the corner to join Poppy and Cruz.

"Lilah tells me you are the queen of dirty jokes," I challenge grabbing the seat next to Poppy. She looks fucking good tonight. Still wearing the same black jeans and Chuck Taylors as earlier but she changed into a cropped tank top under an oversized teal-and-black flannel with the Bandits logo across the back.

"I have been known to tell a dirty joke or two." Poppy leans in, crooking her finger at me and drawing me forward.

The look she gives me tells me she doesn't know how not to have a little fun. "What did Cinderella do when she got to the ball?"

Taking a drink of my beer, I think about it for a minute. "She's the one that turns into a pumpkin at midnight, right?"

Poppy nods and lifts her glass nonchalantly to take a drink. "She gagged." A slow smile takes over her face as she innocently twirls a braid between her fingers like she didn't just drop a filthy joke about a fairy-tale character. My fingers itch to feel the silky hair slip through my hands as I tug on those braids.

"Sounds like she needs more practice," I say before I can think better of it. I brace for Poppy's reaction, expecting her to recoil at my crudeness.

She grabs a napkin and covers her mouth. "Warn a girl, Hendrix. My beer almost came out my nose. I love a good one-liner as much as the next girl, but it's not worth snorting my drink."

After Poppy recovers from her near miss with the beer snort, we talk about the game and how I'm adjusting to the city. Several teammates and their significant others drift in and out of our conversation as they stop by. Poppy asks questions about how I have been spending my time outside of baseball. We talk about our favorite places to hike outside the city and find common ground in chasing down new adventures.

"Have you ever tried urban hiking?" I ask as Poppy raises an eyebrow. "I know it sounds dumb. One of my teammates in LA made me try it with him. The idea is to simulate a regular nature hike while exploring a city. You plan out a route that includes stairs, parks, and walking paths to see new parts of the city."

"Okay, that makes sense. What kinds of things did you explore in LA on your *urban hike*?" she replies clearly intrigued but still carrying some skepticism in her voice.

"Mostly architecture and outdoor sculptures. He was trying to plan a date for this girl he was seeing and made me his guinea pig," I explain with a shrug. "I learned a lot, and I made him buy me lunch, as a gentleman does on a date."

"As one does," Poppy echoes. "You basically got a free date out of your buddy. That didn't emasculate you or anything?" she says in a teasing tone. I like that she isn't afraid to bust my balls a little. Most of the women I have met shy away from giving me a hard time or trying too hard to impress me. She's just effortlessly herself.

"Absolutely not. There's nothing more manly than being a good friend. Give me a trophy for being the world's best wingman," I insist playfully. Poppy laughs at my ridiculousness. The more she laughs, the more I crave it.

After an hour, we put Poppy and Lilah in an Uber back to their respective apartments. The early hours of the coffee shop caused Lilah to yawn earlier than most. Lilah tried to convince Poppy to stay, but she refused to let her leave alone.

Rejoining a few remaining teammates at the high-top table, we share orders of wings and appetizers as we talk through our upcoming schedules and travel plans.

"Braxton, were you able to find a dog walker for Tiny?" Dean asks our rookie pitcher about his not-even-remotely small Saint Bernard.

Nodding, Braxton wipes wing sauce from the corners of his mouth. "The neighbor has a teenage son looking to earn some cash for college. He's going to walk him during road trips."

"You live close to us. Think he'd want to water some plants for me?" I take a sip of beer to wash down the wings. The idea of having a stranger in my apartment makes my skin crawl, but it's unavoidable with my job. The amount I travel during the season means regardless of my issues, I have to suck it up. I'd rather it be somebody one of the guys know than a random person.

"I can check. He's in wrestling and I know his schedule is packed already but college is expensive."

"You should have Poppy do it. She takes care of all the plants for Lilah and has kept them alive so far. She doesn't live far from you," he interjects, looking pleased with himself and the suggestion.

"There, I sent you her number. She's changing careers and saving up money before she makes the transition."

My phone vibrates in my pocket. When I pull it out, I see the contact info from Cruz and a picture my nana sent. She's pretending to sleep, and thankfully she's alone in bed. Although, I wouldn't be surprised if she made her partner hide under the blankets while she sent me proof of life.

"You really think she'd be interested? She's not going to sell my used cup on eBay or anything?" I ask dryly.

I like Poppy. She seems funny and down for a good time, but I don't really know her. And letting her into my apartment without some reassurance makes me hesitate. My privacy is important to me and no one besides my family and

Cruz has been inside my new apartment. I was burned in the past when I let people get too close.

"Yeah, man. She's totally cool. Not even a hint of under-wear sniffer in that one."

My eyebrows bunch together, and I glare across the table at him. "If she's a nutjob I'm coming after you," I threaten more serious than I let on. Cruz is aware that I have issues with people in my space and I know he wouldn't put me in a position to be taken advantage of again. The fact that he's willing to vouch for Poppy helps ease some of my concerns over allowing her into my space.

Beer and wings gone, I pocket my phone and pull out my wallet. I lay down enough cash to cover my part of the tab and a generous tip.

"I'll text her tomorrow. I'm heading out. You don't get this good-looking without enough beauty sleep," I deadpan gesturing to my face.

CHAPTER 2

POPPY

Last night was the most fun I've had in a while, starting from the game and ending in drinks at Draft with the team. The energy at the game was electric, and when Dean hit that walk-off home run crowd noise was enough to make my insides vibrate. Once we got to the bar, conversation and laughter were flowing along with the celebratory drinks. When it was time to get Lilah home, I was struggling with a serious case of FOMO.

We've been best friends for almost three years and there isn't much I wouldn't do for her. Ever since I walked into her coffee shop and found her with bloodshot eyes, clearly going through something, I defaulted to humor — it's my go-to coping mechanism. I was hoping it might make her day better, and after breaking the ice with a dirty joke, she poured out her heart (and my coffee).

Turns out her fiancé was a cheating bastard and she had just called off her wedding while he ran away with one of her bridesmaids. I went back daily for two weeks, mostly to check on her, but also because we just clicked. Plus, she makes amazing coffee and the playlist in the coffee shop is killer.

This is why even though our jobs have us working completely different hours, I left early with her last night. The conversation with Hendrix was great, and it was fun to get to know a new person in the city. But Hendrix is just that, a new person, and no matter how hot he is that doesn't trump best friend, ever.

The bonus to coming home early was productivity. I was able to talk to a few clients before bed and still get up early enough for a run this morning before work. Popping in my ear buds, I push through the doors to the apartment complex and head toward the park to run on the Cherry Creek Trail, my favorite spot to get outside in the city.

It's one reason I picked this building. That, and I love I can walk to all my favorite shops and restaurants. Finding my best friend while exploring coffee shops nearby was an unexpected bonus — one I'm especially grateful for.

Working my way through the park toward the trailhead I see a runner stopped on the side tying his shoes. He's a real-life Adonis with his muscular back glistening in the sun.

It's warm for an April morning and he has his shirt tucked into the back of his shorts to reveal a dark tattoo wrapping around his shoulder and bicep. It is a remarkable sight. I slow my pace as I approach when he looks over his shoulder and spots me.

"Poppy?" a deep voice says.

Forcing my gaze to travel away from his arms and back to his face I register that the man in front of me isn't a stranger. His sharp jawline peppered with dark stubble and his bright blue eyes are familiar. In the sunlight, I can see that they're the most stunning shade of aqua blue — like the surface of an alpine lake. The slight variation in hues almost makes it look like ripples on the water.

If I thought he looked good the last two times I saw him, it's nothing compared to the sight of him shirtless, with his tanned and corded muscles on display. He stands and turns toward me, flipping his baseball hat around giving me an even better look at his handsome face.

If I listen carefully, I can hear the distinctive sound of my ovaries exploding at his use of the ultimate man-flex, a backwards hat.

"Hendrix, what are you doing running today? A late game last night and another today? Are you a man or machine?" I quip praying I'm not drooling.

"Maybe a bit of both. Want to join me? I actually have something I wanted to ask you."

"Sure, let's do this, Mr. Stark." I catch his smirk at my Ironman reference before I fix my gaze in front of me, so I don't end up embarrassing myself by tripping. Pretty sure I could watch his muscles work all day. *Nope, eyes ahead, Poppy! Do not let those abs distract you. You are a strong woman. You can run with this man without ogling him.*

"I was going to text you today. Cruz gave me your number last night after you left. I hope that's okay," he explains interrupting my mental pep talk.

We jog along the creek, falling into step side by side. "Cruz said you might be interested in making some extra money, and I think you might be able to help me out while I'm on the road."

That causes me to stutter step and almost trip over my own feet. My heart drops into my stomach. Hendrix seems like a nice guy and I've enjoyed getting to know him better. I really don't want him to sour all of that if he's about to say something demeaning about what I do for a living. If he does, I'll be forced to take back everything I just thought about how attractive he is. Nothing kills allure quicker than being a pig.

I'm not ashamed of my business. It's just that sex work is still taboo and even though I don't have any face-to-face interaction with my clients, people — men especially — tend to believe other things about my sex life. Mostly because I run an adult phone line for a living that I'm an easy lay, which isn't an accurate depiction.

"I got you," Hen reassures as his arms shoot out landing on my hip to steady me as I right myself before I go down.

"Thank goodness, Ironman was here to save me from the danger of my own feet." I joke uneasily, rolling my lip between my teeth and think back to our conversation last night. I didn't talk about work at all, and it didn't come up. Honestly, I don't think Lilah has even told Cruz what I do, so I'm probably spiraling over nothing.

Recovering as gracefully as a baby giraffe, we keep pace down the path. I'm not sure where he's going with this, so I stay silent. Resolving to hear him out, before I fall any further down the rabbit hole.

"I have a plant collection that I need cared for while I'm on road trips. Only the longer stretches and probably only once each trip."

My eyes go wide. Now I feel silly. That's the last thing I was expecting. Not even close. If my past has taught me anything, it's that guys want one thing from me — a good time. As soon as people find out that I'm a phone sex operator, they stop taking me seriously.

Even though Hendrix doesn't know about what I do for a living, it's the first place my mind goes. Blame it on years of experiences and one disastrous relationship where I was the butt of everyone's joke. Now it's a defensive reaction to assume the worst in situations like this.

"Plants." Yep, that's all I say, like a parrot. Maybe, "Poppy wants a cracker" will come out of my mouth next. *Nice moves, Poppy. Super smooth. Follow me for tips on how to engage in stimulating conversation with the opposite sex.*

"They're more sentimental than hobby," he explains glancing at me as he continues to explain how his nana buys them for him.

"That's unexpected — and sweet. I think I could manage that. Plants are easy enough and they rarely talk back to me." I'm rambling, why am I rambling? I'll chalk it up to the way his muscle move with every step. I'm torn between asking him to put his shirt back to see if my brain cells return or continuing to enjoy the distraction, even if it means I can't form coherent thoughts.

His warm chuckle vibrates through me. He gives me a quick side-eye like maybe he thinks my brand of crazy is cute.

"We have our first road trip next week, and it's a longer one. I'll be gone for eight days. I can send you my schedule? That is if you are in."

"Sure. I work from home, and you live close to Cruz, right?"

"I do. His building is just down the street from mine," he explains.

"Perfect, it's close to me then. Send me your address with the schedule. I'll need a key as well, and any specific care instructions for the plant babies."

"They're all pretty low maintenance." He glances toward me with a smile playing on his lips as he talks about his nana again. "I think she gives me plants as a passive-aggressive way to help keep me grounded. If I have to keep her plants alive out of my devotion to her, how irresponsible can I be?" He shrugs as the trail turns.

"You guys are close?"

"She raised my sister and me after our parents took off, so she's the only parent I've ever really had. She's amazing," he says, leaving me in awe of his admiration for her.

Hendrix eyes the runners approaching from the other direction and reaches up, turning his hat forward to tug it low again to shadow his face. It has me wondering if he's not a fan of the attention.

"She sounds amazing. What does she think of you play-ing professional baseball? She must be proud of you." I picture Hendrix with his arm around an adorable little old lady that barely comes up to his chest with short gray curls and glasses perched on her nose. The kind with the strap so she can hang them around her neck while she cross-stitches baseball-themed wall hangings. The mental image makes me swoon.

"The most amazing, but she never fails to humble my sister and me. Her brand of tough love keeps us grounded. If I ever got an over inflated ego, she'd be sure to shut it down."

"I like her already," I say, wishing that I had that kind of parental influence in my life.

"You two would get along. You remind me of her. Sharp tongue and all," Hendrix muses as we round a corner in the trail. "She knows I appreciate everything she's done for us way too much to fuck up my career by going wild. But I think the plants are just extra insurance for her after my wild streak in the minors."

"So, your feral days are behind you?" I tease, taking a second to look over at him. He looks so good in that hat it should be criminal. Dark hair damp from his sweat curls out from beneath it. Being shorter than him, I can still see those killer blue eyes under the brim that remind me of a bluebird day in the mountains, clear and bright. So full of warmth.

"Mostly. There's a time and a place. I'm more careful with who I let in and where I let loose. It's hard to know who to trust. Who likes you for you or just wants something from you. I have seen too many teammates forfeit their hard work to bad decision making over the years. I owe it to my sister and Nana to be better."

"It's clear they mean the world to you. I'm really feeling the pressure to make sure those plants thrive," I state honestly as we round the bend, bringing us off the trail and back into the park. "Tell me more about these feral days."

"Maybe someday. You need to stick around and get to know me before I'll give away all my secrets," he teases with a wink. "I have an extra key I can get you. Our flight leaves Wednesday. I was getting nervous about finding someone before we left. I'm glad Cruz thought of you. The idea of a stranger in my apartment weirds me out."

"You're saying I should cross making hair dolls off my list of approved activities?" I deadpan. His face freezes, eyes wide with fear. "You should see your face right now."

When we slow to a stop, he lifts his leg to the bench in front of us and reaches for his toes to stretch. He's bent forward with his strong body lengthened and twisted slightly to the side, putting his broad chest and obliques on display. The amount of carved muscle on this man is wholly unfair.

Lifting the hem of my shirt, I bring it up to wipe the sweat from my forehead, hoping it keeps him from noticing the blush creeping up my neck and face. Hendrix switches his stance to stretch out the other leg and I have to work to keep my gaze on his face.

"No hair dolls, and please don't steal my underwear to sell on the black market." He laughs, but it's strained, the look on his face that tells me he's serious. "I had someone in my life that I trusted steal some sports memorabilia and personal items in Los Angeles." His lips drawn in a tight line, hurt and anger flash in his eyes.

"Hendrix, that's awful. What a terrible way to violate your trust." I release the shiver running up my spine and put my hand on his shoulder to comfort. "What a creep. I hope Karma gets them in the end." He smiles at me and puts his hand on top of mine. It's a friendly gesture, but the contact sends butterflies soaring in my stomach.

"Thanks. It was eye opening and did a number on my faith in humankind for a while. It still probably does. If I'm being honest. I don't trust easily," he explains and comes to a stand next to me. Now that he's upright again, I have to look up at him, something I didn't really notice before when we were running side by side. He's tall. I'd guess 6'3" to my 5'5".

"I'll water the plants and be on my way. I won't touch anything of yours," I promise, trying to ease some of the concern that still lingers on his face. If anyone understands the desire for privacy, it's me. "I'm heading to the coffee shop to say hi to Lilah and grab my daily caffeine fix before starting work for the day. Are you heading that way?" I say, changing the subject to something lighter.

"Not today. I caffeinated before I ran. Besides, It's almost nap time for me. Snack time first, but then I need to start on my gameday routine. Baseball superstitions," he says in explanation, his shoulders lifting toward his ears. Taking a step back from me, he pulls out his phone and starts typing something out.

My phone vibrates in the side pocket of my leggings. I grab it out, giving him a quick questioning look.

"Now you have my number. I need to get you a key this week." He smiles and starts backing away to head in the opposite direction. "That was a good run. I'll text you later this week — about the key."

Watching him back away, I nod sliding the phone back in my pocket. It's on the tip of my tongue to tell him that he can text me anytime but stop myself. It's not like I date anyway. Something about Hendrix makes me wish I did.

"Hendrix," I say, grabbing his attention just as he turns away.

He pauses looking over his shoulder at the same time he grabs the shirt out of his waistband and brings it over his head — damn, that was hot. I bet it would be fun to watch him undress.

"Let's see if we can make it two and oh tonight?" I suggest with a smile.

He nods and pulls his shirt the rest of the way down hiding the work of art that is his abs and chest.

"Bye, Poppy."

"Later, Hen." I call as I turn to head the opposite direction to Buns and Roses.

When I get to the coffee shop, I pocket my AirPods and spot Lilah sitting in the corner booth. Her laptop and inventory checklist are spread out in front of her. She has her hair up in her signature messy bun and her apron is folded neatly on the seat next to her as she focuses on the work in front of her.

Her eyebrows are scrunched in concentration, and she's spinning a pencil around her finger as she stares at the computer on the table. We've dubbed these her office hours.

Over the years, it has conveniently shifted to match my post run coffee time. She works, and I provide her with a brain break when I stop by to caffeinate. Lilah looks up as I approach and slides my standard coffee order across the table with her work set aside for now.

"How was your run today?" She stops spinning her pencil and tucks it into her hair as she greets me.

"The view was amazing," I say without elaborating as I take the chair opposite her bench.

A puzzled look passes over her face. One eye squinting while she twists her mouth to the side. "Did you change routes?"

"Nope. I bumped into an unexpected running partner," I explain taking the first glorious sip of my drink, the spiciness of the chai tea hitting my tongue. "So good. You are a goddess, my friend."

She thinks through the possibilities for a moment and her face falls. "Poppy Ann, please tell me it wasn't Paul. He might be fuck hot and have an enormous dick, but that guy is a grade-A jackass. What a complete fool to treat you the way he did," she scolds keeping her voice low but scary so her customers don't overhear.

She's not wrong. He had a huge dick but lacked the ambition to use it properly. It was almost like he thought because it was big, he didn't need to know how to use it. False. So, so false. Looking back, I can't find one redeeming quality in that man, and after everything he put me through, not even his good looks make him physically attractive to me. He reminds me of a sleezy Ken doll these days, not the blond-haired, blue-eyed, meticulously put together man I once cared for.

We met the old fashion way in a bar, and at first he was charming, but he broke me in a way no one else ever has. I thought we were building a relationship. While I was busy falling for all the ways he made me feel special, he was making me the punch line in all his jokes with his friends. I'm not sure I'll ever be able to open myself and be that vulnerable with anyone else.

I trusted him with my heart and my secrets, but it was all a joke to him. He had no intention of building a future with me like he made me believe. Even the memory of him puts a bitter taste in my mouth.

"So much time and energy all wasted on that man. No, it wasn't him. Not even in the same realm. So much hotter, and at this point, he's much less of a douche canoe. Although he has big dick energy, but I feel like he can back it up." I say smiling as I remember his boundless adoration for his grandma coupled with those stacks of abs.

She looks at me blankly. Blinking, it's almost like I can see the wheels turning but coming up short.

"Cruz."

She finally tries knowing that while he is very attractive, I'm not attracted to him. Besides, I'm pretty certain he's meant to be with someone else — even if they're too blind to see it.

"So close, but so far away."

Her blue eyes light up, realization dawning that I'm talking about our newest Bandit. A smile crosses her face as her hand slaps the table startling me.

"Hendrix James. Spill, now!" she demands practically shouting at me. Not waiting for me to confirm that she has indeed guessed correctly.

"Woman, calm your tits." I tell her, shaking my head. I push the strands that came loose from my braid behind my ears and take a nice long sip from my coffee to see just how far I can push my friend.

"Poppy," she growls tapping her pen against the table.

"Okay, sheesh! There really isn't much to tell. I saw him in the park, and we ran together for a while. Cruz gave him my number last night, and he had planned to call me, but we bumped into each other first." I shrug.

"And..."

"He wants someone to water plants during road trips," I tell her anticlimactically. Lilah's eyebrows furrow, but she stays silent waiting for me to continue. "It's actually really adorable. His grandma — or Nana, as he calls her — gifts him plants when she comes to visit. Has for years. They are sentimental to him more than anything."

"That is unpredictably cute. I wouldn't have thought he was a softie. He has that bad boy appeal with the leather jacket and the tattoos."

"You have no idea. I almost tripped over my own feet when I got an up close look at him shirtless. And the way he talks about his grandma. *Swoon*. This sweet little old lady is buying him plants as a way to give him responsibility for another living thing. And he just eats it up because he loves her so much." One hand cradling my cup, I use the other to fan myself as I remember the way he looked turning his hat backwards. A sigh escapes me, and I bring my chin to my fist, elbow resting on the table. "Alas, he only wants me for my green thumb."

Lilah balls up a napkin and throws it at me, batting it away I put on my affronted face.

"How dare you? Kicking me while I'm down. Some friend you are," I joke, placing my cup on the table and crossing my arms for maximum snootiness.

"Oh stop. That man would be stupid not to want a bigger piece of your pie."

I chuckle because my sweet best friend is thinking with her baker brain but it's not the way I interpret it. Nope, I hear it through the filter of a twelve-year-old boy. "It's for the best. I need to focus on launching my demo and getting my shit together to make this career jump." I down the last of my coffee and check the time on my phone.

"Who are you trying to convince?" Lilah asks with a raised eyebrow.

"Speaking of... duty calls. A girl's gotta girl boss," I say pushing off my chair and bringing our cups to the washing station.

"Who do you have on the docket first, Lady Penny?" she asks using my pseudonym.

"Fuzzy Fred is up first today." I tell her using my best phone sex voice, making my voice all low and raspy when I refer to my first client of the day. The first time Lilah heard me use "the voice" she made me order all my coffee for the entire week in my phone voice. It was ridiculous and exactly why we work so well together she's my favorite kind of weird.

"Last week all he wanted to talk to me about were his wife and his job. Didn't have to tell him even once how much I liked the feel of his back hair under my fingers." That thought causes an involuntary whole-body shudder.

Lilah pulls a face, setting her half-eaten scone down. She pushes it away, looking like she might just gag.

"The time I told you about his hair braiding fantasy lives in my head rent free — you know the one where he asks me to describe how I would braid his —"

"Nope — not today, Hades," she cuts me off. "You finish that sentence, and I will ban you from this coffee shop for life."

Laughing, I walk toward the door looking over my shoulder to blow her a kiss. "Time to go make all of Fred's dreams come true. Bye, friend." Sweetness drips from my voice in an effort to win her over after pushing her buttons.

Seltzer water in hand, I walk toward the guest bedroom that pulls double duty as my home office. It's got everything your modern phone sex operator needs — which is more than most people realize. Setting the scene to help clients feel immersed in their fantasies means the difference between getting hung up on and securing repeat callers. Sometimes that means I make the sound of heels walking across the floor or a whip cracking when I'm on the phone.

Popping my ear buds in and opening my laptop, I glance over my schedule for the day. It's light which is intentional. I started working for a phone line when I was nineteen and going to school for my marketing degree. After a night of nachos and margaritas, my roommate and I wandered into a sex toy shop — because why not. In the back corner of the shop there was a bulletin board with a bright pink flyer looking for adult phone operators.

When I was in high school, we were required to have fine arts credits for graduation. I took drama to meet the requirement, but turned out to be good at it. Which I naively figured made me qualified to act out phone sex. Because how hard can it be to fake an orgasm. *Am I right, ladies?*

I was hung up on more times than I could count for months, but even with the constant brush off from clients, the pay was enough to cover tuition, books, and weekly nacho night. About three months in, something my theater teacher told me after a miserable rehearsal came back to me.

It was a quote from Dame Judi Dench, "'I think you should take your job seriously, but not yourself. That is the best combination.'" I was so focused on acting the way I thought sounded good or saying the right thing that the experience was unnatural. It felt forced and ungenuine to my clients — not sexy in the least.

Which I'm one-hundred-percent certain was not how Mr. Finch or Dame Judi Dench saw that quote being used for inspiration. But we all draw our inspiration from different places and that quote spoke to me. It changed the way I thought about my job.

I stopped taking calls in ratty sweatpants and dressed in things that made me feel sexy. I stopped caring how I sounded and just had fun in the moment. Listening to what the client wanted to get out of the call, asking them questions and leading with fun.

If I didn't know how to do something, I asked them to teach me which turned out to be a big hit — because men are easy in bed. Clients stopped hanging up on me, and I built relationships with them that went beyond phone sex. They started confiding in me about their lives, which was rewarding because I felt like I was helping them in a more tangible way.

After a year of working for a line, I went freelance and some of my clients followed me. It gave me freedom to say no to callers that made me uncomfortable and build my business to suit me. The adult industry put me through college without student loans and gave me a great life for the last six years but it's not what I want to do forever. I make more than enough that I can afford to live in a great building complete with security and beautiful views of the city.

It was never the long-term plan. Which is why my schedule is lighter than it has been in years. The goal is to transition to narrating audiobooks as a voice over actor. I have been saving money as a safety net while I'm building my brand and slowly purchasing the equipment I need to record from home. I'm so close that I can taste it. But before I can go all in, I need to wrap up the next few weeks before I close down the line.

After a quick shower, I leave my hair down to air dry and slip into my silky pajama set. It's a black short and tank set with lace trim. It's comfortable but helps put me in the right mindset to talk with my clients.

Fred isn't in the mood to talk about his wife or job today.

"I love the way your hair feels under my fingers. So coarse and rough. Oh god. It makes me so hot," I croon for Fred in the way I know drives him crazy making my voice deeper and a little raspy.

"Penny, I love your voice. It makes me so hard," his groan echoes through the phone.

"You like it when I talk dirty, Fred. The sound of your name on my tongue drives you crazy." I say on a moan. It's a little loud but not obscene. I have learned you need to project a bit more to set the scene over the phone.

"I'm so close, Penny. Tell me you're right there with me."

This is my least favorite part of the job. I don't get any satisfaction out of my calls. It's all about the clients fantasies and what *they* need. Nothing about what I do is arousing for me, while it may be phone sex to my clients, it is not like that for me.

With my new business, I plan to focus on books with some spice because it's fun and I'm good at it. Whether they're fantasy, romance, or suspense, I want to feel that same joy in giving someone an escape, but my audience will be mostly women. Letting them step out of their skin and into their fantasy world. Empowering my listeners to lose themselves in the stories.

"Oh god, Fred, that feels so good. You feel so good." I tell him moaning and slapping my hand against the wall because

I know he gets off on praise and feeling like it's as real as possible.

"Fuck, Penny!" he grunts out. Then it's quiet on the other end of the line.

Fred's breathing is heavy, coming through in short bursts that make the speakers in my headphone rasp. I sit cross-legged on the bed and wait him out. There's rustling on the other end of the phone when he finally speaks.

"How many more weeks?" he asks, disappointment coloring his sated voice.

He's tried to talk me into staying. After five years, he's developed an attachment. And he even offered to pay twice as much to continue speaking with me. It's not about the money, it's about building a life that brings me happiness.

"Two more." Which he damn well knows.

"And there's nothing —"

I cut him off, we have had this conversation before and he knows my boundaries. "I'm going to stop you there, Fred. If you want to keep your last three calls with me, you won't try to talk me out of this. We've been over it before," I scold him, leaving no room for argument.

"Sorry, Penny. You're irreplaceable."

"Thanks, Fred. That means a lot." And it does, I wouldn't lie to him about that. I know that the time we have spent talking over the years has helped him be more open with his wife about his desires.

He disconnects. I take a deep breath, letting myself fall back into my pillows. I have time for a quick break before my next call.

CHAPTER 3

HENDRIX

Superstitions in baseball can get weird real fast. I have never been prone to believing my socks or underwear are winning me games. But I'm not immune to it either. I stick to a routine on game days. I'll be the first to admit that disruptions to it make me cranky. It gives me something tangible that I can control going into a game and puts me in the right head-space.

As I cross the room to finish packing my bag for tonight, clothes in hand, I hear pounding coming from the other side of the wall.

Not sharp like the headboard yesterday, this is softer and less persistent, maybe a hand on the wall. Then a soft moan comes through the wall, and my muscles tense in frustration. As I pack my bag for the stadium, I hear some muffled talking, but thankfully it stops quickly and goes silent next door. There's some hope yet for an uninterrupted nap today.

Relieved that my routine won't be disrupted, and I'll get a full nap today, I zip the bag and make my way across the room, pulling down the covers and sliding into bed. The clean crisp sheets are cool and feel great against my skin.

My eyelids are heavy with sleep when loud noise filters through the wall. I run my hands over my face, rubbing my eyes with the heel of my palm. Judging by my disorientation, I must have napped hard, but I feel like I just fell asleep.

"I'm going to make you work for it today, Clark." The voice is louder and more commanding than earlier as it echoes from next door.

There's a sharp slapping noise followed by a laugh. The kind you hear from villains in movies. *What the fuck was that?*

"Not again," I grumble to myself. Looking at my phone, I see it's only been thirty-five minutes since I laid down. My hand fists the sheets. My mind is running through scenarios. Do I go over there, and interrupt God knows what? Before I can decide I hear the voice again, still in that same stern tone.

"You like it when it hurts, don't you?" There's a pause and cracking noise. "Yeah, you do. I bet that makes you hard."

Fuck me, definitely not going over there and interrupting that. My imagination runs wild as I picture a full-on dominatrix answering the door with her sub gagged at her feet. There is no way I'm going to get back to sleep listening to this.

"Now you're going to sit there, hands under your legs while I make myself come. Don't even think about moving a muscle." The voice through the wall says a little quieter but still unyielding.

I swallow roughly. "Shit," I groan aloud. That was kind of hot. Time for Plan B. I sigh loudly, shoot out of the bed, and grab the noise canceling headphones from my nightstand.

I practically stomp off the field like a toddler throwing a tantrum and whip my glove at the wall of the dugout. My teammates steer clear, giving me space as they move around me. Today's interruption to my nap left me with a shit attitude. One that I carried over to the field.

I just let a routine double play turn into an error when I bobbled the ball. Instead of recovering like the high paid veteran I am and catching the ball, I looked like a minor league rookie. I'm too experienced to let my off the field problems impact my game play like that. My teeth grind in frustration, I'm pissed at myself and aggravated as fuck with my neighbor.

I shove my batting helmet on and pace as I wait for my turn at bat. I see Cruz approach cautiously out of the corner of my eye. My glare should tell him back off, but he ignores it. Hardheaded asshole.

"Dude, you're like the Hulk out there. One wrong move and you're self-destructing. What is going on with you?" Cruz probes.

"Not now," I bite out.

"Hen, you have two choices; talk to me or go out there and strikeout. You're not focused, and you'll swing angry. You know as well as I do that if you don't channel that shit you won't hit. I don't think I need to explain that we need you to perform. This is a young team and you're a veteran. Act like one."

Ouch. Not that I blame him, but it stings when Cruz pulls the captain card on me and treats me like his floundering teammate instead of his friend. He's not wrong. I take a deep breath in and exhale. Focusing on what I can control, I close my eyes and go through a visualization exercise in my head. It's part of my routine every at bat and the exercise calms my frayed nerves.

"I'm good. Promise. It's just an off day."

"Push all the garbage aside. Head in the game. You can deal with the neighbor later. Talk to the building manager or whatever, but it can't impact your game." He meets my eyes and gives my shoulder a squeeze. Turning back toward the field, we move to the edge of the dugout and wait for our place in the batting order. He sticks to my side like I'm on the verge of losing it until he's up.

"You had me sweating there for a minute," Cruz tells me dropping down on to the locker room bench next to me after Coach's postgame speech.

"I owe you one," I admit with a sigh. "Not sure I would have pulled myself out of that funk."

He scratches the stumble on his jaw as if thoughtfully appraising me for a moment. "You would have. This game is too important to you. You wouldn't have let a shit afternoon and dominatrix fuck up your game," he declares with a smirk, standing up and grabbing his towel and shower bag.

"I probably would've let it impact that at bat." I shake my head "And it ended up being a turning point in the game."

"Just get your shit straight at home — I don't like cranky Hen very much. He's too damn whiny," he tells me over his shoulder.

Even though we won, and I pulled my game back from the brink, I'm not in the mood to go out. The guys meet at Cruz's place for a game of poker and pizza while I head back to my apartment alone for my nightly phone call with Nana.

Settling into the couch, Thai takeout on the coffee table, and ESPN on mute in the background, I hit dial on my phone. Straight to voicemail. Panic bubbles up inside me. We always talk after a game. Just as I'm about to dial Mia, my phone buzzes with a text.

NANA:

I'm on with Mia. We will triple call you.

My phone rings with Mia's number calling me. I answer it on speaker and grab the container of pad Thai and a fork.

"Triple call?" I ask playfully when the call connects.

"I don't know what the hell it's called," Nana huffs. "Are you telling me you're too dense to figure out what that means?"

"Come on, Hen, don't be a dummy." Mia chastises as the two of them gang up on me.

"Oh, you're going to pile on too. Why do I put up with this?" I pout, stuffing a fork full of food in my mouth.

"Someone's got to keep your ego in check. Otherwise, it would grow uncontrolled, and you wouldn't fit through doors." Mia explains sharing all her sisterly wisdom with no filter as usual.

"Is that so?" I ask.

"Yep. Consider it my service to society," she boasts, sounding proud of herself for putting me in my place.

"What was with the error and dugout meltdown tonight?" Nana asks, concern in her voice. It's rare that I let my emotions get the best of me during a game.

"You noticed that?" I sigh, setting the container of food back down.

"I notice everything, boy. You ought to know that by now."

It doesn't surprise me, not really, I could never hide things from her. She always knew when I was up to something when I was younger. Checking in to monitor our moods and emotions was her second job — always making sure we were okay. After she took over custody, she did everything in her power to make sure we knew she was there for us, for anything. She shouldn't still be worrying about me. That ramps up my guilt.

I run my fingers through my hair tugging on the strands while I gather my thoughts. I launch into it from the beginning, telling them about the neighbor and how she's been keeping me up, throwing off my routine. "She's really messing with my mental game," I say trying to summarize how I'm feeling.

They laugh so hard I am sure they're both in tears when I give them a rundown of some activities I have overheard.

"So let me get this straight, your sex kitten of a neighbor, whom you haven't met, is derailing your game?" Nana summarizes breathless from laughter. "Because she might be a dominatrix or a furry?"

"I mean — I wouldn't put it —" I start but Mia cuts me off.

"I never thought I'd see the day Hendrix James let a girl get under his skin. Wouldn't it be funny if it wasn't even a woman but a man that just likes really loud porn?"

"It's not, and she's not under my skin, Mia. At least not in the way you are suggesting. She's interrupting my routine and I don't like it." My face scrunches up. That sounded whiny even to me. Shit, Cruz was right. Am I being ridiculous? "And I don't care if she's a dominatrix or a furry." I add just so we are clear that my dislike of the woman has nothing to do with her kinks.

"Oh no. Not your *precious* routine," my sister prods. Mia thrives in chaos, working best under the pressure of a deadline. Which is perfect considering she chose a career as an author. "If you ask me, you need some commotion in your life. Something to come in and mess up your order."

"Maybe Mia is onto something. You should thank this woman for making your life more interesting," my grandma piles on. "Who knows maybe she'll invite you in for some light spanking. Not sure you could handle her, Henny."

That last bit earns some fake gagging from Mia. "Ack! Hard stop. I'm going to hang up if we are going to talk about Hen's sex life," she exclaims dramatically.

"Don't be ridiculous, Mia. You literally write about sex for a living. We can talk about mine instead. Last week, during movie night in the clubhouse, I let Harold Davis act out the scene from your latest book—"

"Bye, Nana!"

"Good night!"

Mia and I both shout at the same time before ending the phone call. Grabbing the garbage from the takeout, I head to the kitchen and dump it in the garbage. The key I set out earlier for Poppy catches my eye on the counter. Before I can do anything with the key, my phone buzzes with a text from where I set it on the phone screen in front of me.

NANA:

I love you, Henny. Before you go to your building manager, consider knocking on your neighbor's door and talking it out with her first. Give her a chance before you assume the worst.

HENDRIX:

I'll think about it.

NANA:

Do more than think about it. I know Kylie broke your trust, but this woman probably has no clue you can hear her.

HENDRIX:

You make a valid point.

NANA:

Of course I do.

NANA:

And be nice. Chances are that poor girl is going to be mortified when she finds out you heard her getting her kink on.

HENDRIX:

I'll talk to her, but no more of Mia's books for you. I love you.

NANA:

Fat Chance, that girl's got a dirty mind, and I'm here for it. Love you too, Henny.

We have a day game tomorrow, so I decide to head to bed and see if I can catch up on some of the sleep that I have missed out on in the last few days. Sitting on the edge of the bed, I mentally go through my to-do list before our first road trip. Now that I have a plan to speak with my neighbor, that key looms at the forefront of my mind. Looking through my contacts, I navigate to Poppy's number.

HENDRIX:

Hey Poppy. It's Hendrix.

POPPY:

Hey Ironman.

HENDRIX:

How was the rest of your day?

POPPY:

No complaints here. I got my post run coffee fix, crossed a few things off my checklist. Watched the Bandits win a baseball game.

HENDRIX:

You watched me play?

POPPY:

Sure if that makes you smile. I watched you play.

HENDRIX:

Let's go with that. I like the idea of a pretty girl watching just for me. What kinds of things did you cross off your checklist?

POPPY:

Just some work stuff. Nothing interesting.

HENDRIX:

Sounds like a productive day.
Speaking of to-do lists. You're on mine.

Three dots appear. Then disappear and appear again. I re-read that last exchange. Oh fuck, that sounds like I want to do her. I don't hate that idea, but it's not what I meant. I panic as I quickly try to undo the damage. *Why can't you unsend a text message?*

HENDRIX:

Wait that came out wrong... Let me start over. I promise that was not me trying to perv on you.

POPPY:

Start from the top.

HENDRIX:

When can I get you the key for my apartment? I leave on Wednesday.

POPPY:

Lilah and I are going to the game tomorrow. Or you can leave it at the coffee shop with Lilah next time you go in?

56

HENDRIX:

I can bring it to the game tomorrow. Lilah has a family pass, right?

POPPY:

Sure does.

HENDRIX:

Want to meet up in the family area after the game?

POPPY:

I can do that.

HENDRIX:

Thanks for your help.

POPPY:

Don't mention it.
Serious question...

POPPY:

Chocolate or chips... I'm having a snack attack and can't handle the pressure of this decision.

HENDRIX:

Decision fatigue. I'm well acquainted with it. Chocolate hands down.

POPPY:

You are a knight among men, Hendrix James. Chocolate it is.

HENDRIX:

Night Poppy.

POPPY:

Goodnight Ironman.

POPPY:

Hey Hen...

POPPY:

I'm okay with a little perving.

That last text makes me smile. Poppy is gorgeous, funny, and a little flirty. Without being over the top, it's a combination that makes me want to get to know more about her. The possibility of spending more time with her is enticing. It's hard to have relationships and get to know someone new during the season.

As a rule, I have avoided relationships since I was drafted for that reason. It never feels like I can give enough to the other person. It's hard to be there for them in the way I want to be, and the girls I have come across haven't been able to handle that aspect of the lifestyle or they're interested for all the wrong reasons.

At least that's why I didn't date early in my career. It's compounded by the fact that the last time I tried, it was a total disaster. The lack of time together made it hard to really know one another. As it turned out, I didn't really know her at all. I gave her an all-access pass to my life, and she took advantage of the situation. The red flags were there, but I willfully ignored them. Never again. Kylie made sure of that when she shattered my trust.

CHAPTER 4

POPPY

I survey the mess around me. It looks like a tornado went through my spare bedroom. There are boxes and sound equipment parts scattered haphazardly across the room. And I'm sure if I look in the mirror, my hair will be sticking out in all directions from running my hands through it in frustration. Lilah and I have plans to meet at the coffee shop and walk over to the stadium together later. But right now, I can't see beyond the chaos that is my office.

Until I get this all put together and working, I can't record my demo. On top of that, my sound booth still hasn't arrived. I hoped it would be delivered already so when my new neighbor moved in I could start using it for calls without worrying about disturbing them. I have attempted to stop over and introduce myself since they moved in, but we must be on opposite schedules because they never answer the door.

They've got to have some questions if they've heard me working.

Right now, it feels like my entire future hinges on my ability to put this equipment together and the missing booth shipment.

My fingers press into my temples, massaging them, making small circles as I try to concentrate on the directions in front of me. *Focus, girl.* The instructions for the microphone and pop filter are giving me a headache, but I start over at the top working through it step by step. Ticking off each part and piece that is scattered around me until it's all put together and all that's left is the piles of discarded packaging.

I wipe my hands on leggings and stand up. My muscles are tight from sitting on the ground hunched over. "Ouch," I groan to myself as I bend over to collect the trash and cardboard off the floor. My arms are overflowing with all the garbage as I walk through the apartment to dispose of it.

That was a lot more work than I expected. Hopefully, when the soundproof paneling and booth come, it's not a complete shitshow assembling it. There was an option to have it installed, but I'm nothing if not determined.

I want to do this on my own and prove to the people who don't take me seriously that I can do it. That I am more than the sex phone operator whose boyfriend was only with her because the idea of dating me thrilled him. A challenge, a wild oat to sow, not serious girlfriend material. I'm more than the girl who never lived up to her parents' expectations for her. I need to do this to prove it to myself.

Maybe I can convince Lilah to help me. We can drink margaritas and put it together. As I take the last load from the guest bedroom to the garbage in the kitchen, the time on the microwave catches my eye. Shit! I'm going to be late.

I rush to the bedroom to change for the game and whip my tank over my head before I'm even through the door. My leggings end up in a pile in the closet as I riffle through my shirts, looking for my Bandits jersey.

When I find the jersey, I yank it and a fitted long sleeve black shirt off the hanger before I reach for my favorite jeans. They make my ass look like a juicy peach, and after being on the struggle bus all afternoon I want to feel good about myself. I hop around the closet and pull it all on as fast as possible. Only slowing down to ensure my braid stays intact.

On my way out of the closet, I slip my feet into a pair of low boots and vow to pick up the trail of clothes when I get home. Leaving it a problem for future Poppy. As I dart back through the apartment, I pocket my phone and grab my purse. Almost crashing into the doorframe in my rush.

Lilah sees me coming and meets me on the sidewalk in front of Buns and Roses. With a coffee in hand, like the goddess she is. I pop a quick kiss on her cheek as I take it from her.

"Come to Mama. You have no idea how much I need this." I bring the coffee to my lips and fall into step beside her. We make our way toward the stadium alongside other fans rushing to get there in time for the first pitch.

"Death by audio equipment?" Lilah asks, she glances over at me with one eyebrow raised.

I slip my arm through hers and nod. "It was a close one. You almost had to eulogize me before I accomplished my dreams. That would have been depressing."

"Mhmm… Sure would have. Today we honor the life of Poppy Ann Byrne. She was one of the good ones. The kindest, strongest, and baddest bitch I ever met. Always down for a dirty joke and some caffeine. Loved a good dicking but hadn't had one in ages. She taught me everything I needed to know about plants and margaritas. May she rest in peace."

"Please write that down and use it at my actual funeral. My mother would be appalled." But almost everything I do causes that reaction from her. I stopped trying to live up to her expectations a long time ago. She wants a prim and proper daughter. One that dutifully marries her high school sweetheart and stays home making dinner every night and doting on her family. There is absolutely nothing wrong with that life, if it's what you want. But it's never been my dream, and that's something the two of us have always clashed on.

Lilah has her hair down in all its gorgeous long blonde glory. She's styled it in loose curls. I give one of her stray tresses a tug. "Hair down today. I thought that was only for holidays and hot dates. Any reason or just feeling frisky?"

"You act like I've been on a lot of hot dates in the last three years. Any I've been on have been slightly above freezing at best." She sighs and squeezes closer to me as we make our way across a particularly busy crosswalk. "I'd really like to put an end to my dry spell. My elbow is getting sore from all the self-love." Her laugh is hollow, and it sounds like there might be more truth in there than she would like. Geez, I hope her elbow is okay.

"Okay, wow. I love that you are comfortable sharing that with me. Let's make sure we fix that with an ergonomically correct vibrator. Maybe try switching up your position?"

We pause at another stoplight, waiting to cross. I make a mental note to send her a hands-free toy.

She smiles but says nothing before the signal changes, allowing us to cross with the crowd. "Do you have anyone in mind to end the dry spell?"

Lilah pulls out her phone and navigates to her wallet to pull up our tickets, completely sidestepping my question.

"You do. Don't you?" I accuse, my voice getting higher than it was a minute ago, my excitement for her taking over.

She looks at me over her phone, nibbling on her bottom lip nervously. "I had a dream last night that I can't get out of my head — but I need to," she rushes to explain.

"Did you have a sex dream about Cruz?" I ask her as we get in line to go through security at the gate. She might think they're just friends but I see the way they ogle each other.

Blush creeps up her neck and she shushes me dramatically while nodding quickly. "God, it was hot. I woke up sweating and out of breath," she gushes, fanning her face. "It had me so amped up that I needed to come a second time."

"Is now a good time to tell you I told Hendrix we would meet them after the game? I need to get the key to his apartment."

Lilah clutches my arm tightly. "I can't pick a guy up in front of him, and I absolutely can't hook up with a Bandit. I'm not even sure how I'm going to function around him after that dream. My plan was to avoid face-to-face interactions until after their road trip. Give me time to gather myself."

"Solid plan. Do you want me to figure something else out with Hen?" I offer to appease her distress.

"Ugh — No. New plan. Hang with me here, I'm just spitballing." She pauses as if the wheels of deceit turning in her head. "I'll duck into the bathroom while you grab the key. You make up a story about needing a girls' night and get rid of them. Her hands flutter with gestures as plots how to avoid Cruz. Lilah is too sweet to be seriously devious.

"No way that works without him getting suspicious," I tell her truthfully.

"Please, Poppy." She clutches her hands together in front of her chest as we approach the security checkpoint.

"Of course I'll do it, but he's going to know you're avoiding him. Maybe you should just tell him."

Panic freezes her in place. "No — I can't. Absolutely not. He doesn't see me like that. He treats me like I'm his sister." That earns an eye roll from me, but Lilah goes on. "Besides, even if he saw me like that, I would never risk our friendship." Her face looks pained as she continues. "You saw me when Brad broke off the engagement. You and I had just met, but Cruz was there every step of the way. He took care of me, let me cry on his shoulder — so many times." She shudders with the memory.

Her voice shakes, and I can tell she's terrified of losing him. "Hey, Delilah. Look at me." I tell her, using her full name for emphasis. "You won't lose him. No matter what happens. You mean just as much to him. You were his rock after his brother died," I remind her how she helped him through his darkest days.

"So, I can hide in the bathroom?" She laughs, her eyes comically wide with panic.

"If that's what you need, we'll hide you in the bathroom."

Lilah grabs my hands in hers and gives them a squeeze. "Thank you, Poppy."

"That must have been some dream," I comment offhand-edly to lighten the mood. That gets a smile out of her.

"You know that joke, what's the difference between a golf ball and the g-spot?"

"Of all the jokes I have told you, why do you remember that one?" I laugh.

"It always stuck with me. Brad was a golfer but couldn't find my g-spot with a map and compass. It was one of the first ones you told me. I was a mess, but you were always there to make me laugh in those first few weeks after I ended things."

My chest swells with appreciation for Lilah and if we weren't in the middle of a busy concourse I would pull her into a tight hug. Instead, I nod knowingly, he was such a loser. "Good riddance."

"Let's just say dream Cruz had absolutely no prob-lem finding my g-spot or clit several times. He knew all the right buttons to push," she says quietly as we approach our section.

We stop at our favorite beer stand. It's right at the top of the stairs that lead down to our seats. Betty works it, and she's the most awesome seventy-seven-year-old in history. Her hair is dyed teal to match the Bandits team colors and has a double nose ring. It doesn't hurt that she laughs at our dirty jokes every game without fail.

Her stories are the best. The kind that can only come from a life well lived. Betty was in a polyamorous relationship with three men for most of her thirties before she left the country to travel through Europe for several years. I've never met someone more comfortable in their own skin, she's my hero.

"Afternoon, ladies! You both look stunning today." Betty grins at us when we get to the front of the line. She doesn't even ask for our orders anymore. She knows what we like and starts filling up two tall cups with the local IPA they have on tap today.

"Right back at you, Betty. Nice bolo," I tell her of the black-and-silver tie she has hanging from her neck.

She beams in reply. "That's a story for another time. Remind me to tell you about the man who gave it to me when I was hitchhiking through Arizona." She leans in close so that only the two of us can hear. "He had this piercing on his penis. Being with him was an out-of-body experience." She holds out her hand with her pointer and middle finger pressed together and draws four lines across the top of them before wiggling her eyebrows at us. Lilah and I both gawk at her hand for a moment before pulling ourselves together.

Betty looks at me with an expectant smirk on her face. She sets both our beers down in front of her and wiggles her fingers toward her chest in a give it to me motion. I take a quick glance around to make sure there are no kids in ear shot.

"What's the best thing about gardening?" I ask her, indulging in the ritual we started when she began working this section.

Betty props her elbow on the beer cart leaning in close as she studies me closely. "Is this one of those dirty jokes that aren't really dirty? Like a pig rolled in the mud?"

My shoulders shrug casually, and I hand her my card to run for our beers without looking away. She blows out a breath causing her teal bangs to float up and off her forehead momentarily. When she hands me the receipt and pen,

I sign my name and Lilah drops a twenty in her tip jar over my shoulder.

Betty glares at her but doesn't say a thing. She knows better than to argue with us about how much or frequently we tip her. At this point, she just begrudgingly accepts it.

"I give up. What's so great about gardening?"

"Getting down and dirty with your hoes." I wink at her as she slides the beers across the metal cart. "Bye, *ho*, see you later."

Lilah and I make our way down the stairs to our seats as the players run out on the field to warm up. Cruz tried to get her to sit with the wives and girlfriends when we first started coming to games regularly, but Lilah wasn't interested. She told him she wanted to sit in right field where he plays.

Her logic was what's the point of coming if he can't hear her heckling him during games. He's gotten her seats in the outfield for the last two seasons. Scooting past the handful of fans that have already taken their seat, we find our seats in the first row.

As soon as we sit, Lilah brings her thumb and pointer finger to her mouth and lets out an ear-piercing whistle. I know it's coming, so I set my beer between my feet and clap my hands over my ears just in time. The fans around us aren't so lucky which results in a few dirty looks. *Oh well — can't make everyone happy.*

Cruz doesn't look up immediately because he is still warming up with Dom, the Bandits' rookie center fielder. Dom nods in our direction and says something to Cruz. Whatever he says puts a sour look on Cruz's face. If I had to bet, I'd say he made a comment about Lilah.

He is making his signature don't-fuck-with-my-girl face. His jaw clenched and his eyebrows knit together. I know that if I were closer, I could see his nose crinkling and the vein in his neck popping. He looks over his shoulder at us quickly and then directs his attention back to Dom. He shakes his head sharply and Dom throws up his hands in defeat, but he wears a boyish grin.

They finish warming up and Cruz jogs over to the warning track as Dom heads back out to center. The seats are raised too high above the field for him to reach us, but he crooks his finger at Lilah signaling her to lean down.

She stands and sets her beer in the cup holder before bending at the waist to talk to him. Whatever he says has her cheeks turning pink before Cruz turns to jog back to the dugout.

"Was that so bad?" I ask when she drops into the seat next to me. Before she responds, she takes a long pull from her beer.

She rolls her eyes at me before replying. "I don't know, you tell me. I can feel the heat in my cheeks, so I know they're flushed."

"So sassy… Just blame it on the gravity of leaning over the railing. Are we sharing?" I ask about the exchange between them on the field, giving her the option to keep it to herself. The way she nibbles on her thumb I can tell she's anxious.

"He made me promise to meet him after the game," she tells me in a rush.

"There's no way that made you blush. You're holding out on me." My voice is soft, not pushy but trying to support her. She shakes her head, blond hair moving around her shoulders with the motion.

"He told me he likes my hair down like this. And said —" she pauses, glancing toward the dugout, her eyes finding Cruz before starting again. "I looked incredible and that he wants to hang out after the game. He called me gorgeous in Spanish." The color on her cheeks flares brighter.

"Damn, I swoon every time I hear him speak Spanish to you."

She nods. "Me too. He suggested a movie night and pizza at his place. We have movie nights all the time. It's not weird at all, right?" I pat her back reassuringly as the players step onto the field and remove their caps for the national anthem.

The Bandits take the field first, and it's a rough inning with two runs scoring in no time. By the third inning, we are down by three, but Dean turns the tables with double and a stolen base to put the Bandits in scoring position. When the team's catcher, Xavier, steps up to the plate, he gives us a base hit, which is enough to bring Dean in. Lilah and I jump up and down, sending our popcorn flying everywhere as we cheer for Dean when he crosses the plate.

I am on the edge of my seat when Barrett steps up to the mound and gets us out of the fourth inning with three up, three down. But frustration takes hold when the Bandits strand three runners on base not scoring any runs.

Tensions are high as they take the field in the fifth. The guys scrape by with no additional runs from the Knights, thanks to a double play, including a diving throw from Hendrix to the second baseman, who rockets the ball to first to get the runner out in time.

With a two-run deficit in the fifth, Cruz hits a solo homerun bringing the Bandit's within a run of tying the game up. The team isn't able to capitalize on it and the Bandits end up losing by one. Despite losing, both Cruz and Hendrix played well.

We hang out in our seats for a few minutes after the game, letting the crowd dwindle before we make our way through the concourse and take the stairs down to the first level. When we get to the entrance, security checks our passes at the door before letting us into the area where friends and family with credentials wait.

"Lilah," I say setting my hand on her bouncing knee to calm it. "You can say no to movie night. Tell him we have plans for a girls' night." It's not really a lie. We never finalized our plans for the night.

"No, you are right," she explains, her attention darts to the door as it opens. It's not Cruz or Hendrix. "He'll know if I'm avoiding him, and I can't do that to him. I just need to suck it up."

"What if I invite myself along for movie night?" I ask only half seriously because it sounds awkward as hell, but I'd do it for her. Her face lights up. *No backing out now.*

"Um, yes, please." The stress drains from her body and her shoulders relax. "Just follow my lead," she exclaims in a way that gives me zero faith that she has an actual plan.

CHAPTER 5

HENDRIX

After a quick shower, I find a quiet corner to check in with my nana before we head out to Draft. Even if we can only talk for a minute, it's habit to call her after every game at this point. When I finish I find Cruz, and we head over to the waiting area to meet the girls. All the families have cleared out and there are just a few people scattered around the space. Hiking my duffle bag higher on my shoulder, I head toward the couch with Cruz where Poppy and Lilah are waiting.

"Nice game tonight, sorry it didn't go your way." Poppy says, her voice unsure as she looks up at me with those big green eyes. She's clearly uncertain how I handle a loss or more accurately how to handle me after a loss.

"Thanks. Losing always sucks but there wasn't much else we could have done." I'm happy with the way I played. There are some things we will work on as a team in the batting cages this week to improve but we know we can't win all one hundred sixty-two regular season games.

I reach into my back pocket and pull out my wallet where I stashed the key for her. Gripping it between my fingers, I hold it out to her. Poppy takes the key and turns it over in her hand.

"I have the keys to the castle," she teases. Her easy smile returns. She tucks the key into the bag hanging across her chest. The movement draws my eye down, bringing my attention to her jersey. Jealousy zips through me, catching me off guard. I wonder whose name is on the back.

"Use them wisely," I tell her fighting to keep the possessiveness I'm feeling on lockdown. She isn't mine to lay claim to regardless of how attracted to her I'm.

"What do you say, Poppy?" Lilah asks out of nowhere with an unnaturally large smile plastered to her face. Honestly, she looks a little unhinged. I scrub my hand over my jaw, clueless to what the hell is going on.

"Hmm?" Poppy asks, pulling her attention from where her eyes were tracing the movement of my hand. "Sorry, what was that, Lilah?"

"Cruz invited us all over for a movie night." Is her eye twitching? I hold back a laugh at Lilah's obvious discomfort.

"Oh, um, sure. I could do that." Poppy's gaze swings back to me. There's a silent pleading there when she grinds out, "How about you, Hendrix. Join us for movie night?"

I look over at my friend, trying to figure out what is happening. He just shrugs and shakes his head, looking equally confused. Lilah and Poppy are both staring at me. Poppy's mouth turns down in the slightest frown and her pupils shift uncomfortably. Lilah still has the unnaturally large smile plastered to her face as she bounces on her toes. Even though I'm just getting to know Poppy, I know yes is the only acceptable answer to their question. I grew up as the only male with two females in the house learning how to read cues was critical to my survival.

I rub the back of my neck glancing between the three of them when Poppy suddenly speaks up.

"Pizza — we can order pizza. And Cruz always has beer. It'll be a fun night in," she explains going for the hard sell. She catches my eye, pleading with me to save her. "You won't have to deal with fans asking about the game." Poppy continues, clearly not wanting to be the only one crashing what is sure to be an awkward evening with this tension between Cruz and Lilah. It's endearing the way she's bargaining to get me to agree.

"Sure. Pizza, beer, and a movie." I concede. I don't have other plans and the idea of spending more time with her is appealing, even if I feel like we might be intruding on Cruz's plans. Thoughts of Poppy in the dark, snuggled up under a blanket next to me isn't a hardship at all. "But I get to pick the movie," I add at the last minute.

Lilah and Cruz head out of the family room with Poppy and me trailing behind. I hold the door for her and get a glimpse of the back of her jersey. Sticking out from under the red braid — a braid that has my fingers twitch to touch it, tug on it, wrap it around my hand — "Tellez" is spelled out across her shoulders. Cruz's name on her back has the jealousy from earlier clawing at me, trying to get out.

My hand rests on the small of Poppy's back as I guide her through the double doors that lead out of the stadium into the players' parking lot. When we step out into the cool night air, Poppy steps in closer to me, shivering at the chill.

I tip my head down toward her ear as I tell her, "Don't worry, Poppy, I'll keep you warm."

Just as she looks up at me with a small smile pulling at the corner of her lip, flashes go off around us. I hold in my grumble as I take in the photographers, fans, and reporters that have gathered there to see if they can snag time with any of the players. Being photographed with Poppy isn't the cause of my annoyance. It's always felt invasive to have my photo taken unexpectedly like this, even more so since Kylie.

Poppy is perched on a stool in the kitchen at Cruz's apartment, scrolling through her phone looking over the menu for the pizza place. Her forearms are resting on the dark countertops, making her creamy skin stand out in contrast.

"How do we feel about chicken as a pizza topping?" she asks, turning to find me over her shoulder where I'm leaning against the wall.

On his way to the living room, Cruz grabs four beers from the fridge and hands two to me before he joins Lilah who is looking at movie options. I twist the top off both beer bottles and cross the room where I lean my lower back against the island next to Poppy. She looks up at me and I hand her a beer.

"What kind of sauce are we talking about?" I ask, watching Poppy as she brings the bottle to her full lips. Needing to restrain myself from reaching out and running my thumb along her bottom lip, I clench my fist at my side. Damn, I want to test the softness of it and see how she reacts to my touch. Would her breath hitch? Maybe her nipples would pucker under that thin black shirt she's wearing beneath her unbuttoned jersey.

Poppy's attention shifts from her phone over to me as she slowly trails her gaze up my body before making eye contact.

"I love a good barbeque chicken pizza," Lilah chimes in from her spot on the corner of the couch. "Cruz — meat lovers for you?" she says, looking over to where he's seated next to her, thumbing through movie choices.

"Yeah, but get whatever you guys want too," he says absentmindedly, too focused on Lilah to have any real input.

Leaning in toward me, Poppy shows me the pizza menu on the phone screen. "What's it going to be, Hen? You're the deciding factor."

"I'm not picky about pizza toppings. What's your favorite?" I question, noticing the way her eyes have a darker ring around the outside of her pupil, instead of the menu options.

"I could go for the buffalo mac pizza," she says, glancing up at me through her lashes. "Shall I place the order?" I nod and reach out with my hand, holding it in front of her. When she places her hand in mine, I pull her up off the stool and gesture toward the living room.

She follows me to where Lilah and Cruz are snuggled up in the corner of the sectional talking about movie choices. Cruz is sitting at the end of the overstuffed sectional with Lilah tucked under his arm. I have seen the two of them in the same position several times. For two people that insist they're just friends, it doesn't look that way. I doubt they'll be "just friends" much longer. They both seem to be giving into the tension between them.

"Pizza will be here in an hour. What movie are you picking, Hen?" Poppy asks as she settles into the opposite end of the couch from the other two.

I smirk at her before responding. "Avengers."

"Stop. Really?" she says with a laugh. Cruz and Lilah look at us like we've lost it. "So original, *Ironman*." Poppy continues under her breath just for me. She reaches her arm behind me and pulls the blanket off the back of the couch.

This end of the sectional is shorter, putting Poppy right next to me when she tucks her feet up on the couch next to her and snuggles in under the soft blanket. The movie starts and Poppy leans into me nudging my shoulder.

When I look at her, she brings her lips to the shell of my ear. "Thanks for coming tonight. I know it was an awkward invite. You bailed me out of being the third wheel."

Her breath is warm on my neck, tickling the sensitive skin below my ear. It makes me want to pull her into my lap to get her closer and feel her against me everywhere. Instead, I lower my chin and bring my face toward her.

"What exactly is going on here?" I ask, tilting my head slightly toward the other side of the couch while the opening of the movie plays on the screen.

Her throat bobs as she swallows but she stays silent. Her gaze drifts from mine and she shrugs. She knows something but she's not willing to say.

"Okay. We can play that game. I like the loyalty to your friend." Not everyone is as loyal as Poppy. It's nice, one of the many things I'm coming to realize that I like about Poppy. "Did something happen? Cruz told me they have never —"

"They haven't. They're just friends," she cuts me off quietly, careful not to let her voice carry. She's not very convincing as her gaze darts toward her friend.

"But not for long?" I guess. Poppy stays silent, meeting my eyes again. Being this close I can see all the different shades of red and copper weaving through her braid. It's a kaleidoscope of hues and I want to unbraid it. See it let loose for me to run my fingers through. I bring my hand up to her cheek and brush a strand of hair back that's fallen free. She's captivating and I can't help myself.

Her head tilts into my hand. It's such a small move that I almost miss it. I certainly don't miss the way her lips part, letting out a long, shaky exhale when she responds. "I guess we will just have to wait and see. You can only fight attraction so long." She pats my chest and lets her hand linger there for a moment as she gazes up at me. When she removes her hand, I have to force my focus back on the movie instead of how that innocent move lit me up on the inside.

The movie starts and we settle into a comfortable silence. After a while, Lilah holds up her beer to Cruz, signaling it's empty. I catch the movement out of the corner of my eye and get up to grab another round for the group.

"I got them," I offer, and Cruz nods he needs another. When I look at Poppy, she twists her lips and contemplates her empty bottle.

"Are there still margarita supplies from the last time we were here?" Poppy asks, still frowning at the empty beer bottle hanging between her fingers.

"There are. And I even stocked up on fresh limes this week. Delilah, beer or margarita?" Cruz answers before looking to Lilah for her decision.

"Is that even a question?" she responds without bothering to lift her head from where it's resting against Cruz's chest. "Margarita."

Poppy reaches her hands out and I take them in mine to pull her up off the couch. I tug her into my space and her scent surrounds me. It's sweet like honey and lavender. So very Poppy.

Poppy leads the way to the kitchen, knowing where everything is from having spent time here with Lilah. Seeing her so at home in Cruz's kitchen triggers a vision of her comfortable in my apartment. I haven't had a woman that isn't a relative in my apartment since Kylie. The thought of Poppy in my apartment doesn't cause chills down my spine. Instead, it sends warmth through my veins, lighting me up from the inside out.

Poppy moves through the kitchen, grabbing the margarita mix and a shaker from the cupboard. I retrieve the beers and limes from the fridge.

"Can I help?" I ask as she reaches across the counter in front of me to grab a knife from the magnetic strip lining the wall. I step back just enough to allow her room to maneuver, which causes her ass to brush against my thigh. I clamp my mouth shut so I don't groan aloud.

She slides the cutting board and limes over, so they're in front of me, and sets the knife down. "Want to cut these for me, and I'll juice them?"

Moving away from me to grab the glasses, she leaves all the places we were just touching begging for her return. I watch her out of the corner of my eye as I finish the last lime. She's on her toes leaning into the cupboard, the glasses she wants just out of reach.

Quietly, I move in behind her, bringing my chest against her back, and reach into the cupboard to retrieve the glasses. Her breath catches at the contact. My ego grows at the way these little touches affect her.

"I got it," I tell her softly, dropping my hand to cradle her hip.

Poppy lowers to her heels, and it causes her ass to drag down the front of my pants. I let out a rough groan, not even bothering to hide it this time. I want her to know how she affects me, and I'm thrilled that she's giving it right back to me. When I set the glasses down, my chest rumbles with laughter. The two glasses say "If you're going to be a salty bitch, bring the tequila" printed across an outline of a lime.

"I gave those to Cruz as a Christmas gift last year. I was sick of drinking my margarita out of his boring glasses every time we came over." Poppy explains as she finishes mixing the margaritas. When they're finished, we bring them back to the coffee table along with the beers.

Poppy takes a seat on the couch and pulls the blanket over her lap, feet tucked back under it. When I go to take my seat next to her, she lifts the blanket, offering me some of it. The cushions shift with my weight to bring her against my side. I look over at her just as she looks up at me. I quirk a brow silently asking if this is okay. Poppy just smiles sheepishly in return, so I bring my arm around her shoulder, keeping her there.

CHAPTER 6

POPPY

Everything feels right. The awkwardness from being forced to tag along and then coaxing Hendrix into crashing movie night long is gone. Melting away with the effortless connection between us. We have been toying with the chemistry between us all night.

His light touches have sent my pulse through the roof. Coupled with flirtatious smiles that send shivers of anticipation straight to my core. The way he pressed into me, covering my body with his when we were making the margaritas. All those moments combined have me on edge in all the best ways.

Just as I relax into Hendrix's hold, the buzzer goes off, signaling the pizza delivery. I reluctantly peel myself away, irrationally annoyed that I can't stay there all night.

Cruz and Hendrix hover over the pizza boxes and eat standing, hips cocked against the island, as they talk about the game today. Going over what the team needs to work on, and the upcoming away trip. Lilah and I opt for plates and a seat at the table because we are civilized — and want to girl-talk without being overheard.

"How are you feeling?" I ask my friend tentatively before taking a bite of my buffalo mac pizza.

Her eyebrows pull together as she takes a drink of the margarita, darting her tongue out to lick some salt off the rim. "Honestly, I'm confused. And tired. Cruz has always been affectionate with me, but lately it feels different, like there could be more." Lilah explains, keeping her voice low.

"You don't think it's worth exploring or having a conversation about? That man loves you." Her face pales. My hand drops to her knee under the table, and I squeeze it. "I'm just saying that he wouldn't stop being your friend over some confusing feelings."

"I'm not sure I'm ready for that. But I don't know how much longer I can sit in limbo with him. Thank you for coming tonight to be a buffer. I know it was awkward earlier, but I would have been a mess, second guessing everything I said or did. I'm in over my head." She takes a bite of her pizza and realization spreads across her face, her cheeks flushing pink. "Do you think he touches me a lot?" *Oh, sweet, oblivious Lilah.*

My lips pull into a thin line because I cannot laugh at my friend right now. Her observation skills are seriously lacking when it comes to Cruz. He's her biggest blind spot. She sees everything he does as protective or platonic. But from the outside looking in, it's easy to see that it's more for both of them.

He takes every opportunity to touch her. Deciding maybe this is the nudge she needs, I lay it out for her. "He's never been shy about touching you, Lilah. That man takes every chance to brush up against you or hold you. It's been that way for years. It could pass as platonic if you aren't paying attention, but he looks at you like he wants to devour you."

Her gaze travels over her shoulder and lingers on where he is standing with Hendrix as she responds, "You mean how his eyes don't stray even when I'm across the room? Or how he radiates heat and desire anytime he is near me, so much so that it's a real living thing taking up oxygen and space?" Her description is spot on, and it makes my pulse race. I realize I want to be the focus of someone's attention like that.

"That was oddly specific, and a little hot, but yes, exactly like that." A smug smile pulls at her lips. I follow her gaze and see it's not Cruz that she's looking at. She's looking right at Hendrix, and he has his gaze trained on me. He's looking at me so intensely that it causes my skin to heat. The prickles of fire skate across my entire body before settling in my core.

"Mhmm. I've seen that look before," she explains, looking away from the island before downing the rest of her margarita in one gulp. "I think you are about to have your hands full. The way Hendrix is looking at you screams dirty sex and multiple orgasms. And I for one am jealous."

I swallow, my throat suddenly dry at the attention. She's not wrong and I'm not complaining. Our attraction is simmering right under the surface, just waiting for the opportunity to boil over.

Lilah's hand rattles my mostly empty glass. "Why don't you go grab us another round of margaritas and Cruz and I will restart the movie," she suggests with a little nudge of her shoulder. Not even attempting to pretend she's not meddling to push us together. Crossing the space to the island where I left all the margarita supplies, I grab another slice of buffalo mac pizza and step into the space that Cruz just left.

"Did you try any of the buffalo mac pizza yet? So good. The perfect mix of gooey and hot," I explain, picking the pizza up off my plate and folding it in half to keep the toppings from escaping. Hendrix shakes his head and turns his body, so he's angled toward me. My eyebrow lifts in question and he tilts his chin down to bring himself closer to my height.

He opens his mouth, and I bring the pizza to his lips. Watching his mouth close around the bite and lick the stray cheese from his bottom lip is the most erotic experience I have had in a while. Which speaks volumes about my sex life and priorities as of late.

"You weren't kidding, that's good. I think chicken on pizza is the winner tonight," he says around the bite.

"Or maybe I'm the winner," I say to myself. My voice barely a whisper.

Turning the pizza back toward me, I bring the slice to my lips and bite from the same spot. Hendrix's gaze drops to my mouth. The space between us shrinks, I'm not sure who made the move. Tension crackles like wildfire between us, hot and uncontrolled. The way he is looking at me has me fighting the urge to push up on my toes to press my lips to his.

As tempting as his full lips are, this isn't where I want to have our first kiss — in the middle of Cruz's kitchen with our friends across the room. I fight the urge not allowing myself to give into the moment. Hendrix's attention stays on my mouth, but he doesn't move any closer. Instead, his hand comes up settling under my chin, the rough pad of his thumb swipes across my bottom lip.

So slowly.

A whimper escapes without my permission as his thumbprint leaves a scorching path in its wake. Desire trickles from the spot on my lip to the tips of my toes. I watch in awe as he brings his thumb to his mouth, sucking the sauce off his finger. The sound of an explosion in the movie jolts me back to reality and breaks the spell.

"Want to help me with the margaritas?" I struggle to keep my voice from sounding breathless. Hen just nods wordlessly and joins me as we make another round.

When we take our spots back on the couch, he lifts the blanket up so I can take my seat and then carefully arranges it so that it covers my feet before he slips underneath it. This time he sits close enough that we are pressed tightly together, my side connecting with his chest and my head resting on his shoulder. We stay like that silently watching the movie for a while.

At one point during the movie we all get into a debate about which action hero has the best abs. The argument is between Thor and Captain America. But I disagree. "My vote goes to Ironman." That causes Cruz and Lilah to look at me like I'm nuts while Hendrix dips his head and laughs into my hair.

"Is that so? Even better than Thor?" Hendrix asks quietly, his lips tickling my ear and his nose pressed into my hair. It spurs me on, giving me the bravery I need to slide my hand across his stomach letting it come to rest on the body part in question.

"Yep. Ironman all the way, fight me on it. But be warned this is the hill I will die on," I proclaim loudly enough for everyone to hear. The laughter bubbling out of Hendrix causes the muscles under my hand to bunch and I know my vote went to the right place when I feel the divots and valley twitch beneath my palm. I go to pull my hand away and his fingers wrap around my wrist holding me there.

"Leave it. I like your hands on me."

"If you insist," I answer softly, looking up to meet his eyes. His pupils are blown wide, leaving little of the familiar aqua blue behind. I feel my face flush with heat. What started as playful banter fun has quickly turned molten hot.

Hendrix grips my chin between his fingers, tilting it up so he can see my face. I resist, afraid that if I look up and see the need in his eyes again that I'll crawl into his lap here and now. *God, this man makes me I.*

He doesn't relent, gently forcing my chin to leave his shoulder. "Go on a date with me." His hushed voice is firm as if leaving no room for argument. It's said with confidence that he has no doubt it's what we both want.

I nod and he releases his grip on my chin, allowing my face to rest back onto his shoulder.

I stay glued to his side for the rest of the night and savor the feel of his hard body pressed up against me. Eventually we start another movie, but I only make it through the opening scene before falling asleep on the couch tucked against Hendrix.

♥

Sometime around sunrise, the glow coming in from the window causes me to turn away from it to bring me face to face with Hendrix. Overnight, we shifted in our sleep so that we are both lying horizontally on the couch. His leg is draped over mine and somehow I ended up cradled in his arms. I settle my head back into his shoulder and drift back to sleep, wanting just a little more time like this before the rising sun wakes up everyone in the apartment.

Low laughter and shuffling in the other room has my eyes slowly fluttering open. The sound is muffled by the door, but it's enough to disrupt the peaceful sleep I'd fallen back into. My eyes slowly open and close a few times. The warmth of the body next to me on the couch wills my subconscious to fight waking up.

Hendrix runs his palm up my back and his hand tangles in my hair as he tenderly grips the back of my neck. "Good morning," he rumbles with his voice gravely with sleep in a way that has me clenching my thighs. His lips press to my forehead as he says, "You look so fucking good like this. Wrapped up in me first thing in the morning."

My hands sneak up his shirt and run over his chest. I press myself against him, knowing that we probably only have minutes before the cavalry comes marching out of the master bedroom and ruins the moment.

For a second, I'm distracted by the realization that Cruz and Lilah shared his bed instead of her taking the guest bed. I quickly push that thought aside as Hendrix groans, flexing his hips into me with delicious pressure. He is hard and thick where he presses against my hip. "Fuck, you can't do that right now."

Not one to relent, I meet his eye, my breath catching. "What do you think the chances are that they'll just stay in there for another hour or so?" I have never wanted Lilah to ditch her fears about hooking up with Cruz and go for it as much as I do at this moment.

Still gripping the back of my head with one hand, his other snakes out from under me and slides up my rib cage pulling the hem of my shirt from last night with it. A stream of goose bumps blossom along my skin. His hand stops, leaving his thumb resting right below my breast.

My hips shift again, chasing any friction they can find as my nipples pull tight from his touch. "Poppy," he grunts, but I can't tell if it's a warning or an invitation. "There is no chance we have more than a few minutes. They have been giggling for a while." My pulse hammers wildly at the slip that he's been awake for some time but chose not to wake me.

"You're probably right," I tell him, bringing my forehead to rest against his. It would be so easy to kiss him right here and now. "I want more than a few minutes with you."

Giving in to my impulses, I bring my lips to the corner of his mouth and brush a light kiss there while tilting my hips up one last time before I force myself to break contact.

He growls, his grip tightening around my neck and ribs. Suddenly he shifts, rolling me underneath him. His athleticism pays off, somehow he keeps our bodies aligned and our foreheads pressed together. "When this happens," he breathes out, grinding his erection into me and stealing my breath away. "I want you alone and hours to take my time with you," he says, rotating his hips again as if to prove a point. And I'm here for it. An audible moan escapes me. He responds by taking a page out of my book laying a quick kiss on the corner of my mouth. "You and me, it's going to be so fucking good. I can just feel it. When I get back from this road trip, you're mine. I'm taking you out. Alone. No double dates. No Cruz or Lilah. Just you and me." He places a kiss on my forehead. "I'm going to get up now, but I want you to know it is physically killing me to do it."

I whimper but nod as he releases me and pushes up to get off the couch. I watch as he gives himself a squeeze through his joggers, seemingly trying to get a handle on the situation in his pants.

"I'm going to start some coffee. Do me a favor and stay here for a minute or I'll end up pinning you against the island in our friend's kitchen?"

"Promises, promises." I chant under my breath. Looking over his shoulder, he raises his eyebrows almost like a dare to try him.

Hendrix crosses the living room and starts riffling around for the coffee. Turning on the couch, I watch him searching but stay put. Just enjoying the view. I need the space just as much as he does. I can still feel the pulse between my legs and my face is hot. Sucking in air, I take a few deep breaths to get myself under control before I push myself off the couch.

"It's in the cupboard next to the fridge," I tell Hendrix, moving to the other side of the island, hoping the solid object between us will be enough of the barrier.

"Thanks," he replies, grabbing it and continuing with the task at hand. "I meant what I said last night." He says not offering any additional details, but I know what he's talking about — the date. Once the coffee is brewing, he comes to stand opposite me and leans over on his forearms, getting as close as he can with the barrier.

"This," he motions back and forth between us with his hand. "It's hot and needy. I like that about it —" he pauses, and his lips tilt into a smile "— but I like you, Poppy. This isn't just a physical thing for me. I want to get to know you."

"You're not so bad yourself, Ironman." I tease to keep things light because that's what I'm built for. But the door to Cruz's bedroom opens, and Lilah comes out with Cruz following close behind to cut our conversation short.

"Do I smell coffee?" Lilah asks, interrupting the conversation unknowingly.

"Hendrix just started it. Like the hero he is," I tack on the end, making eye contact with him from across the room.

Blissfully oblivious, Lilah comes over and takes a seat next to me at the island while Cruz fills coffee mugs and passes them out. Hendrix waves him off when he starts pouring one for him.

"Nah. I'm going to duck out for a run before the gym. Are we still meeting up later to lift?" he asks Cruz as he slips his shoes on.

"Sure. I'll see you in a few hours."

"Enjoy your day off," I tell him as he finishes tying his laces.

"I'll text you."

He pauses to look up at me. Lilah's eyebrow raises but she doesn't say anything.

"About the road trip," Hendrix covers with a smirk, and I see my friend's face fall in disappointment. I nod and bring the coffee mug to my lips to blow on it. He watches the movement. His attention laser focused on my lips, before rising to his full height and opening the door to leave.

CHAPTER 7

POPPY

I groan as I read through the shipping notification for my sound booth. It's delayed again, this time by a week. Not only does that mean I won't be able to record my demo, but it also means that I need to keep taking calls with my current clients with nothing to reduce the disruption to my new neighbor. I have stopped over several more times to make introductions with no success.

The previous owner only used the apartment for business travel to Denver and was rarely in the apartment during the hours I work. My new neighbor seems to travel a lot too, or perhaps they work an off shift so our paths haven't crossed yet. I make a snap decision and walk next door to introduce myself again.

The walk is short, but the nerves roll through my body at the thought they might already have formed an opinion about me if they heard any of my calls. But I straighten my spine and knock once, waiting to see if they'll answer. I can't even imagine what they must think goes on in my apartment. An apology and an order of scones from Buns and Roses might be a good idea to smooth things over. I bite my lip nervously before I raise my hand to the door knocking a second time.

Maybe the fact we seem to be on opposite schedules is a good thing. If they aren't around much, then maybe they haven't overheard any of my calls. I haven't seen them coming or going at all.

Once the sound booth is assembled, I'll feel more comfortable knowing that I'm not disrupting them. Other than the booth, everything else is ready to go in my new recording space.

I plan out my day as I make the short walk back to my apartment. My goal is to spend today working on branding and networking. I need to get my name out there which means building up a following on social media for my narration accounts, creating content, and getting exposure in the writing community.

One thing that really drew me to become a marketing major was the creativity and design side of the work. The sense of accomplishment when creating something that helped to establish how consumers react to a brand, product or service fills my jar. I'm excited to do more of that on this new career journey.

Growing up, I did things my own way, never following the path laid out in front of me. My free spirited nature frustrated my parents to no end, not because I was unruly, I just did things my own way. Despite the fact that my creativity was stifled as a child, I've learned how to embrace it.

Without that side of me, I wouldn't be successful at the business I built. Being in the adult industry has made me acutely aware of the people I let into my life. I surround myself with people who are open minded and don't judge me for my work. If someone doesn't support me I don't have space for them in my life. Unlike my parents, my friends respect my boundaries, allowing me to disclose how I make a living to new people on my own terms.

My phone buzzes next to me on the couch to pull my head out of the designs I'm working on for my new logo. I'm about to switch it to Do not disturb so I can focus on my work but see that it's a text from Hendrix. I haven't heard from him since he left Cruz's yesterday morning. Tapping the chopstick against my lips, I open the message.

HENDRIX:

Hey Poppy. How was the rest of your day yesterday?

POPPY:

Once I hiked off all that unresolved tension that I woke up with it was good. Productive. You?

HENDRIX:

Tell me more about how you worked off this tension. Was it just hiking?

POPPY:

Nice try. That's not a conversation I'm having before you buy me dinner.

HENDRIX:

Speaking of dinner. I get back in town late next Wednesday. We don't have a game on Thursday. Any chance I can take you out then?

POPPY:

I probably shouldn't tell you this.

HENDRIX:

Tell me anyway. I want all your secrets.

POPPY:

I don't want to wait that long.
But yes, Thursday night works.

HENDRIX:

I know. This road trip came at the worst time. Can I text you while I'm gone?

POPPY:

Please.

HENDRIX:

If we are doing this thing Poppy, it's just me and you. I'm not seeing anyone else. I want you to know that. I don't share.

POPPY:

There's no one else I want.

POPPY:

I think I found a loophole.

HENDRIX:

I have no idea what you are talking about, but you have my attention.

POPPY:

The loophole to your question earlier.

The three dots dance on my screen as I wait for him to catch on.

HENDRIX:

Poppy, don't mess with me right now.
I'm on a plane with a bunch of guys.

POPPY:

You paid for pizza the other night.
That counts as dinner, right?

HENDRIX:

Pretty and clever. Let's revisit this conversation later when I'm not surrounded by teammates.

HENDRIX:

I was actually texting you about plants. Now I feel foolish even bringing them up. I'll email you my address and details. Because I don't want to ruin this by talking horticulture with you right now.

POPPY:

Poppytalks@zmail.com

HENDRIX:

Good talk gorgeous.

POPPY:

Later Ironman.

With do not disturb activated on my phone, I get back to work on my logo. Once I'm happy with the design, I open my content planning software to work on my social media marketing strategy for the next month. The sun is setting out the window, and I realize that I have been wrapped up in work all day with no human interaction aside from my text messages with Hendrix.

My phone is resting on the coffee table in front of me and the screen is filled with notifications. This couch undoubtedly has a permanent indent of my ass sitting crisscross applesauce with how long it's been since I moved. Stretching my arms above my head, I link my fingers together, palms facing the ceiling and lengthen my muscles. They scream in protest, angry that I have made them sit hunched over this computer for so long.

Deliberately I shift my legs out from underneath me, allowing the blood back into my feet. They prickle as I stretch them out in front of me and grab my phone. Scrolling through the notifications, I see the email from Hendrix but don't open it right away. I'm hanging onto the sexy vibe from earlier as long as possible. Besides, I won't need to water plants for him until the weekend.

As I'm hovering my finger over the email from Hendrix, contemplating whether to open it, a text from my mom comes through distracting me. She's checking to make sure I'm alive. I send her a quick text promising a phone call later this week and a quick selfie as proof of life. Our relationship is tenuous at best and holding her off is an art form I have perfected. Maybe it makes me an asshole, but I have to protect my joy from her toxic negativity.

Next, I tackle the pile of texts from Lilah. She's bored with Cruz being on a road trip and wants to make plans. I respond and we go back and forth but ultimately make plans to get ramen at a place down the street, followed by wine night at her apartment.

Lilah rubs her stomach making circles with her hand as she groans. "I'm so full. There isn't any room in here for wine," she protests as she unlocks the door. "That's a lie. There's always room for wine, but it will be a hardship."

A tote bag of wine that we picked up on the walk back in one hand, I pull the door shut with the other. "Once you have sweatpants on, it won't be a hardship. Go make Joey proud and pull on your best Thanksgiving Day stretchy pants." I set the wine down so I can slide off my boots. Lilah pads down the hall to change.

When she returns, she has an extra pair of sweatpants in her hands. She tosses them at me and twists her hair up in a bun as she goes to grab wine glasses. "Go get comfortable, babe. If you want anything else just grab it."

"Cue up some tunes while I'm gone." I tell her, walking backward toward the bedroom to change. My pants are in a pile at my feet when I hear Miley Cyrus "Flowers" coming from her Bluetooth speaker. Dancing toward her closet, I decide to lose the bra and grab an oversized Bandits sweatshirt. Wearing anything that she snagged from Cruz feels like a weird betrayal of Hendrix, so I pick one I know she bought for herself.

The thought brings a smile to my face. Acting on impulse, I snap a quick selfie in the mirror. It's me smiling over my shoulder. Before I can second guess it, I add a quick message wishing him good luck and hit send. I pocket my phone and make my way out to the living room.

Lilah has couch cushions, throw pillows, and blankets piled up on the floor of the living room between the coffee table and the TV. It's our standard setup for when we watch away games together. It's sloth-level comfortable. We can reach the snacks and drinks on the table behind us while we lounge around watching the game. On several occasions, we have fallen asleep in our gameday cocoon.

Before I take a seat, I adjust the pillows, getting them just the way I like. Once I have them piled up recliner style, I plop down next to Lilah. She's got one of Cruz's warmups on with her sweatpants. She looks adorable, his number on the sleeve and his name stamped across her back.

I launch my sneak attack when Lilah gets up to turn on the TV to prepare for the game. When she has her back turned, I snap a candid picture of her and send it to Cruz with the message, "your girl is watching."

"Is it time for share and tell?" Lilah wiggles down under the blankets and props herself up on her side to face me, her brow cocked in question.

"Are you sure you want to go there? I have no problem sharing, but are you going to feel the same when it's your turn?" I grab the loose pillow next to me and toss it at her with a smirk on my face.

Lilah's cheeks blush and she glances away picking at nonexistent lint on her shoulder. "There's not much to share. We're just friends."

"The kind of friends that share a bed. Are you going to pretend that you and Cruz sleep together regularly, and it's just never come up?" I accuse sarcastically. "It's okay I can start while you think of some more nonsense to sling my way."

Lilah's mouth opens and closes several times her lips moving like a fish. I finally throw her a bone and change the topic back to Hen and me. "Hen asked me on a date at movie night."

Lilah sputters, almost choking on her wine. She uses the sleeve of her shirt to wipe the tears gathering in the corner of her eyes. I continue as she recovers. "God, Lilah, when we woke up together on that couch it took everything in my power not to strip him naked — even with the threat of you and Cruz walking in on us."

Lilah is staring at me, mouth hanging open at that. "What the hell happened under that blanket during Avengers?"

"You and Cruz were so wrapped up in each other neither of you noticed me going down on Hen during the second movie." I deadpan taking a sip of my wine as I watch her tilt her head to the side before her face splits into a grin.

"That I don't believe. I can't see you being into exhibitionism." She eyes me curiously as her hand swirls the wine in her glass. Narrowing her eyes at me like the simple act gives her a window into my brain, she muses. "You'd get jealous too easily to be into someone watching." Her trick works because she's not wrong about that.

"You're right, that didn't happen. But I did definitely feel up his six-pack under the blankets during our debate." I smile, able to recall the feel of his toned stomach under my fingers — warm and carved with hard muscle. I have thought about it so many times that it's a core memory now.

"What was with lobbying for Ironman's abs?" Suddenly distracted by that detail.

Laughing, I bring the wine to my lips for a sip before setting it back down over my shoulder. "It's a nickname I gifted Hendrix when we ran into each other at the park."

"Oh my god, you're ridiculous. Ironman really, of all the Avengers, that's who you picked?" Her head tips back with laughter before refocusing on the TV. "Don't you dare speak ill of Robert Downey Jr." My rant is cut short when a clip of the team warming up flashes on the screen while the game day announcers talk in the foreground. I catch sight of Hendrix stretching, his white baseball pants pulled tight across his muscular thigh. When they zoom in he's laughing with Dom looking handsome as ever.

Her gaze shifts back to me, and her face softens. "You really like him."

"I really do. It feels different this time," I sigh. "The attraction is nuclear hot, but it's more than that." I contemplate how to explain it. It's all very new, but we have had several long conversations over the past week. "He is kind and I like spending time with him. The love he has for the women in his life, his grandma and sister, it's so — unyielding. The idea of being loved unconditionally by someone—" I pause and look at the screen again. He's gone and it's a commercial now. "It wrecks me emotionally in all the best ways. I want that in my life, and I'm not saying he's the one, but he makes me want to chase it. Try for something meaningful instead of just being the short-term casual or fun girl for once."

Lilah brings her hand to my shoulder and squeezes. "So, are you ready to try after Paul? Because you deserve all of those things, and as your friend, it's killed me to watch you shut down to the possibility of more for the last two years. You deserve someone to see you for who you are and to love you because of it. Not in spite of it. Like I do." Her lips turn down and I know she's thinking of my parents right alongside my ex.

"I'm getting ahead of myself. We haven't had a conversation about what I do for a living. That's always been a sticky conversation with guys. It ends up changing everything for them not to mention we haven't even been on a date yet."

"Have you thought about when you are going to have the big job talk with him?" Lilah asks.

"I'm nervous about it, but I want to do it face to face. So, I'll talk to him next week when he's home. I'll only have a week left by then. It's not like the work itself is going to interfere with a potential relationship like it has in the past." I sigh, thinking of Paul. Lilah understands what an issue it's been with guys and as a result, I just haven't been dating seriously. "He needs to accept that part of my life — of me — even if it's ending. I don't want to be with someone who can't deal with or is ashamed of it — of me."

"I slept with Cruz," Lilah says but doesn't elaborate, giving me conversational whiplash. My eyes bug out at her bold statement.

"That's not new information. But care to clarify? Are we talking platonic snuggles or P in V style?"

"Shared a bed, nothing happened— not really?" Her brows furrow in question like she's not really sure. "After we fell asleep, he carried me to his bed. He was going to go back out to the couch, that way if you or Hen wandered into the guest bedroom, it was open."

"That was thoughtful of him, but completely unnecessary." I muse, thinking about the fact that a herd of wild horses couldn't have pulled me off the couch with Hendrix that night.

"I woke up when he laid me down in his room. He went to leave, but I asked him to stay." She takes a long drink from her wine as if gathering her thoughts before she goes on. "He stripped down to his underwear and crawled in next to me, like it was no big deal. Like he wasn't about to sleep next to his best friend looking hotter than anyone has a right to."

"Shit. What did you do?" I ask, knowing that to Lilah, it probably was a big deal with how she's been conflicted about her feelings for him lately.

"I shimmied out of my pants, did that fun trick where you remove your bra from under your shirt, dropped it all off the side of the bed and went to sleep. What was I supposed to do?" She shrugs but doesn't elaborate.

My mouth drops open how easily she handled the situation, leaves me feeling astounded. "Are you still feeling confused?"

"Yes. Still confused and terrified, but I don't think I care anymore. Do you know what I mean?" She looks at the TV where Cruz is jogging out to his spot in the outfield. He spreads his legs and stretches from side to side, reaching for his toes before snapping his feet together and jumping in place.

"You know you won't lose him. He won't cut you out. No matter what happens. You know that, right?" My hand makes circles on her back, trying to reassure her he won't walk away like her ex did.

"I want to know if he feels it too. The magnetism between us. I don't want to pretend it's not there anymore." Lilah worries her bottom lip.

I roll into her and tackle her in a hug and give her a big smooch on the cheek. "I'm proud of you, Lilah. Look at us both trying to put our pasts behind us." I pull back so she can see I'm serious. Taking a chance like this after Brad is a big deal for her.

We fall silent and watch the boys go three up, three down in the field before hitting. Neither of us takes our attention away from the game as Cruz and then Hendrix bat, and both of them get on base. The inning ends before either score. But that doesn't last long. In the third, Cruz makes a play in the outfield that shifts the momentum to the Bandits, stealing a homerun from the wall.

They carry that energy over to their hitting and Cruz hits a deep line drive giving him a double before Hendrix sneaks one through the gap in right field, scoring a run and making it to second himself. The rest of the team feeds off it, pushing themselves harder and it's an easy win from there. Lilah and I are on our feet cheering as the team celebrates the win on the field and Dom leads the charge to dump yellow Gatorade all over Cruz's head. Lilah and I laugh when he tips his head back, shaking the sticky liquid off like a dog.

When the game is done, I walk back to my apartment, taking my time and enjoying the walk. The wine has me feeling a little warm and fuzzy, so the cool air feels divine against my skin.

By the time I'm stepping into the lobby of my build I'm revitalized from the brief trip home, leaving me with too much energy to sleep. I power on my laptop to get a little work done before bed and return to the kitchen while it boots up to get something to drink. Tea sounds good. Maybe it will help me get in the headspace for sleep and mellow me out. I put some water in my electric kettle and grab a chamomile lavender tea bag. As I wait for the water to heat and the tea to steep, I move around the kitchen, cleaning up from the day. Then change into a pair of soft sleep shorts and a cami.

Cradling the warm mug of tea in my hand, I return to the office. There's no shortage of work that needs to get done so, I take a minute to run my finger down my to-do list. Weighing where I want to start and what I can realistically accomplish tonight. I check my email for responses from publishers, authors, and editors about upcoming projects. As I move through the inbox, I come across the email from Hendrix and skip it to focus on my work, leaving it for when I'm finished.

My inbox dwindles down as I continue working on responses to the emails and then switch to working my way through social media messages and notifications. The tea takes hold after about an hour, making my body feel heavy. When I rub my eyes and cover a yawn, that's my cue to call it quits for the night.

Feeling relaxed from the tea, I fall into my bed. Laying there and just enjoying the stillness and sense of accomplishment from tackling so much of my work. When I feel myself slipping off, I reach across to my nightstand to plug my phone in. Few things are worse than the regret of waking up to a dead phone.

A notification catches my eye. It must have come through when I was working. I smile when I see that it's a text message from Hendrix. Rolling onto my back and propping myself up against my pillow, I can't help but smirk. *I could stay up just a few more minutes for this.*

When I unlock my phone, I see the text includes a picture.

HENDRIX:

Thanks for the text earlier, hope you had a good night.

It's the picture that really captures my attention. He's in his hotel room bed lying on his back, with his arm under his head — no shirt — smirking at the camera. It's a standard issue fuckboy pose, and I'm not even mad about it.

POPPY:

That pose is giving I send unsolicited dick pics.

HENDRIX:

Does it now. Noted... no more shirtless pictures for you. Sorry to have offended your sensibilities my lady.

That's not the results I was hoping for. *Abort.* Opening his contact up, I hit call.

"Hey, Poppy." Hendrix says smoothly, like he knows he's got me riled up with his last message.

"Nowhere in that message did I say I disapproved of your text message antics."

"Hmmm... your response was giving a respect-my-boundary vibe," he says, throwing my teasing back in my face. I live for this banter between us. The fact that he doesn't take life too seriously is one reason I enjoy spending time with him. He keeps things light and fun. That's something I can do without putting feelings on the line.

Pulling my phone away from my ear, I click to switch the call to FaceTime. Just to make sure we are clear that seeing him shirtless in bed isn't outside of my boundaries. Not at all. *Please, sweet baby Jesus, let him be shirtless.*

"FaceTime? So, my nakedness isn't off-putting?" His voice dances with amusement as he continues to let my request go unanswered.

"Hendrix, accept the damn FaceTime." I say with faux irritation in my voice.

His face, inked shoulders, and broad chest fill up the screen of my phone. A layer of dark stubble covers his jaw, making me think he hasn't shaved on the road. It makes me wonder if that's part of a superstition. His hair is messy from being in bed. It softens his rugged look with the facial hair and tattoos. The man on my screen is a literal fantasy.

"Hey, Beautiful. It's good to see your face," Hendrix says with an unguarded smile.

"You too, for the record, you can send me shirtless pictures anytime. You look like all of my fantasies rolled into one right now. Cozy and a little dangerous." I gesture with my hand to the screen as my eyes roam his chest, to focus on those tattoos that get me so hot.

"Let's come back to that comment, but first tell me about your night."

My heartbeat picks up at the knowledge that he wants to hear about my night when we could have so easily slipped into flirty banter. Instead, he wants to know about the mundane details of my day.

I tell him about the dinner with Lilah, raving about how delicious the ramen was. We talk about our favorite kinds of wine and learn that he doesn't care for it but also that he's never tried any decent ones.

We're both laughing when I learn that his introduction to wine came from stealing his nana's sherry. He doesn't get butthurt over my teasing that his distaste makes sense if that's his baseline for good wine. That's how it is with us, the conversation flows like we've know each other for much longer. No matter what we're talking about he always finds a way to make me smile.

I ask him about Phoenix and if he's done anything outside of baseball. He tells me about a hike he and his teammates are planning to go on before they need to be at the stadium tomorrow. When Hendrix explains the match up for the next two series on this road trip, his love for the game is written on his face. We go back and forth like that for a while when Hen falls quiet. I roll from my back to my side and prop up the phone on my nightstand.

"Want to share with the class?" I ask him to break the silence. Before he speaks. He mimics my move and sets his phone off to the side, tucking his arm under his head.

"I was just thinking — you look so pretty like this, all sleepy and relaxed. Tell me more about those fantasies you mentioned earlier." His gaze travels down my face and neck to my chest and then sweeps back up.

His voice is rough and a little hitched. The sound of it combined with the intensity of his gaze on me sends heat straight to my core.

My fingers toy with the hem of my cami. "Right now, I can't stop thinking about that pizza from the other night. It was so good."

His forehead crinkles before his eyes widen. The text messages we exchanged earlier click into place. Hendrix's voice is low and rough when he demands, "Tell me how you worked through the tension after movie night."

"What do you want to know?" My hand moves higher and pulls my tank up with it just enough that a sliver of skin is showing under my bunched-up top.

He drags his hand down his face, peeking out at me from between his fingers. "Fuck Poppy, I can't even think straight with your hand under your top right now. Don't toy with me."

"But it's so much fun," I say, pulling my hand away. He squeezes his eyes shut, rallying himself.

"I didn't mean for you to stop. It's just distracting as fuck. All I can think about is replacing your hand with mine." He shifts on the bed, so he is propped up against the headboard giving me a view of his sculpted abs. If he were here I'd drag my tongue across each one, tracing the pattern they make before they form that perfect v. "Did you have to touch yourself to get rid of the tension, Poppy? I know I did. Tell me how you got yourself off thinking of me."

The way he says my name and commands my attention with his words is intoxicating. I watch his every move with rapt attention as his hand dips below the camera screen. If I close my eyes, I can see him cupping himself over his underwear. All his muscles and bare skin are on display for me. "I'll tell you, but I need you to promise me something."

"What is it?" he asks urgently, like he would give me anything to keep playing this game.

I swallow, my throat suddenly dry, and consider how to explain what I want. It's a struggle to find the words. My mind seems to have melted. "The first time I see you — I want to touch you. Keep that camera on your handsome face."

"Same. Tonight, I want to hear you, get to know the sounds you make. See what you look like when you fall apart with my name on your lips."

Jesus, that hits me right where I'm already throbbing for him.

"Yeah?" I've never done this before. Which sounds absurd considering my career, but it's true, touching myself like this for someone else on the phone is new to me. My hand shakes with nerves as it trails down from my neck. My breasts are heavy and achy. I tweak and pull at my nipples through my top trying to get some relief. He has me so worked up and we are just getting started but this already feels exceptionally intimate.

"That's it, Beautiful. You have me so hard right now. I can't stop thinking about the way you felt in my arms when we woke up together. So soft and warm."

"I wanted you so badly. After you left, I made an excuse to leave before I finished my coffee. The walk home was torture." It was almost painful. The way he pinned me to the couch replaying on a loop in my head. As I walked home, every touch of my thighs together escalated my need.

"I know, when I got home it was like I could still feel you under me." The muscles in his forearms flex and veins strain as he moves his hand slowly off camera. *Why are forearms so sexy?*

I would do just about anything for Hendrix to be here with me, I'm not sure I have ever been so turned on in my life. My hand dips back under my top pulling it up so that most of my stomach is exposed. The cool air against my heated skin makes me shiver as I pluck at my nipple working it into an achy bud under my shirt.

"I came home and took a shower. My skin felt like it was on fire. Nothing helped to cool it. Every time I closed my eyes you were —" I can't hold back my moan. "Right there. I imagined you being there with me. I couldn't not touch myself."

"Did the shower help?" Hendrix demands, the muscles in his chest and shoulder twitching with every stroke of his hand.

"No, it couldn't touch the fire you started within me." I admit breathlessly.

"Tell me how you did it. Did you have to touch yourself to get some relief?" He asks, sounding on edge himself.

I swallow down my nerves and give him what he's asking for. I know how to do this. That's not the problem. I haven't been this vulnerable with anyone in a long time, but for Hendrix, I want to. "Yes. I did — I came so fast thinking of you. I used the detachable shower head and imagined it was you with your head between my legs," I tell him, struggling to focus on anything other than the insistent pulse between my legs.

"Poppy, I'm barely hanging on here." he grits out, sounding pained. "If I slid my hand down your shorts, would you be wet for me?"

Keeping my eyes on Hendrix, I slip my hand down my shorts, letting my finger circle over my clit before dipping lower. "Soaked, all for you. If you were here, would you make me come with your fingers or your tongue?" My finger sinks in giving my body what it needs, and a tremble rattles through my body.

"Both. Poppy, I'd give you everything and just know you'd take it so beautifully. I'd keep going until you were squirming and begging for me to fuck you." A low groan releases from Hendrix chest. "Add another finger and fill yourself up. I need you there with me." His breathing is ragged now like he's just as desperate for this as I am.

The sound of my name on his lips alone is almost enough to push me off the ledge. My toes are hanging off the edge, and I'm so close to falling. I use the heel of my palm to put pressure on my clit. My mouth drops open and my eyes drift closed.

"Poppy, eyes on me. I don't want to miss a thing when you shatter for me." he commands. His voice brings my focus back to those devilish blue eyes. "That's my girl."

His praise does it. I dive right off the ledge, my whole body collapsing in on itself before it explodes into a divine weightlessness. Shattering for him just like he said I would.

"Hendrix — Oh god." I breathe out. A strangled cry leaving my mouth. "Hendrix…" His name on my lips sends him tumbling right down after me. He comes with a grunt uttering my name under his breath.

We lay there silently catching our breath for a moment. Both our chests heave with exertion. My nerves from earlier at being this vulnerable with him over video long gone. This is an experience that exceeded my wildest expectations. The way we played off each other to give the other what they need, I wanted more of it.

After working in the business for so long, I never thought I would enjoy phone sex. I was very wrong, but I'm certain that it was solely because of my partner. Pushing it out of my mind for another time, I roll to my back and tilt my head toward the phone.

"Hey, Hendrix."

"Hhhmmm," he mumbles as his hand sweeps through his hair, pushing the dark sweat damp strands off his forehead.

"That was like next-level good. I don't think I have ever come that hard before. Just thought you'd like to know."

He chuckles, turning his head so he's looking at me. His smile lights up the screen. "Thanks for sharing. And Poppy?"

"Yes?" My mouth opens in a yawn I cover with the back of my hand. Sleep is about to steal me away.

"I wish I could kiss you right now," he says sweetly.

"I'd really like that too. Why is Thursday so far away?" I curl into my pillows and reach for the phone bringing it closer. Hendrix's eyes look as heavy as mine feel.

"I know. I'll be reliving tonight until then. I made a mess of myself, so I should probably clean up and get some rest. Can we talk tomorrow?" His hand waves carelessly at his crotch, like the effort of the motion is too much. Uncertainty creeps into his voice like he doesn't really want to do either of those things.

"We can. Get some sleep, Hen."

"Good night, Beautiful," he tells me with a wave as we disconnect the call.

My phone never makes it to the charger. Sleep takes me with my phone still in hand. And I wake up with zero regrets about the low battery or anything else.

CHAPTER 8

HENDRIX

I blindly grapple for my phone, hand searching the night-stand to snooze the alarm. By the time I drag myself out of bed there are only minutes to spare before I need to meet the guys for our hike. Cruz, Dean, and Dom are waiting for me when the elevator door slides open.

We pile into an Uber and head through the city toward the trailhead. Dean and Dom clamored to the back and are laughing about some girl Dom tried to pick up last night. From what I gather, he was shut down hard.

Good for her.

"Did you go out last night?" I ask Cruz, motioning over my shoulder to the others in the back. He's a bit of a home-body and tends to stay in while we are on the road, but he mentioned needing to get out of the hotel yesterday. His attitude turns surly anytime his personal life or dating comes up these days.

"No, I stayed in. Lilah and I talked, and then I binge watched a documentary on deforestation in the Brazilian Amazon." His attitude is still firmly in place.

"You're going to have to talk about it, eventually. If you don't, this shit with Lilah is going to blow up in your face." He's been quiet with what's going on between them. But the tension between them has been steadily climbing.

Cruz looks out the window and says nothing. Deciding to wait him out, I shift in my seat and watch him.

"You're not going to let this go? Are you?" His eyes meet mine in the reflection on the window before facing forward again.

"Not a chance. Want to roleplay? I'll pretend to be Lilah and you can practice on me?" He grunts but doesn't tell me to shut up, so I keep talking. "You liked Lilah when you met, right? But it was right after her fiancé cheated and Jarrett had died that year too. So, the timing was fucked."

"I'm not roleplaying with you; I'm a full-grown man." Cruz mocks looking back out the window.

"But I'm not wrong, am I? It's because of those two clowns, if we were alone you'd jump on that."

Cruz rolls his eyes, but I can see it there on his face. I'm right.

"Lilah friend zoned you right off the bat, and you didn't pressure her for more. Now you two are besties, braiding each other's hair and shit." This earns me a headshake and a smile from Cruz. *Progress, I'll take it.*

"That was one time. You should be impressed, braiding is complicated. There's no way your sausage fingers can do it?" he scoffs, wiggling his finger between us.

"Master braider, right here." I point both my thumbs at my chest. "My sister broke her arm in middle school. I learned how to do it to help her because I'm an awesome brother." Suddenly I'm struck by a vision of Poppy in bed and me braiding her hair. I push the thought aside for now.

"Where was I? You and Lilah are besties now, and you are both mostly healed from your respective traumas. You never really stopped wanting her. Instead, you just suppressed it, but it's creeping to the surface, and you can't stop it. How am I doing so far?"

He rubs his hand down his face before replying. "Annoyingly well." Cruz sighs deeply. "I don't think she's ready yet, and I'm not sure she'll ever be."

"I think Lilah's closer than you realize," I tell him honestly. Thinking about the times it's come up with Poppy, she's kept it pretty close to the chest but given me the distinct impression that it's on Lilah's mind as well.

"I'm terrified that if I push her, it'll freak her out and I'll lose her. Christ, you saw what happened with the movie night fiasco." His voice is tight and pained. "I was hoping I could get a better feel for where she was at, but she freaked out and made it a group thing."

"I thought movie night was awesome." A sly smile splits my face.

Cruz whips his head in my direction, nostrils flaring. "I bet you did. Getting felt up on my couch while Delilah was a nervous wreck over by me."

"There was no —" I start and then stop. That's not strictly true but also not a lie. "There was a little PG groping under the blanket."

"Is it time to talk about your problems yet?" he asks as the driver turns into the parking lot for the trailhead.

Grabbing my water bottle from the cup holder, I open the door. "That depends on what problems you are referring to."

The gravel crunches underneath the tires of the Uber as it pull away and we walk toward the trailhead. "Which problem should we start with? How about the fact that you don't date but you were awfully cozy with Poppy the other night and then asked her out?"

"I don't — Or I didn't. I haven't dated anyone since Kylie." Hooked up on the road, yes, but never at home because I don't trust anyone in my space.

"She fucked you up good," he says with a whistle.

She really did.

"I should have known from the minute I met Kylie that it was doomed. We were introduced by a teammate's girl-friend. Both her and Kylie were cleat chasers, hanging out around the stadium and the club the team frequented in LA. But that was the scene with the guys on the Diablos. Most of them were young, unattached, and a little reckless. They all hung out with girls from the club. She was always around and persistent as hell. Eventually, I just kind of gave in and we hooked up. That's all it was it first."

I lift my hat off my head, smoothing my hair back. It's easy to see now how things got so out of control, but back then it all just happened so fast that I got swept up in the idea of coming home to someone, having the companion-ship.

"We went from hooking up to her posting pictures of the two of us on social media and I just kind of went with it. Having someone to come home to was nice. Being in LA was the first time I was far away from Mia and Nana. And it wasn't all bad with Kylie. We had a lot of fun together. She was the life of the party. Her personality just kind of sucked you in."

"How long were you together?" Cruz questions as we step over a fallen cactus on the trail.

"Almost two years. The first six months were strictly hooking up but it eventually turned into more. I had bought an engagement ring the week I found out she had been selling memorabilia behind my back. My sister was the one who tipped me off."

Cruz's eyebrows shoot to his hairline. "Oh shit, I didn't know that."

"I thought we were in love. She was lying and using me since the start. Turns out I was more in love with the idea of being in a relationship than I was with her. After we ended things, I was angry and hurt, but I didn't really miss her. I missed having another person to share my life with, but I wasn't in a place where I could trust anyone. It was too fresh. I stopped dating altogether."

"How did Mia end up finding out?"

"A friend of hers saw a posting on eBay for a game-worn jersey, and she recognized the username of the seller because it matched Kylie's Instagram handle. She showed it to Mia, sensing that something wasn't right."

"Jesus, that's brutal."

"You think? Now imagine your little sister has been warning you about your girlfriend from the start — claiming that she was trouble and you refused to listen." I shake my head as Dean and Dom walk ahead laughing and joking without a care in the world. In some ways, they remind me of my teammates on the Diablos. They're younger and more care-free but not nearly as destructive. The tone here in Denver is more laidback, and I'm grateful. It's a better fit for me.

"Are you ready now?"

"Maybe? I like her. She's funny, easy to talk to. She's the first girl I have wanted to ask on a date in the last four years. That's gotta count for something."

Cruz's eyes go wide. "You need to be pretty sure about this, don't fuck around with Poppy if you aren't. Find some-one else to try with if you still have doubts about dating."

I cringe at the way he breaks it down. It's not like that with Poppy. At least I don't think it is.

She makes me want to try, and I know I have some trust issues to work through.

"I hear you, but I really think this could be different."

Cruz shakes his head. "This is all going to blow up in your face if you're not upfront about your past and trust issues with her from the start."

I nod. We follow Dean and Dom down the trail. Dom looks over his shoulder at Cruz. "Are you finally going to go for it with Lilah?" he questions, having picked up pieces of our conversation over their replay of last night.

Cruz gives Dom a look before answering. "Don't even fucking start. One word and I'll lay you out," he barks, jaw tense.

"Is that a yes?" Dom asks, like the dumbass he is. "Cause if you don't lock her down someone else will." He winks at

Cruz provoking our captain about his best friend is Dom's favorite pastime.

"Let's not poke the bear," I ready myself to grab Cruz before he can lunge at Dom.

When I hear Dean tell Dom, "If Cruz snags Lilah before you get the chance, you could see if the redhead she brings to the games is single. She's a fucking smokeshow."

My jaw clenches and my fists ball at my side. And just like that, Cruz has his hand on my shoulder keeping me from tackling Dean.

"Or not. Chill, man. I didn't know she was your girl. I won't take her from you," the cocky motherfucker taunts like he could snap his fingers and make her his.

"So, you're going to do this, aren't you? Date Poppy?" Cruz asks as we make our way around another switchback. Dean and Dom take off ahead of us again like puppies let off their leash.

"I want her, Cruz, and not just because she's so pretty it hurts. It's still new, but we aren't seeing other people." I'm not really sure how to classify my relationship with Poppy. Even though it's early, she just makes it so damn easy to want more with her. I want to see where this can go.

Cruz looks over at me with a knowing grin. "We could do a double date —" he starts, but I cut him off.

"No, we can't. The blue balls I earned from movie night were bad enough. There is no way I'm sitting through a double date with you and Lilah before I get her alone."

"What are you going to do, throw her over your shoulder, caveman style, and lock her away?"

I consider it, the idea has merit. I'm desperate for some one-on-one time with Poppy. "No, I think I'm going to cook for her at my place."

"I guess that means neither of you are going to come out with us after the game," Dom grumbles.

"Did you need our help with the ladies? Dean doesn't have any wingman game?" I mock as we work our way up a switchback.

"Like I want help from you two. Old maids — both of you. If this is our future, Dean, we better enjoy ourselves now before we turn into them," Dom shoots back as we reach the top of the plateau.

I swallow a drink of water and look out over the landscape, taking in the scene in front of me. Phoenix is off in the distance with the desert and cactus blooms dotting the landscape with color. My first thought as I take in the view is that Poppy would have loved this hike. I pull my phone out and snap a quick selfie, typing out, "The view from up here is beautiful. The switchbacks were brutal but worth this view. Hope you're having a good day."

There's a knock at the door as I get out of the shower. Knowing that it's probably the room service I ordered, I wrap my towel tightly around my waist and grab the tray from outside the door. Scrolling through my notifications while I eat lunch, I see a text from Poppy.

POPPY:

It looks so warm there. I'm glad you got outside to enjoy it before your game.

The message is accompanied by a photo of her sitting in front of the window at Buns and Roses. Her lips are turned down in an exaggerated frown. It looks cold and rainy outside. Spring in Denver is unpredictable as fuck. One day I'm running in just shorts and the next day it could snow. But she's adorable, all bundled up in a thick sweater with a stocking cap on her head. Her long red braids hang out the sides with a coffee in her hand.

I save the picture to my phone. Those braids just fucking kill me. She looks so damn good. Once I finish my lunch, I pull together everything I need and pack my bag to leave me some time to kill before I get my nap in. Mia and I haven't had a chance to talk lately. I'm not used to going this long without at least a quick check in. Scrolling to her name, I hit the call button.

"Hey, brother. How's Arizona?" Mia asks when she picks up.

"It's good. The guys and I went for a hike this morning. It's almost naptime, but I wanted to call you first. I feel like we haven't talked in a while," I tell her, stretching out across the bed. Mia and I were really close as kids. We still are, but I miss living close to her. I keep trying to convince her to move to Denver. So far, she's been resistant, but I think I am wearing her down.

"Other than the call last week with Nana, you and I haven't talked in over a week. What's up with that? No time for your sister?" Mia teases, her voice light as her fingers tap away on her keyboard in the background.

"I always have time for you, but it's been busy with the start of the season and moving. The phone works two ways. Tell me how the new book is coming. Your release date is right around the corner."

"It's in six weeks. Working on proofreading and marketing this week. It's in pretty good shape. Other than baseballing, what's new in your world?" she explains before changing topics.

"I have a date next week with Poppy. She's a friend of Lilah and Cruz."

"That's huge, Henny. You haven't dated since Kylie. What are you doing for your date? Fancy dinner to impress her?" She knows that's not my style. "Wait, is this the girl from the picture?"

"What picture?" I ask before adding, "let's not make a big deal of it. I just went through that with Cruz."

My phone vibrates in my hand. I look down to see the picture Mia was referring to. Poppy and I are exiting the stadium, trailing Lilah and Cruz. My hand is on her back as I guide through where photographers and fans are waiting near the players' exit. She has her head tilted toward me, smiling as I whisper something in her ear. I think I was teasing her about the way she was shivering and offering to warm her up. We were heading over to Cruz's for movie night, but to an outsider it looks like we are a couple in love.

"Yeah, that's Poppy." I confirm for Mia, who squeals in my ear.

"She's adorable, and she doesn't look like a viper. Kylie always gave off predator vibes. Ick."

"Want to give your big brother some girl advice on the date? I was thinking maybe I'd cook her dinner. Or maybe cook together at my place? I don't want the interruptions of being in public. I just want to relax and talk. Is that dumb? Do you think she'll be disappointed?"

She laughs at my nervous chatter. "Girls eat that stuff up, Hen. You're a professional athlete, and you can cook. If she would rather go out so she can be seen with you, then she's not someone you need to worry about. It's actually kind of sweet if you think about it. You would rather spend the time together one on one to get to know her." Mia muses her romantic side shining through and causing her voice to get all wistful on me.

"Thanks, Mia. You made my decision easier. I'm glad we talked."

"Me too. I want a follow up after this date. Let me know how it goes. I'm invested now," she demands like the nosey little sister she is. Ironic considering she won't move to Denver because she thinks living in the same city as me might be too much of a good thing. She's afraid she'll lose her identity and become "Hen's little sister" all over again. Something she struggled with when we were younger.

"I will. She's great, Mia. I think you would really like her. She's nothing like Kylie," I say, running my hand down my face at the memory of that dumpster fire. My sister tried to warn me. Mia never trusted her.

"Kylie is literally the worst. You're not setting the bar very high if you're just looking for better than her," she rants, her tone full of disdain for my ex and the hell she put me through before adding. "As long as she makes you happy and is deserving of a spot in your big heart."

"I think she could." A smile lifts my lips as I think of the way Poppy felt in my arms the other day "Thanks for the advice, Mia. Let's talk again soon. Love you, kid."

"You deserve to find that with someone. Love you, big brother," she says, ending the call.

Like every sister, Mia can drive me crazy sometimes but she's also one of the best people I know. She never fails to give me solid advice. And even though most people might think being in the MLB makes me more successful that's not at all how I see it. She's arguably more famous than me as a New York Times bestselling author. Beyond her ambition, she is just a really good person. I navigate back to the photo Mia sent earlier of Poppy and I leaving the stadium and save it. We look good together, like she belongs by my side.

Trading pictures with Poppy throughout the day has sort of become our thing during this road trip. We are swapping them and sharing parts of our days. Before I plug my phone in, I snap a selfie of myself on the bed. Still in my towel because I know she loves shirtless pictures. Before I hit send, I type out a message replying to the text she sent earlier.

HENDRIX:
Sorry to see a frown on your beautiful face. That weather is garbage. Maybe this pic will cheer you up.

Once I hit send, I set the alarm and switch my phone to Do not disturb.

♥

After the game, the guys and I meet at the hotel bar for a celebratory drink. Dean and Dom bail quickly to hit up another bar — one that's featuring a ladies' night. Cruz only sticks around for a little while before heading up to his room to talk to Lilah before it gets too late to leave me alone to finish my beer before I head back to my room. The only thing I'm interested in now that the game is over is going upstairs to talk to Poppy.

"Can I get you another?" the bartender asks, pulling me out of my thoughts as I set down my empty glass.

"No, thanks." I leave a twenty on the bar and head up to call Poppy. When I get back to my room, I wash up and get ready for bed before I lay down and make the call that I have been looking forward to all night.

"Hey, Hendrix." Poppy says when she answers. "Good game tonight. I saw your bomb in the fifth inning."

"You watched me play again?" There's a little teasing and some awe in my voice.

She laughs, and it sounds warm and sweet. "I did, but don't go getting an over inflated ego. I watch a lot of the games. Seeing you was an extra incentive. Your hike looked amazing today. Did you see a rattlesnake?"

"Fuck no," I shudder. "There's something you should know about me. I'm afraid this might ruin my image —"

"Ironman, are you scared of snakes?" There's an evil amount of teasing and joy mixed into her voice over my irrational fear.

"I'm not — not afraid of them," I begrudgingly admit. "There is a very good reason."

"This is going to be good. It's going to make me see you in a new light, isn't it?" She's giddy. Even though it's at my expense, her enthusiasm for my discomfort is amusing. Her voice is light, filled with laughter, and I could listen to the sound of her teasing me all night.

"Probably. My grandmother took Mia and me to the zoo. I must have been around six. It was such a fun day. It was one of those times that your cheeks hurt from smiling nonstop." One of those times that even though you're exhausted from all the activity, you can't help but be happy at the time spent together. "At the end of the day, I asked to go see the snakes. My grandma was hesitant because I wasn't listening very well, and Mia was starting to drag. But I begged, tugging on her hand until she finally agreed. Once we were in the serpentarium, I wandered away to another room to look at one of those huge yellow-and-white pythons and we got separated. When I realized that I couldn't find her, I panicked and sat down in a corner. The snakes were everywhere; it was dark and creepy. The longer I stayed there, the more I was certain they were watching me." I shiver at the memory of the cool, damp floor under me as I sat balled up with my knees to my chest.

"I was afraid if I left she would never find me if I moved, so I stayed put. But I could feel their beady eyes everywhere, watching me. I tried closing my eyes, but then it was like I could feel them crawling all over me. I just sat there huddled in the dark corner waiting for her to come back for me."

"No one tried to help you? You must have been so scared!" Poppy's voice breaks all the giddiness gone.

"I'm sure they would have, but it was dark and loud. Being huddled in the corner, no one even saw me. That's why it took so long for her to find me. She told me she had looked for almost thirty minutes before she spotted me."

She switches the phone to FaceTime. "I felt like I needed to see your face after that to make sure you are okay. It made me so sad for little Hen. You must have felt so alone."

"My grandmother felt terrible. She was worried I'd think she left me like my mom did. I was spoiled rotten for the rest of the week. The nonstop treats dulled the pain, but I still hate snakes."

"That seems like a legitimate reason to be afraid of snakes. I allow you to keep your nickname."

"Your turn, Poppy. What scares you?" She comes off as fearless, living life at her own speed and with confidence to spare. I can't really imagine her cowering to anything.

She thinks for a minute. "I don't really have a physical fear like snakes. Mine is less tangible," she laments. "My parents are very rigid. Not strict, but they have specific expectations and dreams for me that never really meshed with what I want out of life."

She takes the tie out of her hair and unbraids it. She's looking down at her lap and working her fingers through her soft strands while she continues. "They have a hard time relating to me. Not that they really try, so I guess I fear not being understood and accepted for who I am. Having to take up less space or make myself smaller to be loved." She sighs with the heaviness of her words.

"We're still getting to know each other, but there's nothing I'd change about you. Please don't hide yourself from me — or the world. I want every part of you. Show me all of it — the messy, loud parts that they can't handle." I mean every word; Poppy is warm and joyful. She makes the world a better place. The thought of her feeling like she wasn't enough as a child causes a ripple of anger to run through me.

She smiles, but it doesn't reach her eyes this time. "Ugh… too heavy," she groans. "Talk to me about our date. What are your plans for me?"

"I was hoping we could stay in. And I could cook for you, or we could cook together." I start. "Whatever we decide, I just want to spend the time with you, no distractions." I finish, tugging on the back of my neck, hoping she doesn't hate the idea. "I'm actually a decent cook. Mia and I spent a lot of time helping in the kitchen growing up. I was thinking of chicken carbonara or shrimp tacos. Lady's choice."

"Tough choice. I love tacos, but I eat them at least once a week. A good pasta dish that's a rarity," she contemplates, twirling her hair with her finger. Her smile is back in full force now.

We talk for a little while longer about our date. She tells me some happier stories about her childhood and her best friend, Indie from back home. She's coming out to visit soon. I don't miss the way Poppy's face lights up when she talks about Indie and her family. I tell her about some of my friends from LA and the minors that I have stayed close with.

Eventually our conversation turns to flirting. She looks so beautiful encased in the fluffy pillows and blankets with her hair fanned out in coppery waves, cheeks flushed and green eyes shining with lust. Her voice is raspy and my name on her lips as she comes is the hottest thing I have ever heard.

If I can't be with her in person, this is the best way to fall asleep. None of the guys like to sleep in the hotel rooms on the road, but I'm sleeping better than I have since I moved. Without the interruptions from my neighbor at home, my naps and gameday routine have all been just how I like them.

CHAPTER 9

POPPY

I squeeze my eyes shut and I pull the blanket over my head shielding myself from the harsh light shining through the window. My limbs are heavy like they're filled with lead, rolling to the side of the bed requires more effort than I care to admit. I blindly feel around my nightstand for my phone.

There's a new notification something that's become a regular occurrence.

HENDRIX:

Hope you slept well, Beautiful.
Enjoy your day.

POPPY:

Someone kept me up late but it
was worth it. Call tonight?

HENDRIX:

I can't wait. Talking to you at night is way better than sitting across from my teammates at some random bar.

POPPY:

Are you sure about that? Dean is SO pretty.

HENDRIX:

He's not my type.

POPPY:

Oh yeah?

HENDRIX:

I prefer redheads with legs for days and that sound like heaven when they moan my name.

POPPY:

Well, then. That's a nice way to start my day.

HENDRIX:

Let me know if there are any other ways I can be of service.

POPPY:

Ok, now you crossed the line into cheesy.

HENDRIX:

You're right I should have stopped while I was ahead.

POPPY:

Get out of here you cheese ball.

HENDRIX:

I'm going to the gym if I can't charm you with my swagger, maybe my muscles will do the trick.

My heart swells at his message, he wants to charm me. Mission accomplished I might have given him a hard time but I look forward to his cheesy lines. The last three nights of staying up to talk with Hendrix for hours after his games are taking a toll, but every midday yawn is worth it — especially after the last two nights. Watching him as he lay there on the other end of the phone, a perfect contrast of hard and soft. His hard expanse of corded muscle against the fluffy rumpled sheets with his dark glossy hair in a sexy disarray.

Each time we talk, I feel myself growing more smitten. We have talked about mundane everyday things like our favorite places to eat in the city, where we want to travel to. I confided in him about how Indie's family impacted me growing up and the riff with my mom.

He shared a lot about his grandmother. I feel like I know her through our conversations. From the stories I have heard, she's feisty and wise. If I ever get to meet her, I know I'm going to love her mischievous spirit. Not everything has been innocent conversation, there has been plenty of sexy time too.

This road trip feels like a blessing and a curse. It's forcing us to slow down and get to know each other without our physical attraction ruling over our decisions. At the same time, I crave the feel of the coarse stubble on his jaw under my fingertips. When he gets back, I know the chemistry is going to be just as electric as it was the morning after movie night.

My body is begging me to lay in bed a little longer, but I need to water Hendrix's plants this morning before my client calls later today. Like a gold medal procrastinator, I haven't opened his email yet. Every time I thought about opening it, I prioritized my work or got interrupted by something else. My mom texting or work pulled me away the last two times. Shuffling across the bedroom, I slip my fuzzy robe on as I make my way to the kitchen to start the coffee.

Barely alert, I muddle across the apartment and settle into the couch. The warmth of the mug cradled in my hand is sublime. Pulling the laptop on to the couch next to me, I open my email. Scrolling down I find the message from Hen at the bottom of the email, he included his address.

I read it over several times in disbelief before it sinks in. I blink at the address and rub my eyes making sure that they aren't playing tricks on me. The words swirl on the screen in front of me, and the back of my neck prickles with the discomfort of what I'm seeing. When I finally accept the truth in front of me my stomach lurches at the realization.

Hendrix is my neighbor. Not just a neighbor in my building, but right next door — the one I was worried about hearing my calls. This can't be happening. Panic fills me immediately and I feel sick to my stomach. What's he going to think when I tell him I live next door?

Will this be just one more example of a person I was coming to care deeply for not understanding who I am?

Part of me wants to just say fuck it and call him right now to tell him. Spill everything about my career and the fact that we are neighbors. But I just know I need to do this face to face. To see his reaction, even if he is understanding of my career choice. I want to know that this won't come back down the road to tear us apart. If I'm going to pursue a relationship with anyone, they need to be all in.

Hendrix needs to be willing to accept all of me. I can't repeat what happened with Paul. My heart won't recover this time.

But it's not just up to me. Hendrix needs to decide if that's a risk he's ready to take with his career if the media finds out about what I do for a living he could take a hit. Even with my career change, it needs to be his decision to pursue this, knowing everything. He said he wanted the messy parts, but when he finds out just how messy what will he do?

It has to wait until he's back. I'll tell him then.

My coffee tastes sour going down. The client calls I have today are going to be a struggle with this overwhelming sense of dread hanging over my head. I may as well just get this over with and go water Hendrix plants. Once that is done, hopefully I'll be able to focus on the rest of my day — at least that is what I'm telling myself.

When I walk through the door, I notice that Hendrix's apartment is set up similar to mine but appears to be flipped. The watering can is right on the counter where he said it would be. Underneath it there's a note from him. The blood pounds in my ears and my hand trembles as I pick it up.

"Poppy— Thank you for giving me peace of mind by taking care of my plants. I appreciate it and I can't wait to see you when I get back. Take care. Hendrix."

My throat grows tight with emotion. In such a short time, I have so much hope for a future with Hendrix, or at least the opportunity to try for one. It's not something I have even entertained since Paul, and I am not ready for that to disappear. Hendrix made me want to try. He unlocked that part of me that I had sealed up when Paul broke my heart.

A picture of Hendrix as a teen in a baseball uniform with his sister catches my eye as I move through the living room watering plants. He has his arms around her shoulders and admiration shining in her eyes as she looks up at him. It's almost more than I can take. With shaky hands, I replace the frame on the shelf where I found it and move on, turning away from it.

The hollowness in my chest that had felt a little less lately is now more pronounced than ever. Seeing that picture, I want that. The feeling of unconditional love and family with someone. For the first time in a long time, I'm willing to put myself out there because of Hendrix, but will he want the same with me after he finds out who I really am?

When I'm finished in the living room, I move on to his bedroom. There are a few plants scattered throughout his space. Hendrix's masculine scent surrounds me as I step further into the room. It's undeniably him done in browns and grays with a leather headboard. Black-and-white photos of baseball stadiums and historical plays line one wall.

The art on the wall isn't what sticks out the most. It's the fact that his bedroom is set against my office. Knowing his schedule, he is home during the day before games. He has undoubtedly heard my client calls. It hits me like a punch to the gut, causing my breath to woosh out of me.

My insides twist with dread that as soon as Hendrix finds out I'm his neighbor, he is going to jump to conclusions. This feeling, that fear of judgment from Hendrix, mimics so much of what I feel when I'm around my parents and so much of what I experienced with Paul. Always questioning whether I'll be enough, if I say or do the wrong thing how harshly will I be criticized or not taken seriously?

I rush through tending to the plants in the bedroom. The oppressive feeling of being here is too much. My heart feels like it's in a vase, and my throat is burning with the emotion of it. This isn't how it's supposed to be. I should be imagining the way he looks when he undresses for the night or the way he would look hovering above me the first time we are together here.

I can't be here one more minute. Grabbing my things and the key, I replace the watering can where I found it, pocket the note, and bolt out the door. When I make it back to my apartment next door, I feel like I can barely breathe. Crumpling onto the couch in a heap, I pull my phone out scrolling my contacts desperately. Lilah is out of the question, she's too close to the situation, and I don't want to pull her into this. She has enough going on with Cruz already.

Scrolling back up, I stop on the person I need. Indie answers on the second ring and I thank the Lord that my friend is the only millennial that answers the phone unprompted. She's always been able to talk me down when I'm in a panic, and she knows the impact my parents and Paul had on my ability to open myself up to someone. The best thing about Indie is she doesn't pull any punches. If I'm being dramatic, she'll tell me with no coddling, but if I'm hurt and the reaction is justified, she'll hand me the lighter fluid and encourage me to burn the world down.

"Hey, Poppy."

"Indie — I need to talk." My voice breaks. The phone shakes in my hand as I try to gather my thoughts.

"Pops, what is going on? Are you okay?" she asks, her voice soothing and filled with concern.

"No — yes. I'm not really sure. Physically I'm fine." Indie lets out and audible exhale on the other end of the line before I launch into the explanation.

Her family and house were my safe haven growing up. I went there to escape the constant criticism at home. They let me hide from my problems when I was overwhelmed with the expectations placed on me. And she was there for me even from across the country when Paul broke my trust. Indie has been the one stable presence in my life since kindergarten.

"I'm so scared that I screwed this up without even knowing. I can't tell him over the phone."

My mom's voice echoes in my mind, *"This is the kind of dilemma you get into when you try to build a life that you're not meant for."* I push it out of my mind mentally cursing myself for falling into the trap of her negativity and focus back on Indie.

"No, you can't." Indie confirms her voice calm where I'm still ragged. "Even if you tell him over the phone and the conversation goes flawlessly. You'll need to see it firsthand. With your past, you won't trust that reaction if you can't be there to see it for yourself. Paul messed you up, Poppy, we both know that. He used you. Worse yet, he was callous and sneaky about it. What he did left behind deep wounds, the kind that scar." I can hear the anger in her voice as she talks about Paul before she takes a deep breath and continues. "Are you going to trust that he is being entirely up front with his feelings on your work and living next door if you tell him over the phone?"

"No, but what if he is mad that I kept it from him?" I give voice to my second biggest fear out loud for the first time. But I can already feel Indie's pep talk giving me back some of the strength that the memories of Paul and my mom had washed away. Each sentence from her gives me a wave of courage and I let it build me up again.

"He might be. But that's something that you'll have to work through," she says, confirming what I have been feeling. I might be setting myself up for more heartache before things get better. "I know you don't want to hear this, but I think it's time to talk to your parents. They need to know how much their behavior has hurt you. Paul is out of your life for good, but they're still hurting you and it's time to enforce some boundaries."

"I thought I did that with moving across the country." My voice is stronger now, tinged with anger that I'm still battling against these feelings of distrust and unworthiness from across the country and years apart. Indie has been telling me to lay ground rules out with my parents for years, but it feels like I won't be able to push aside this confrontation much longer. The kicker is that I don't think my parents have a clue the impact their criticisms and dismissiveness have had on me.

"Am I being a coward by waiting until he's home?" I crack my knuckles in my lap while I brace myself for her honest answer.

"No way. You're doing what's right for you. And do you really think telling Hendrix face-to-face is taking that easy way out?"

"No."

"No, it's not. Telling him over the phone would be the easiest thing to do." Indie spends another few minutes calming me before we talk about her visit this summer. When we hang up, I feel stronger than I have since I opened that email, but there's nothing I want to do less than take client calls.

I strongly consider canceling them and the rest of my remaining calls. The money will go toward padding my savings while I secure my first few audiobook projects. It's too much of a risk to cancel. Besides, none of this is a result of any shame I have in my career. I just wanted to be able to tell Hen on my terms. I'm angry that option has been taken away with him having overheard my calls. But anger is better than the fear and guilt I was feeling earlier. Anger I can deal with, and I use it as fuel to get me through the calls.

Later that evening when I am done with my client calls, I order takeout, locking myself away to work on the content and networking. When I finish, I have several notifications. I open the one from Hendrix first.

He sent me a picture of a t-shirt in a shop window that says, "What the Fucculent." It's funny and sweet that he is thinking of me while he is on the road. Before today it would have made me feel lighter, but it only makes my heart crack wide open. A reminder that this could all be fleeting and over before it really gets started.

When Hendrix calls me later that night, I almost let it go to voicemail. The appeal of ignoring my problems for the next four days is pulling at me. Ghosting him until he gets back will only make things worse. It wouldn't be fair to him, and I'm not sure I could do it either. Talking to him for the next few days and not telling him that we are neighbors doesn't seem right either. My stomach aches with the way this all tumbling out of control.

"Hi, Hendrix." I say when I answer his call, picking up right before it goes to voicemail. I'm crossing my fingers that he doesn't switch the call over to FaceTime today. If he does, I'll force a smile and he'll know something is wrong.

"Hey, Poppy. It's really good to hear your voice. It was a rough game tonight." He sounds tired and a little bummed. I couldn't bring myself to watch the game. That's just one more thing to add to the list of the ways I'm letting him down. Guilt floods me, causing a heavy feeling in the center of my chest.

"I didn't catch the game tonight. Time got away from me while I was working on my new project." The lie slips out too easily.

His laughter is weary when he says, "I don't expect you to watch every game. Hell, you don't have to watch any if you don't want to. And you never need to justify it to me. I want to hear more about what you were working on."

Hendrix knows my career is in flux, even if I haven't told him outright how I make my living yet. The right time to tell him I'm a phone sex operator hasn't come up yet. We haven't had the privacy for that conversation. It's never an easy conversation to have with someone new. It's always awkward to bring it up and then work through the misconceptions.

Which is why I rarely tell someone unless I trust them and can imagine them being an important part of my life.

Once I decide to tell someone, I just go for it — like a band-aid rip that sucker off and get all the painful parts over. But with Hendrix on the road, I can't do that.

"I'm working on marketing and social media content to break into audiobook narrations as a voice over actor. I can't record my demo until some more equipment arrives," I explain, giving him as much information as I can without getting into the adult hotline piece over the phone. It immediately gives me the icks that I'm not telling him everything, but I feel stuck like this is all out of my control. It's an impossible choice. Tell him now and risk doubting his sincerity or wait and risk hurting him. Either way, I'm certain that this is going to break my heart.

"Babe," he says excitedly. My throat closes up at the nickname. It's the first time he has used a term of endearment like that with me. "How did this not come up already? You should talk to Mia. She's an author. She writes romance books. Her release date is coming up for her next book, but she would make time for this. But she can help you navigate the ins and outs of the industry." Hendrix's voice is vibrating with excitement and admiration as he talks about his sister.

"Hendrix. I appreciate that you are trying —" I stop as the dots connect in my head. Hendrix's last name is James. Making his sister's name Mia James. *Holy shit.* "Wait, Mia James is your sister? Like Mia James, bestselling romance author?" My voice wavers as I ask for confirmation of what I already know must be true.

"The one and only," he confirms proudly. "She loves mentoring indie writers and people trying to break into the business. She would eat this right up. Let me send her your number?" He is going a mile a minute. It would be so fucking sweet if it didn't just make me feel like more of an asshole right now.

Trying to navigate my mixed emotions, I stop him. "Slow down. We have only known each other for a few weeks, Hendrix. It's a lot to ask your sister for help with my career. I don't even know her." Fuck. How is this happening? I don't even really know Hendrix that well. As much as I want to get to know him better, I may not get that chance now.

This should be great news. It has the potential to be life changing, but right now it feels like I would be taking advantage. Hendrix doesn't need more people like that in his life. He has had enough people do that to him. My stomach flips and I think I'm going to be sick. "Hendrix — I need to call you back. I don't feel well. Sorry." I rush out the words as I hang up the phone and toss it carelessly on the couch.

As I dash to the bathroom, I hear my phone clatter to the floor. Skidding to a stop in front of the toilet, I come down hard on my knees. The sharp pain is nothing compared to the way my stomach lurches. I have just enough time to lift the lid before all the takeout I ate earlier comes back up.

When I'm done, I sit back on my heels and pull the towel from the bar behind using it to wipe my mouth. That's when I feel the hot tears tracking down my face. I hate this. How did everything get this messed up? Did I do something in a past life to anger the gods? Is this me being punished? Pushing off the ground, I clean up and toss the towel into the hamper. Or is it just everything my mom has ever told me coming true, am I just a girl going after a life that will never be hers?

Fuck that.

She's wrong, and I deserve the life I have built.

These are just shitty circumstances, I tell myself not letting the destructive thought creep in any further. Even though I'm able to combat the years of negativity with my positive affirmations, I don't call Hendrix back. Instead, I text him.

POPPY:

Sorry for the hang up. I think I had some bad takeout. I'm just going to go to bed.

HENDRIX:

You're sick? Tell me what you need. Can I send some medicine or Gatorade?

POPPY:

That's really sweet but I'll be okay. Just going to sleep it off. Talk tomorrow?

HENDRIX:

Night Poppy. Feel better. Please let me know if you need anything.

After I read the text from Hendrix guilt consumes me and I bury the phone under my pillows. I can't stand to look at it after reading his sweet messages. I pull a blanket around me tight and stare up at the ceiling. I'm not sure how long it's been when I'm jolted out of my daze by a knock at my door. It takes some effort, but I drag myself out of bed wiping my nose with the back of my hand as I pear through the peephole. Marv is standing in hallway his weathered face pitched together with a concerned look holding a takeout bag.

CHAPTER 10

HENDRIX

I know Poppy said she didn't need anything, but I can't help feeling like I need to do something. She's sick, and I'm stuck here on the other side of the country. I don't even have her address to send her anything. Not wanting to disturb her if she's sleeping, I twirl my phone around in my hand debating what to do next as I sit on my hotel bed after we hang up.

When I was not feeling well as a kid, my nana always made soup. I want to do the same for Poppy, even if I can't be there to make her the soup myself.

HENDRIX:
Hey Cruz. Do you have Poppy's address? She's not feeling well, and I want to send over soup or something for her.

CRUZ:

I don't. I have never been to her place.
We always hang out at mine or Lilah's.
But I know someone who does.

Three dots appear on my phone as I wait for his reply. After a minute, it vibrates as I stare down at it.

CRUZ:

Lilah said she can help you out. There's
a place down the street that deliv-
ers she'll have it sent over now.

HENDRIX:

Tell her thanks for me. I'll owe her a favor
for this.

CRUZ:

You really think she's going to cash in
that favor if you're taking care of Poppy?

The atmosphere in the locker room is melancholy. We have lost the first two games of the series against San Francisco, not able to carry over the momentum we had in Phoenix. I haven't been hitting for shit and my plays in the outfield are passable at best. It's been two days since I have heard more than a quick reply to a text message from Poppy.

She's been ducking me since our call was cut short the other night. It feels like she's pushing me away. I can't figure out why and it's impacting my focus on the game.

When I checked in the next morning to see how she was doing, she thanked me for the soup and said she was feeling better but tired. To make matters worse, we haven't been able to talk over the phone since then. Our schedules just haven't lined up. Tonight, she has plans with Lilah, which means we won't be able to FaceTime or even talk later.

The only bright spot is that she hasn't canceled our date tomorrow, but something has changed. I can't figure out what it is, and I can't afford to let it distract me from baseball any longer. I need to set it aside until tomorrow when I see her. We have one more game left in the series this afternoon and we need to win. No one wants to get swept in a series to start their season.

Turning on the bench, I reach into my locker and pull out my phone. I pass it back and forth between my hands, debating if I should just let it ride or text her. Ultimately deciding that whatever happens, I want her to know that I'm thinking of her. Sliding my thumb up the screen I open our thread to send her a message before I put my phone away for the game.

HENDRIX:
Hey Poppy. I hope you and Lilah have fun tonight. I can't wait to see you tomorrow after we get home.

It's simple, to the point, but most of all true. Even with Poppy being withdrawn, I can't wait to see her. I miss her smile and the sound of her laugh. Going without video calls the last few nights has sucked. It left me feeling like I was missing out on something I didn't know I needed.

In the past, I have always kept things casual because there wasn't anybody that was worth the distraction from the game. Kylie was the exception, but look how that turned out. She always made me feel guilty about not being there or not flying her out to see more games. She wanted to be on the road with me. Her only concern was having access to the WAG lifestyle. I wanted to keep my personal and professional life separate. I also never craved being near her like I do with Poppy. If I had, maybe things would have been different.

It's a difference that wasn't clear until now.

In a short time, the way Poppy makes me feel surpasses what I thought I had with Kylie. Our relationship, if you can even call it that, feels more balanced. Poppy couldn't care less that I play ball for a living. When we got caught by the photographers, her eyes were on me, not on all the cameras going off around us.

Small things like asking about the other person's day when we talk. Or the way she didn't jump to take advantage of the offer to connect with my sister, careful to be sure she wasn't overstepping. With Kylie, it was never that way. She always wanted more from me. She rarely asked about my days when I was on the road. I know now that what we had wasn't genuine.

Whatever this is with Poppy feels real.

This lifestyle doesn't come without challenges. I have seen my teammates struggle with being separated from their wives or kids. The video chats with Poppy, having her there for me, made the loneliness more bearable. That's not something I'm ready to give up.

I hope she feels the same. For a long time, I thought I'd put relationships on hold until after I retired, but she makes me want more.

I don't want to wait for retirement. I want to see where this goes with Poppy.

♥

Cruz walks past and takes the seat next to me. His face is stony with determination. "Let's wrap this up with a win and go home." Cruz reaches over and holds out his fist to me. I ball my hand into a fist and tap the top of his. There's nothing I want more than to finish this series on top and get home to my girl so I do what I need to prepare myself to do just that.

Next to me Cruz goes through his own process of getting mentally prepared to play while I pop in my earbuds and work on visualization. Eyes closed, letting the music pump me up with each passing song.

By the time we step on to the field, I feel better than I have for days. My reasons for being here are crystal clear and at the forefront of my mind the whole game. I want to finish this damn series with a win and get home to figure this out with Poppy.

Relief fills my chest when I walk off the field, knowing that we could turn it around and that I was able to contribute to my team tonight. The night gets even better when Coach announced we are flying straight home after we finish with the media.

I have never been more grateful for a change to the flight schedule. The team bumped up our departure time because of incoming weather. They're flying us home tonight instead of tomorrow to make sure we get a full day of rest instead of being delayed. I rush through my shower and head to the team bus eager to get home.

Grabbing a seat on the bus next to Cruz, I fish my phone out of my duffle bag before I stow it and look at it for the first time since before the game. There are several text messages waiting for me.

NANA:

Looked like you had fun out there tonight. It was good to see you enjoying the game again. I'm proud of you. Go Bandits!

MIA:

That's how you do it! Great game tonight, glad I can finally claim you as my brother again after the pitiful performance the last two games.

POPPY:

What a game! You looked like a stud out there.

It doesn't escape me that she didn't return my earlier sentiment about being excited about our date. Whatever is going on with Poppy it's not a conversation I'm going to have over text on the team bus. I type out a quick reply to Mia and my grandmother then slip my phone into my pocket and look over at Cruz, who is texting next to me. He must feel me looking because he slides the phone back in his pocket and levels me with an annoyed glare.

"Am I interrupting something?" I challenge when he just stares back at me like I kicked his puppy.

The bus fills in around us. Everyone has their hoods up or earbuds in giving serious don't talk to me vibes. It's typical at the end of a long road trip. Everyone is overstimulated and ready to be home.

Cruz's jaw tightens. I can almost hear his teeth grinding. "Unfortunately, no." He pushes his hair off his forehead. "I was going to call Lilah, but she must already be asleep. She said she would text me after the game if she was still up."

"She gets up before the sun; you can't fault her for falling asleep." I remind him as the bus pulls out of the parking lot for the short drive to the airport. "How's it going with her?"

"You tell me," he challenges. "How's it going navigating things with Poppy in the middle of our first long away stretch?"

I grit my teeth. He's got me there. "It was going really fucking well but, the last few days something has definitely changed. I can feel her backing away. It's frustrating as hell not being able to be there to understand what is going on with her."

Cruz blows out a low whistle. "Feels good to get that off your chest. Lilah mentioned Poppy has a lot going on with work right now, so they haven't seen each other much either." He looks confused for a moment; his hand comes up to scratch the scruff on his chin before he continues. "I don't even really know what she does, but I do know she's shifting gears with her career. Maybe she's just wrapped up in that."

He's not telling me anything I don't know. Although it strikes me as odd that we haven't really talked about what she does and that he doesn't know either. She shared some things about how she's trying to get into audiobook narration, but she never really talks about what she's doing now.

The doubts start to creep in that there's something she's keeping from me.

"Is it strange that I don't know what she does now? We talked about her career change. She's trying to get into audiobooks, but that's it." Why haven't I asked her these questions yet? Everything has been accelerated with meeting and then going on the longest road trip so far this season. A lot of our interactions have been limited to texts and calls.

Cruz tilts his head to the side considering. "Not really, I've known Poppy for years. I get the feeling she's almost — protective of her career, but I don't get the impression that she's actively hiding anything. It just doesn't define her."

I don't get the sense that she's hiding it from me either. But even as I say the words my uncertainty builds in the back of my mind. We openly talked about her career change before she got sick the other day.

"I don't know, man. Something has changed on her end, my gut tells me that it's all connected, how fast we moved, not knowing each other well enough." I make a note to ask more questions about her life and to slow down so I don't end up repeating past mistakes. One thing is clear, I want to get it right with Poppy and I want to know all these things about her life.

CHAPTER 11

POPPY

When I wake up on Thursday, I'm unsettled. Being simultaneously enthused and panicky about my date with Hendrix tonight is a real mindfuck. On top of my mental state, my body is still tired and aching from a lack of sleep as I slip on my running shoes. Maybe I can run off the emotional turmoil and wake up my body at the same time.

I grab my phone off the charger, glancing at it before sliding it into my pocket. A notification catches my eye at the last second.

HENDRIX:

Morning, Beautiful. I'm excited to see you tonight.

So damn sweet, but my guilt keeps me from soaking it in the way I want to. The only bright spot in my morning is that Hendrix doesn't fly in until later this morning. So, I can run without fear of bumping into him and take my calls this morning without worrying about him hearing.

This run is needed for my mental health today by any means necessary. My legs are slow to start. It's a very one-foot-in front-of-the-other day. My mind is still running full tilt over seeing Hendrix tonight.

The excitement of our first date is tainted by how he's going to react when he finds out where I live and what I do. If I could have a do-over, I'd have gotten his address and had this conversation before he left. And skipped all this turmoil. One way or another I would have known if he was going to be able to accept this piece of my life. After a few minutes of trying to focus on my breathing and cadence, my legs come alive and the anxiety in my chest loosens.

As I start the second mile winding through the city streets, I focus on pushing myself. Thriving on the feeling of taking all this emotional frustration and funneling it into something physical. By the end of the third mile, I'm covered in sweat and the endorphins are doing their job — keeping my mind off this evening. For now, at least.

When I start the run back to my apartment, my head feels clear for the first time in days. Runs are a coping mechanism I picked up in my teens to help me deal with my family and the anxiety they caused. I'm grateful it still works and that I have this tool to help me manage when things get to be too much.

I take my time in the shower washing, shaving, and moisturizing. Procrastinating to the very last second before I have to start my client calls. I'm so ready to be done with this stage of my career. I want to build something new and watch it flourish.

By the time lunch rolls around, I have finished two client calls and managed to stay focused better than earlier this week. Both were mild, mostly just reminiscing over their favorite calls, or interactions with me. They did most of the talking and I was just able to listen and respond without much heavy lifting on my end. Each client that I wrap up with this week lightens my load and I feel relief at knowing that I am one step closer to being done.

I have some time before my next call, and I figure there's no better time to call my mom back. I may as well get it over with instead of dragging it out and dreading whatever criticisms and negativity the conversation will bring. Each ring of the phone causes my pulse to spike, equally dreading that moment when she answers and excited that maybe she won't.

"Hello, Poppy." My mom answers on the fourth ring. Her voice is tight, and it doesn't sit well with me. What could I have possibly done to upset her already?

"Hey, Mom. How are you?" I'm cautious in my approach, feeling out the situation.

"Fine. I'd be better if my daughter could make time to call me once in a while. You know I'm at the soup kitchen this afternoon." Making it clear that she's disappointed with the timing and frequency of my calls. *Just add it to the list.*

"I can let you go if it's not a good time," I offer knowing she will turn it down. She just wanted to voice her discontent. It's always like this with her.

"I can make it work. As long as you don't mind the background noise." There is literally no background noise. She's alone in the kitchen doing prep work for later today when the rest of the volunteers arrive. "Did I tell you I saw Eddie Barton the other day? He was with his mother having lunch. Such a nice boy."

Eddie is the exact opposite of a nice boy. For one, he is a grown-ass man. He is also a jackass. He used to grope me every chance he got in high school. I reported him several times, but nothing was ever done. Senior year he was caught trying to lace girls' drinks at a party, but his mom is a judge and could keep it quiet.

"No, Mom, you didn't." I don't bother pointing out that Eddie sucks or that she and I haven't talked in weeks. Putting up a fuss would just cause her to accuse me of being dramatic.

"If you would move home I could set you two up," she offers like she would be doing me a favor. The thought of being set up with Eddie literally makes me gag.

"Mom, we have been over this. I'm happy in Denver with my friends and the life I built here. I am not moving home, not now, and probably never." I tell her, exasperated that we are having this conversation again. My fingers rub circles on my temples trying to massage away the stress. "And I don't need you to set me up with anyone."

She scoffs at that — actually scoffs — like me finding someone to date on my merit is absurd. "I don't know why you have to be so difficult. Why can't you come home and settle down, get a job here? The high school is looking for an office clerk. You're always chasing after something more, like you are too good for a life here. The life we tried to give you," she says, an edge to her voice that tells me she's more than disappointed.

She's hurt that I won't cave and live the life she envisions for me. Move home, marry a local boy, and raise his babies. She wants me to be a carbon copy of her. The cheerleader that married her high school sweetheart, then raised his baby and planned church fundraisers. Instead, she got a daughter who fled her hometown the moment she could, works in the adult industry (not that she knows that), and has no plans to get married or bring a baby into this world anytime soon.

Working hard to keep my voice calm, I take a deep breath. "Mom, I love my life here." If I focus on what I love here instead of everything I don't love about my hometown in Illinois, she can't get mad at me for talking poorly about my upbringing or how she lives her life.

I use every trick I have learned over the years to handle her. "I have great friends and I'm happy." Because as my mom isn't that what really should matter to her?

It's not, but it should.

"I can't with you, Poppy. You just don't appreciate the life we live and how we raised you. Your head is too far in the clouds. You have lost sight of what matters," she gasps and her voice shakes. "Your family, the church, and community we raised you in."

My eyes roll so hard it hurts. I haven't attended church with my parents since I was sixteen, the community couldn't care less that I moved away, and my biological family consists of two people who can't stand my life choices because they don't mirror their own. They stopped supporting me as soon as I started asserting independence. Indie, Lilah, and even

Cruz feel more like family than my parents do. This is exactly why I haven't told them about my career choices. Now I'm even less sure that I want to.

"Mom, I do appreciate it, but it's not where I'm the happiest. Does that even matter?" I'm beyond irritated now and need to be done with this call. "I'm sorry that I upset you, but it would be nice if you could try to be happy that I'm in a place in my life where I'm thriving."

"Thriving because you are away from your parents?" she accuses with a huff. "I can't do this right now. I need to get back to work."

"Fine. Bye, Mom." I tell her as the phone disconnects without a goodbye. Leaning my head back into the cushions, I rub the heels of my hands into my eyes. I spend the rest of my time before my last two calls of the day using cat videos as mental bleach to rid my brain of the memory of that inter-action.

Me working in a high school, what a joke.

Only it wasn't a joke.

Because she doesn't get me at all.

CHAPTER 12

HENDRIX

I would have preferred to sleep in on my rare day off, but a text from my grandmother wakes me up before I'm ready. Especially since she interrupted a particularly interesting dream involving Poppy and a sleek little silver toy she used on herself earlier this week before everything went to shit. One that I really would have liked to finish.

NANA:
Stop lazing around in bed and call me.

She's feisty because, with my travel schedule and time zones, it was hard to find a good time to call her on this road trip. It should warm my heart that she gets cranky when we go too long without a phone call, but right now, I really want to stay in bed for a little longer.

I sit up and unplug the phone from the charger, then adjust myself in my briefs. The morning wood I was sporting when I woke up immediately deflating at my grandmother's demands to call her. Before pulling up my favorite contacts and tapping my nana's contact info, I quickly type out a message to Poppy, something that's become a daily ritual. The call to Nana connects almost immediately.

"Turn on your FaceTime, Hendrix. We need to have a serious conversation." A good morning would have been nice seeing as she woke me up on my only day off for a while. But she gets a pass. I always give her a pass for everything she has done for Mia and me.

I hit the button to switch the call over. "Better?"

Her eyes survey me. Taking in my disheveled hair and the scruff on my face, she says, "You really should work out more. For a professional athlete, I'd expect more muscles." Her light blue eyes give away the joy she gets from ribbing me.

"Is this our serious conversation?" My eyebrow raises, knowing damn well there are plenty of muscles on display right now, even though all she can see is my shoulders and face. Everything else is out of the frame and safely covered by the sheets.

"Mia sent me an interesting photo the other day."

I roll my eyes, not the least bit surprised my sister ratted me out for being pictured with a woman I'm actually interested in. "And I bet it was painful to wait this long to call me about it."

"It really was. You have no idea the sacrifices I made. Now, tell me about her. Mia says you're dating."

"Nana, is that really what she said?" My younger sister has many annoying qualities, but she wouldn't have given our grandmother false hope. She would have tempered the shit out of her delivery so Nana didn't get her hopes up. Because if there is one thing that's not annoying about Mia, it's how much she loves her family.

"Not exactly, but if I don't manifest a girlfriend for you, it may never happen," she admits, looking over the top of her purple glasses at me.

"Poppy and I met through Cruz. She's Lilah's best friend."

"Henny — what happened last time you let one of the guys introduce you to a girl?"

"Come on, Nana, you have met Cruz? Is he anything like the guys on the team in LA?"

"Well, no, they're called the Diablos for a reason." That last part is said under her breath. She was never a fan of my teammates in LA, there was a noticeable uptick in the number of visits and plants while I was there. "What about Poppy? Is she anything like Kylie?"

"Do you really think I'd ask her on a date if she was?" She knows me better than that, but I can see the concern in the way she has her pink lips pressed together. "She's nothing like Kylie. We are still getting to know each other but I like her enough that I asked her on a date. We are having dinner at my place tonight."

"You are having her over?" Her eyebrows pull so high on her forehead that it's almost comical. She's well aware of the fact that aside from Poppy watering my plants this week, I have had no one but close friends and family inside my place in years, not since Kylie.

"Yes, she's been in the apartment already. She helped water the plants while I was gone."

"Oh." It's barely a word, but it's loaded.

"Yeah, oh." I tell her, mimicking her tone. "I can't really explain it. Our connection is just easy. From the moment I met her, I was comfortable around her. Not guarded or on alert. She's sweet and funny".

Even as I tell my grandmother that the concern that Poppy's been pulling away sits in the back of my brain, I'm not ready to share that with her. It could be nothing and I don't want to taint her impression of Poppy because every-thing I said is true. I think Poppy is great and I want to try dating her.

"You look absolutely smitten when you talk about her. What's that they call it in Mia's books?" She twists her lips to the side as she thinks. "A boy obsessed. That's what you are. I can see it in the way she looks at you in the picture too."

"You can see all that in a picture?" I laugh, letting my head tilt back and rest against the headboard.

"Yes. The picture, your face, the way you talk about her. I know you, Henny, what Kylie did destroyed your trust. You wouldn't even entertain the idea of dating this girl if she wasn't something special. Or if you didn't already see a future with her. You have closed your heart off for so long. Afraid to open it up to that kind of hurt and mistreatment again. But you have a beautiful heart that deserves to be loved."

"You think I'm closed off?" I am — was? But I didn't think anyone else had noticed the damage that Kylie had done.

"Oh, sweet boy, you can't hide these things from me, I see it all. Treat her right, Henny. If she's managed to even crack those walls around your heart, this girl is special, and you'll regret it if you let this slip away."

The thought that she might already have slipped away crosses my mind. How she was pulling away makes me question how much more I should share with my grandmother. The idea that Poppy could slip through my fingers causes my chest to tighten, but I keep that to myself. I don't want to get her hopes up.

"I won't," I tell her, but I'm not so sure it's a promise I can keep.

Nana gushes about Poppy asking a few more questions about her and our plans for the night before she lets me go so I can workout before my call with my agent later this morning.

My hair is still damp from my lifting session in the gym as I grab a protein shake before my call with Clay, my agent. The office still isn't setup from my move earlier this season. It's not ideal, but I grab a notebook and sit on the chair in my bedroom for the call. When the phone rings, I answer on speaker, so I'm free to take notes as we talk.

"Hey, Hen, great game last night. Glad to see you were able to bring it back after a few rough games," he says, assessing my performance earlier in the series with a nervous laugh.

"Thanks, Clay." I'm not sure what else to give him there. It's not like I planned to suck the first two games of the series. "You wanted to talk about some endorsement today?" Pushing to move on from why I was distracted during the series.

"I got a call from Caper Watches. They are considering you for an endorsement and want to set up some time to meet. If everything goes well, it will include a photo shoot for advertising. They were flexible to work around your schedule —" His thought is cut off when a voice comes through the wall. *Not fucking now.*

For the first time in my life I miss being on the road, I had almost forgotten about my obnoxious neighbor.

"Right there. That feels so good." Loud moaning echoes through the wall.

I jump up to move to the living room and stub my toe on the small table next to the chair. "Oh fuck!" I groan and land on my knees with a thud.

Jesus, can you imagine me explaining to Coach why I can't play. *Sorry, Coach, stubbed my toe trying to escape the noise of my neighbor having sex.*

"Hen, everything okay there? We can reschedule if now isn't a good time." Clay laughs awkwardly at the suggestion.

"No, it's okay. It's not what you think — my neighbor," I start to tell him, grasping for a quick explanation that doesn't sound like a bullshit excuse. There's no way to play this off. He's never going to believe it even if I can get an explanation out.

"So good. Harder. Just. Like. That." The voice next door cries as the headboard bounces off the other side of the wall. Then there's a long, loud, very fake sounding moan. She doesn't sound the least bit satisfied.

"Fuck," I mutter. "Clay, it's not what it sounds like." I tell him as I hobble out to the living room and drop onto the couch. Bringing my foot on to my thigh and squeezing the big toe to try and stem the pain.

"I'm going to let you go, Hen. You take care of — that. And we can connect on this later. I'll text you later today to reschedule," he says right before the line disconnects.

"God dammit." My fist wraps tightly around the phone, and I have to resist the urge to chuck it across the room. Clay is a pretty understanding guy and a good agent, but he's busy and doesn't have a high tolerance for bullshit from his players.

I need to get the fuck out of here before I go next door and make a scene that will inevitably land on the gossip sites. That would piss my agent off even more and I need him working hard to get me endorsements.

On my way out of the apartment, I grab a baseball hat, keys, and my shopping list for dinner tonight. The time in the car calms me down enough that my blood no longer feels like it's boiling, but I'm still aggravated that I was put in that situation. I should have dealt with this neighbor weeks ago.

Have you ever aggressively grocery shopped? No? It's a terrific way to keep people from approaching you. Right now, I'm sending major back off vibes. Drawing looks from moms with young kids and the elderly alike as I stew through the store, grumbling as I toss my purchases in the cart, and stomp down the aisle. It's the grocery story equivalent of "Get off my yard."

My tantrum comes to an end when I too roughly place the eggs in the basket cracking them. The mess is the wake-up call I need to remind myself why I'm here in the first place. My date tonight with Poppy is enough to readjust my attitude. I let go of my irritation with the neighbor for now. Once I have everything on my list, I grab a bouquet of brightly colored flowers.

Poppy wouldn't let me pick her up tonight. She insisted she could get there on her own, but I'd still like to have flowers for her when she gets to my place. I don't do this dating thing often, but I want to get it right. Poppy deserves that much.

After adding the flowers to my haul, I make the last-minute decision to grab some chocolate, remembering how she made me choose salty or sweet for her. That seems like it was months ago, not just a few weeks. After the way Poppy has been distant the last few days, we might need the chocolate and flowers to smooth over whatever has her pulling back.

CHAPTER 13

POPPY

By the time I am dressed and ready to walk next door to Hendrix's apartment my nerves are frayed, and my hands are shaking. The calming effects of my run this morning are long gone and once again I'm a mess.

I've changed my outfit no less than a dozen times. Finally deciding on a black skirt that hits mid-calf and has a slit up the side. Pairing it with a graphic tee and pair of boots. It's casual and comfortable while still being cute. Opting to go light on the makeup and leave my hair down in loose curls. It's not like I could manage a dramatic eye with how anxious I'm anyways. I was lucky to make it through the curls without burning myself.

Assessing myself in the mirror one last time, I decide it's time to walk away before I throw the whole thing out and start over. A quick swipe of lip gloss to finish it off and I grab the bottle of wine from the kitchen counter on my way out.

It might be a short walk, but I'm painfully aware of each step as I walk down the hallway from my door to Hendrix's. The sound of my footsteps seem to echo through the hallway before I pause in front of Hendrix's door. I bring my fist in the air to knock, taking deep breaths to calm my racing heart and nerves as much as possible. Lowering my hand, I close my eyes and shake my hands out before bringing it back up to rap it against the cold metal of his door.

The sound of his muffled steps reaches me through the door and my heart rate picks up. When the door opens, Hendrix is staring down at me with the biggest smile on his face. He reaches out and takes the wine, then steps back just enough so I can enter. Our bodies brush as I step into his apartment, sending sparks to my core. Wine set aside for now, he turns back to me, shutting the door. His body towers over me and caging me in.

Hendrix's hands land on my forearms, skating up to my shoulders and leaving goose bumps in their wake. "You look gorgeous, Poppy."

God, I missed him. The thought takes me by surprise. It's surreal after keeping my heart on lockdown for so long, but he has quickly cracked the walls I erected around it to keep it safe after Paul. I bring my hands to his pecs and trace them up to his shoulders, savoring the feel of him underneath my fingertips. Slowly his hand wraps around the back of my neck as he brings his face to mine. He runs his nose along the side of mine.

"I missed you." There's no point in hiding it. My gaze drops to his lips, right there for me to take, finally. Looking back up, I see the same desire reflected in his eyes.

"I can't wait any longer," he whispers against my cheek. Before I can make my move, he answers me with his own. Bringing his lips down on mine in a rush. The kiss is hard and hungry. My hands fist in his shirt, holding on and holding him to me at the same time. Hendrix licks at the seam of my lips and I open for him, relishing in the minty taste of him. A moan slips past my lips at the feel of his tongue gliding along mine.

Kissing him is like a runaway train with a broken brake, there is no stopping it. My body feels like it's lit up from the inside out with the intensity of it as we barrel down the tracks.

Hendrix's hands slide down my back and grip my ass, lifting me off the ground. Instinctively, my legs wrap around his waist, and he turns away from the door, moving to the countertop behind him. The coolness of the surface seeping through the fabric of my skirt is welcome against the raging fire that's taken over my body.

His lips move to my jaw and then my neck. "Is this okay?" His lips move against the skin below my ear.

"Yes, so much, yes." My hands shift through his hair, the dark strands glide through my fingers. Being able to touch him and feeling his hands on me after the last week apart has me completely caught up in the moment pushing all the nerves and worry aside for the moment.

Rhythmically, his thumb draws circles on my stomach where his hand rests on my waist. "Fuck, I have wanted to kiss you since the moment we met. You taste even better than I imagined," he groans as he layers little kisses, nips, and licks down to my collarbone before descending on my mouth again.

When his lips meet mine he's slower, taking deeper pulls from me, like he's savoring it. Savoring me.

This kiss is different than before. It adds a whole new dimension of longing. It's sweet and thorough. Both of us pouring all that we feel into this moment. All the phone calls and texts exchanged over the last week building up to this one kiss. My hands find his jaw and caress the stubble there, mapping out the feel of his face in my hand.

When Hendrix nips at my lower lip, changing the pace again. The teasing action sends a jolt of impatient longing straight down my spine and my hips tilt up, chasing any friction they can find. My center finds his hard length and Hendrix groans into my mouth.

He slows the kiss before pulling back just enough to rest his forehead against mine. "I'm probably going to regret this," he starts to say before mumbling something under his breath that sounds a lot like, "Such a dumbass."

I pull back to look at him. His pupils are blown, and it bolsters my confidence to know he is feeling the same need I am. Hendrix exhales deeply, his dark hair tumbling over his forehead. "My plans weren't to maul you the second you walked through the door."

"Not sure if you noticed but there were no objections coming from me," I tell him, running my hands down his chest, smoothing his shirt where my hands crumpled it in our rush earlier.

Hendrix lowers his forehead to mine. "Should we cook?" he suggests quietly, like he's not entirely sure that's what he wants. I don't blame him; I'm feeling all the temptation to continue down our previous path.

Nodding, I tell him, "Probably, but let the record show that I'm conflicted about it."

The low chuckle that leaves his body vibrates through me. Without warning, the hands around my waist pluck me off the counter, setting me down in front of Hendrix. He dips down for a chaste kiss and leads me further into the kitchen. Our hands joined.

All the ingredients are laid out on the island in preparation for cooking. Looking around I see the table is set and complete with flowers. Hendrix nods toward the table.

"Those are for you. Since you wouldn't let me pick you up." My cheeks heat with embarrassment knowing the reason he couldn't pick me up is also what is likely to sabotage the evening.

"Thank you, they're beautiful." I tell him, coming up on my toes to kiss the corner of his mouth before asking, "Where do we start?"

I can't focus on why he couldn't pick me up.

Not yet.

"Would you rather chop or separate egg yolks?" Hendrix holds up the pancetta in one hand and an egg in the other. I reach across his body and grab the pancetta.

He slides the cutting board, pancetta, garlic and herbs my way while he starts cracking eggs and separating the yolks into a bowl. I get temporarily distracted by the movement and the way his hands work before shaking it off and focusing back on the knife in my hand. Losing a finger on our first date would be a real mood killer.

"Such a modern man. You have plants in your apartment and know your way around the kitchen. I know your grandma is responsible for the plants. Did she teach you to cook too?" This isn't the easiest recipe in the world. Given Hendrix's schedule, I expected his cooking skills to be more along the line of from the jar spaghetti sauce, not fancy Italian bacon with fresh chopped herbs.

"You already know that it was just the three of us when we were kids. Mia, me, and Nana." he explains while he adds cream to the bowl of yolks. "When my grandma picked up extra shifts at the hospital to pay for baseball camps and writing camps, Mia and I would pitch in with cooking. The two of us would take turns making dinner. It started off as mac and cheese or grilled cheese for dinner. It wasn't long before we got sick of the same simple things on rotation. Mia made these lasagna rolls she had seen some on a cooking show she was obsessed with at the time." A smile tilts his lips up at the memory as he whisks the cheese and herbs I cut into the bowl.

"My expectations were pretty low, but it was amazing. Instead of just thanking her, I turned it into a competition. It escalated pretty quickly, each of us picking dishes that were more complicated than the last. By the time we were out of high school, both of us felt at home in the kitchen."

"Remind me to avoid any competitions between you two. Your grandmother sounds like an amazing woman. I have enjoyed all the stories you have told me about her," I tell him as I finish chopping the pancetta. Hendrix moves to the stove where he adds oil to the pan.

"We owe her everything. Neither of us remember our parents. After they took off and signed over their rights, they never looked back, but my grandmother made sure we knew from that moment that we were hers and she would never leave us behind. That she wanted us." There's no doubt lingering in his voice when he says it. Hendrix continues moving around the kitchen with ease and comfort.

He takes the pancetta from me and adds it to the oil along with the garlic. "Can you grab me a pot from that cupboard and fill it about halfway with water?" Hendrix points to a lower cabinet and I move across the kitchen to grab it.

"She made sure we went to therapy at a young age to work through any trauma or abandonment issues, but I have always felt lucky. All we've ever known is a parent that was present and wanted the best for us."

Bending over, I reach into the cupboard, grabbing the pot to fill. When I turn around, I catch him staring at my ass. He knows he is caught, but it doesn't deter him.

"See something you like?" My voice comes out more gritty than normal. Following his instructions, I move to the sink and fill the pot.

His hands come down on the counter. One on each side of my body as he brings his chest to my back, eliminating any space between us. His lips drag along the side of my neck, and he pauses there before he inhales deeply, nosing into my hair.

"I noticed your perfect ass that first day at the coffee shop. You were wearing these tight black jeans that hugged your perfect body. When you reached under the counter to get the watering can, I knew I wanted to make you mine."

Mine. The word reverberates through me.

If we can get through this night can I manage to open myself up to him after everything I went through with Paul?

The appeal of being his seems too strong not to consider the possibility.

Hendrix punctuates the statement with a pulse of his hips against my ass. His hand leaves the counter, and he reaches around my body to turn off the water. Next, he takes the pot from me and sets it down on the counter. After that is out of the way, his other hand comes to my jaw tilting my mouth up to his.

My hand comes up and snakes around the back of his neck as he deepens the kiss. In this position with his chest pressed against my back, I'm totally at his mercy, so I press my ass back into him. Pulling his lips away, he breaks the kiss too soon. "If I don't stop now, I'm going to start a literal fire," he says, stepping away to deal with the food. I follow him with the water, setting it on the stove top.

"I wasn't done kissing you," I grumble.

"You'll thank me later when your stomach is full. Then I'll let you do whatever you want to me."

Heat surges through me at his words. "Promises, promises." I chide playfully before thinking that he might not feel the same once I tell him where I live and explain what I do for a living. My blood cools immediately dousing the fire he had stoked.

"You okay, Poppy?" he asks, picking up on the change in my demeanor. He turns the heat off on the pancetta as he wraps his arms around my waist.

"I will be. It's been a long day." Leaning my head into his chest, I inhale his scent trying to commit it to memory. He smells of soap and leather. "My mom and I don't see eye to eye — on pretty much everything. We got into it this afternoon." It's not the full truth, but I want to enjoy this meal together before I blow everything up.

Grabbing my hand, he brings me over to a stool and sits down on it, tugging me between his legs. "We have a few minutes while the water boils, want to talk about it?" he offers, brushing a stray hair behind my ear. His ability to shift so effortlessly between smoldering to sweet has my heart thumping hard. It beats out a tempo inside my chest that sounds a lot like Hendrix's name.

I shake my head. "Not really, but there's something else you can do for me." Placing my hands on his shoulders, I lace them together behind his neck as he looks up at me.

"Anything." His blue eyes on me emanating the truth in his statement.

"Take my mind off it," I say as I slant my mouth over his.

He pulls me in tighter. Sliding his tongue against mine, giving me exactly what I asked for. Hendrix James is the best kind of distraction, but he is already so much more than that to me.

His rough palm slides up under the back of my shirt, searing the skin as it dips under the band of my bra. His other hand palms my ass.

I lengthen my neck, giving him better access as his mouth leaves mine to pepper kisses in a line down the side of my throat. My shirt slides down giving him more skin and work with and he seizes the opportunity, nipping at the tattoo on my shoulder.

"This tattoo is so sexy," he soothes the bite with a soft kiss.

"They're Virginia bluebells," I pause before deciding to open up. "When I was maybe nine, Indie's mom found me crying next to a bed of them that she planted in their yard. I had run to their house after my mom had said something to upset me. Farrow sat down next to me in the grass, and instead of asking what was wrong she told me about the flowers. How they were resilient even though they looked delicate." Warmth spreads through me at the memory of how Farrow was always so good at building me up when I was down. Hendrix's hand runs up and down the length of my back as he listens patiently. "My tears dried up as I stared at the beautiful little blue flowers and listened to the sound of her voice calming me. Then she gave me a hug and sent me into the house to find Indie."

"I like it. They fit you." he says, laying a soft kiss to the juncture of my neck where the tattoo ends. "Now, how good of a distraction are we talking?"

The way Hendrix goes straight from sweet to dirty and back again makes me want him even more.

"Do your worst." The words are shaky with need as I arch into him bringing me into contact with his hips and chest.

"Fuck, Poppy. Let me take care of you," he groans, sliding his hand out from under my shirt and trailing it down my hip and to my knee. His fingers gather the fabric of my skirt up and he hitches my knee up over his hip and uses the hand on my ass to drag me down to him. With my skirt hitched up, it leaves just his jeans and my thin lace panties as a barrier.

My hands grip his shoulders as I press down on him, my center finding his hard length. A whimper escapes me at the first pass. The friction is almost too much. "Oh god, Hendrix. I have been craving the feel of you all week. It was torture being able to talk to you and see you but not have this."

Keeping one hand on my ass to help steady me, the other comes up to grip my breast over my shirt. He works the nipple into a peak between his thumb and pointer finger. The added roughness of my lace bra only adds to the sensation.

I slant my mouth over his and kiss him. My kiss matches the rhythm of his hips as I grind my clit against the rigid length of him. Hendrix groans into my mouth before pulling back, his hand coming to the hem of my shirt. He raises it slowly savoring every inch of skin he reveals.

"I can feel your heat through my jeans. So hot for me." His dirty words cause me to flush more than I already am. The tendrils of an orgasm wind through me as my core starts to tighten.

Hendrix lowers his head, bringing his mouth to my nipple through my lace bra. Sucking it into his mouth and then tugging on it with his teeth. "You're close aren't you, Poppy?" His voice is deep and rough when he asks.

The one leg I'm standing on is shaking and I'm struggling to hold my weight on it as I grind into him. Hendrix stands up without warning, wrapping my other leg around his waist as he moves us to the couch.

Laying me down under him, he pushes my skirt up to my hips and runs his finger up my slit. "So wet for me, too."

"Please — Hen." It's all I can get out. His hands on me are causing my brain to short circuit. He shifts my underwear to the side and when he sinks a finger in slowly, my back bows off the couch.

As he hovers over me, his mouth comes down on mine as he pulls his finger out and sinks back in, adding a second. He crooks them hitting me just right, and I detonate. Light bursts behind my eyelids. My body tightens and fragments all at once. He kisses me softly, working me through the waves of my release slowly before withdrawing his fingers. I ache at the emptiness and sink back into the couch in a boneless mess. *Holy shit, no one has ever made me see stars like that before.*

Resting his forehead against mine, he gives me one last slow kiss as his fingers leave me. "Fuck, Poppy, that was so sexy. You look gorgeous when you come for me," he tells me as his eyes rake over me before he lowers his head, kissing the tip of my nose. "Stay here. Let me finish up and then I'll feed you."

He adjusts my underwear back into place. "Give me a minute and I'll come help you," I say from where I lay, letting my heart slow as Hendrix climbs off the couch to go finish in the kitchen. I hear the water running as he washes his hands and I decide to get up and help. If this is all we have, I'd rather be there with him.

As I push up off the couch to join him in the kitchen, I realize that this is really going to hurt if he reacts poorly to the news that I'm his neighbor. And it's not just the stellar orgasms that I'm going to miss.

Hendrix makes me feel different.

I can't exactly put my finger on it, but it just feels like he gets me. Like there's this shared connection between us. Maybe it's that we have both had our trust broken by someone we cared about. We are both a bit guarded and that links us somehow. Our flaws recognize each other.

I come up behind him at the sink and loop my arms around his waist. My throat tightens at the thought of not being able to do this after tonight. "Thank you. Best distraction ever."

ALL ON THE LINE

"I'm glad I could help you relax. Dinner is almost done. I cooked the chicken earlier so, once the pasta is cooked, everything just has to simmer for a few minutes then we can eat."

Hendrix finishes the cooking with little help from me. When everything is done, we sit side by side at the table and his hand falls to my thigh as we eat.

"This is really good, Hendrix. All that practice with your sister paid off," I praise after the first bite.

"I had this really sexy helper and I think it made all the difference," he says around a bite of chicken. "Having her here added some extra steps to the recipe, but I think it really improved it."

"I'll never cook the same way again," I tease as I twist my fork in the pasta. "How do you like the wine?" I ask as Hendrix brings his glass up to his mouth.

"It's better than sherry." His nose wrinkles, making him look boyish. "I'd still prefer a beer over wine, but with the right food it isn't bad."

"Anything is better than sherry. Do you think maybe your grandmother did it on purpose? Kept the sherry in the house knowing you guys wouldn't touch it?" I muse as I take a drink.

His eyes widen, hand frozen with the fork halfway to his mouth, and he looks at me shocked. "That is something she would have done. I bet she hid the good stuff from us." He laughs. "I'll have to ask her about it." He leans over to lay a light kiss on my temple. "Tell me about Indie's trip. What are your plans for her visit?"

"We talked about going to Breckenridge for the weekend. We're going to do some hiking, see the Maroon Bells and explore the village."

He tilts his head toward me like he is weighing the words about to come out of his mouth. "Would she want to see a game while she's here?"

"You know baseball isn't everyone's thing? Right?" His face falls for a second. And I hate that my teasing put that look on his face. "Hen, I'm kidding — I mean not everyone does like baseball, but she would love to come to a game. She's a big fan of baseball pants."

"Baseball pants, huh?" He raises an eyebrow. "Is that something you're into?"

"There's not a woman on the planet that isn't into baseball pants, and you know it. I didn't take you to be the type to need his ego stroked."

"There isn't a man on the planet that doesn't want a gorgeous woman to stroke his ego," he tells me, giving my teasing right back. Twirling a strand of hair around his finger, he gives it a light tug, rubbing it between his fingers. "If you decide you want to go to a game with her, let me know and I'll get tickets for you two. Preferably on my side of the field."

CHAPTER 14

HENDRIX

When I offer to get her tickets for Indie's visit, Poppy goes silent and her smile falters. The change in demeanor combined with how she pulled away when I was traveling has me concerned. Something is bothering her, and I think it's more than the fight with her mom. All of this reminds me of Kylie and how she used to keep things from me. The way she's avoiding eye contact is what Kylie used to do when she was hiding things from me.

I can't ignore the déjà vu that trickles through my body. My defenses immediately come up, but I remind myself that this is Poppy, not Kylie, and try to tamp them down while I figure out what is going on with her.

Turning in my chair so I'm facing her, I push a strand of hair behind her ear and lift her chin to me gently. "Hey, what's going on? You got quiet on me again. I think it's more than the conversation with your mom. You did this when I was on the road too."

She tries to look away from me, her gaze cast down. My stomach drops out. She won't even make eye contact. Those defenses that were flaring up just a second ago roar back to life. My hand clenches at my side with the urge I push the subject harder.

"There's something I need to tell you, but I'm afraid it's going to change things —" Her hand motions back and forth between us. She's still struggling to meet my eyes as she talks.

My jaw is tense as I try to be patient. "Poppy, I need you to tell me. I can't do this if you are hiding things from me. I can't be with someone that keeps things from me." I blow out a breath before I lay it all out. Cruz was right I need to be upfront about why honesty is so important to me. Having this conversation is hard, I feel stupid when I think about how Kylie took advantage of me. "The person who stole things out of my apartment was my ex-girlfriend; she was selling things and tipping off paparazzi anytime we went out to make money. I was going to propose to her. The week before I planned to ask her, my sister got wind of what she was doing and told me."

Her eyes widen in shock. "When I confronted her she didn't even try to deny it. The only thing she ever really cared about was the lifestyle being with me had afforded her. She got impatient waiting for me to make it permanent. It's the reason I haven't dated for years. I haven't been willing to put myself out there like that again. Until you."

"Oh god, Hendrix. I'm so sorry." Her voice breaks and I can't tell if she's apologizing for the past or for what she's about to say. Everything in me tells me that whatever is coming is going to be bad. It's going to hurt. I brace myself for the impact of it.

"I need you to be upfront and tell me what's got you so upset." My voice has an edge to it now. Bringing up Kylie has me expecting the worst. I scoot my chair back, giving myself some distance like it will lessen the blow. My hands cross over my chest so I don't reach out to Poppy. I can tell she is distressed, but I can't be the one to soothe her until I know what she's hiding.

"I didn't know, Hendrix." Her eyes franticly search mine. She's panicking and it makes my stomach bottom out because she wouldn't be reacting like this if she didn't think that she had already lost me. "Not until a few days ago when I came over to water your plants. If I had known I wouldn't have —"

"Wouldn't have what?" I cut her off, my voice sharp now. Any patience I had earlier is gone. Whatever she's about to tell me, she's known for days. She's been keeping something from me since she started pulling away. I opened myself up only to find out that Poppy is no different from Kylie.

She looks away and then looks back finally making eye contact. "We're neighbors."

That's all she says and for a second I'm not following. I turn it over in my head a few times. "We're neighbors." Not sure why this has her freaked out. I'm missing something, a key piece of information. And my brain feels so scattered from the last few minutes and explaining my past with Kylie that none of this is making sense.

"We're neighbors. I live in the apartment next door."

I repeat her words back in my head. *We're neighbors. I live in the apartment next door.* It all clicks together. The noises through the wall. The voice that sounded vaguely familiar, but was just muffled enough that I couldn't place it. Poppy is the loud neighbor next door. The possibilities swarming around in my head are enough to make me recoil in anger.

Stunned, I stand from my chair fast enough that it falls back to the ground. Poppy's eyes go wide as it clatters loudly off the floor. That's not what I was expecting. I thought maybe we were moving too fast; she was having second thoughts.

Not this.

How many times have I heard her through the wall with someone else? Was it always the same person? Multiple people. Fuck. The dominatrix next door is Poppy.

"Let me explain. Please, it's not what you think. I swear," she begs, her voice is strained and cracking with each word. I can tell she's holding back tears, but right now I can't bring myself to care.

How could I be this fucking stupid? Again, after Kylie I should have learned a lesson. I never should have opened myself up to someone I didn't know well so easily. I trusted her and she has been sleeping with other people this entire time right on the other side of the wall. The kicker is that this feels so much worse. I should never have trusted Poppy.

"You need to leave. Now." I tell her, pointing toward the door. Not willing to hear any more lies. Jesus, how many times since movie night have I heard her through the wall with someone else? Today even, the realization freezes me in place. My fists clench at my side and my jaw pops with tension.

Poppy sits in the chair frozen for a second before she moves to the door. Turning to me one last time with her eyes pleading. "Please, Hendrix."

"No, Poppy, go. How stupid do you think I am? I told you if we did this it was me and you. I heard everything." She turns toward the door, shoulders shaking as she pulls it open and walks out.

Fuck! How did I get played this badly again? Taking the dishes from dinner to the sink, I dump them unceremoniously. They clatter and break. Not bothering to clean them up, I move to the pantry to grab a bottle of whiskey.

As I walk past the table whiskey swinging at my side, the flowers catch my eye. Vase and all, I shove them in the garbage. So angry that I fell for the lies again. Hurt that Poppy betrayed my trust.

I skip the glass and carry the bottle of whiskey with me to the couch, uncapping the top and taking a long drink, letting the burn settle in my chest. I set the bottle down with a thud as my phone vibrates.

"What the fuck did you do?" Cruz growls from the speaker before I can even say hello.

"Me? She used me. Played me for stupid," I shout back angry that he is taking her side. My hand comes up, raising the bottle back up to my lips for another drink. The burn going down is nothing compared to the hollow ache in my chest. I rub my sternum with my knuckles, trying to ease it. But nothing works, not the amber liquid and not the pressure of my fist.

"I don't know what the fuck happened, but Lilah got a frantic call from Poppy and then kicked me out to comfort her." His voice is laced with frustration.

"I see, so this is about me cockblocking you, not actually about Poppy or me."

"Watch how you talk about Delilah," Cruz barks, his voice escalating to match mine.

"Fuck! That wasn't cool. I'm sorry. I know it's more than that between you two." Cruz isn't the problem here. The last thing I need is to isolate myself from my teammate and best friend.

"No, Hen. I didn't word that right. Delilah was upset when I left. It's got my guard up. What the hell happened between you two?"

"She's my neighbor, Cruz. My fucking neighbor… The one that I can hear through the wall having sex at all hours of the day." I bring the bottle up to my lips, taking a long drink.

This whiskey needs to do its job and numb me from the inside out.

I hear Cruz say, "Oh, shit."

Before he can continue, I end the call and toss my phone over my shoulder. It falls to the ground some place behind me.

My head is pounding and there is banging. *Of course, there fucking is.*

I guess this whole thing was one sided, it had to have been if she's back at it again next door. I groan as I lift my heavy head up from the back of the couch. Shit, my neck hurts. Rubbing my knuckles into my eyes, I see the half empty whiskey bottle wedged between my legs. Open but upright. At least I did something right. Passing out on the couch, though, that's another story. Bad move.

The banging has to stop. I set the whiskey on the coffee table and stand to go bang on the bedroom wall. Maturity be damned. I'm halfway there when I realize the banging is getting further away.

Front door, genius, for once it's not coming from Poppy's apartment. "Go away," I grumble still moving toward the bedroom with every intention of passing back out until I have to get up for practice.

"Hen, open the fucking door." Cruz hollers. When I pull the door open, he pushes past me, not waiting for an invite inside. "Jesus, man, you smell like a distillery." He thrust a coffee into my hand.

"No good coffee for me today?" I gripe, noticing it's not from Lilah's, but from the corner store. Great, this coffee is just as bitter as I am.

"She refused to make you one." He shakes his head.

"You can leave now. I'm not in the mood for a lecture."

"I'm not going to lecture you. Just tell me what happened, and we can figure it out." He leans against the island giving the dishes in the sink the stink-eye and making it clear he's not going anywhere. Reaching into his pocket he takes out a bottle of ibuprofen and throws it at me.

"There is nothing to figure out. Poppy's my neighbor," I tell him, popping three pills into my mouth and swallowing them with a gulp of coffee. "This coffee is terrible."

"We covered that part last night before you hung up on me," he says urging me to continue.

"She's the neighbor. You know the one that's been fucking someone at all hours of the day since I moved in. Even yesterday, before she came over here for a date." I explain more slowly than necessary because I feel like a real prick today.

"Christ, I know it seems bad when you spell it out like that. What did Poppy say?" he challenges.

"Nothing."

"Nothing," he repeats like a confused parrot.

"What excuse could she possibly have that was going to make it okay that she was fucking someone else after we promised not to see other people?" As annoying as it was to have the constant disruptions next door at this point I don't even care about that. What or who Poppy did before me isn't the issue. The thing that has me thrumming with outrage is the fact that she was screwing around on me this whole time.

"Look, man, Delilah insists it's not what it seems. She won't talk to me about it. But she's furious with you."

"I heard her. Several times. Fuck, even Clay heard her when we were on a call yesterday. He hung up because he thought I had a girl over. Newsflash, it was Poppy screwing someone else hours before our date on the other side of the wall." I assert pointing toward where our bedrooms butt up.

"I'm sorry, Hen. I know you really liked her. Don't you think it might be worth hearing her out? What if Delilah is right and it's not —"

"I'm going to stop you right there. I can't. Not after Kylie. She showed me who she is, and I need to take it for face value. I won't get fucked over again."

"Okay. I hear you. What can I do to help?" he asks, hanging his head resigned to the fact that I'm not willing to budge on this.

"Trade me coffees for starters?"

"Nope, not happening. I'll let you do this your way, but I'm not going to put myself between you and Delilah." Cruz tells me as he takes the stool beside me.

"Fair enough. Give me a few minutes to get myself together and then help me run off this whiskey before practice?" I request standing from the island.

"Sure, man. Can't have you showing up smelling like a frat house basement," he tells me, finishing the last of his coffee.

I'm still wearing last night's clothes and my mouth tastes like the inside of a whiskey barrel. The first step to feeling human today is going to be a quick shower before I run this alcohol haze off. When Poppy walked into the apartment last night I had envisioned us having a lazy morning together.

Instead, Cruz is sitting in my apartment while the woman I thought I was starting to care about sits next door. How I ended up in this situation again is beyond me. Evidently, my picker is broken, and I can't be trusted to find someone that won't take advantage of me.

My plan of putting relationships aside and focusing on baseball was working just fine after Kylie. *Lesson fucking learned.*

Stepping into the shower, I turn the knob and duck under the spray from the shower. It's too bad this water can't wash away the memory of how good it felt to have her, even just for a few weeks. I give myself a half assed scrub down, just enough to wake me up.

When I'm done with my shower, I find Cruz sitting on my couch, brow furrowed as he looks at his phone. He looks up when he hears me approaching and pockets his phone.

"Everything good?" I ask, slipping on my shoes. He has to be getting some backlash from Lilah because of my drama with Poppy. Cruz has been a good friend since I moved, and I don't want to see his friendship or relationship — whatever it is — be impacted.

He rubs his hands down his face and stands. "Not really, but let's just run. We aren't going to solve my issues today."

When we exit the building, I lead him away from the park and toward another multi-use path. I'm not mentally prepared to chance bumping into Poppy. And equally not wanting to face the memory of our run a few weeks ago.

Cruz, to his credit, is smart enough to leave my route choice well enough alone. "How badly did my night with Poppy fuck up your plans with Lilah last night?" I ask, wiping the sweat gathering on my brow with my forearm.

"You didn't really interrupt anything. We were just catching up from the last week when Poppy called her." His jaw tenses at what he's leaving unsaid. She rushed out to be there for her friend, leaving Cruz behind before they got a chance to talk. "Do you have your head straight for the game tonight?" he questions, changing the focus back to me.

I kick the pace up. "Yes. Won't be a problem." I mean every word. I won't let this impact my game. My emotions need to be on lockdown. It seems to be the only way to keep myself from being played for a fool.

"Good," Cruz comments, surging ahead of me down the path. "Let's flush out the whiskey and get to practice."

CHAPTER 15

POPPY

"Lilah, I'll be fine. Please just go to the game tonight. I don't need a babysitter," I plead with my best friend as I push her toward the door. She's been hovering since I called her last night. I love her for it, but the last thing I want is to have her skip out on her life to watch me mope around. Besides, I could use a bath, a glass of wine, and a little alone time to decompress.

"I can give the tickets to Mikey. It will thrill him and Mitch to go to a game. You know how much they love baseball," she justifies her plan to give the tickets to one of her employees and his husband at Buns and Roses even as she slips her shoes on.

"More like baseball players," I mumble under my breath while I push her purse into her chest.

"Was that a joke I just heard?" Lilah places her hands on my shoulders, giving me a serious once over. "You'll text if you need something?"

"I will, I promise. Just go have fun. Say hi to Cruz for me. I'm just going to take a bubble bath and relax." Shrugging out of her reach, I open the door.

Lilah sighs, giving into my demand. "Fine. I'm going, but I'm leaving under duress."

I grab her hand, pulling her to me for a hug. "I know —" Squeezing her tightly so she knows I mean it. "Thank you, Lilah. For rushing over here and for having my back. You're a good friend."

She gives me a squeeze and pulls back. "Damn right I am. It's what we do. You've always been there for me, and I'll always be there for you. Hoes before bros, and all that."

"I don't think that's how that saying goes, but I like it." I wave goodbye and shut the door as she starts down the hallway. When it latches, I lean against it, sliding to the floor and letting out a longer exhale. When I left Hendrix last night I was so hurt and angry. The sadness blurred by the disappointment in his reaction and refusal to hear me out.

I knew he would probably be upset and confused, but I didn't think he would be so cold. As soon as I told him we were neighbors, he shut down. The minute he figured it out I could see it in his eyes. His emotions shuttered, and it was over. He was done with me.

My career has caused issues with men feeling insecure in a relationship with me in the past. They couldn't deal with the fact that I owned a business in the adult entertainment industry and my role in it. They felt like I was cheating or that I just wasn't girlfriend material. I'm not the girl guys want to get serious with and take home to meet their families. Tears roll down my face, burning my cheeks as I remember the first time this happened two years ago.

Right after I had moved to Denver, I met Paul. He'd taken me out to a club to meet some of his friends. We had been dating for a few months at that point, but kept it casual. A few weeks before, I had told him about my job and he seemed supportive, promised it didn't matter to him. And it didn't seem to. Nothing changed. There was no dramatic shift in our relationship, it just kept on. After dancing and a few drinks, I needed to excuse myself to the bathroom.

When I came back, Paul and his best friend were talking with their backs to me. They didn't see me approach before I overheard their conversation.

"A phone sex operator? Fuck, man, I bet she's wild in the sheets. You lucky asshole."

My stomach bottomed out at the callous way his friend spoke about me. I stopped dead in my tracks, waiting for Paul to come to my defense.

Instead, he crushed my spirit in a matter of seconds. "It's not like it's going to go anywhere. Poppy's not the girl you bring home to meet the parents and marry. But damn, is she fun."

I haven't dated anyone since. Two years, I waited, refusing to put my heart on the line, to have it mistreated by someone in that way again. The second I let my guard down and try, Hendrix reinforces that message with how easily he cast me aside. He may not have found out about my career, but his dismissal hurt me all the same.

When Lilah came over last night, she was shocked to find out that Hendrix was my neighbor, but more stunned to hear about his reaction. I still can't believe that we never put the pieces together, but I'm not close enough to Cruz that he has been to my place. We hang out a lot at his place, Lilah's, or Draft. Lilah and Hendrix have only known each other a short time and all their interactions are tied to their shared friend-ship with Cruz.

If Lilah had gotten her way, she would have marched over there and reamed him out. I had to beg her not to, positive it would only make things worse.

Right now, I'm not sure I want Hendrix to know what I do. His actions last night, and the way he just dismissed me. His thoughtless reaction broke my trust in him too. I don't want someone who can discard me so easily when they find out details about my life. I refuse to have them used against me again. Pushing up from the floor, I grab the wine and run a warm bath.

Once I'm reclined in the tub with a few sips of wine down, I prepare to call Indie back. She had called earlier today for an update on date night. I hadn't been in the headspace to fill her in then.

"Hey, Pops." Indie answers in greeting, her voice warm and welcoming.

"Hey, Indie."

"Are you in the bathroom? Your voice is echoing." Indie asks.

"Bathtub, to be exact. Drinking wine and soaking my worries away." I bring the wine to my lips for a fortifying sip.

"Did it not go well?" Concern laces her voice. This is why I called her. Indie has been my biggest supporter and protec-tor since we were five. As much as I don't want to rehash last night, I know she'll help me through it in a way no one else can.

"It did not. Not at all," I tell her and then recall the first hour. Cooking together, the earth-shattering orgasm, dinner. Groaning, I add. "That's actually not true. It was going really well. Like the best first date ever. Until it wasn't."

By the time I have unloaded the story on her, the water is cooling and my wine is gone. My head is all buzzy from the generous pour and Indie has me feeling more like myself already.

"Pops, if Hendrix came knocking tomorrow apologizing and wanted to hear your side, what would you do?" Indie challenges me as I sink lower into the water letting it lap over everything but my face.

"That's not going to happen. He was pretty clear. But if it did, I don't even know if there's enough trust left there for me to tell him what he was really hearing was me talking to clients."

Indie hums her agreement on the other end of the line but otherwise stays quiet to let me continue.

"And I think that's what hurts the most. At first, I was just really angry. Now I am equally sad for what could have been. I really liked him, Indie. And I could see us having a future. I can't be with someone who writes me off like that. My parents did that for as long as I can remember. I won't do it. He doesn't deserve to know that part of me." Saying it aloud is cathartic. I feel the heat of a tear rolling down my face and wipe it with the back of my hand.

"Do you think you are ready to have the conversation with your parents yet? You need to give them boundaries. It's never going to get better if you ignore it." Her voice is soft. She's only pushing it because she has seen the toll it's taken firsthand. And she's right. I harbor a lot of baggage from my relationship with my parents. I recognize that my need for privacy comes in part from them. Paul made things worse, but even before him I kept my work separate from my personal life, careful to only tell those I trusted. Making it impossible for others to use it against me.

"I think I am. But maybe in a few days. Let me have some time to deal with things one at a time."

"A reasonable request. You're going to be okay, Pops. No matter what happens. You are one of the toughest people I know."

"Thanks, Indie. I can't wait to see you in a few weeks."

Somehow I manage to make it through the next two weeks without bumping into Hendrix in the hallway or at the coffee shop, but I know my luck is bound to run out eventually. I have gone over that next interaction in my head dozens of times and let it play out. Even envisioned how I will respond and what I want to say to him, but I still have no idea how I'll actually react when it inevitably happens.

I haven't actively been avoiding him outside of skipping Bandits games with Lilah. Something I don't plan to do for much longer. I love going to the games. I miss that time with Lilah. The team goes on a road trip tomorrow and when they come back, I want to be back in the stands with her. Even if I know it will sting to see him.

My client calls are all finished, and it was a bitch getting through them all. Each call was like a pinprick to my tender heart reminding me of him. Now I'm just relieved that they're done so I can focus on getting ready to record my demo.

The recording booth I ordered is still not here and I need to check the tracking for it. When I open the email and see the newly estimated arrival window, I push back from my chair and start pacing the room. It won't be here for another two to three weeks.

The ding of my phone stops my pacing and I grab it off the desk already aggravated about the sound booth. The text notification is from Hendrix.

HENDRIX:

We leave on a road trip tomorrow. Can you drop my key off before then?

I read over it a few times, the hurt and sadness bubble back up but right alongside it is rage. The urge to march over there and bang on his door until he answers and say — I don't even know what — is almost as loud as the blood pounding in my ears.

Fuck him. This is not the man I thought I knew. Not the fun, kind man I was falling for. If this is who he is, then I want nothing to do with him. I let my temper cool for a moment nibbling on my thumb as I think through my response.

POPPY:

~~Take your key and shove it up your ass Hendrix.~~

POPPY:

~~You're a real tool Hendrix James. Hope you get chronic hemorrhoids.~~

POPPY:

I'll leave it with Marv when I go tonight.

My response is short and civil, deciding he is not worth my time or energy. I grab the key and bring it down to the lobby to drop it off with Marv. When I get to the lobby, Marv has the Bandits game on the radio and they're talking about a play involving Hendrix. I do my best to tune it out.

It's next to impossible with the announcer raving about Hendrix's play this last week. Saying he has never seen him this amped up. I guess he's figured out how to channel his frustration into his game. Or maybe he's just already over it and everything I felt was one sided.

Not my monkeys, not my circus.

"Hey, Marv. This is for Hendrix James when he gets in tonight," I tell him, sliding the key across the counter.

Frowning, Marv shakes his head at the radio before he turns and looks at me. "That boy has been downright cantankerous this week. Walking around with a scowl all week, but he's been playing ball like it's game seven every day. Going to burn himself out," he mutters that last part more to himself than me.

Not my monkeys, not my circus. I repeat the mantra over in my head before giving Marv a tight smile. "He should be expecting the key. I told him I'd leave it down here." Stepping back from the counter, I turn to head back upstairs. As I'm pushing through the door to the stairwell, a text from Lilah comes through.

LILAH:
Are you ready to re-enter the world?

POPPY:
That's a little dramatic.

LILAH:

Is it? Have you left your apartment today?

POPPY:

As a matter of fact, I'm not in it right now. And I went for a run today.

LILAH:

Good, if you are already out, meet us at Draft.

LILAH:

You-know-who won't be there.

POPPY:

He's not Voldemort Lilah. More like Nagini, a slimy snake. I refuse to give him dark lord level power.

LILAH:

See you soon?

My hair is in a messy bun from my bath earlier, but a quick change of clothes and I could be ready to go. My fingers type the response before I can second guess anything.

When I get to the bar, I make my way past the hostess to the roped-off section and wave down Lilah, who comes to get me. She grabs my hand and pulls me through the crowd to where Cruz is sitting with Dean, Dom, and another teammate. Even though she told me Hendrix wouldn't be here, part of me is still expecting to see him when I walk in. My muscles relax when I look around and don't find him anywhere. I need a night out to relax after the last week. I'm not sure I'd be able to do that if he had shown up.

Lilah takes the seat next to Cruz, leaving a seat open between Dean and the other Bandit. Sliding into it, I look over to find Dean smirking at me and running his eyes over me appraisingly. I'd roll my eyes at his bold move, but I know he is completely harmless.

"Poppy, you've met Dean and Dom, right?" Cruz gestures to the two of them. "And that's Xavier."

"Hey guys. Nice to meet you, Xavier." I say politely. Lilah slides a beer toward me. Xavier smiles at me and it's a look that I bet gets him whatever he wants. He's attractive in a pretty boy sort of way. Dark hair, square jaw, light green eyes, young but just enough stubble on his jaw to make it clear he's not a boy.

He does nothing for me.

Knowing he wears a Bandits uniform is enough to make me steer clear. That's not the kind of drama I want in my life. Even without him being Hendrix's teammate, he isn't what my body craves. My foolish body needs to get onboard with my heart and mind. Both of which want nothing to do with blue-eyed, sharp-jawed outfielders.

"I'm surprised to see you out without Hen," Dom says with a playful smile. Lilah whips around to face him. The scowl marring her pretty face should be enough to scare him, but Dom's oblivious. I smile at her trying to silently communicate that it's fine. *Really, everything is fine.*

"Why is that?" I innocently ask while taking a drink from my beer. I can pretend not to care all day, but my curiosity still gets the best of me. I look to Cruz, whose gaze is pinballing back and forth between Lilah and me with concern, like he's not sure if he should jump in. Dean stares slack jawed at Dom, but he just continues on.

"Your boyfriend almost took Dean's head off in Arizona when he suggested I should try to hook up with you." Dom glances at Dean, seeing his face for the first time. His laugh turns nervous as he reads the room.

"I'm not his to claim." Dom's eyes widen, and he clears his throat as he looks over my shoulder with his gaze fixed beyond me.

Goose bumps run up my arms and I know he's there before I even see him. My attention is focused on Lilah, who is wearing a shocked look on her face. I will myself not to look. But I lose out to my morbid curiosity. When I glance over my shoulder, I see him leaning against the bar propped on his elbow, looking like he might murder Dom and Xavier for talking to me. It's a look that would normally melt my panties, but I am so pissed at him that it only intensives my anger.

The fucking gall. For him to stare another man down for talking to me after he pushed me away.

Threw me out like yesterday's leftovers.

How dare he.

I'm not good enough for him, but he's angry that I'm talking to someone else. That's not how this works.

"Does he know that?" Dom asks, his eyebrow raised.

"He should. It was his fucking decision."

Dom's hands raise in front of him, palms facing me, clearly not wanting to get himself in anymore hot water. Shit. I'm all flustered now, and Dom didn't really deserve that even if he was being an instigator.

"He said he wasn't coming out tonight. I didn't —" Lilah starts, looking apologetic, but I cut her apology short.

"It's fine. We are bound to run into each other. I know you wouldn't spring this on me," I tell her, laying my hand on hers across the table to reassure her. She doesn't need to feel guilty. As much as I didn't want to see him here tonight, this is his team, and it's going to keep happening. With a sigh, I pound my beer, sliding it over for Lilah to refill from the pitcher. All I can do is make the best of it. I'm not running away. I'll leave that to him.

CHAPTER 16

HENDRIX

My body aches as I walk across the locker room with a towel cinched around my waist after our win against Tampa Bay. I have been pushing myself harder than I ever have and although it's paid off on the field with four wins in a row this week, it's taking its toll. I did this after my split with Kylie too. If I'm not in the gym training, I'm in the cage taking extra reps it's the only way I know from letting the anger consume me.

My exhausted body sinks to the bench and I run my hands down my face. The locker room is mostly empty, all the guys having cleared out to celebrate with their families or head to Draft. Cruz, Dom, Dean and Xavier all rushed through their showers to meet Lilah there.

I'm not going, I just don't have it in me tonight. Despite my success on the field, everything else in my life feels like it's falling apart.

NANA:

Hendrix James, I know you are off that field. You better call me the second you are out of the locker room.

Great now I am in trouble with her as well. I finish dressing and call her as I walk out the door to the player's lot. As I head toward my apartment, I wait for her to pick up. I know exactly why she's calling. Mia and I spoke earlier, and she wanted an update on my date with Poppy. I didn't rehash all the details. I just told her that the date didn't go well and that there wouldn't be another. She let it drop without a fight, but I knew it wouldn't be that easy.

"Hendrix," is my grandma's one word greeting. Her voice is soft and tentative, like she's not sure whether to ask if I'm okay or get on my case. "What happened?"

"Are you really going to make me give you all the details?" I ask, not really wanting to relive the entire night.

"Yes, I am because I love you and I want the best for you. The last time we talked, you were so happy. Nothing compared to the stone-faced man I watched on the television the last few days. All that joy that was in your eyes is gone. You might have had a good game, but you looked like a robot."

I start at the beginning as I continue the walk back to my apartment. I tell her how it felt like Poppy was pulling away, then go over the date and talk about how we laughed and cooked together, leaving out some of the more intimate details, like the way Poppy clung to me when I made her come on my fingers. The vision of her like that still assaults me daily, even though it's the last thing I should be thinking about. When I tell her about the bomb Poppy dropped on me I expect her to be as outraged as I am.

"So what?" my grandmother asks when I am done.

"So what?" I balk back at her. Clearly, I'm going to need to spell it out for her. "She's my next-door neighbor. As in, we share a wall."

"Okay. I guess I'm still not seeing the problem." She pushes back her voice firm.

"She was sleeping with someone else. God, maybe even more than one person judging by what I heard."

"Was she really?" Her voice is too sweet when she asks. It sets me on edge, but I keep my cool.

"Can you just say what you mean?" I ask careful to keep my tone in check. She's not who I'm really upset with, but I'm tired. Fucking exhausted actually from this conversation and from the way I'm punishing my body.

"Did she tell you that she was seeing other people?"

"What? No. Of course not." I sigh annoyed that she's not immediately taking my side. "You remember when I was in kindergarten what was the comment from Ms. Brown on my report card?"

"What does that..." her voice cuts off as she chuckles on the other end of the phone. "Oh. Henny."

"Hendrix needs to work on his ability to share with his classmates. Fun fact, I still don't share well."

"No, you don't, but that's not what I meant. When you asked her for an explanation, what did she tell you?"

"She didn't. I asked her to leave. I'm not interested in hearing anymore lies from her."

"What did you say to me the other day, Hen?" she asks pausing for a moment. "'She's nothing like Kylie.' Those were your exact words."

"Clearly I was wrong."

"Were you? Or are you just so trapped by your past and how Kylie hurt you that you refuse to see what's in front of you?"

"And what's that?" I challenge not sure where she's going with this. What possible explanation could there be for what I heard?

"That Poppy made you happy. For the first time in four years, you found someone that was worth the risk, and you couldn't even give her the benefit of the doubt long enough to explain before you cut her loose. What if it was a simple explanation, maybe her version of self-care involves watching porn or she has a roommate and that's what you were hearing? You know it's not just men that watch porn. Don't jump to conclusions that could cause you both a boat load of heartache."

"Are you still going to come see me next week or are you so annoyed you have canceled your plans?" I complain growing tired of the conversation revolving around Poppy and me.

"Now that you mention it, maybe I should hop on the earlier flight and come out this week instead. You could use my guiding presence in your life now, more than ever. I think I'll change my flight and make sure you get this sorted out," she says lightly, but I can tell the idea is taking root. "I'm sure there's a red eye tonight and my bag is already packed." There's no doubt that when I wake up tomorrow morning, I will have a guest waiting on my welcome mat.

After that she says her goodbyes, claiming she'll see me soon and asking me to think about what she said. I know Kylie screwed with my head. I'm not oblivious to the fact that she is the reason I haven't dated or allowed anyone into my space in years.

But it hadn't crossed my mind that the reason I didn't give Poppy a chance to explain was more to do with Kylie than her. A lot of what my grandmother said is true, and she's not the first person to point out that this could have easily been flipped. Lilah gave me a heated lecture the other day when I stopped at Buns and Roses for some decent coffee and to make good on my bet with Marv. She sold me the coffee, but I think it was only because I was picking up scones for Marv at the same time.

"You're the worst kind of idiot, Hendrix James. Poppy is one of the best people I know, and if she ever decides to let you back in and tells you what actually happened, you are going to kick yourself for pushing her away." She ranted while she held Marv's scone hostage.

"You think you know what happened?" I asked, careful not to be an ass to her even though she was irritating me. I don't need Cruz to skin me alive for upsetting Lilah.

"Oh, I know what happened, mister. But it's not my story to tell. That needs to come from her. And I'm not sure it's a truth you are worthy of hearing." She said, turning up her nose at me and shoving the pastries at me across the counter. "You just gave up the best thing that will ever happen to you."

I'm still livid that I was lied to again. Everyone chirping at me has me questioning my decision not to hear her out. It's making me more uncertain of my decision every day. Now that I have heard it, I can't unhear it. My head is going in circles, debating if I have made a mistake. That, coupled with the fact that my grandmother thinks I have messed things up so badly that she needs to fly out to help me get my life in order, has me slowing to a stop in the middle of the side-walk. I halt my progress toward my apartment suddenly not wanting to be alone with my thoughts and turn toward Draft.

My snap decision to detour to the bar backfires, I came here to get away from my thoughts of Poppy. What I wasn't expecting was to walk in and find Dom flirting with her. She looks relaxed and happy next to him. It makes me feel like fire is running through my veins. I want to walk over there and knock that stupid smirk off his playboy face.

Forcing myself to calm down, I remind myself that she's not mine. That I don't want her to be mine, but even as I think it, my hand tightens dangerously on my glass. Before I know what's happening, my feet move me across the bar to the table they're seated at. When Dom sees me approaching, he gets up.

"I see an old friend. I'm going to go catch up," he mumbles, nodding toward the bar. Xavier stands to join him.

"Good plan." I roughly pat his back, encouraging his exit and drop into his chair. Not a clue what the fuck I'm doing. Lilah stares at me, mouth gaping like she can't believe I'd have the nerve. I watch as Cruz's hand dips below the table and her attention returns to him.

Fuck, this is awkward, but it's better to just get it over with. I have no intention of avoiding my friends and team-mates, so we are going to have to figure out how to coexist.

"Poppy," I grunt out in greeting. She turns to meet my gaze. Why does she have to look so damn good? Even if she's looking at me like the shit on the bottom of her shoes. Not sure I deserve all that disdain when she's the one that lied.

"Hen," she says brusquely, using my nickname, not my full name like she used when we were together. Her eyes flick over me once and then turn back to Lilah. Dismissing me from the conversation.

"How did interviews go? Any promising candidates in today's batch?" Poppy asks Lilah, her voice much lighter and happier than it was for our brief exchange.

"Yes, actually. My last interview today, Willa. She's finishing her master's degree and looking for some extra cash while she's in school. She was perfect. So sweet she'll be great with customers. And she has baking experience so she can help with some baking and prep too," Lilah gushes. I watch Poppy as her face lights up for her friend. My heart pangs remembering being on the receiving end of her warmth.

"Thanks for dropping my key off," I mutter, and everyone at the table turns to look at me. Staring at me like I have two heads. *What the fuck, did I lose my brain-to-mouth filter today? Why am I even talking?*

Poppy turns to me, eyes blazing. "Seriously, Hen?" Her lips are pulled into a tight line that looks out of place on her face.

I run my fingers through my hair, pushing it back, frustrated with myself. "Yeah. That was dumb. Maybe I should go," I say as I push my chair back.

"No, stay." Poppy practically growls at me. "You did this to yourself. Don't run away because it's uncomfortable now." Her eyes are wild like she might rip me a new one and part of me wants her to. For us to fight this out, do anything other than what we are doing right now. But she just shakes her head. Disappointment washes over me.

She doesn't even care enough to fight me on it.

She's resigned and for some reason that doesn't sit right with me.

A foot connects with my shin under the table, and Cruz throws his hands up in the air. I just tilt my head down and take a drink of my beer.

"What are you going to do with your free time once Willa starts?" Poppy asks Lilah, returning to the conversation that my verbal diarrhea just interrupted.

Redness creeps up Lilah's cheeks before she responds. "It'll be a few more weeks before she's trained, but I'm hoping I can travel a bit. Just a long weekend here or there."

When I glance over at Cruz, he has a goofy smile on his face and I notice his hand has disappeared back under the table. These two aren't fooling anyone. Poppy smirks across the table at them, picking up on the same cues I am.

"Any place in particular?" Dean asks, completely oblivious to what's going on.

"Chicago, Milwaukee, or St Louis on your itinerary?" I muse mostly to myself, thinking of our upcoming travel schedule. Dean's face crinkles with confusion for a moment before his face lights up with understanding and a quiet, "Oh," pops out.

"No — Nothing is set in stone," Lilah stumbles over the words, and Cruz frowns for a second before jumping in.

"Let her finish hiring the girl before you start planning out all her free time," he suggests, effectively ending that line of questioning.

"I'm going to go grab another pitcher. Anyone need anything?" Poppy asks, pointedly looking at everyone but me. Glancing over my shoulder, I watch her head to the bar. She's wearing the tight black jeans I love so much, and I'm not the only one that notices the way they hug her ass, making it looking fucking phenomenal.

As she approaches, Dom and Xavier make room for her to get to the bar, sandwiching her between them. While Dom keeps his distance, I see Xavier lean in and whisper in her ear. Her head tilts back in laughter and I hear a low chuckle from my right where Dean is seated.

"Someone's got a death wish," he gloats through his laughter. Eyeing me up and reading my reaction like the button pusher he is.

"Shut the fuck up, Dean." I grit out through my teeth. Eyes glued to where Poppy's hand just came down on Xavier's forearm. His gaze travels down her body before he catches me looking and comes to his senses, discreetly stepping back from Poppy and excusing himself from the bar.

Confusion crosses Poppy's face before she looks over her shoulder and finds me. She catches me staring at her, but I don't look away. Not breaking eye contact, she pulls out her phone and types something out. Across the table Lilah grabs her phone, brows furrowing together before she levels me with an icy glare.

My feelings for Poppy are dizzying. She broke my trust in the worst possible way, but I still feel pulled to her. Seeing her with anyone else kills me. The jealousy running through me is making me act like a jealous boyfriend, not someone that just walked away from her.

"Poppy's heading out," Lilah says, her gaze still on me, disappointment tinges her voice, and it makes me feel like shit. I wasn't trying to chase her away. I rake my fingers through my hair before I push my chair back.

"Tell her not to bother. I'll go." I try to tell myself that it's an olive branch more for Lilah than anything else, but it's not. There are still feelings for Poppy buried under the hurt. I don't want me being here to hurt her.

When I exit the bar, Poppy is standing outside the door, phone out. Her ride is nowhere in sight and as much as her actions hurt me, I can't just leave her alone out here to wait. It's not how I was raised, and it doesn't sit well with me, even if I know she has no interest in my company. My nana would never let me hear the end of it if I left her out here alone to wait. Especially after how we ended things, she would encourage me to take this opportunity to try to figure things out.

I lean against the wall on the opposite side of the entrance, giving her space as I debate my next move. My friends and family have given me a hard time for not hearing Poppy out. In the heat of the moment, I was too angry to give her that chance. Even now there is nothing she could say that would excuse the lies and deceit. Still, there is that nagging doubt in my head from everyone else.

"Why did you do it?"

She turns toward me just realizing that I'm there. Poppy shakes her head and returns her eyes to the phone in her hand.

"If you didn't want to be exclusive, why didn't you just tell me you wanted to keep things casual?" Pushing her to give me something, anything. Even though I know there is no way I'd have gone for a casual fling with Poppy. I already felt too much for her for things to ever be casual.

She pockets her phone and turns toward me, arms crossed defensively over her chest, which only serves to push her tits up. My body reacts, and it's frustrating as hell that she still has this hold on me. I plant myself more firmly against the wall. Determined to stay put, not to give into what my dick wants.

"Do what exactly, Hen?" Her tone is defiant, and her eyes are blazing with fury that is visible even in the barley lit night.

"Come on. Don't play dumb, Poppy. We both know you're not." The words slip out before I think better of them. Her reaction is immediate, the emotion leaving her eyes. Her walls come down and she's in full defensive mode now. *Shit, if I wanted a genuine answer my shot is blown.*

"That's rich. Coming from you. You have zero fucking clue what you are talking about. Aside from not telling you as soon as I read your email that we were neighbors, I did nothing wrong." she spits back at me. Her voice is cold, and her posture is closed off with her shoulders turned in. She turns on her heels and starts walking toward our building. Not even waiting for her rideshare.

I should let it go, but I don't because this woman makes me stupid.

"Nothing wrong? Poppy, I heard you fucking someone earlier in the day. It was so loud my agent could hear you while we were on the phone. I cared about you and thought we were on the same page. I let you in and you decimated that trust." I stop myself before I tell her more than I actually mean to.

She whips around coming to a halt in front of me, her green eyes are wild with anger. "If you cared about me, you would have heard me out then. Instead, you wrote me off. Made the worst possible assumptions about me and pushed me away. I thought you were different." Her shoulders are shaking and she's holding back tears when she adds quietly. "I haven't even looked at another man since we met. Forget sleeping with someone else. It was just you, Hendrix."

I flinch at her quiet admission, not sure what to make of it. But before I can process it, she is on the move again, walking away. Last time I watched her leave I pushed her away. This time she's going on her own. Head down and shoulders shaking with rage and hurt. "It's over, Hen. You are the one who broke us, not me. Leave me alone," she finishes, and I fall back watching her go and feeling more conflicted than ever.

CHAPTER 17

POPPY

"Morning, Miss Poppy." Marv croons at me when I exit the stairwell. He's leaned over his desk talking to a woman I don't recognize, his soulful dark eyes are focused on her. She's wearing a pair of tailored pink pants and a sheer white blouse that she has tucked into the front of her pants on one side. She finishes off her look with chunky gold jewelry around her neck and wrists. Her hair is styled in a sleek gray bob that gives her an edgy look despite her age. Bright purple glasses perched on her nose and hot pink lipstick staining her lips. As she watches Marv, her pale blue eyes shine with flirtation. I know without even speaking to her I want to be just like her when I grow up.

She exudes confidence and grace as she twirls her hair around her finger, looking Marv up and down like he might just be her next meal. Lord help him, I'm not sure Marv can handle this woman if she sets her sights on him. I watch in awe as she leans across the desk and grabs a pen. Brazenly, she takes Marv's hand and flips it, palm up, before scrawling her number across it with a sly smile.

"Morning, Marv. Need anything from Buns and Roses? I'm running over to grab some coffee. Did you get your daily scone fix yet?"

His attention stays glued to the woman in front of him when he replies. "No, I haven't. The team left on a road trip, so sadly my supplier is gone. I was just giving Janet directions to the best coffee shop in Denver. Would you mind walking with her?"

She smiles at me warmly putting any trepidation I might have had to rest. I'm outgoing by nature and walking with Janet seems like a great way to meet someone new and hear their story.

Leaning up against the counter next to the woman extending my hand, I say, "I'm Poppy. I'm heading there now. I'd be happy to walk with you."

Her knowing eyes sparkle and I get the distinct impression that this woman has my number. There's mischief in her eyes when she says, "Poppy, what a unique name. I love it. It fits you perfectly, darling. You are just as magnificent as the flower. What can we grab for you, Marv?" Janet might just be the most charismatic person I have ever met. Her personality sets me at ease immediately.

"That's sweet of you, Janet. I do love Lilah's scones. Just pick me up whatever she has on special today," he says sliding a bill across the counter.

"Not a chance, Marv. This one is on me," I chastise as I push the money back at him. I turn toward Janet and ask, "Ready?"

"Let's do the damn thing!" she exclaims, pushing off the desk and winking at Marv. "I'll see you later."

Marv's eyes widen at her blatant flirting but his mouth lifts in a boyish smile before he nods.

When we step out onto the sidewalk Janet dramatically fans her face. "Hot damn that man is fine. Please tell me he is single?"

Considering Marv is as asexual to me as a container of hummus, I have never considered his relationship status. Tilting my head, I try and remember if he's ever mentioned anyone special. "I'm not sure. He isn't married, never has been, if that helps."

"Tell me about yourself. We may as well get to know each other as we walk." She loops her arm through mine like we are old friends.

"What do you want to know?" I ask with a chuckle. Janet is a trip, and I'm here for it. Her energy is refreshing. She's so warm I'd probably tell her just about anything without a second thought.

"Are you from Denver, or did you move here?"

"Moved here. I grew up in Illinois. Only child, stifling parents. That whole story," I explain, waving my hand in the air like my family dysfunction is no big deal. "I moved away for college and never looked back. Denver is home now. What about you, do you live in Denver or just passing through?" I ask, hopeful that she's sticking around for a while.

"I'm not sure how long I'll be in town, I have family here and they needed some— help. So here I am. They're incredibly lucky to have me." Her laughter is contagious, making me break into a smile. "What did you go to school for?" she continues with her questions.

"Marketing. I wanted something that allowed me to be creative while still earning a living," I tell her, pointing toward the next intersection where Buns and Roses is located.

"Is that what you do now? Sorry, I'm being nosy, but I can just tell you and I are going to be friends."

Her statement about being friends catches me off guard, but not because it's sudden. It's surprising that I feel the same way. Typically, I'll keep people at arm's length getting to know them, but not sharing as much about myself. With Janet, there's an instant connection, like I already know her even though we just met. She reminds me of Indie's mom in the way she puts me at ease. There's no judgment in her eyes or tone. Janet is asking with an open mind to get to know me.

"Well then, if we are going to be friends you need to know these things. Right now, I'm in the middle of a career change. Up until recently, I owned a business in the adult entertainment industry running a phone sex line. When I was in college, I worked for a popular hotline, but I branched out on my own so that I had more control over — well, every-thing."

Her pace slows and something passes over her face that I can't quite place. It's not judgment or disappointment. More like understanding. "Thank you for sharing that with me. I can't imagine that everyone is open-minded about your career. I bet you have some great stories. What is it you do now that you are done with that?"

Her unequivocal acceptance of my past warms my heart and makes my throat tighten with emotion. I have to swallow to clear it. "I have certainly had some interesting clients over the years. Right now, I'm working on getting into narrating audiobooks."

Her face lights up. "You have the perfect voice for it, so rich and sultry. It's going to work out for you. I just know it," she tells me.

This woman I just met seems to have genuine faith in my ability to achieve my dreams. I haven't even told my parents yet. It's a conversation I'm not looking forward to knowing they'll not be supportive. But Janet openly accepts and encourages me. Suddenly I find myself wanting to wrap her in a hug and ask her to stay forever.

When we get to Buns and Roses, we grab the booth by the window and sip our coffee as we laugh and wait for Lilah to bring our orders. Willa, the newest employee, is behind the counter with Mikey getting trained, so Lilah said she would come out and sit with us.

As we wait, Janet fills me in on her plans while she's in town. "So, tell me, Poppy, where is the best place to get the ganja?" My mouth falls open at the unexpected ask and she misreads the situation and rephrases. "You know devil's lettuce, the green goddess."

My head falls into my hands while I try to rein in my laughter. "I know what ganja is. I just wasn't expecting that." Lilah picks that exact moment to walk over and chooses violence, inciting the situation further by probing. "Janet, are you looking for some lady joints?"

"You know a guy?" Janet asks, her voice filled with hope. She's clearly excited about letting loose while on vacation.

"I think we can point you in the right direction," I tell her as Lilah slides into the seat next to me and sets our coffees and a plate of scones down to share.

"You know what would be fun? We should have a girls' night in. We can order far too much take-out, watch movies, tell dirty jokes, and have some brownies for dessert. The whole shebang." Janet wiggles her eyebrows when she mentions dessert.

I'm immediately and without question up for this plan. Janet is exactly the energy I need in my life right now. She tips that balance of good vs. crappy in my favor. I'm not about to turn her down. Lilah looks and I shrug. "Why not?" I say before asking "Lilah, are you in?"

"My only plans were watching the Bandits game, but I like this idea better." she says picking up a lemon scone and taking a bite. "I'm a genius in the kitchen. This is to die for. You have to try it."

Biting into the scone Lilah holds out, I moan around the bite. "So good. I have all the ingredients for brownies but, Lilah, you are on baking duty. No one wants me to make brownies. Should we meet at my apartment, that way Janet doesn't need to go far?" I volunteer assuming she's staying in the building. Both ladies nod, their mouths too full of scone to verbally respond.

Janet and I leave the coffee shop together but split when she stops in a bookstore she saw on the walk over. She wraps me in a hug before we part. "This tattoo is beautiful, what kind of flowers are those?"

"Oh, they're Virginia bluebells." I tell her, reaching out to take the scones as she passes them to me.

"I thought they might be. Strong and resilient, but beautiful too. Just like you," Janet says, squeezing my hand. "You'll get these to Marv and let him know I'll stop by after I finish my errands."

♥

Lilah shows up first when I open the door for her I find her standing on the other side, and her arms full of goodies for our girls' night in. She sets the tote bag she's carrying on the island and excitedly starts unpacking it.

"I grabbed some snacks and brought everything for pedicures," Lilah rambles, setting chips and dip on the counter before pulling out a cosmetics bag for nails. The two of us haven't had much time together over the past few weeks and I think we both really need this spontaneous girls' night."

Genius, Lilah. No girls' night in is complete without manis and pedis. This is going to be so much fun," I exclaim moving through the kitchen to grab bowls for the snacks. "I really need this tonight. Janet seems great but I'm looking forward to hanging out with you. It's been a few weeks since we have really gotten to spend any time together."

"We should really consider moving to some sort of women-only commune. Someplace free from the drama of men," Lilah jokes, moving through the kitchen to get supplies out to bake the brownies for dessert. She pulls cocoa and chocolate chips out of the pantry, bringing them back to the island where I have the mixer set up for her.

"Your plan sounds good in theory. There are some aspects of the male species I'd miss." My brain involuntarily flashes back to the night on Hendrix's couch and movie night at Cruz's. Just the thought makes my pulse quicken. Even if Hendrix is the world's biggest asshole, what we had physically was combustible.

My vibrator just doesn't compete, and trust me I've tried — every setting, every angle.

God, have I tried.

Nothing feels as good as he did.

I can't even imagine what it would have been like to actually have sex with him. The man has ruined me. That single orgasm will be the one all future climaxes are measured against.

"Tell me about it," she mumbles, and it's quiet enough that I almost miss it. As soon as it comes out of her mouth Lilah's face freezes in shock.

"Oh really? Are you enjoying some benefits from a certain Bandit lately?" I watch her face soften at the mention of Cruz as I hand her the eggs and butter.

Lilah stops unwrapping the butter and turns her body so she is facing me. She hesitates for a second, worrying her bottom lip before she speaks. "He kissed me the other night, and it was everything, Poppy. That one kiss was hands down better than any other encounter I've had with a guy, and it was just a kiss."

Lilah lowers her head into her hands and looks up at me after a moment. I am smiling like a fool, ecstatic for her that she is finally open to taking a shot with Cruz. "It wasn't just the kiss either, which was hot enough to scorch the earth, in case you missed that part. It was how it made me feel, like kissing Cruz was what I was always meant to do. All of these other guys out there who have left me feeling blah. There was a reason. It was never supposed to be them. Cruz was always it. This entire time. Why did we wait this long?"

Her words resonate with me, and I'm not sure I like where these feelings are taking me. What she's describing, how Cruz makes her feel like he is made for her. That's how it felt when I was with Hendrix like there was no one else that could match me as well as he did. He was the missing piece in my puzzle. That thought has me longing for what we could have been. Before I can tumble too far down that rabbit hole there's a knock at the door.

When I open the door, Janet is standing there looking every bit as stunning as this morning, even in a pair of hot pink leggings and a loose white sweater. Her smile widens when she sees me. It's genuine and warm, like there is no place else she would rather be.

She wraps her arm around my shoulder giving me a side hug as she passes. "Hey, Gorgeous. Thanks for indulging my whims and hosting tonight." Janet breezes past me and wraps Lilah in a hug as well. "I brought us something from my shopping adventures today. Thank you for the recommendations." While she flits around the kitchen taking the space in, she reaches into her purse and pulls out a container of cannabis-infused butter wiggling it in front of her.

Lilah laughs when she realizes what it is, throwing her head back. "Janet, are you interested in adopting any adult children?" she asks through her laughter.

"Or taking on any fairy godmother responsibilities?" I add, thanking my lucky stars that fate brought Janet into my life.

Janet points her polished finger at me. "Fairy godmother. I like that. It seems right up my alley. I'm not interested in raising any more children, adult or otherwise. But bestowing blessings of the fairy godmother variety is something I could be interested in. Especially for two goddesses as deserving as the two of you. What's up first on the fairy godmother journey you speak of?"

"I believe you owe us a dirty joke, Fairy Godmother." Lilah teases.

"I made that promise when I proposed girls' night, didn't I?" Janet taps a finger on her chin dramatically while she considers her options. "What's got three holes and gets stuffed in all of them every night?"

My mouth falls open as I look to Lilah, unsure how to respond. Before either of us can pick our chins up off the ground and hazard a guess, Janet adds, "A bowling ball, you pervs. What did you think I meant?"

The three of us let out peals of laughter. Lilah clutches her stomach as she doubles over. I have to grab a napkin to dab the tears out of the corners of my eyes by the time we gather ourselves.

"Janet, I'm not sure what I did to deserve running into you today, but you appeared in my life at the perfect time." I tell her, winded from my laughter. Her presence in my life makes me feel more like myself than I have since Hendrix and I had our falling out. It soothes some of the ache that was left behind when he pushed me away.

The way she's open and accepting of someone she just met gives me the push I need to speak with my parents. She freely and gladly embraces me for everything I am. She's the exact opposite of the two people who raised me. My parents, who should support me this fiercely, have done nothing but demoralize my spirit and dreams for as long as I can remember.

That thought makes my chest ache, but my head is clear. I need to set aside time to talk to my parents. They need to know how I'm feeling, and I need to put limits on our relationship if they aren't willing to change.

"Oh, my sweet girl, I'm the lucky one. I know you will be in my life for a very long time. You and I are going the long haul with this friendship." Janet pats my hand softly before saying. "Now, what are we watching? I vote for *Beaches*."

"You really went for it with that suggestion. I was going to vote *Legally Blonde*, but there's no competition." Lilah announces as she beats the cannabutter into the sugar to make the brownie batter.

"We have one last decision to make before we neglect all our responsibilities for the rest of the night. What are we ordering for dinner?"

"Gourmet Grilled Cheese."

"Loaded Nachos."

Lilah and Janet exclaim at the same time, resulting in the three of us breaking into a fit of giggles again over the complete randomness of their choices. We decide the only reasonable solution is rock, paper, scissors for a final decision. They square off for the best two out of three, looking far too serious.

"Okay, ladies. Keep it clean, we shoot on three. One… two… three…"

Janet lays down paper with Lilah picking.

"Rock wins. One for Janet."

"Eat that you, little master-baker." Janet lets out a playful whoop and shimmies her hips. "Too much?"

"No, never. Don't dull your shine on account of us. Let's go again. Ladies, take your spot. Although I'm not sure Janet can fall into the ladies' category after that outburst."

"Total hooligan," Lilah agrees.

Squaring up they go again.

"Scissors takes it. That's one win a piece. Winner takes all in the final round," I announce as Lilah wipes her brow looking at Janet with fierce determination.

"You're going down, Janet. Try not to break a hip."

Both Janet and I turn to Lilah, whose eyes go wide.

"That was too far, wasn't it?"

Janet cracks a smile, and her shoulders shake with laughter. "No, dear. I love a good old lady joke. But I'll have you know these hips work just fine."

Then Janet turns to the side, hands on her knees, and gives us an impressive twerking demonstration.

"That was. Wow! I'm impressed. Marv is a lucky man."

They shoot on my count and Janet wins the final round.

"Grilled Cheese it is," Lilah concedes before refocusing on whipping up the brownies.

CHAPTER 18

HENDRIX

When I get back to my hotel room in Boston, I try calling my grandmother. The phone rings twice and then goes to voicemail. Frustrated by being shut out, I decide to call Mia. Maybe she can shed some light on why our nana is ignoring my calls tonight.

"Hey, Brother." Mia says cheerfully when she answers the phone.

"Hey, Mia. Have you talked to Nana tonight? She's not answering my calls. I know she's pissed at me about Poppy, but I'm getting worried." I ask her, dropping onto the hotel bed and reclining against the pillows.

"Don't be such a drama queen. She's fine. I talked to her earlier. She was excited about plans she had for a girls' night with some ladies she met," Mia explains making light of my concerns. "Leave it to her to make friends wherever she goes."

"She could at least text me if she doesn't want to talk to me, so I know she's okay." I grumble into the phone at my sister.

"Are you feeling sorry for yourself, Hen?" Her voice oozes derision. It's been weeks since everything went down with Poppy, but Mia and my grandmother haven't let me live it down. For two people who have never met Poppy, they seem to think the world of her. If I didn't know better, I'd think they loved her more than me.

As if their tactics to wear me down aren't enough, after our confrontation in front of Draft I have some serious doubts about my decision making when it comes to Poppy. She has worked her way into my dreams each night, giving me glimpses of what it could be like if I hadn't walked away.

"No, I'm not. I just want to know she's safe," I argue, but we both know that I'm a little sore about being brushed aside by my grandmother these last few weeks. "If you talk to her just remind her I worry about her and ask her to at least text me so I know she's okay."

"I'll let her know — and Hen, you know she's just as worried about you. She saw how happy you were with Poppy. The way you talked about her, it was clear she was special to you. You could hear the admiration in your voice. You never talked that way about Kylie and you guys were together for two years," Mia says softly. It's not the first time I've heard this. Both shared they think I'm letting a good thing slip away by not hearing Poppy out. After the other night, I don't think Poppy has any interest in telling me her side of the story.

"Mia, even if I was willing to give it another shot, Poppy wants nothing to do with me. She made that clear the last time I saw her. She's pissed that I didn't give her the benefit of the doubt. When I asked her what happened, she told me to get lost."

The memory of Poppy walking away from me that night is etched in my mind and each time I'm forced to relive it, my gut tightens with regret a little more. I'm starting to see that I acted out of fear. Things with Poppy were blending with what I experienced with Kylie. The way she was keeping parts of herself from me, the pace at which things took off. Then the lies happened. And as soon as I felt deceived, I shut down any chance of a future with her.

But there's something else there taking shape in the back of my mind. With Poppy, I trusted her and cared for her from the start. It wasn't like that with Kylie. She was just always hanging around and I had people in my ear telling me to give it a shot. It wasn't an organic connection; it was forced. So, when I found out that Poppy was hiding things, I erected those walls around my heart, trying to protect myself from failing at this again, from feeling stupid for being duped into a relationship with someone who was using me.

Maybe I should have listened to Poppy. She's not Kylie, she's is the girl that sees someone struggling and goes out of her way to make them smile, like she did with Lilah. On the outside, she seems tough, but deep-down Poppy's sensitive, just craving acceptance for who she is, the way Indie's mom did for her when she was younger. She's everything Kylie was not. I push my hands through my hair, frustrated with the inability to see it sooner.

"Oh, Hen. You big dumb man. What did you do?" she asks me with a pitying laugh.

"Nothing." My voice is defensive. Not quite ready to admit my mistakes out loud. They all see the mistake I made so clearly. I've run through our fight repeatedly, trying to sort out my feelings. Maybe it's time I listen to what everyone is trying to tell me.

Tugging on my neck, I sigh before admitting, "I asked her why she did it."

As soon as I hear the words out loud again, I am embarrassed that it took me this long to see the issue. My grandma's words flash through my mind. "Poppy made you happy for the first time in four years. You found someone that was worth the risk, and you couldn't even give her the benefit of the doubt."

Everything becomes clear all at once. Poppy just wanted the chance to explain herself and I took that from her because I was wrapped up in the mistrust from Kylie.

I groan.

Mia groans. "Do you see a problem with that?"

"I didn't at the time, but now that I've heard it out loud again — Fuck. I'm a dipshit." My idiocy is clear as day. "I fucked up, Mia."

"You sure did. Really stepped in it. You can't change what has already happened, but what are you going to do about it now?"

Do I want to do anything about it? What if everyone is right and I should trust Poppy? Hear her side of it? Lilah insists that it's not what I think, that Poppy wasn't seeing anyone else.

I've felt the universe tugging me toward Poppy since we ran together in the park. Movie night, the texting and phone calls only cemented that for me. If I don't hear her out, I'm walking away from that without knowing what really went down.

I think about the conversation I had with Mia when Poppy and I met. Even then, I defended Poppy, claiming she was nothing like Kylie, when my sister questioned her intentions. Yet here I am lumping her in with the lies my ex told.

"I need to know," I tell Mia with conviction. As soon as the words are out of my mouth, I know it's true. While I don't know what that means for me and Poppy, I want — no, I need to know her side of the story.

"She hates me, Mia, and I don't blame her. My reaction was so cold. I shut her out completely like she was nothing to me. When that couldn't be further from the truth."

"If she gives you the chance to hear her out you need to listen without judgment. After that, if you decide to walk away there's no turning back. She's not going to give you a third chance."

"I hear you," I pause before adding, "Do you have any romance book scale grand gestures in your back pocket to help your brother out?"

"Grovel, Hen. Tell her you're sorry and mean it. She's going to need a reason to trust you. You're going to have to open up to her about what Kylie did. Tell her the whole story."

"Thanks, Mia. You really think it will work?"

"All you can do is try. And, Hen, it never hurts to bring presents when you grovel."

Mia is right. Poppy isn't going to share anything with me until I earn her trust back. The irony of the situation isn't lost on me. It was my trust issues stemming from Kylie that made me push Poppy away. My fear of being taken advantage of, combined with the feelings I already had for Poppy, sent me into a panic. We may not have openly talked about our feelings or our future, but things were moving fast and, in that short time, Poppy had more power over me than Kylie ever had.

There is nothing I can do about the groveling right now, but I can work on the present. I send a quick text to Tank, our equipment manager. If I can get Poppy to give me another chance, I want everyone to know she's mine.

HENDRIX:

Hey Tank, can you do me a favor and have a spare Jersey in my locker for me tomorrow?

TANK:

Sure thing, Hen.

HENDRIX:

Thanks, I appreciate it!

There's a knock at the door as I finish sending my text. Cruz is standing on the other side of the peephole with Dean and Dom.

"Let's go grab some food. I know you have to be as sick of hotel rooms as I am," Cruz demands without even a hello for a greeting. *Grumpy ass.*

I rub my hand down my face. The distraction is probably for the best. Otherwise, I'll sit here stewing over my apology and end up calling Poppy, but this needs to be done in person. "Let me grab my shoes. The room service here sucks anyway," I agree, needing a change of scenery before I cave and making everything worse with Poppy.

We walk down the street to an Italian place that we have been to before when we played in Boston. The corner booth that the hostess sits us in gives us a little privacy. Cruz pulls his phone out across the table and his brows furrow in confusion before his face splits into a grin and he's laughing.

"Dude, what am I looking at?" Dom asks as he peers over his shoulder, looking puzzled.

Instead of answering Dom, Cruz swings his gaze up from his phone to look at me. His phone slides across the table toward me as he says, still laughing, "Care to explain, Hen?"

Confused, I grab the phone and look at the picture. It's a text from Lilah. And holy fuck, it's my grandma, Poppy, and Lilah all lying in a heap of pillows. They're laughing as someone's arm extends to take the selfie.

It's such a jumble of body parts I can't tell whose arm it is. They look like they're having more fun than should be legal. Huge smiles spanning across all three of their faces. My eyes roam over the picture, taking it all in. Warmth spreads through my chest at the thought of Poppy and Nana together. Right before I pass the phone back, I spot the plate of brownies sitting just at the edge of the shot.

I look up at Cruz, who has a knowing smirk on his face. He's just staring at me, waiting for me to catch on. "Are they?"

I pause and look at the picture again. Poppy clutches her stomach, and her head is thrown back in laughter. She leans against my grandma's shoulder. Her red hair is splayed against the cream throw pillow under her head. Lilah is curled up on the other side of my grandmother, looking the most innocent of the bunch, which isn't saying much. In the middle, the woman that raised me has her arms wrapped around both women smiling, her face crinkling with pure joy and her blue eyes are glassy.

"They're high." A laugh bursts free from my mouth. When Mia told me my grandmother had made a friend and was excited about her plans, this was not what I had envisioned. I imagined she found a card game to join or something similar — not hunting down Poppy, and crashing a girls' night with Lilah.

Cruz just shakes his head laughing, and Dom snatches the phone from my hand to take a look.

"So, fucking high." Dom confirms as he hands the phone to Dean.

"Should we place bets on whether my grandma got the girls high or whether one of our girls is the guilty party?" Once the words are out of my mouth, I realize what I said. There's no regret. That's what I want, for Poppy to be my girl again.

Cruz doesn't call me out for it, but I see his lips twitch into a quick smile of understanding before he wagers, "My money is on Janet."

"Who is Janet?" Dean asks. Looking over the photo quickly before handing Cruz his phone.

"My grandmother. The woman in the middle," I clarify as I pull my phone out and type out a quick text.

HENDRIX:

You look like you are having fun tonight. Too high to answer the phone when your grandson calls? You're a very sneaky woman.

NANA:

So much fun, my new friends are delightful.

HENDRIX:

Don't I know it. Be good.

NANA:

Never.

CHAPTER 19

HENDRIX

The hum of the coffee grinder in my kitchen pulls me out of my dream. After a late flight back into Denver last night, I was hoping to sleep in a little longer, but my house guest has other plans. The soft pad of footfalls approaches my door. There's one sharp knock before my grandmother's voice penetrates the bedroom door.

"Get out of bed, Hen. We need to talk." The cold shoulder from my grandmother has been a theme over the past few weeks, but it's gotten more obvious since she met and befriended Poppy. Sliding a pair of joggers up my legs, I make my way to the kitchen.

"Are you done giving me the silent treatment?" Dropping onto a stool I reach for the coffee mug resting on the island. My hand is slapped away. I pull it back, holding it to my chest protectively as she rolls her eyes at my dramatics.

"Not for you." She brings the mug to her lips and inhales the aroma before taking a drink. "You deserved every second of my ire, Hen. The way you treated Poppy was not how I raised you. You were raised to be a compassionate human. To give people a second chance. I know that you have your own issues with trust, your mother and Kylie made sure of that. But it's not who you are. Listen to the girl. You're a fool if you think there's a better woman out there for you."

"You barely know her." I'm not sure why I am arguing with her. I've already decided to hear Poppy out, but I part of me wants to know why my grandma is so adamant about this.

"But I know you, and that girl made you happy. Happier than I've ever seen you. And I know enough about her to know you two are a pair."

I lower my head to my hands. "I know," I admit before looking up at her. "I screwed up, but I'm going to fix it."

"Well, what are you waiting for?" my grandmother challenges, her eyebrow raised. It's the same look she gave me as a child when she was daring me to try her.

"For starters, I thought Poppy deserved an in-person apology." I explain, standing to grab a mug and coffee for myself. When I reach the coffee machine, the pot is empty. I look over my shoulder and my grandmother wears a smug look on her face. "You are a cruel woman."

"You love me, and you don't deserve coffee. Not yet," she boldly claims, her arm extended with a polished finger pointing at the door. "Go apologize and I'll make you coffee."

"You want me to —" I start but her hand gesticulates toward the door again. "Can I put a shirt on?"

She considers me for a second. "I'd be more willing to accept a shirtless apology. Go."

"Now you're pimping me out for my body?" She glares thrusting her finger at the door taking none of my bullshit.

CHAPTER 20

POPPY

The stretch in my tight hamstrings feels delicious when I push my heels into the floor, reaching my tailbone toward the ceiling of my living room. The yoga mat is slick with sweat under my palms. As I lower into plank, a knock at my door startles me out of my yoga trance. My eyes shoot open, and I drop to my stomach for a second before getting up to answer the door.

Janet mentioned stopping by this morning on her way out for a walk to see if I was around to join. So, I don't hesitate to open the door in just my bike shorts and sports bra, sweat dripping down my spine. Only it's not Janet standing in the hallway. Hendrix is there with an arm casually propped against the doorframe.

He is clad in only a pair of low-slung gray sweatpants. At least if we are going to have another verbal sparring match, I get some eye candy out of it. Like a magnetic pull, I'm drawn to the expanse of his broad chest and stacked abs. Resisting seems pointless.

"Please don't slam the door," Hendrix pleads, reminding me that regardless of how good he looks standing in my doorway, he's not my favorite person. His hands come together in front of his chest, requesting that I hear him out. He looks contrite and stressed, the worry lines on his forehead more pronounced. His ocean blue eyes are sad, lacking the normal spark of joy I'm used to seeing there. His mouth is pressed into a tight line.

Fuck, he looks miserable.

Stepping back, I sweep my hand across the space in front of my body, inviting him in. "I thought you were someone else. My friend Janet was going to stop by," I mumble, not sure why I'm telling him that. Would I have opened the door if I had known it was him? Maybe? I'm not as mad as I was outside Draft the other night, but I still haven't forgiven him. Not that he has tried to apologize.

"Not Janet."

Definitely not Janet. My mind betrays me as I take in his broad back when he walks past me. Why does he have to be shirtless? It's distracting me from all the reasons I'm mad at him. I step around to the other side of the island, wanting to put some space between us so I don't do something stupid. Climb him like a tree and lick that stupid tattoo, for example.

"What do you want, Hendrix?" The question comes out more hostile than I intend overcompensating for still being wholly attracted to him.

He runs his hand through his hair and hangs his head. "I owe you an apology. A couple actually." He brings his gaze back up to meet mine, looking me in the eye.

I can see my pain reflected back at me on his face. We have both been so angry that it's easy to forget we are both hurting. Even though we'd only known each other for a short time, the feelings between us were already growing. We were creating something together that had the potential to be life changing, only for that to be ripped away. That realization makes me unexpectedly sad for both of us.

His admission that he wants to apologize surprises me, up until now he's taken no blame for his role in this. I stay silent, waiting for him to continue. He needs to take the lead here if he wants a shot at redemption.

"That night at my apartment, I should have asked you what happened. I'm sorry that I shut you out and made assumptions. My past experience clouded our relationship, and I hurt you because I was afraid to be taken advantage of again. I hadn't realized how much Kylie messed me up."

He looks at me for a moment like he is trying to read my reaction, but my emotions are locked down tight. "Then the other night at Draft, I knew I had made a mistake letting you go, and I fucked it up even more — I should have apologized then. We may not know everything about each other yet, but I know you well enough to know you aren't Kylie. You would never intentionally hurt me. But instead of apologizing and hearing you out, I acted like an ass. I was scared of letting you back in and getting hurt again."

He steps forward like he wants to come to me but catches himself and thinks better of it. Unexpected disappointment settles over me. My mind and body are at odds, still holding on to the anger in the way he dismissed me while also craving a physical connection with him. "And what do you know about me?" I need him to keep talking before I let my emotions spill over.

"You are nothing like her. You are honest and kind, even if you keep some parts of yourself private. Poppy, I'm sorry that I lumped you in with her. I know that what we had was as real to you as it was to me. You're exceptionally compassionate and empathic, even if you hide it behind your feisty attitude, nothing like anyone I've met before."

I release the breath that was stuck in my chest and drop onto the stool. That was everything I didn't know I needed to hear from him, and I am physically aching to go to him, but I can't. He still doesn't know everything. His eyes rake over me like he just realized I'm barely dressed. He leans against the island, elbows propped on the cool surface. The move brings us closer together.

"Thank you." I finally break the silence, but it's all I say for a moment as I weigh all my options. If I want another shot with him, I need to show him all of me. The apology is a step in the right direction, but he still hasn't said what he wants. "Is that all?"

He looks dejected for a moment, and he doesn't speak right away. He rubs his hands down his face before he comes around the island. My heart is in my throat as he rounds the island and stops right in front of me. Hendrix's hand cups my face, stroking my temple with the pad of his thumb. He tilts my face up to him and his eyes soften. "I miss you. So fucking much. No matter what you tell me, I won't hurt you like that again. I don't know what's going to happen between us, but I will listen to whatever it is you want to tell me when you want to tell me. Please, just give me another chance to get this right with you."

I think about what I know about Hendrix. What I learned before everything went to shit. The way he loves his people, how he offered to help me connect with his sister. At his core, he's a good man. I know he has his own trauma, but he is also kind and loving. He struggles with trust, but not with love. If he trusts and cares about you, he will go to the end of the earth for you.

My breath stutters with that realization and I rise to my feet, wrapping my arms around his waist and burying my face in his chest. My anger evaporates with the realization that I want a chance to be one of those people he cherishes.

His arms come around me, holding me tight to him, and I soak in the feeling. This is where I belong, and I need to tell him everything. Tilting my head back, I look up at him. The urge to push up on my toes and kiss him is overwhelming, but before I can do so there's a knock at the door.

"Janet," I mumble to myself. Hendrix's hold on me loosens, and he follows me to the door.

Opening the door, we find Janet standing in the hallway, a bright pink carry-on next to her and a potted plant in her hand. My face falls, she's leaving.

"You're leaving."

"You're leaving?"

Our voices mingle when Hendrix I both speak at the same time. I look over my shoulder and see Hendrix's face. His brow is furrowed with concern, but his eyes are soft with love and admiration. When I look back at Janet, she shakes her head at us.

"Don't be mad, love." Janet says stepping toward me. She hands the plant to Hendrix and wraps me in a hug. "Let me in to say goodbye — to both of you."

"You're Hendrix's nana." As soon as I saw his reaction to her in my doorway, it all clicked into place. Hendrix drops his hand to my waist and gives it a light squeeze. "I pictured you... different." I say mostly to myself.

"The one and only," Janet confirms before adding. "I'm more fabulous than you expected, right?" She gestures to herself before tapping her foot and glancing pointedly into the apartment behind us. "My Uber is going to be here in ten minutes. Are we doing this in the hallway?"

"So much more fabulous." I confirm stepping back from the door to allow her inside.

Janet and Hendrix trail me into the living room. I take a seat in the armchair, giving myself some space and distance from both of them. My gaze bounces between the two of them, trying to get a read on the situation. Stopping momentarily on the plant cradled in Hendrix's large hands. There's an envelope tucked into the leaves.

"Did you know who I was? Why didn't you tell me?" I'm not mad, not really. Confused, sure, but I'll hold off on being mad until I hear Janet's explanation. How could I be mad at her after everything that happened with Hen? She deserves a chance to explain her actions, just like I do.

"My sweet girl, I needed to meet you in person. When Hendrix told me about you, I could hear the affection in his voice. When I saw the photo of the two of you leaving the stadium, I could see it in the way you two looked at each other. I knew you were special if you meant that much to him after everything he went through. Those walls of his have been up for so long only someone amazing would be able to break through. I wasn't trying to bamboozle you," she explains, keeping her eyes on me while she talks.

When she pauses, she looks over at Hendrix, who is sitting next to her on the couch. "And then you went and fucked it all up." Her voice is soft, but her gaze is steely. Leaving no doubt, she will put him in his place if he dares to step a toe out of line right now. I cover my laugh with a cough at the way she scolds him.

I love this woman.

"There was no yelling this morning and we all know these walls are thin." Her lips quirk into a smile, and a moment of panic hits me.

Janet must see the worry on my face before I can cover it up. She shakes her head. The movement is so quick that Hendrix doesn't notice. It's a message just for me. She didn't tell him anything.

"Why are you leaving?" Hendrix places a hand on her knee, setting the plant on the coffee table in front of him. "You know you don't have to go," he adds with a squeeze.

Dropping her hand on top before she responds, "Yes, I do. You need space to figure this out. I'm not going to be a third wheel while you do it. Besides, Mia will get all jealous if I only visit you." Her phone vibrates with a notification. "That's my ride. There's a note in the plant, it's for both of you." She reaches over and gives Hendrix a kiss on the cheek.

I stand and move to where she is sitting, wrapping her in a tight hug. "Thank you, Janet." I whisper just for her to hear. It's so much more than a simple thank you, and she knows it.

She pulls back from me, placing both hands on my face. "Anything for you, darling."

"I'll walk you down," he says, standing and reaching for her suitcase. She pulls it out of his reach.

"Like hell you will. Stay here. Talk to each other." It's not a request. Janet turns on her heels and walks out the door.

"She's a force, Hendrix." I say when the door closes behind his grandmother. My gaze sweeps over him. "Go get a shirt and we can talk."

He smirks down at me, his hand tugging on the back of his neck. Thinking better of making the cocky remark that I know is on the tip of his tongue, he nods. His eyes rake over me before one last time before he says. "I'll go put a shirt on, but only if you promise not to change."

"Go, before I change my mind about this whole thing." It's an empty threat. His apology opened a door back up that I'm not willing to close. Not until I figure out what's behind it.

Hendrix is only gone for a minute before he's pushing back through my door, this time fully clothed and carrying two mugs of coffee.

"My grandmother made these for us before she left," he says in explanation as he follows me to the couch. "Should we open the note?" He tips his head toward the plant still on the coffee table as he takes a spot on the couch.

"I guess it's as good of a place to start as any," I say, taking the mug from him and lowering myself to the cushions. I sit facing him with my legs crossed and cup cradled in my hands. Hendrix reaches for the plant and plucks the note from the leaves, bringing it between us so we can both see it. He slides a small card free from the envelope before reading it aloud.

"Hendrix & Poppy, this plant will do best on Hendrix's balcony in the shade. It's a hardy plant but will still require some love and attention from both of you. Just because something is strong doesn't mean you can neglect it. Be sure to nurture it so that it can thrive, growing to its full potential. Take care of it and each other. All my love, Nana Janet. "

We look at each other and then at the plant. "Did she just make us plant parents?" I say to break the silence.

Hendrix looks just as bemused next to me, a crease settled in his forehead as he looks at the note. The plant is a sweet gesture, even if it's her way of meddling. But until we talk about the real issues between us, the plant and how well we nurture it doesn't matter. Deciding to rip off the band-aid, I go for it.

"I didn't know you were my neighbor until I opened the email you sent with your address. And maybe I should have told you right away, but there's more to the story that I didn't want to explain over the phone." I pause and consider Hendrix for a moment.

He is more relaxed than I expected, and it puts me at ease. He's listening intently, but his legs are extended in front of him and crossed casually at the ankles. The lines of his broad shoulders are relaxed with his arm slung over the back of the couch. Nothing about his demeanor is defensive or on edge. It's a complete reversal from the Hendrix that jumped to the worst possible conclusions about me a few weeks ago.

"I wasn't cheating on you, Hendrix. What you were hearing through the walls was just me alone in my apartment working." His brows furrow in confusion, like he is trying to work through a puzzle in his head, but he remains silent, allowing me to continue on my own terms.

"When I was in college, a friend and I came across a flyer for a company hiring phone sex operators. We took a tab off the flyer as a joke, but the more I thought about it the more it made sense. I had control over my hours, the pay was way better than any job on campus, and it was rewarding. It also gave me financial independence from my parents that I desperately needed to get out from under their thumb and preserve my mental health. It was one of the best decisions I ever made."

The last bit makes his jaw tense, but he catches it and schools his features quickly. I can tell Hendrix is making an effort to really listen to me and understand where I'm coming from. That flash of jealousy isn't a detractor like he thinks. My hand drops to his knee reassuringly.

"Not rewarding like you are thinking, perv." I say, trying to lighten the mood.

"Sorry, I — the idea of you doing what we did with someone else —" His jaw muscle twitches again, and he clenches his fists on the couch. "It — fuck, I can't even think about it without wanting to rip someone's head off."

"Ninety percent of what I do is more therapy and listening than it is phone sex. I've never actively participated in phone sex until you." It's important that he understands that this is a job for me. It's not something I do for pleasure.

"When I was hearing you, those were calls with your —" he pauses, not sure what to call them.

"Clients," I supply for him. "I'm not ashamed of being a phone sex operator, but it's caused issues with guys in the past. I wanted to tell you in person, to see your reaction. I've had people tell me it's not an issue for them, only to turn around and hold it against me or cut ties. Not just guys," I clarify because people I thought I was forming friendships with ghosted me when they found out about my job in the past as well. "My ex and I had been together for a few months when I told him. A few weeks later, we were out with some of his friends, and I overheard him telling his best friend about my job. He was bragging, it was repulsive." A shiver runs up my spine as I remember the look on Paul's face as he told his friend.

"'A phone sex operator, fuck, man, I bet she's wild in the sheets. You lucky asshole.' That's what his friend said about me. My stomach bottomed out at the callous way his friend spoke about me. I stopped frozen in place as I waited for Paul to come to my defense, but he didn't. Instead, he smiled. God, he looked smarmy, he said it's not like it's going to go anywhere. 'Poppy's not the girl you bring home to meet the parents and marry. But damn is she fun.'"

Hendrix's jaw ticks as he grinds his teeth, but he stays quiet and lets me continue. "When I confronted him about it later, he claimed it wasn't a big deal and that he still wanted to see me but suggested an open relationship since I was seeing other people and it obviously wasn't going anywhere."

Hendrix opens and closes his fist at his side several times. "He tried to use your job as an excuse to sleep with other women while he was still with you? After he spoke that way about you?"

"Yep. I need you to know my job is just a job. Nothing about what I do gets me aroused. There's no connection with my clients."

He nods before saying, "He must have been really fucking stupid. You know that you are more than just fun, right? You are kind and beautiful. Smart and a great friend. You are also funny as hell, but it's not all you are."

I nod. It's the only response I have right now. I'm too raw from what I just shared and his response.

Hendrix looks me in the eye, his hand reaches around to grip the back of my neck. "Come here, Beautiful," he requests when his other hand comes to my waist as he guides me into his lap. "Thank you for telling me. I'm so fucking sorry that I didn't give you this chance earlier. I guess we both have some baggage to work through. But that's what I want to do. Think we can figure out a way to work through our baggage together?"

His thumb strokes the skin in front of my ear as he cradles me against his strong chest. "Hendrix." I bring my hand to the nape of his neck, filtering my fingers through his hair. "I'm really regretting asking you to put a shirt on right now." His chest vibrates beneath me with laughter. His lips find my temple for a quick kiss.

"Can we start over?" he asks his voice raw with emotion.

I shift in his lap, so I'm straddling him, knees on the side of his hips. I roll against him and feel him harden below me. "Do we have to start all the way over?" I ask right before my lips brush against his. The fact that he openly accepted my past and didn't judge me for it makes my stomach flip. I trust that he wants to try to that he meant what he said. He doesn't want to hurt me. Maybe it's naïve of me to jump right back in with him, but I want to know where we can take this. What we have is too strong to ignore.

"No, Poppy, we can start wherever you want." He says, his lips a whisper against my skin. His hands snake up my back, blazing a trail over the bare skin there.

"I had my last client call two weeks ago." It's not a test, but I am curious to see if he is relieved, so I pull back just the slightest to look at his reaction.

His expression morphs into one of confusion. "You don't have to—" he starts to say, but I cut him off. My heart swells with an appreciation for this man. It's like nothing I've ever felt before. No one I have dated has ever been openly accepting of my career before.

"It's got nothing to do with you. That's been the plan long before I met you. It's time for me to move on to something different."

CHAPTER 21

HENDRIX

Nothing has felt as right as this moment right now with Poppy in my lap. The last thing I want is to ruin it, but I need to know we are on the same page. I want to get it right this time. When Poppy grinds down on me, I almost lose my nerve.

"Hold on. We need to finish this talk." My voice is as shaky as my resolve to do the right thing, but I know it will protect us both from any more pain and confusion.

"What else is there to talk about?" Her fingernails scrape across my scalp in the most distracting way.

"When Kylie did what she did, it messed me up more than I realized. I was closed off for so long and then you came along, and I let my guard down. But the minute something went wrong, I shut down not wanting to be hurt again. I'm still learning how to trust again, but I want to try. You make it worth the risk. I know you're not Kylie and that you never intended to hurt me. We are both going to make some mistakes along the way, but I want you to know I trust you. I'll always hear you out — I'm yours, Poppy."

I want her to know that this is as real as it gets. Bringing my hands to the sides of her head, I rub the pads of my thumbs along her cheekbones. "Come to the game today and let me take you to dinner after. If we aren't starting over, let's at least get a redo on that first date that I messed up so badly."

She answers me with a kiss. Her lips slant over mine. The hardened peaks of her nipples graze my pecs through the thin fabric of the shirt I grabbed. Her kiss is soft and tentative like she's getting reacquainted with me, with us. When her tongue sweeps across my bottom lip, I open for her. She lets out a barely audible whimper at the first brush of her tongue against mine.

"Is that a yes?" I ask between kisses. She nods but continues kissing me. Grabbing her hips, I stand with her in my lap. She squeals and wraps her bare legs tightly around my waist before halting the kiss.

"Where are we going?" she asks breathlessly with her face buried in my neck, dropping little pecks there. The sensation tickles the sensitive skin and even though the move is innocent enough it causes my dick to twitch between us.

"Field trip," I tell her while I walk us toward her front door. When I push through my door and set her down on the couch, Poppy looks confused.

"Wait here. I have something for you." Standing up, I look down at her for a second. She looks so fucking good that I have to force myself to walk away.

Quickly moving through the apartment, I grab what I need from the bedroom. The superstitious baseball player in me was nervous that I was about to jinx myself when I grabbed this for her the other day before I had hashed out my apology. I quickly pushed those thoughts aside, knowing that if I was lucky enough to get a second chance, I wanted her to have this.

When I walk back out to the living room, box in hand, Poppy is lounging against the back of my couch, her long legs encased in tight spandex and looking like the most beautiful vision I've ever seen. Her red hair is pulled back in one of the messy braids that she favors letting the light filtering through the window play up the freckles decorating her face.

Setting the box in her lap, I take the spot next to her and pull her to my side. She fits there in the crook of my arm like we are two pieces of the same puzzle. "Open it," I tell her gesturing to the box.

Poppy lifts the top off and her hands part the tissue paper. She stops for a moment before she pulls the black Bandits jersey out of the box, holding it up in front of her. Her gaze finds me for a second before turning it around to see the back. The back of the jersey has James spelled out between the shoulder blades.

When her eyes find mine she's grinning. "And now I'm yours," she says repeating the words I told her earlier back at me. She leans forward and slips the jersey over her head, not bothering to undo the buttons.

"This is just the beginning. I want everyone to know you are mine. I'm going to spoil the shit out of you. I'll do everything in my power to show you how sorry I am."

I lied before. This is the most beautiful sight I've ever seen. Poppy draped in my jersey, knowing that it's my name she's wearing, with only a hint of her bike shorts peeking out from under the hem.

Pushing back on Poppy's shoulder, I lay her underneath me on the couch. "Fuck. Do you know what you do to me?"

"I have an idea, but you should probably tell me." Her voice is low and breathy as she arches up into me.

"Right now, you have me hard as hell. There is nothing I want more than to strip this jersey off you and bury myself inside you so deep you can feel me for days," I groan bringing my forehead down to hers. My cock nestled against her thigh. "But I have to leave for the stadium in fifteen minutes. That's not enough time for what I want to do with you."

Now that Poppy and I are on the same page and all the drama is behind us, I want to take my time with her. When I fuck her, I want to have all night. Not a rushed quickie where I leave her to get to the stadium.

Tilting my mouth over Poppy's, I dive in for a kiss to hold me over until after the game. Our touches as we kiss are featherlight, but I feel them deep in my bones. A brush of her fingertips over my back, or a gentle tug on the strands of hair at the nape of my neck. It's not grinding and frantic like most of our kisses have been. It almost feels like a first kiss given our fresh start.

I pull Poppy up with me when I sit up. My head tilts toward the box on the table. "There's a family pass in there for you and tickets for the game. You can sit in Lilah's seats or those. Wherever you're more comfortable. Hell, you can swap back and forth between innings for all I care as long as you are there."

Poppy and I make it to the door of the apartment where we lapse back into kissing for a few more minutes before I have to force her out the door. I take the world's fastest cold shower, so I'm not late reporting to the stadium. My gameday routine is completely screwed, but I can't be bothered to care because I got Poppy back and right now that's more important.

CHAPTER 22

HENDRIX

"I can't believe I've never been there before. Tacos are basically a food group for me. I thought I had tried all the best places in the city. Those Tacos De Cochinita were like an orgasm in my mouth. The pickle red onions, chef's kiss," Poppy declares adorably as I hold the door to my apartment open for her.

"I'm glad you liked it. Should I be jealous of the taco for giving you your first orgasm of the night?" I tell her as I push her back against the door, caging her in. My lips drop to her neck and Poppy tilts her head giving me the access I need to kiss a trail down to her collarbone.

"Who says the taco gave me my first orgasm of the night?"

Her eyes are focused intently on me, but her lips are tilted into a lopsided smile. It's her tell when she's being playful. And it makes her look innocent, even though I know she's not. Poppy's the most sensual woman I've ever been with, partly because she doesn't try too hard. She just says and does what feels good to her. The combination is my personal brand of kryptonite.

"Care to explain?" I push my hips forward, letting her know two can play this game. Her mouth drops open in a cute little "O" at the contact.

"You see, there's this guy that I like, and he got me all worked up earlier today. Then he just left — poof — without taking care of me." She runs her fingertips lightly down my chest before sliding them under my shirt to toy with the waistband of my briefs.

"Poof, huh? Could it be that he had to go to work even though he would have rather stayed with you?" I hover over her lips just a breath away as I talk.

"It's possible he had to be somewhere, but it doesn't change the fact that he left me feeling very needy." She presses up on her toes, bringing us even closer.

"Can't have that, can we?"

"No, we can't. I tried to focus on work but couldn't get the image of you above me on the couch out of my mind. You really left me no choice but to take matters into my own hands." Her hand dips further into my waistband, so close to grazing the head of my cock that it's almost painful. I have to hold myself back from tilting my hips up to seek out the contact.

My hands grip her waist and I walk us both through the kitchen, backing Poppy up to the island. Dropping down to my knees in front of her, I look up at her while I work the button on her jeans loose. My lips skim across the satin-soft skin on her stomach as my hands tug the material of her jeans down revealing her smooth legs.

When her jeans fall in a puddle at her feet, I lift her onto the counter, parting her legs when I step between her thighs. "I'm going to need a demonstration, for science." My fingers slowly pop each of the buttons of her jersey, causing it to fall open.

Poppy's hand trails down my chest, over my stomach before yanking at the hem of my shirt up. "Lose some of these clothes first. I take direction better when you're naked," she demands, her hand moves to my belt. Her fingers graze my stomach as she works the leather free. The touch sends a jolt of desire straight to my cock.

In awe that I get a second chance at this, seeing her on my counter with my jersey parted with nothing, but a deep purple lace bra and matching panties is almost enough to tempt me to haul her to the bedroom right now. The lights are still off, but the moonlight bathes the room in a soft glow. "Poppy, you look so fucking sexy like this. You in my jersey, like that." I bite down on my knuckle giving myself a second to soak in the sight of her.

Poppy coaxes my zipper down before working my jeans over my hips. Once she has rid me of my pants, she leans back on her elbow and trails her hand between the valley of her breasts. They're not overly large, a good handful. Her nipples are tight against the purple fabric, and I bet they're pale pink matching her fair skin.

She takes time to give each one a squeeze before dipping her hand lower and tracing her fingertip along the lace at her hips. Her mouth opens, releasing the slightest moan before she pulls her bottom lip between her teeth.

My attention stays on her as my hands drop to her knees. I run my hands up her legs, pushing them wider as I go. "About that demonstration? I want to see how you made yourself come thinking of me. Show me what you like."

"You want to see me this time. Greedy, greedy man." Her voice is raspy, but her hand dips lower under the waistband.

"Only for you, Poppy. You make me greedy for everything you're willing to give me." My thumbs trace circles along the crease of her leg slowly working down and then back up making her legs break out in goose bumps.

"Do I get to be greedy too?" she asks with a moan. Her head tips back exposing her neck. I take full advantage of the access and lean forward, hovering over her and placing kisses along her neck before moving down to her breast. I pull the cup of her bra down with my teeth and trap her nipple in my mouth, sucking and swirling my tongue around the hard tip. Her hips clamp tight around my waist as she writhes underneath me.

"You want to watch me?" I ask, moving my lips across her chest to give her other nipple equal attention.

"God, yes. I haven't stopped thinking about it since that first time we FaceTimed." She's a panting mess and I'm barely hanging on. This day has been a tease from the moment she let me back in her life. I let her nipple go with a pop, running my hands along the curve of her waist until I reach the top of her underwear. When I give them a tug, Poppy lifts just enough for me to slide them down her legs. Her eyes trace down my body, stopping to stare pointedly at my hard cock. I quirk an eyebrow at her in question.

"You want me naked, Beautiful?" She nods desperately before sliding her hand back between her legs, and running her fingers over her folds. She doesn't look away as she dips one finger inside her. Pumping in and out before circling for clit again.

I push my briefs down, taking my cock in my hand and give it a squeeze. Watching her like this, all slick and spread out for me while she makes herself feel good. I need to get inside her like I need my next breath.

"I need you to touch me. It's not enough," Poppy cries, adding another finger, slowly pumping them in and out. I shake my head and give myself a slow tug.

"You can do it, Poppy. Make yourself come for me and then I'm all yours."

"Please, Hendrix, don't make me wait any longer. Give me something. I need to come," she whimpers continuing to work her fingers in and out. She makes the most beautiful sounds I've ever heard. Her frenzy to have me pushes me into action.

"So needy for me. What do you want, Poppy? Tell me what you need, and I'll make you feel good." I ask, toying with her and letting my hand join hers as she fucks it. I let my fingers brush her folds and clit but not entering her as she works herself into more of a frenzy.

"Make me come — please. Fingers, tongue. I don't care," she stutters, moving her fingers to her clit to rub circles around the swollen bud.

"How about this?" I ask before dipping my head down to lick her from opening to clit while her fingers continue their work. She gasps and her legs bracket my head holding me there. "Was that a yes?"

"Yes — fuck, yes. Don't you dare stop." She commands. Lowering my mouth to her, I resume with long languid licks.

When I feel her legs tighten around my head, I push two fingers inside her curling it to reach that spot that I know will send her soaring. Her legs tremble around me as Poppy pulses squeezing my fingers. I continue to work her pussy with my tongue and fingers as the waves crash over her until she's tugging at my hair, pulling me up toward her.

"Hendrix?" Poppy quietly pleads as I kiss my way up her stomach. I mumble a response against her stomach. "Get me off this hard counter and take me to bed to fuck me properly," she demands sifting her fingers through my hair more gently now.

CHAPTER 23

POPPY

"Gladly," Hendrix replies when I order him to take me to bed.

He bends forward, picking me up and hauling me over his shoulder. I laugh at the unexpected playfulness of the move. Reaching down, I smack his ass in retaliation. "I didn't know I was dating a caveman."

"Would you like me to go full caveman and turn that spanking around on you?"

My pulse quickens at the idea. "That's not the threat you think it is."

"I'll remember that for another time." Hendrix sets me on the edge of the bed, bringing his cock level with my face. My palms land on his thighs, itching to touch him. I run my hands up his thighs, feeling his strong legs under my fingers. When I look up at him, Hendrix is looking down at me with wide blue eyes.

"I can't wait to taste you." I wrap my palm around the base, testing the weight and feel of it in my hand. I was right about him being able to back up his BDE. He's long and thick in my palm, and his tip is beaded with precum. His skin is smooth and hot as I pump him once slowly.

Without breaking eye contact, I dart my tongue out for a taste.

"Poppy — oh shit. If you keep that up I'm going to make a mess of you," Hendrix groans, his rough thumb finding my bottom lip and rubbing across it. "Any other time and my cock is all yours to do whatever you please with, but right now, I need to be inside of you. It feels like I've been waiting forever for this moment."

"Then get over here and fuck me." I give him one more lazy stroke before dropping my hand and scooting back on the bed.

Hendrix hovers over me as I move to the top of the bed. His forearms envelop the sides of my face, and his lips drop to mine. His kiss starts slowly but grows deeper with each swipe of his tongue. I mirror his movements and bring my leg up to wrap around his hip.

He groans into my mouth when his length comes into contact with my slick center. The sensation of him gliding over my slippery center is indecent. He grinds down on my sensitive clit.

"You feel so good. I'm not sure I have ever wanted anyone the way I want you," he praises as he moves his mouth down my body to my breast.

"Hendrix, don't tease me. I can't handle it right now." My voice sounds desperate and on edge. He's got me so worked up that I don't think I can stand it anymore.

"Relax," he mutters against my skin as he drags his cock along my center again and again. "I want you good and ready for me."

"I'm — ready. So ready. Stop this torture and get inside me already." My body is like a live wire, every touch is almost too much. Hendrix bites down on my nipple, trapping it between his teeth as he rolls his hips again. Out of nowhere my orgasm barrels down my spine. There's no stopping it when he drags against me one last time.

"That's my girl, I knew you could give me another. So fucking responsive." Hendrix buries his face in my neck as he stills on top of me, letting me catch my breath. "You did such a good job. Now you're ready." His voice is barely audible over the pounding of the pulse in my ears. He places a quick kiss on my temple and then sits back on his knees to roll the condom down his length.

"It's unfair how sexy you look putting on a condom," I grumble breathlessly as I let myself fall back to the bed, a boneless mess.

"Speak for yourself. You look like a goddess laying there all wrecked from your orgasm. I've never seen anything more perfect than the way you fall apart for me." He hooks my leg in his arm as he moves to kiss me covering me with his body. Stretching me open for him.

"Thank you, Poppy. For giving me another chance. I might screw up, but I promise to always see you. I won't lose sight of who you are again," Hendrix promises, bringing our foreheads together as he notches himself against my entrance.

"That's all I ask." My fingers tug on the hair at the nape of his neck as I pull his lips to mine, and he finally sinks inside me. He stills for a second, giving me time to adjust to him. "I need you to move."

He drags out slowly before thrusting back in. "Fuck, you feel amazing. So fucking tight." His head dips to take my nipple in his mouth as he repeats the pattern dragging out slowly before thrusting back. His pace is slow and deep, it keeps on the edge, but it's not enough.

"I need —" I start but then he thrusts back in, and a moan cuts off my words, "More, Hen." The way he fills me is damn near overwhelming, but I want to feel him everywhere. I can't get enough.

He sits back on his heels, bringing me with him and changing the angle. "Like that?" He pushes down lightly on my lower stomach as he continues to pump in and out of me. I'm already so full but the new angle and the added pressure increase the sensation with every thrust.

"God — yes." I chant as I bring my hands up to palm my heavy breasts. My orgasm is building so slowly it's almost painful. I tug on my nipples asking Hendrix for what I need. "Hendrix, fuck me harder."

Sweat beads at his temple as he amps up his pace and gives me just what I asked for. "You like that, Poppy?"

"God, yes, just like that. Don't hold back." And he doesn't, his deep thrusts push me up the bed.

"Squeeze my cock, Beautiful. Give me everything you've got." And with that, my stomach drops out and tingles explode across my body. I moan out Hendrix's name and plummet so hard when my orgasm hits it steals my breath away for a moment.

"Fucking hell, Poppy." Hendrix groans as he stiffens above me. He lowers his forehead to mine as he slows to work through his climax.

We stay like that breathing hard until Hendrix rolls to the side quickly taking care of the condom before pulling me back to his chest. "Stay tonight?"

"You couldn't drag me away." I place kisses across his chest, feeling his heartbeat under my lips. "There's going to be more of that, right?"

"Abso-fucking-lutely. Now that I have you, I want to make up for lost time. I hope you didn't plan on getting dressed or sleeping." He makes good on his promise. Never bothering to get dressed, we alternate between sleep and sex until we finally rinse off together and crawl back into bed to sleep for real this time.

The sound of coffee beans grinding and the smell of bacon drift into the bedroom, pulling me from sleep. Stretching my arms over my head and glancing around the room, I see one of Hendrix's shirts folded on the armchair in the corner, along with my clothes that were discarded in the kitchen last night.

I pad across the bedroom with a pleasant ache between my legs, a reminder of all the orgasms Hendrix gave me. I lost count after the fourth one. Holding his shirt up to my nose, I inhale his scent before slipping it over my head and joining him in the kitchen.

Hendrix is standing in front of the stove, clad in only a pair of joggers resting low on his hips, flipping the bacon in the pan. I lean my hip against the counter and watch him work. My sleepy brain is mesmerized by the way his back muscles flex while he works.

"I could get used to this. Especially the shirtless part. Can we make that a condition of our relationship?"

"All breakfasts must be cooked shirtless? Sure, I can agree to that. You understand that goes both ways, Poppy. Are you going to make me breakfast topless too?" Hendrix turns the heat down on the burner and stalks across the kitchen to where I stand. "Maybe we need another rule about only wearing my shirts and nothing else when we are in the apartment. You look so goddamn good like this. Makes me want to drag you straight back to bed and peel it off you."

His fingers toy with the hem brushing against my bare thighs as they move back and forth. "That could be arranged."

"Sit and let me feed you first." Hendrix drops a kiss on my forehead before stepping back to plate the food. I get a glimpse of the plant which we relocated to the balcony after our field trip the other day. It's started to blossom, and my mouth drops open when I see the little violet hued bell-shaped flowers just starting to open. I'd recognize it anywhere.

Hendrix sees me staring and follows my gaze to where it's fixed on the flowers. He looks from the flowers to where his shirt has slipped down on my shoulder revealing part of my tattoo.

"Those flowers are the same as your tattoo?" He's got the cutest look of confusion on his face, lips twisting to the side with his head tilted faintly.

"It is. They're Virginia bluebells. Janet asked me about my tattoo the day we met."

"Beautiful and strong just like my girl," Hendrix says sliding the plate in front of me and taking the chair next to me.

"They grow even in the shadiest spots and come back year after year. But mostly they represent a safe haven. A place where no matter what happened at home that I always felt loved and accepted," I say as I stare out the window at them.

"I'm grateful that Indie and her family were able to give you that." Hendrix leans over and places a kiss at the spot where my neck and shoulder meet right where my tattoo ends.

"Have you heard from your grandmother?" I ask, not wanting to talk about my childhood any longer.

"She texted me after she got to Mia's. The two of you really hit it off?" Hendrix raises an eyebrow as he bites off a piece of bacon.

"We did. She's really amazing. Is that a problem?" The look he's giving me has me confused. He slides his phone across the table screen down.

I pick it up tentatively. When I see the picture on his lock screen, I bring my hand to my mouth to cover my laughter. It's the picture from our girls' night that Lilah took and sent to Cruz. He's cropped Lilah out, but Janet and I are draped across each other on a pile of pillows in a fit of giggles after consuming our brownie dessert.

"That depends, am I going to get a phone call from the county jail while I'm on the road to bail the two of you out?" Hendrix reaches over pulling my hand down. "Don't hide that smile from me, Poppy. I'm glad the two of you get along so well. Once you meet Mia, I'm really going to have my hands full with the three of you."

"You want me to meet your sister?" The butterflies in my stomach explode into a flurry of wings at the thought of making plans like that with him.

"Maybe I wasn't clear enough yesterday. This is real. It's the most real relationship I've ever been in." His voice is low and serious.

The tone and meaning send those butterflies soaring even higher. I drop my fork on my plate and stand from my chair, pushing back on his shoulder until he scoots his chair back from the table. I slide on to his lap and kiss him, channeling all the things I am feeling into it.

When I pull back, I look him in the eyes. "It's the same for me, Hendrix. These last few weeks have been miserable. As mad as I was at you, I couldn't get you out from under my skin. There was still something there beneath the surface begging for me to recognize it."

Hendrix picks up his fork and spears some eggs before bringing them to my lips. "Eat, I'm not done with you yet." Staying in his lap, we take turns feeding each other bites of food. We both need the calories after last night. When both plates are empty, Hendrix slides his hand up my thigh. He freezes before he grabs my chin, turning me to look at him. "No underwear this whole time. It's like you're just begging for me to fuck you senseless before breakfast. My greedy girl didn't get enough last night?" I shake my head still gripped between his fingers. His arm bands around my waist, holding me to him while he lifts his hips off the chair enough to pull his joggers down.

"Should we go get a condom?" My breath catches as I grind down on his hard cock. "I have an IUD and I'm good. I tested at my physical a few months ago. There hasn't been anyone else," I add, swallowing my nerves down.

"Fuck, Poppy, are you sure? I — I mean I am. Sure that is." His hands pull my shirt up over my head, leaving me completely naked in his kitchen for the second time in twenty-four hours. "We get blood tests all the time, but I've never gone bare before. But fuck, do I want to with you."

Lifting, I position him underneath me and sink down slowly. Groaning at the delicious stretch and ache from last night. "So sure. God, you feel so good like this." I breathe out on a groan.

"You like the way my cock fills you when you ride me, don't you, Beautiful." His words are dirty, but he doesn't try to take control. His fingers grip my hips as he lets me control the pace, taking things tortuously slow until he dips his thumb down to my clit working me in tight circles just like he saw me do to myself last night. When I start to feel the first tingles of my orgasm, Hendrix takes over and fucks up into me faster and harder, driving me over the edge before he follows right behind.

CHAPTER 24

POPPY

Closing the door behind the delivery man, I squeal in delight. It's finally here. After countless delays, my sound booth arrived. It's been almost a month since I wrapped up my business with the hotline. While I have kept busy working on other areas of the business, I can't move forward with launching my career as a narrator until I get this bad boy built and record my demo.

I pull my phone out of my pocket and take a selfie of me enthusiastically, pointing at the box and send it to Hendrix.

POPPY:
It's finally here!

HENDRIX:

That's awesome. I can help you put it together when I get back.

POPPY:

I'll have it done before you're home. How hard can it be? Good luck today. I'll be watching.

HENDRIX:

I love it when you watch me play.

As if that isn't enough good news for the week, Indie flies in tomorrow. We have plans to head to Breckenridge for the weekend, which is perfect because Hendrix has an away series for the next few days.

It's been over a year since the last time Indie was out here. We've seen each other briefly over the holidays when I have flown back home for a few days and talked on the phone a few times a week, but I can't wait to have her all to myself for the next five days.

Hendrix and I have been making up for lost time, squeezing in day dates before games and spending the nights together after his home games. The fact that he is gone for most of her visit will make it much easier for me to focus on Indie.

I grab a box cutter and slice through the strap on the boxes of materials for my sound booth. As I'm gathering up all the garbage from the way the boxes were wrapped, my phone rings. Glancing at the counter, I see Indie's name light up the screen.

"I need help packing," she whines before I even get a greeting out. "I have half my closet spread out in my living room and I can't make any decisions."

"Do you have anything packed? If I'm going to help, I'll need to assess how dire the situation is." I switch the call over to FaceTime so I can see what she's working with. There are clothes scattered everywhere, with one neatly packed backpack in the corner.

"Just my hiking gear and clothes for Maroon Bells. It's all the other stuff that's giving me problems. Do I need fancy going out clothes for Denver and casual going out clothes for Breckenridge?"

"Yes to both, but maybe we can mix and match things. You can always grab out of my closet," I tell her, shoving the straps and packaging from the sound booth into the garbage. I watch as Indie pans across the options she's got in front of her. We pick out some staples that she can mix and match.

"The day after we get back from Breckenridge, there's a Bandits' game. Hendrix got us tickets for the game, and we can go out afterwards. That will be super casual and should work with the options you already have packed. You can borrow a jersey from me," I say, knowing that there are a few options in my closet without the names James on the back for her to choose from.

"How are the guys on the team? Are they decent, or are they all a bunch of pigs?" Indie's voice drips with loathing. Her ex-boyfriend from college was a baseball player and a total tool. He cheated on her habitually with her roommate.

"Most of them are pretty great. Cruz is a solid guy. I've known him for years, and he is one of the nicest guys I've ever met. There are a few guys on the team that are a little wilder and more known for their off-field antics. None of them are like Noah," I assure her, referencing her ex.

"Just don't let me sleep with any of them. The last thing I need is another player in my life. That phase is over. Give me all the boring guys. They don't cheat." She rants. "Oh shit — Poppy. I didn't mean I thought Hendrix would cheat."

"It's fine, Indie. I know that's not what you meant." Hendrix and I are solid. After what Kylie did to him he understands the impact of betrayal better than most. We talked about what is important to each of us in a relationship and what we need from each other to feel secure.

"I think I feel good about our packing decisions. And I can't wait to see you tomorrow," she squeals on the other end of the phone before we hang up.

I should have paid to have someone install this sound booth for me, but I'm stubborn and wanted to do it myself. After wrestling the paneling into the guest bedroom one by one and assembling the frame, all my muscles are screaming. I can feel sweat dripping down my spine as I struggle to hold up one of the side panels of my recording booth while bending at a weird angle to attach it to the frame. There's no point in struggling through this, it would take a fraction of the time with help.

Accepting defeat, I swipe the back of my hand across my forehead and looked at my watch. Indie's plane should be landing any minute. My goal had been to get it done before she got here, but at this point I'd be lucky to get it done before midnight. Standing up slowly, I stretch out my legs before setting the paneling down and acknowledging that I need help to get this done.

Indie, Lilah, and I have dinner plans tonight before we head to Breckenridge tomorrow. I really should shower before she gets here. Abandoning the sound booth, I step under the warm spray of the shower head, letting the pressure of the water ease my muscles.

My mind wanders to my date with Hendrix last night. After his afternoon game, we grabbed dinner at a food truck and then went glow-in-the-dark mini golfing. I don't remember the last time I laughed so hard. As a professional athlete, Hendrix is obviously competitive by nature.

I did my very best to distract him every opportunity I got. My tactics resulted in him pushing me up against the wall in a dark corner and kissing me stupid before threatening to tie me up when we got home if I didn't play fair for the rest of the night. He failed to realize that was not a deterrent. It only encouraged my antics.

We made it through three more holes before I dragged him out of there. Frantic to get him alone after his promise to "lick every inch of me until I was begging for him to let me come."

And holy shit did he deliver.

With my hands secured to his bedposts using two of his baseball belts he explored every inch of me at an agonizing pace. I was a whimpering mess. Tears tracking down my face, writhing and pleading with him to make me come by the time he finally gave in and fucked me.

Afterward, he carried me to the bath where he washed my hair before we crawled into bed. We snuggled up and talked about his upcoming schedule trying to plan out a trip home for me.

"Why don't you join me on our away series to Chicago in a few weeks? We have a day game and then an off day. I could stay an extra day and fly home with you."

"You want to come home with me? You know this isn't going to be a particularly fun trip. I'm basically going home to tell my parents that I'm not going to put up with their judgment and pressure to live the life they planned out for me."

He wrapped me up tighter, pulling me against him. "I know that. I want to be there for you no matter how it goes. You don't have to do this alone."

My throat tightens with emotion at the memory. The night was the perfect mix of sweet and sinful. Since we got back together, Hendrix has been the attentive and supportive partner I got a glimpse of when we first met. He has broken down each of the walls I had erected around my heart. Gradually, making me fall for him a little more each day.

Rinsing away the last of the soap, I turn off the water and grab a towel off the rack, wrapping it tightly around my chest. I towel off my hair and grab a pair of terry cloth shorts and a sweater to throw on while I wait for Indie.

The knock at the door has me dashing through the apartment, toothbrush dangling from my mouth to the front door. When I open the door, Indie launches herself at me and we are a tangle of arms and legs as we hug each other and jump up and down.

We spend a few minutes exchanging rapid-fire greetings and questions about her trip here.

"This place is adorable. I love the little sushi boats." Indie grabs a small plate off a boat floating around the miniature lazy river while the chef works in the center of the hollowed-out bar. "Lilah, you picked a winner. Ten out of ten, would recommend."

"Cruz introduced me to it. He knows all these eccentric little places in Denver." Her lips turn up in a smile as she talks about him.

"What's the deal with you and Cruz? You've been friends for a long time, but I always thought that eventually you two would get together." God forgot Indie's filter when he built her and it's one of my favorite things about her. She tells it like it is.

"Can we talk about literally anything else? Cruz and I — it's new and scary. I'm not ready to talk about it." Lilah's face flushes pink as she says it.

"I think you two just need to fuck it out," I offer as I grab a spicy shrimp roll off the passing boat. Evidently my filter is missing tonight too, but I am going to blame it on the sake.

"You're in an orgasm haze from Hendrix. Your opinion can't be trusted. Indie, when was the last time you had a good dicking? I need someone that hasn't been fucked into oblivion for the last month." Lilah laughs, bringing her wine glass to her lips.

"I'd give my left tit for some hairpulling toe curling sex. Maybe I'm not the best person to talk you off that ledge either. But I can recommend an excellent vibrator." Indie raises her glass in cheers to Lilah.

"That's already taken care of. Isn't it, Lilah?"

I bite my lip to stop myself from laughing. Lilah glares at me across the countertop. After she confided in me about her elbow, it's possible I sent her a gift. A brand new ergonomically correct vibrator to add to her collection. "I gifted her a new toy and addressed it to her Lady Garden. Cruz found it on her doormat and hand delivered it." I summarize for Indie, but I can't stop the laughter as it barrels out of me in the form of a snort.

Lilah swats me, throwing her head back with laughter. "You're such an asshole. But my elbow thanks you."

"Oh, you love me. Don't even pretend. You and Cruz just need to go for it. You'll thank me. The two of you are endgame. You just need to take that leap." I can't stand the sexual tension between the two of them. It's hard to even be in the same room as them right now and it's gotten even worse since they kissed. I think there's more to the story, but they're both keeping it under wraps as they figure it out.

"Athletes are on my no-bone list, but I can't wait to meet these guys. They must be something to have the two of you all tied up in knots. Besides, Hendrix and I need to have some words." Indie says, trying to look menacing. And it works, I'm nervous for Hendrix, but the feeling is fleeting.

I roll my eyes at her. She means well and I'll let her say her piece with Hendrix because he was a jackass and earned her wrath. But I also know that if he makes me happy, she'll crumble like a stale cookie and be his biggest ally. She just needs to see the way he treats me firsthand after our rocky start.

"If you keep measuring every man against Noah and his douchebaggery, you might miss out on a great guy." He really

messed her up, and she has held it against every guy since —
closing herself off to finding someone.

"I'm going to side with Lilah here, you're getting laid
way too regularly to give relationship advice to the scorned
women of the world."

I stick my tongue out at her before I take a drink. I'm
happy and not willing to apologize for it. Naturally I want the
same for my girlfriends, but they both have a Louis Vuitton
store full of baggage to unpack first.

We all made a deal when we came out tonight that we'd
put our phones away. Mine's been tucked in my purse since
we stepped in the restaurant, but I can feel it buzzing against
my chair. My lips flatten into a thin line thinking about who it
could be. The girls are all here, and Hendrix should be getting
ready to take the field. The only other person that calls is my
mom.

When I finally check my phone after we leave the restaurant I see a barrage of texts from my mom.

MOM:
We need to talk about this visit home.
MOM:
*Your father and I talked about it and I'm
not happy about driving into the city.*
MOM:
*I'm not sure if we'll be able to make this
work.*
MOM:
*Just call me so we can talk about you
coming here instead.*

Just reading the messages is exhausting but I'm not going to let her ruin my night. I slip my phone away without a reply. I'll call her later this week and explain why we can't come to her. It's not going to change her attitude, but I'll be able to say I tried if they decide not to come into Chicago.

Indie slips her arm through mine, "Everything okay?"

"Mhmm, nothing worth worrying about." I tell her and for the first time in a long time I mean it. I'm still dreading the conversation with my parents but they're either going to listen or they won't.

CHAPTER 25

POPPY

I use the key to unlock Hendrix's door. After we figured things out together, he gave back the key so I can water his plants like originally planned. I loved the meaning behind the jersey he gave me during our reconciliation. Hendrix was claiming me, telling everyone I was his. It was possessive and made my lady bits tingle. But when he gave me the key it hit me right in the feels because he wouldn't have handed it back over without complete trust.

Even though this isn't how he intended I use the key, I know he won't be mad. We've grown so much in how we communicate with each other. This will be a secret he'll be happy I kept when he comes home to find me here. Indie and I got home from our weekend trip to Breckenridge earlier today. Even though the hike was grueling, the mountains were gorgeous and worth every step. She was ready for some downtime after two days of backpacking in the heat as the spring fades away and summer takes hold. When we got back today, her priorities were a long cold shower and then an early night with one of her serial killer books. *Shudder.*

I had something a little different in mind for my night. Hendrix gets home from another away series today, but his plane isn't scheduled to land until close to midnight. So, I'm sneaking into his apartment to wait for him so I can be here when he gets home from Texas. After my cold shower of course.

I debated between waiting for him in lingerie or just crawling into bed naked. We always sleep naked when we are together, so the lingerie just seemed like an unnecessary step. Stripping down, I fold up my sleep shorts and tank, setting them on the chair in the corner.

I slide into his bed and open up the Kindle App on my phone, the anticipation of seeing him again after almost a week apart has me too wired to sleep. I was going to read Mia's newest book, but it feels weird to read her book while I lay in bed naked, waiting for her brother.

Instead, I'm reading the debut book from an indie author that she recommended. The book is fantastic. It's a spicy romance about a billionaire and his best friend's little sister who end up in a fake dating relationship to save his family's company. I can hear the female main character's voice in my head as I read with the inflections she would use. It has me buzzing with excitement to record my demo.

Eventually the buzzing and nerves from sneaking in wear off, and my eyelids get heavy with exhaustion from the weekend. After my phone slides out of my hand mid-page for the fourth time, I decide to put the book down and give into the pull of sleep overtaking me.

CHAPTER 26

HENDRIX

Our flight was delayed due to weather and we spent an hour on the tarmac waiting for the go ahead to take off. By the time I kick off my shoes inside the entryway to my apartment, I'm exhausted. My bed is calling to me.

Not even willing to haul my bag to my bedroom, I dump it inside the doorway. There's nothing I need right now other than the comfort of my own bed and Poppy's arm wrapped around my waist. The latter isn't going to happen. It's after two in the morning and she's been asleep for hours already. Even though I'm aching to be near her, I'm not enough of an asshole to get her out of bed.

Running my hand down my face, I shuffle my way through the dark hallway into my master bathroom. I strip down to my briefs and brush my teeth. When I make my way out of the bathroom, I freeze at the sight of my bed.

The ambient light filtering through the windows is enough to highlight the red hair laid out across my pillow. My breath catches in my throat at the sight of her waiting there for me. Her eyelids flutter at my movement but she stays sleeping.

I don't deserve this woman. She knew what I needed tonight without me saying a thing. I slide under the covers, careful not to disturb her. When I lift the sheet, more of her creamy skin is exposed and I groan softly. My girl is in my bed naked. I slide my briefs down and drop them off the side of the bed.

Poppy sighs next to me and shifts so that she's flush up against me in her sleep. Wrapping my arms around her, I inhale the honeyed scent of her hair. Brushing a strand of hair off her forehead to place a kiss there before softly telling her, "You have ruined me, Poppy. If it's not you, I don't want anyone else, ever." She nuzzles into me further but gives no other indication that she's heard me. I watch her sleep for a few more minutes before I let my heavy eyelids fall shut.

The rumble of a groan working its way out of my body causes me to stir. Poppy has invaded my dreams for almost three months now, but this one is the most vivid. In my sleep induced fog, I lower my hand to my cock but stop short when it connects with the silky texture of hair.

Flashes of coming home to find Poppy in my bed filter through my consciousness as I peel my gritty eyes open. Her soft warm hand slides up the flank of my thigh and I weave my fingers through it as I look down at Poppy, who is perched between my legs dropping kisses on my hips and pelvis while she lightly strokes my hard cock with loose tugs of her fist. Just teasing me enough to wake me.

She's soft and playful and still a little sleepy herself. "Mhmm." My voice is rough from waking up. "Good morning, Beautiful. Thank you for being here last night. It was everything I needed." My fingers tangle in her hair while my other hand clings to hers.

"You're what I need." Her tongue darts out to lick her lips and her eyes drop to my cock before she looks back up at me through her lashes. "I missed you. All of you."

Then she lowers her head and takes me in her mouth. A shudder runs down my spine at the sight in front of me — my cock disappearing between her pink lips. "Fuck. Your mouth feels so good." The praise eggs her on and she takes me deeper, flicking her tongue along the sensitive skin under my head. My hands fist the sheets as she brings me to the back of her throat.

Not being around her the last few days on the road has me coiled tight. Her hand untangles with mine and trails down her stomach to play with her clit. At the contact, she hums around my cock, sending shivers through me. I gather her hair on top of her head and tilt her face up to look at me.

"Come here, baby. Let me take care of you the way you did for me when you showed up last night." My voice breaks when she sucks hard and twists her hand at my base. "Fuck, Poppy. Get your ass up here and sit on my face," I urge more forcefully this time. Trying to stave off my release until I can take care of her. I tug on her hair enough that she releases me with a pop before kissing her way up my body. My hands go to her hips, and I pull her higher.

"I want to taste you, Hendrix. You're ruining my morning fun."

"No, I'm improving it. Turn around," I tell her when her knees are straddling my head. She looks down at me nervously biting on her bottom lip. Her cheeks are flushed. It's not a look I'm used to seeing on Poppy, she always owns her sexuality. My hand connects with her ass, smacking it playfully and stoking her into action as my lips move along the inside of her thigh.

"Give me a taste of that sweet pussy."

She rolls her eyes at me but shifts above me, turning so that she can bend at the waist and take me back into her warm mouth. My hands run up her thighs, gripping her hips tightly and yanking her down to my mouth. She cries out at the pressure of my flattened tongue lapping at her clit.

After a few more passes, she relaxes above me, and her hips start moving so she's grinding on my face taking what she needs. The way Poppy gives herself over to her pleasure makes me harden even more in her mouth.

"That's so fucking sexy. Use me to get yourself there," I encourage.

My balls draw up tight against my body, it's a telltale sign that my orgasm is barreling toward me as I sink my tongue into Poppy and rub her clit, working it in tight circles.

Poppy releases me from her mouth, letting my cock slap against my stomach before resting her forehead on my hipbone. Her hand continues to pump me hard, while her thighs shake around my head, and she shouts my name. "Oh fuck, Hendrix. Please — don't stop." Her voice breaks off as she tightens around me.

"What do you want, Poppy?" I ask when she finishes working through her tremors, her hand pumping much more slowly now as her body shifts to the side limply next to me.

"You, I need your cock inside me. I'll finish this later." Her free hand waves absently at my crotch, making me chuckle. I shift up the bed, knocking her hand off me and taking myself in my own hand. When I'm reclined against the headboard, I motion for Poppy to come to me, and she repositions dropping down on me in one smooth motion. My hand wraps around the back of her neck, pulling her forehead to mine. "Too fucking long. Four days is too many without you. Without us," I grunt as I thrust up into her.

Her elbows rest on my shoulders, fingers sifting through my hair as she swivels her hips and drops back down. Her mouth falls open when I'm seated deep inside her. "I'll never get enough of how you make me feel." Is her reply as we move slowly against each other, taking turns controlling the tempo.

Our movements are unrushed and lazy as Poppy's fingers trace the tattoos on my shoulder and chest. She bends her head to bring her lips to the ink following the path her fingers are on. "These get me so fucking hot. Since the first time I saw them on our accidental run." Her voice breaks as her breathing and pace pick up. Then her teeth graze the skin on my shoulder biting down as I feel her flutter around my cock, squeezing me impossibly tight.

My hand comes to her chin, pulling her mouth to mine as I increase my pace fucking her harder. Breaking our kiss as my release rips through me. "Goddamn," I mutter into her hair, holding her close. "It's so fucking good every time with us. You were made for me."

We lay there in a tangle of limbs and panting softly, stroking each other when I hear three taps on the wall and then a muffled voice. "If you two are done, I made coffee. Bring his ass over here so I can meet him, Poppy."

Poppy's eyes widen so much that it's comical before her hand comes up to cover her mouth but it doesn't stop her giggle from slipping out. "Oh. My. God. She did not just do that."

"I take it that's Indie?" My voice is amused as Poppy confirms my suspicions with a nod. Her lip trapped adorably between her teeth.

"Want some coffee, Ironman?" Poppy asks without skipping a beat.

"Yes, but can I shower this plane off first? When I saw you in my bed last night, the shower got skipped because I needed you more."

"Only if I can join you, but no shenanigans." She picks up her phone and sends Indie a text telling her we will be over in ten minutes.

Ten turns into twenty when Poppy insists on dropping to her knees to finish what she started in bed earlier, making me come in her mouth. Try as I might, she refuses to let me repay her not wanting to ditch Indie after sneaking over last night.

Indie is just the way Poppy described her and mostly what I expected after her stunt of shouting at us through the wall. She doesn't pull punches when confronting me about how I treated Poppy the night of our first date. If I didn't feel the way I do about Poppy, she might scare me.

"You have nothing to worry about. Poppy deserves the best and I plan to treat her that way. I might screw up here and there, but I won't hurt Poppy like that again." I assure Indie and it's enough to appease her, but it doesn't deter her fiery personality.

She looks between the two of us before looking Poppy in the eyes and saying, "Congratulations, Pops." Poppy's eyebrows furrow and she stares back at her friend before she continues. "He must have dicked you down good with all the squealing you did this morning. You really need to have the building manager add more insulation to that wall."

"First — Fuck off, Indie." Poppy blurts through a laugh before shrugging at me but making no apologies for her friend's lack of filter. "Second — is it really that bad?"

Indie smirks, "I heard every word, want a replay?"

Poppy's face turns a shade of crimson I'm not sure I've seen on a person before. "That's not necessary." She says pointedly staring down Indie.

Moving on from the topic in an effort to save my girl from her best friend's antics, I ask, "Are you still planning to come to the game tonight?" Not sure if they're still up for it after their weekend in Breckenridge or if they want some down-time. My stomach sinks at the prospect that she might not come, but I want to give her an out if she needs it.

Indie jumps in with an answer before Poppy can even open her mouth. "You bet your tight ass we will be there. I was promised baseball pants on this trip." She tilts her head like she's trying to get a peek at my ass.

Poppy swats her friend. "Knock it off, you psycho. You are going to scare him away, and I want to keep him."

My arms come around her waist from where I stand behind her and I pull her into my chest, my lips hover at the shell of her ear. "Michael Myers himself couldn't scare me away." My voice is low just for her and I place a kiss on her temple. "Thanks for the coffee. I need to head out for my workout and then get ready to head to the stadium. I'll see you both after the game."

"You have a jersey I can wear tonight?" Indie asks as I pull Poppy close for a kiss on my way out the door.

"Mhhh," she mumbles against my lips before she opens for me, deepening our kiss. Before pulling back and patting me on the ass. Mumbling under her breath as I open the door, I hear her say, "All mine."

CHAPTER 27

POPPY

The game is a shut out, but my personal highlight comes in the fifth inning when Hendrix blows me a kiss as he walks past our seats on his way to the outfield. At that point, the Bandits were already ahead by seven and the whole team looked like they were having a blast, complete with dugout celebrations for each of the three homeruns. One from Xavier, Cruz, and the host for tonight's post-game gathering Dean.

We jump in Ubers from the stadium to head to Dean's penthouse, it's further away than the neighborhood the rest of us live in. When we pile out of the cars there's a private elevator up to the building's penthouse.

It's larger than I expected. Hendrix mentioned that Dean's mom is some powerhouse legacy attorney on the east coast, but I didn't expect this level of opulence. His kitchen is outfitted with a double fridge and top of the line appliances. Everything is over the top. While it's impressive, part of me is thankful that Hendrix's doesn't live in a place like this. He can certainly afford it, but I'm not sure I'd feel as at home here as I do at his apartment.

Hendrix backs me against the counter his eyes focused on where our friends are standing on the opposite side of the room. "Where did Indie get that jersey, Poppy?" There's some bite in Hendrix's question, and I look over at Indie, who is turned away from me talking to Dean. The name Harrison was in bold letters across her shoulders.

"Oh that." I bury the laughter that's trying to escape, loving this jealous streak that he's showing. His eyes darken and he steps in closer, like an animal on the prowl.

"Tell me that Dean's jersey didn't come out of your closet." I lift my shoulders in an indifferent shrug. Enjoying this little game and seeing his reaction.

"I wish I could, but I can't lie to you, Hendrix." My hand comes up to pat his cheek like he's a child. I place an overly sweet kiss on his lips. When I first started going to games with Lilah, I grabbed a jersey from a secondhand store, and it just happened to be Dean's. I could tell my boyfriend that, but it's more fun to see him get all territorial about it.

"You are in so much trouble when we get home. You own two Bandits jerseys with someone else's name on the back?" Like a vortex, my emotions swirl. My heart beats faster at the way he said home. It was so casual like we belong together, no questions asked. Meanwhile, my thighs clench at the jealousy in his voice. "You wore Cruz's to that second game on movie night and now this. Are you trying to drive me crazy?"

"Are you jealous? Don't you know by now your threats do nothing but turn me on? It doesn't exactly inspire good behavior," I chide playfully. I turn to head toward the fridge for another drink but only make it a half step before two strong arms band around my stomach, pulling me back into Hendrix's hard chest. His lips graze up from my neck to my ear.

"What am I going to do with you? Pushing my buttons, getting me all riled up on purpose. The way you don't take shit from me, it's such a fucking turn on." His breath is hot against my skin.

"Keep me forever." The words are out before I can stop them. Hendrix freezes behind me but only for a moment before his hold tightens, eliminating all the space between us. His voice is so low and husky that I almost miss it.

"Promises, promises." He says as I tilt my head up to look at him over my shoulder, but he's too quick capturing my mouth in a kiss. He spins me around to face him. All the noise of the party disappears around me and it's just the two of us in this bubble of overwhelming emotion.

I pour everything I feel for him into our kiss — admiration, desire, kinship, respect, infatuation. He matches me step for step, clinging to me tightly, both of us using this to say the things we haven't been brave enough to speak out loud yet.

I break the kiss reluctantly remembering that we are in the middle of Dean's penthouse surrounded by friends and his teammates. Hendrix sighs at the loss of contact and places a chaste kiss on my lips before linking our hands and walking with me to the kitchen.

Hendrix leads me to the fridge and grabs two beers, never dropping my hand. When we rejoin the group in the living room, Indie is holding court with Dom and Dean. Her hands are waving as she tells a story. Both of the guys follow her every move with rapt attention.

Indie is stunningly beautiful and vibrant as hell; I have no doubt she could have the Bandits' two most notorious play-boys eating out of her hand by the end of the night if she wanted.

"You should have seen the two of us trying to put this thing together. Poppy's asking for a wrench, and I'm handing her a screwdriver." Indie chatters on dramatically.

"Someone insisted that we have wine while we work." I stare pointedly at Indie. "That was our fatal flaw. We gave up and decided to watch crappy reality TV after about twenty minutes of failed attempts to get through the first step of the instructions."

"It was really my plan all along. Suck so badly at assem-bling the sound booth that you would let me relax on the couch with wine instead." Her shoulder bumps mine play-fully. "We will try again without the wine after our massages tomorrow morning."

"This sound booth is the bane of my existence, but I need it done. I should have just paid for the assembly. I didn't think it would be this complicated. The instructions are completely useless," I commiserate with Indie.

It wasn't my intention to put her to work while she was here, but she offered to help, joking that it would be good bonding for us. Bonding was the only thing we accomplished.

Between the sound booth being delayed, getting wrapped up in my time with Hendrix when he is home, and

Indie's visit, I'm behind on work. The deadline I had set for my demo has passed and I can't move forward with much else until that is done.

I don't regret the time I've spent focusing on Indie or Hendrix, but I do need to come up with a plan to get back on track, and that includes getting the sound booth put together soon. I know Hendrix would help if I asked, but I don't want to pull his focus on a game day. He hasn't said anything, but his routine is important to him, and he's already made changes to spend time with me when he's in town. I can't ask more from him.

"What time is your appointment tomorrow?" Hendrix asks, absently rubbing circles across the skin at my hip where he is holding me.

"Ten o'clock. We are going to have lunch after and then come to your game tomorrow night before Indie flies home the next morning."

"Thanks for getting us tickets to another game. I really enjoyed the view tonight," Indie adds brazenly roving her eyes over Dom, who is locked in conversation with Dean about the game. Dean catches her gaze and winks. Jesus, I hope she knows what she's doing. For a girl who claims she's not into athletes, she's playing with fire.

♥

"This is heaven on earth. You're a goddess for suggesting it. Best idea ever," Indie groans as the masseuse works on her feet. She's face down on the table, her dark hair piled in a messy bun on top of her head. I groan in agreement as firm hands slide down my calves.

"Genius, for sure. I'm so glad we did this. It should be a standard part of all your trips moving forward."

"Motion seconded," Indie says, hitting the table with her fist like it's a gavel.

We lay in silence, soaking up the relaxation as our masseuses finish out the remainder of the hour. There's a tap on my shoulder, and I realize I drifted off to sleep.

"You alive over there?" Indie says with a laugh. "You got a little drool right there." She brings her finger up to indicate the spot on her face.

"Asshole." I drag the back of my hand across my face, still in a daze. "I do a nice thing for you planning a spa day and you're over here picking on me about a little drool. I heard you moaning over there when she rubbed your feet. It was obscene. Do you have a foot fetish I don't know about?"

"I didn't before, but I might now. Do you think that she's single? I think I might propose?" Indie deadpans as she scoots off the table, clutching her towel in front of her as she slides her leggings up.

Indie's visit has been therapeutic. We have talked about everything from my upcoming visit home with Hendrix, to our careers, and everything in between. The time hiking in Breckenridge gave us hours to just catch up on each other's life and reminisce on some of our favorite memories while building new ones.

I think I almost have her convinced to move out here. We have less than twenty-four hours until she is back on a plane to Chicago, and I want to soak up every moment before she leaves.

"Ready for lunch, Poppy girl?" Indie asks, interrupting my morose thoughts about her leaving tomorrow.

"Always. I worked up an appetite doing all the relaxing," I tell her slinging my arm around her shoulder as we walk out the door.

Lunch passes in a blur of laughter and plotting out a girls' trip for later this year. We agree that we can't go that long between visits again and we should meet up some place warmer once the snow starts. My heart is overflowing by the time we unlock the door to the apartment. I don't think there's room for any more joy inside my soul at the moment.

I stop dead in my tracks when I follow Indie through the door not believing what I'm seeing. Hendrix, Cruz, and Dom are in my kitchen, all of them with their hands full of either tools or packaging. "What's going on, guys?"

"Shit, man, we will get out of your way," Dom mutters under his breath. "What do you say, Indie, want to grab some coffee with me?" He flashes a smirk her way, only to receive an eyeroll in return.

"Let's go, playboy." She says turning back toward the door not bothering to wait for Dom as he gathers up some more packaging to dispose of on the way out.

"Hey, Indie. Thanks for the assist." Hendrix crosses the kitchen in three long strides. His hand reaches out and I see him slide a key into her outstretched palm. Cruz is gathering up tools and stowing them in a worn canvas bag hot on their heels.

"Hendrix James, what did you do?" He crowds my space, threading his fingers through mine and bringing my knuckles to his lips for a kiss.

His gaze doesn't leave mine as he pulls me in, looping his other arm around my waist. "Your sneak attack in my bed the other day inspired me to plan a little surprise of my own. Want to come see?"

"Um — yes, please!" I say, bursting at the seams. His hands drop to my hips, and he turns me around, my back pressed to his chest.

"Close your eyes, Woman." He demands with his lips hovering just next to the shell of my ear. My eyes close as goose bumps travel down my arms from the raspy quality of his voice and the way he's holding me close. "Do you trust me?"

"Yes," I say on exhale, and it's mostly true. I know he has no intention of hurting me. Most of all I know I want to trust him. It seems the man from our first date was a blip on the radar. He has apologized and the spiteful, bitter man that refused to give me a chance hasn't made a reappearance.

Yet there's still something holding me back from letting him all the way in. The hurt inflicted by my parents and Paul still has me in its grip. If I give myself over to everything I feel for Hendrix, he has the power to crush my heart and destroy me.

His grip tightens on my hips, making me feel secure in his hands as he nudges me forward leading me through the apartment. We take a right into the guest bedroom once we have successfully navigated the hallway. The butterflies in my stomach are back and their wings flap wildly as I stand there with my eyes still closed preparing myself for his suprise. The anticipation has my palms sweating and I wipe them on my leggings waiting for his permission to look.

"Can I open my eyes?" I ask, finding his hands on my hips and covering them with my own.

"Yes, go ahead and open them." He whispers into my neck as he lays a gentle kiss there giving those butterflies a run for their money.

Silently, I take in the sight in front of me. My eyes sweeping over the room in awe. My sound booth is assembled. Not only that, but they also took the time to move and hook up my equipment. I'm not an overly emotional person, yet I find myself swallowing the lump in my throat and holding back tears.

This must have taken hours. It's game day— he threw his day off and recruited his teammates to do this for me. That means he gave up his morning run, lifting session, and pushed his nap back to get this all done today. My heart flutters at the realization that he changed up the routine that he's comfortable with for me. When he said he would spoil me, I thought he meant flowers or candy. This is so much more than that. His time is so much more valuable than anything else he could give me.

"*Hendrix*. This must have taken hours. You did this for me? What about your run, and you should be napping, not here doing this." I wave my arm around at the booth. I'm so blown away by his gesture that I am not even sure how to respond. Turning in his arms, looking up at him and looping my arms around his neck. "Thank you. This is the nicest thing anyone has ever done for me. How?"

"I had a little help from Indie. When I heard the stress in your voice talking about it at Dean's last night, I asked Indie for her key and told her my plan to make sure I wasn't overstepping." His hand shifts through my hair as he talks.

"The guys? They gave up their morning on game day. They were okay with that?"

"Of course, They're my teammates. We're a family, and you're a part of that now. They were happy to help because you mean everything to me." His forehead drops to mine on that last part.

"It's perfect. This was such a stressor for me the last few weeks. Thank you." Going up on my toes, I kiss his lips softly.

"I know it's not easy during the season. You are sacrificing your time to be with me in the spaces between practice, games, and travel. It's pulled you away from your work and I don't want my career to keep you from yours. My job isn't more important than yours. I wanted to do something that helped you achieve your goals too."

"Equality is so sexy," I say, craning my neck to kiss him again. This time with a little more heat behind it. His hands travel to my ass, pulling me in tight.

"Fuck yeah, it is. I always want you to feel like my equal. My partner — because you are." He says as his lips move down my neck. "You smell fucking delicious."

I chuckle as he nibbles at the sensitive skin. "You like that massage oil?"

"I like you, Poppy. A lot."

"Enough to christen that sound booth with me?"

"I would be disappointed if we didn't," he says walking me toward the chair they moved to the booth and pulling me into his lap to straddle him.

"Do me a favor and don't tell Indie you fucked me in here. She'll never let us live it down." His eyes darken at my words and he rotates his hips under me. *My man loves the dirty talk.*

We fuck fast and hard in the chair before he crawls into my bed with me for round two and a quick nap before he needs to leave for the stadium.

To think I could have missed out on this if I hadn't given him that second chance. If he hadn't worked to rebuild my trust, starting with his apology I'd have gone my whole life without knowing what it was like to be this entwined with him, mind, body, and soul.

♥

Draft is packed following the win over the Los Angeles Diablos. The main bar is overflowing with fans and most of the players showed up to grab food and drinks together at the back bar. Hendrix has his arm slung over the back of my chair as he draws lazy circles on my shoulder. He looks every bit the hot shot athlete he is — reclining in his seat with his legs kicked out carelessly in front of him as he laughs with his friends. He makes casual and calm look sexy with a pair of black jeans and an open button-up over a white shirt that shows off all his muscles. You think it would be intimidating, but I feel completely at ease like everything is right in the world.

The team was on fire tonight, and my throat is raw from all the cheering Lilah, Indie, and I did in the stands. Watching Hendrix go out there and play well against the team that traded him was exhilarating. He has earned his swagger and confidence times ten tonight. My heart is overflowing with pride that I get to call him mine.

Behind me, I hear high pitched squealing, it's very *woo girl*. When I look over my shoulder to see who is making the offensive shrieking noise, a girl in the world's shortest dress ever shimmies over. She stops on the opposite side of Hendrix and without invitation butts right into the conversation at the table.

"Great game tonight, James. You looked really good out there. Can you sign this for me?" She leans in further than necessary, shoving a napkin toward him. Her position of standing over his shoulder and bending forward causes her breasts to nearly spill out of her top and places them right in front of his face. She continues to be oblivious to the fact he's uncomfortable or that he is sitting with his arm around me.

Hendrix's hand stills on my shoulder and his jaw pops with aggravation at the interruption. I've watched Hen with fans over the past few months. Even if he's a little uncomfortable with the spotlight, he's always been happy to stop what he is doing to talk or sign autographs, but this feels intrusive. His eyes shift to me apologetically for a moment before he stands.

He steps back, giving himself some space before reaching for the napkin. "Sure, want me to make it out to anyone in particular?" he asks with a smile that's a little too wide to be real, but warm enough to pass as not being an asshole.

"Cindy. C-I-N-D-Y," she spells her name out like it's difficult, but it gives her the excuse she needs to lean into him again in case he can't hear her over the crowd.

Hendrix quickly scribbles out a message, his teeth grinding, and I'm afraid for a minute he might crack a molar. I spare a glance at Indie not waiting to act like an insane person even though this interaction is making my blood boil. I want nothing more than to tell Cindy to back the fuck off.

The jealous rage surprises me. Her boldness in approaching my man like this when he's clearly here with me has me slightly enraged. Except there's nothing slight about it.

Indie raises her eyebrow at me. A silent question. *Are you going to just sit there and take this?*

No, I am not. I'm a doormat for no one. Except for my parents, but that's coming to end soon. I know my worth and it's time they see it too. This cleat chaser is no match for the emotional damage my own mother has inflicted over the years. Cindy is going to be disappointed if she thinks she can just waltz in here and flirt with my boyfriend right under my nose.

"Thanks so much for stopping by, Cindy, but as you can see, Hen is busy socializing with his friends." My voice is saccharine in a way that is clear. I am not the sugary sweet girl I'm playing at. Cindy straightens, pushing her tits out further like she's preparing to do battle and her nipples are the bayonets.

Hendrix drops back into the chair next to me and casually slings his arm over the back of my chair before dropping a kiss on my lips. It's quick and not showy at all. The move should be a clear message to disengage from her pursuit of him, but she's not deterred.

Her hand snakes down his chest from over his shoulder. Dropping a slip of paper into the pocket of his shirt. My anger is immediate, but her next move makes every inch of my body vibrate with rage. She drags her fingernails back up his chest, dipping her hand beneath the lapel of his unbuttoned shirt to grope his pec as she passes over it.

Hendrix shrugs her touch off, his head whipping to me, a pleading look on his face. I can't tell if he's looking for help or forgiveness. Indie's mouth is hanging open at what she just witnessed, and it takes a lot to offend my bold friend. Focused on taking deep breaths to control myself, my eyes close and I count backwards from ten as Cindy finally walks away.

All eyes are on me when I reach over and pull the slip of paper out of Hendrix's pocket. As calmly as possible, I unfold it to find a number inked across the scrap. My hands brace against the table, and I push my chair back, causing an obnoxious scraping noise in the process. Bending at the waist, I grab his face in both my hands and kiss him. It's brief and meant to reassure him while serving to fortify me.

A quick glance around the space and I find Cindy leaning against the bar watching the table. One of the guys on the team must have brought her back because Draft is good about allowing the team this private space to gather. My feet eat up the distance as I strut over to where she stands, plastering a fake smile on my face. *Thank you, high school drama.*

I stop in front of her. Her predatory smile falters when she realizes who is standing in front of her.

"Candy, right?" I ask dumbly. Her head shakes and she opens her mouth to correct me, but I push forward not giving her the chance. Jealousy turns me into a petty bitch.

"Candy, Hendrix asked me to return this to you. He won't be needing it. Not tonight, not ever." Her jaw drops at the boldness behind my statement and her eyes flick over my shoulder to the table, but I don't budge.

"Eyes on me, Candy. Hendrix is not interested. Understand?" She looks back at me more unsteady than I thought possible given her brazenness with how she approached Hendrix before.

Careful not to touch her because as angry as I am, I'm not stupid. An assault charge would end the night quickly. I hold the slip of paper up in front of my face considering it for a moment, before I slip it right into her cleavage. "Find your own boyfriend, Candy. I don't share."

Turning on my heels, I exhale for what feels like the first time since she approached our table. I focus on Indie as I cross the bar, nervous to see Hendrix's reaction.

Shit, did I cross a line there? She was a fan. What if he's angry? Doubt creeps in but I push it away and steel myself as I lower into my chair.

Hendrix is on me the second I sit down. Pulling my chair flush against his as his lips descend on my ear. "Poppy, you amaze me. I'm hard as fuck right now; you have never been sexier. All jealous and standing your ground." His voice is rough, and his words set me on edge, my thighs rubbing together at his tone.

I'm quick to finish my drink. I need the cool liquid to chill the fire that is running through my veins for an entirely different reason now.

"Damn, girl. That was a power move. I'm so proud of you," Lilah croons playfully from across the table.

"Remind me not to get on your bad side," Cruz chimes in.

There's a chorus of similar sentiments from the other guys. Hendrix keeps me pulled up tight against him not relenting an inch. I'm dying to get out of here and I know he is too.

"You can get out of here if you want. I'll make one of these guys walk me home." Indie sweeps her hand in front of her to indicate any number of guys around the table. My face must show my hesitance to leave her behind. But she nods toward the door. "Please before the building goes up in flames with the heat radiating off you two. Dom over there is about to pop a boner from all the sexual tension. Don't embarrass him like that."

Hendrix stands, pulling me up with him and dropping a wad of cash unceremoniously in the center of the table.

"Later, guys. Nice game tonight," he calls over his shoulder, pulling me toward the door.

CHAPTER 28

POPPY

"Your place or mine?" Hendrix asks, backing me against the mirrored wall of the elevator. His hips pin me in place as his eyes search mine.

"Mine. I want to be home to make sure Indie gets back okay." His lips drop to my neck and suck hard marking the skin.

"You are so damn sexy. Sitting in the bar with you after that epic display of possessiveness was literally painful." His hand reaches between us to adjust himself.

I take in the sight of us joined together like this in the reflective surface of the elevator doors as the car stops and the doors slide open.

We practically sprint down the hallway to my door, both of us just as unrestrained as the other. When the door shuts behind us, Hendrix drops to his knees in front of me, hands reaching for the button on my jeans.

"I can't wait to get my mouth on you." I love how vocal he is. No one has ever made me feel more desired than Hendrix does with just a few words. My fingers find his hair and delight in the feel of it as he tugs my jeans and underwear down my legs in one motion.

"Spread your legs for me," he demands, trailing kisses along my thighs. My core clenches in anticipation as he works his way higher. "Wider, Beautiful. I want to see all of you."

I shift on my feet, giving him better access, but he's dragging it out, placing more kisses on my hip bones as his hands palm my ass. The dramatic shift from the frenzied pace in the elevator to this deliberately slow progress has my legs shaking beneath me.

"Just like that, Poppy." He stills, halting his kisses and his hands. I groan in protest, needing something.

Anything.

I tilt my head down from where it was resting against the door and almost combust at the sight of him on his knees in front of me. "That's better. Watch me while I taste you."

"Your filthy mouth is such a turn on," I admit, keeping my eyes on him not willing to risk him stopping again.

"I can tell. So wet for me." His fingers slip through my folds as he easily slips one inside of me.

"All for you. Only you." My chest heaves as I pant out the words. Hendrix's tongue darts out, lavishing attention on my swollen clit. My knees buckle underneath the pleasure.

"Only me, I like the sound of that." He hums against my center before adding a second finger and sucking my clit into his mouth.

My hands tug at his dark hair, using it to keep me grounded. If I let go, I'll collapse or float away. I'm not sure which.

"Take your top off. I want to see you play with your tits while I eat this sweet pussy." Releasing his hair, I quickly grasp the hem of my shirt and pull it over my head. My bra follows just as quickly.

"Hold on to the door for me." Hendrix urges as he hooks my leg over his shoulder and uses his bigger body to support me, pinning me against the door as he works me over. My fingers grip the door frame as best they can, and I push my back into the cool metal of the door bracing myself for what's to come. The new angle gives him more access. I feel him everywhere and all at once. Between his finger pumping in and out and the way he uses lips, tongue, and teeth, I'm at the edge already. Begging for him to push me over, ready to fall.

"Give it to me, let go." He spreads my legs further yet with his broad shoulders and crooks his fingers inside me to reach the spot the sends me free falling into bliss.

"Hendrix." It's all I can manage as I grip on tightly to him, my body quaking with the power of my orgasm.

Before I know what's happening, he has me cradled in his arms and he's moving us through the kitchen and down the hall to my bedroom. He sits me down on the end of the bed and I drop back on my elbows, my chest heaving as I watch him strip off his shirt. It's a view I'll never tire of.

"Stop. Let me." I reach for him as he goes to undo the bottom of his jeans. I look up at him through my lashes as I blindly work the button through the hole. "Want to know what I told her?" I refuse to use her name right now, but he knows who I mean. A smirk tilts his lips up, but I continue on before he can answer.

"I told her you weren't interested, not now, not ever." I paraphrase, dragging his zipper down slowly and working his jeans over his hips. When his jeans pool around his feet, he steps out of them, and I pull him closer.

Looping my fingers into the waistband of his briefs, I toy with them. He hisses through his teeth when my fingertips brush lightly against the sensitive head of his cock.

"I told her that you're mine. That I don't share." His hands drop to my hair. His fingers shift through it as I work the briefs down enough to expose the head of his cock. It's swollen and red and a testament to how long he's been hard for me.

My tongue darts out and I swirl it around the head. "Mine, Hendrix." I say, looking up at him one last time before I push his briefs the rest of the way down and take him deeper in my mouth. He fists my hair in his hand as I drop down on his length, letting him hit the back of my throat.

"Fuck, Poppy. Yes, all yours. Only yours." His hips flex, and he pumps into my mouth, gently at first and then faster. Taking over and showing me he owns me just as much as I own him.

I hum around him, enjoying the way he's controlling my head, taking what he needs. My hands reach out toying with his balls. I run my finger along the seam, applying pressure when I reach the spot just behind his balls. He groans loudly and I feel him twitch in my mouth.

"Goddamn, that feels too good." He pulls back on my hair, forcing me to release him. "I don't want to come in your mouth right now."

"No?"

"No." His hands grip my waist, urging me up the bed further. "I want to make you come on this cock, and then I'm going to come inside that pretty pussy." He gives himself a tug as if to prove his point. "Hands and knees, Poppy. Is fast and hard okay this time? I'll give it to you nice and slow next time."

My breath hitches. It's more than okay by me. The pulse between my legs thrums harder at the suggestion. I turn around and look over my shoulder at him, smiling wickedly. He pulls a pillow from the head of the bed and stuffs it under my hips before gently pressing down on my back. The cool air hits my exposed core, sending shivers up my spine.

Covering my back with his body, Hendrix leans in. "I wish you could see the way you look right now. Like a dream. Face down, this pretty pink pussy so eager, just waiting for me to fuck you like a good girl." He kisses me roughly before notching his head at my entrance and thrusting in hard. My breath expels in a whoosh feeling him so deep. If this is his reaction to seeing me jealous, it was worth it.

His grip on my hips is bruising as he fills me up, thrusting in hard and pulsing there before pulling out and doing it all over again.

I have to grip the sheets to hold myself in place. His pace is relentless and so perfect. Each drag of his cock hitting me right where I need him most.

"Hendrix — that feels so good."

"I know. It does. You feel like mine. Every time is better than the last," he groans and my body seizes. The pressure building begs to be released. I reach a hand between my legs, strumming at my clit. The need to come is dizzying. Hendrix slams back into me and my core clenches around him when I break apart, loudly moaning as I come harder than I ever have before.

Hendrix slows his strokes and the hands on my hips curl under me pulling me up to him, so I'm sitting in his lap my back to his front. His hand trails up my stomach as he alternates palming my breast and plucking at my nipples.

"I will never get sick of this," Hendrix admits softly against the shell of my ear. "Never, you hear me?"

The admission rocks me to the core. I swallow roughly, looping my hand around the back of his neck and pulling his face to me. "Me either. It's never felt like this before. There is no one else that could make me feel the way you do."

It's the closest I've come to admitting what I know in my heart. I'm falling hard for Hendrix James. Not wanting any more words to tumble out, I drag his face down to mine and kiss him deeply.

The thought of falling for him the way I am is terrifying. He's made every effort to ensure I feel safe and protected with him, but part of me is still afraid. What if he changes his mind? Or we run into a bump in the road? Will he work thought it the way he promised, or will he shut down on me again? Leaving my heart bleeding on the floor while he walks away like last time?

My thoughts are cut short when Hendrix drops his hands to my clit, working it as he thrusts up into me. That familiar tingle pulses through me again as we kiss and rock together slowly, over, and over. I shatter for the third time. My pleasure triggers his, and Hendrix holds me tight, burying his face in my neck as he roars through his release.

We stay hunched over, me in his lap, both of us breathing hard for a moment before Hendrix uses the arms banded around my waist to drag me down to the bed, so we are laying pressed together big spoon style.

"Should we send Cindy a thank you card?" I say on a laugh, fully exhausted and maybe a bit delirious. Is orgasm delirium a thing? It is now.

Hendrix's chest vibrates behind me with rough laughter. "I think I like you jealous." His breath tickles my ear as he continues. "There's not another woman on this planet that holds a candle to you, Poppy."

I roll in his arms, so we are face to face. My finger traces the tattoo on his shoulder. "I've never understood the phrase seeing red but when she touched you — I got it. But it wasn't just jealousy. She had no right to lay her hands on you without your consent."

His jaw ticks as his teeth clench.

"Does it happen often?" My voice is soft now. Letting my anger go and focusing on how that must make him feel.

His eyes soften as he searches my face. "It happens." He is choosing his words carefully. "But not often. Had you not been there and laid down the law, I would have had the manager ask her to leave. I won't put myself in a situation that could be... misconstrued."

"Hen, I know you would never hurt me like that," I whisper softly as my fingers trace over the lines of his face.

He leans in kissing my forehead softly. "I know, but I don't want to put you in a position where you have to defend us either."

"Hey, Ironman. I'll defend you any day."

"You defending me got me so hot, Poppy."

"I noticed. I think I'm ready for it nice and slow."

His forehead drops to mine. "Yeah, baby? You want me again?"

"I always want you," I tell him as he rolls me under him and does just what he promised. He makes love to me sweet and slow before we both collapse into bed.

While Hendrix sleeps peacefully next to me, the doubts are creeping in now that the intensity of the night has faded. The voices in my head sound suspicious, like my mother. Negative and insistent that it's not the last time women are going to throw themselves at Hendrix. I won't always be there to intervene. I can distinctly hear my mother telling me to be realistic about this. I believe Hen, but no matter how hard I try to drown out the voices with my own positive thoughts about our future they don't let me rest.

x

The heat of Hendrix's body curled behind me when I wake is almost enough to make me stay in bed all morning. That and the fact that I was up half the night talking myself off the ledge. His breathing is even and measured against my back. Cautiously I shift under the weight of his arm and slip out of bed trying not to wake him.

I never heard Indie come in last night, but we crashed pretty hard after the second round. Slipping my arms through Hendrix's shirt, I shuffle into the kitchen barefoot. The door to the guest bedroom is shut, so she must have made it home at some point. Coffee is first on my agenda now that I know Indie is safely tucked into bed.

The click of the latch startles me as I measure out the coffee grinds. Turning quickly toward the front door, I see

Indie attempting to close it quietly. She turns on her toes, bending to slip her shoes off when she sees me.

She freezes in place, eyes wide like maybe she thinks if she doesn't move I won't be able to see her. I'm tempted to remind her that I'm not a dinosaur. "Morning, Indie. Have a good night?"

"Don't look at me like that, Poppy." She says, making her way across the kitchen conveniently avoiding eye contact while she grabs two coffee mugs.

"Like what?" I say, trying but failing to wipe the smirk off my face.

"Your face is all smug like — ugh never mind. You caught me," she rambles on flustered which isn't an energy Indie puts out into the world often.

"Indie, chill. You don't need to explain yourself to me. Just tell me, did you have a good time?" I move around her, grabbing a third coffee mug.

Indie pointedly looks at my discarded clothes from last night still strewn around the kitchen. "Evidently you did." She raises her eyebrow at me. "I made the right decision not to come back. You two animals couldn't even make it out of the kitchen."

I pluck my abandoned clothes off the floor and glare at her over the pile in my arms as I walk it to the hamper in the bathroom. "Deflecting. I see how it is," I call over my shoulder.

"Doesn't really matter. It's not happening again. No matter how good it was."

"Who are you trying to convince me or yourself? Maybe it's time you reconsider your rules."

The bedroom door squeaks open, and I hear Hendrix's footsteps coming down the hall. He's clad in only his jeans from last night. He combs his fingers through his messy morning hair, his muscles bunching with the movement.

"I was wondering where my shirt went." He stops in front of me and pulls me to him for a quick kiss. "Morning, Beautiful."

"Morning, Hendrix." Indie chirps in response with a smirk. Earning a chuckle from him that vibrates against my lips.

"I can go change," I say, ignoring her antics.

"No. It looks better on you." He releases me and grabs the mug Indie has extended for him. "Morning, Indie. Didn't hear you come in last night."

I snort out a laugh as Indie shoots daggers at me with her eyes. Hendrix's gaze dart between us trying to figure out what he missed. I'll keep her secret. It's not like she gave me any information to share.

Indie's lips flatten into a line, but she stays silent. Since I'm a good friend I decide to help her out and take the attention off her, "Did you find out if you'll be in town when the Bandits play in Chicago in a few weeks?"

Indie's eyes soften, thankful for the change in topic. "I won't be. I have to speak at a conference in San Francisco that week and fly out the night before you get in. But I wish I could be there. Are you still planning to talk to your parents while you're in town?"

I groan internally at the thought. This trip is giving rollercoaster vibes. I'm excited to be able to see Hendrix play in St Louis and see his family on the road trip, but I'm dreading the visit with my parents.

"Yes, that's the plan. We're going to grab dinner with them after the game." Hendrix gives my hand a squeeze, knowing the visit with my family is eating away at me.

"You'll let me know how it goes? You need to stand your ground with her. She can't keep trying to lay guilt on you for living your life. She should be proud. You've created something spectacular for yourself, both in your business and your life. You're amazing."

Indie is not being overbearing. She demands that I know my worth and hold others accountable when they mistreat me. Her insistence that I stand up for myself makes my eyes sting with tears. Everyone should be lucky enough to have a friend like her.

She's been my biggest advocate for a long time when it comes to my parents. Had it not been for Indie and her family giving me space to be my authentic self, I think my family would have stifled me into submission.

"My Uber is going to be here in forty-five minutes. I'm going to go make sure I'm packed," Indie says, setting her coffee mug in the sink.

Hendrix takes my hand leading me to the couch as Indie disappears down the hallway. Tugging me down with him he settles me into his lap so that I'm cradled against his chest. "You're not in this thing alone with your parents. You let me know how I can support you and I'll do it."

He runs his nose along my hair line sweetly as he holds me. I shift so I can hold his face between my hands. "Just be there for me. That's all you can do. I don't know how it's going to go. My mom doesn't respond well to confrontation, and she's going to take this personally." I explain with a sigh. "Let's talk about something else. I woke up next to a really sexy man this morning and this conversation is bringing me down."

"I talked to Mia yesterday. She'll be at the game in St. Louis with my grandmother. She decided to fly in for the series when she heard you would be there."

"Oh geez. No pressure on me at all." Hendrix has told me a lot about Mia, and she sounds amazing. If she's anything at all like Janet, the two of us will get along just fine. "I'm glad St. Louis is our first stop. Your family will be a great distraction from what's waiting for me in Chicago."

Hendrix brushes a light kiss on the apple on my cheek holding me tighter to him. "Whatever comes, I'll be there."

"Look at you two being all grotesquely lovey— but so cute." Indie's nose crinkles when she stops in front of the couch with her luggage trailing her.

Hendrix shifts me off his lap and stands from the couch. "I'll get out of your way while you two say goodbye. It was great meeting you, Indie." Hendrix gives her a quick hug as he passes.

"Take care of my girl," Indie says looking up at him.

"Always," Hendrix tells her before slipping out of the apartment.

CHAPTER 29

POPPY

The team plane flew in early this morning, but Lilah and I flew commercial later in the day to join Hendrix and Cruz for this away series. After we dropped our bags at the hotel, we headed out to meet up with Janet and Mia for some pregame food.

I have to lean forward over my plate to keep the juice from spilling down my shirt. "This was such a brilliant idea. These tacos are giving me life." Lilah's eyelash flutter as she savors her birria. Janet bobs her head in agreement across the table from her at a food truck we found in 9 Mile Garden.

"I'm a firm believer that the messier the taco, the better it tastes," Mia echoes mopping her chin up with a wad of paper towels. She flew in last night from North Carolina. Since there isn't a team near there, she makes it a point to come to all Hendrix's games in St Louis.

"You guys knocked it out of the park with this recommendation. What else should we do while we're in town? Aside from the games, we have down time each day after the guys report to the stadium." Janet and I have kept in touch with text messages since she came to visit last month. Mia and I haven't really had much of a chance to talk before now.

"I was hoping we could grab coffee while we were both in town and talk shop. If you're open to it?" Mia offers, and it seems like her desire to help is coming from a genuine place. That even if I wasn't dating Hendrix, she would want to help me get my footing.

Mia's personality is warm and welcoming, which isn't a surprise because it's exactly how Janet was with me as well. I know both of them were disappointed in the way Hendrix handled our situation the first time around. They went to bat for me without having known me because they wanted Hendrix to be happy.

Where Janet is a bit eccentric in all the right ways, Mia is more subtle. Her wit and humor sneak up on you, instead of being punchy and brash. The more I get to know them the more I realize what I've been missing out on. Family for me has been something you find, not something you are born into for quite some time. My family can't be relied on to fill my cup in the same way that Indie, Lilah, and now Hendrix and his family do.

They have made me feel more accepted and loved than my own parents ever have. Maybe that seems a bit dramatic. I know there are people who come from much worse family situations than myself. Knowing that doesn't lessen the emotional distress they have caused over the course of my life.

I've made it my goal to be present and focused while I'm in St Louis, soaking up all the love and kindness they're giving me instead of focusing on the upcoming dinner with my parents.

"I'd love to grab coffee, but you know you don't have to give me business advice to get me to go for coffee."

She knows this. It's not the first time I have put up a half-hearted protest against her offers to help. But I can't help but tell her again. Hendrix keeps reminding me that she wants to help, but I don't want to be an obligation, and I don't want her to feel like I'm taking advantage of her kindness.

"Poppy, don't make me tell you again. I love this shit. It's what I live for. It's my absolute favorite part of the life I've created," Mia chides.

"I know, but I can't help it. It feels too good to be true that Mia James is willing to help me. There's only so much research can tell you. Getting perspective from someone who's got real life experience in the business is invaluable. So yes to coffee, and I promise to chill and stop being a fangirl."

My rambling makes Mia laugh warmly. Her hand lands on top of mine from across the table.

"Nepotism aside, I had a mentor who helped me when I was getting started. We all deserve to have someone who believes in us. I know you can do this. I've seen the reels you have out on social media, you have the talent to narrate. You can fangirl all you want once I actually do something to help, but until then I'm just Mia, your friend."

My chest aches with emotion at her proclamation of her faith in my work. After decades of not getting support from my parents to follow my dreams, I struggle to accept it when others give it so openly.

Mia squeezes my hand and draws it back to take a bite from her taco. I take the opportunity to swallow down the emotion clogging my throat.

After putting down an impressive number of tacos we start the short walk to the stadium. Janet makes suggestions on what to do while we are here. She offers to take the three of us to the zoo because it's her favorite place in the city. That recommendation elicits a laugh from me, and I agree to go on the condition that we don't visit the serpentarium.

Hendrix and Cruz were able to get us seats behind the dugout. It was a compromise so that we could all sit together without choosing a side of the outfield to sit on and hurting someone's precious man ego. The energy in the stadium is high, and the game is a close one making it nerve-wracking to watch.

It's all tied up going into the sixth when Coach Wright pulls the pitcher off the mound. He sends Omar to the dugout and brings in Barrett to relieve him with a fresh arm. It's a smart move getting us out of the inning with no runs scored.

The first batter for the Bandits strikes out, but when Hendrix gives one a ride, sending the ball soaring over the shortstop's head for a double, the momentum shifts. Tension in the stadium rises as the top of Bandit's batting order prepares to do battle.

Cruz smiles as he steps into the batter's box, nodding at second base where Hendrix has a healthy lead off. We are all perched on the edge of our seats, Lilah and Mia clutch my hands as we wait for the pitch. The air around us is buzzing as the pitcher winds up. When the ball comes out of his hand, I hear Mia gasp, and Lilah scream, "No!" next to me. It all happens so quickly it takes me a second to process what's going on, but as soon as I do, I wrap Lilah in my arms, pulling her head into my neck.

Cruz is on the ground at the plate while the opposing catcher waves the trainer over. The crowd goes silent as they wait to see if he'll get up on his own. He lays there in the dirt unmoving as trainers and coaches surround him. When they get him standing, it's evident that he's dazed. The medical staff flanks him as they walk him off the field.

Lilah is distraught, tears streaming down her face as she tries to figure out where to go. It makes my heart ache seeing her like this. Thankfully, Janet is familiar with the stadium and jumps to take control of the situation, directing her to the family area. After having it out with the security guard and providing photographic evidence that she's Hendrix's grandmother, she's able to get Lilah back to Cruz.

When she returns, the three of us watch the rest of the game on pins and needles waiting for an update from Lilah.

CHAPTER 30

HENDRIX

My blood is pumping hot and angry through my veins when I get into the locker room following our game with the Commanders. The pitcher who hit Cruz was ejected from the game, but it did nothing to soothe my frustration. That pitch was reckless and intentional. A throw like that could have done serious damage. He could have ended Cruz's career, and the smug look on his face as he walked off the field tells me everything I need to know about Colby Miller.

The homerun I hit my next at bat helped to take the edge off, but until I hear from Cruz, there isn't much that's going to make me feel better. I rush through my shower, and Coach wisely skips over me in his selection of players to speak with the media. I'd be a liability if asked about the pitch that took Cruz out.

The sight of Poppy standing across the hall when I push through the locker room door makes the tension in my chest ease. She's flanked by my grandmother and Mia. Her head is down looking at her phone. Mia nudges Poppy lightly with her elbow when she sees me, and Poppy looks up.

Her eyes are sad, and she gives me a tight smile. I cross the hall in two quick steps, my strides eating up the space between us. Her arms open for me automatically, wrapping me up in a hug. I nuzzle into her neck, inhaling her sweet scent, trying to keep all my emotions in check.

"He's okay. Lilah went with him to the hospital. He's awake and talking. The doctor wants to keep him overnight for observation to make sure there's nothing more going on besides a concussion. She's going to stay with him until he's released."

The gratitude I feel for her getting me that update without prompting is all consuming. I knew from early on, before we figured our shit out, that Poppy had the power to own my heart completely. That was clear when being apart from her was harder than it ever was with Kylie.

The feelings I have for her have been teetering on the tip of my tongue for weeks. Tonight the words are right there trying to escape me, all because of her need to make sure I'm okay. I hold it in, but I am not sure how much longer I can contain it. All I know is the way I feel about her is like nothing else I've experienced.

"Thank you — for checking on him. For taking care of me." I cling to her hoping that she hears everything I'm feeling in my voice.

Her hands come up to my face, holding me so she can look into my eyes. "Always, Hendrix. You're mine to care for.

Why don't we all go back to the hotel and order room service instead of going out?"

I wouldn't have suggested it, not wanting to let anyone down, but I'd be miserable company if we had to go sit in a restaurant right now. I place a brief kiss on her temple and lace my fingers through hers. Mia approaches from my peripheral and wraps her arms around my middle joining our hug.

"I think that sounds perfect. Who wants to watch everyone fawn over you while we try to eat anyways? Always makes me gag."

She looks up at me from where she's tucked under my arm opposite Poppy and just gives me a grin. The one I know she reserves just for giving me a hard time.

"That sounds like the perfect plan," my grandmother chimes in, registering her vote for Poppy's suggestion.

Some of the tension leaves my body at the prospect of getting to relax in private with the three most important people in my life. We head back to the hotel together and order room service.

Instead of staying in a standard room, like I normally do, I booked a suite so that we would have room for my grandmother and Mia to hang out during down time. St. Louis was my home growing up so it's harder to go out here than a lot of other cities I travel to because I'm more recognizable. While I'll always give the fans attention, it's hard to spend time with my family when we get interrupted so frequently.

Mia and my grandmother sit on opposite ends of the loveseat. Poppy perches on my knee in the chair across from them. Wanting her close, I tug her further on to my lap. The girls talk about their plans to go to the zoo tomorrow afternoon. My feisty girl throws me an amused look when an unintended shiver escapes me at the memory of the last time I went to the zoo.

When Poppy's phone vibrates on the table next to the chair, she glances at the screen before answering the call from Lilah on FaceTime. Holding the phone so that we are both in the frame, the call connects and the image on the screen makes my arms tighten around Poppy's waist.

"Hendrix, man, I hate to tell you this, but you look like shit." A laugh husks out of my chest at my friend. His assessment isn't wrong. My hair is pointing in every direction and my eyes look tired. I do a quick appraisal of Cruz on the screen.

The pitch hit his helmet so while there's not any bruising, he looks pale and tired. His smile looks pained, and his eyes are a bit unfocused. Lilah sits next to him, curled against his side on the hospital bed. There are wires and monitors visible in the background.

"Okay, he saw you. Now turn off the FaceTime and just talk," Lilah tells him her voice soft.

"Shit, Cruz, you know better than to use a screen with a fresh concussion. You should have just called," I say as Lilah's small hand reaches out, taking the phone from him and turning off the video.

"I'll be fine, but between you and Lilah, I'm not sure who was wilder at the prospect of me being hurt."

"You didn't see that hit, Cruz. It was one of the worst I've seen," I tell him, swallowing roughly at the memory while Lilah sniffles in the background.

"Lilah said the same. I'm still waiting on testing, but it'll probably be a couple weeks on the injured reserve before I'm back."

"That fucker hit you on purpose," I say sharply, letting the anger seep into my voice. Poppy rubs my back at the sudden stiffness in my shoulders.

"Yeah, he did. He hates me."

"I hate to intrude, but Cruz needs to get some rest. You two can talk more tomorrow. Plot your revenge on that bastard. I fully support any and all repercussions, but not at the cost of Cruz's health," Lilah interjects with more conviction than she did earlier.

After we hang up, Mia catches us up on the plot for the book she started writing this week. She and Poppy finalize their plan to grab coffee in the morning. Poppy and I exchange a round of hugs with my Nana and Mia before they leave for the night. It doesn't escape my notice that my grandmother clutches onto Poppy tightly and whispers into her ear. Poppy nods and her eyes go all misty for a moment before she sucks in a deep breath and straightens up, releasing her from the hug.

Poppy and I take turns in the bathroom getting ready for bed. I'm sitting on the edge of the bed when she exits the bathroom wearing what looks like a pair of boxers but in a floral print. On top she's wearing a cropped cream lace bra top dips low, exposing the valley between her breasts.

It's not over the top sexy, which makes it even hotter, completely Poppy, casual and cool. Never trying too hard but always outshining the rest. She stops leaning against the door frame; the light forming a glowing halo behind her in the dark room. Her normally bright green eyes look darker, and her pupils are blown wide as she looks at me like I'm the only thing she sees.

Her eyes glide over me and her tongue darts out to wet her bottom lip. The sight of her was enough to make me hard, but the way her eyes are alight with desire as she openly devours me causes my cock to grow even harder. I can't take my eyes off her.

"If you keep looking at me like that, Poppy, I'm not sure I can be held accountable for my actions." My hand grips the base of my cock squeezing it through my briefs because right now my self-control is slipping quickly.

"Normally I'm all for you taking the lead, but let me take care of you tonight." Her voice is sultry and raw.

She pushes off the door frame and drags her fingertips lightly over my thighs as she passes, eliciting goose bumps in their wake. Looking over my shoulder, I follow her path as she saunters around the bed to where her suitcase sits on the floor. She squats down to riffle through it, giving me a decadent view of her round ass peeking out the bottom of her shorts.

"Something I can help you find over there?" My voice comes out strained as I watch her stand. She has a deep purple satiny bag dangling from her fingertips. The sight of it draws a groan deep from my chest. I've seen that bag before. She pulled it from her nightstand during a video call while I was on the road a few weeks ago.

I could have died a happy man that night. She propped her phone up and showed me several of her toys, letting me pick which she used and how. Then she spread her legs and fucked herself with a shiny silver bullet.

The view of her coming undone as I gave her instructions on how to use it and when to turn it up or down almost overshadows the other part of the conversation that night. The look on Poppy's face, as she crawls across the bed toward me, lets me know she's thinking of it too.

"You remember what we talked about that night? How I explained in detail what I wanted to do to you with this vibrator?" She brings her chest to my back and kneels so that her elbows are resting on my shoulders as she reaches around me, holding the bag in front of my face. The movement causes her hard nipples to drag across my back through the thin fabric of her bra.

"I can confidently confirm that was a night I'll never forget. But hearing you talk so boldly about how you would use that to — what were your words? Oh, that's right, make me come so hard I temporarily go blind." I recall as I watch her delicate hands work the bag open.

She chuckles against my ear at the recollection of that memory. Her hand dips into the bag and she pulls out the sleek silver vibrator before flicking it on and trailing it over my collarbone and down around each nipple. The vibrations are gentle on the lowest setting, and she keeps the contact light and teasing.

"You think you can handle it?" Poppy asks as her mouth works along the side of my neck kissing and nipping at the skin there.

"Fuck yes." The words rumble out of me, and I am not even sure if I'm answering her question or reacting to the way she's taking charge.

She stays behind me but drops down, so her legs are straddling my ass and hips. It's equal parts infuriating and hot. I grasp on to the only contact I can control and run my hands along her bare legs. Poppy drops the bag off to the side and brings the bullet down the center of my stomach, causing my abs to bunch at the sensation.

"Your body is such a turn on. I'm not sure if I've ever told you how sexy you are. That first time I saw you running without your shirt on, I was checking you out before I realized who you were. These tattoos — they get me so hot. I want to worship this body so thoroughly that I memorize every inch of it."

As she tells me this, her fingernails drag over the tattoo on my ribs, and she drops a wet kiss on the opposite shoulder where my other tattoo sits. Her slender fingers wrap around the shaft of the bullet, and she holds her knuckles against the head of my cock, letting me feel the vibration through her fingers.

I screw my eyes closed and push my fingers into the flesh of her thighs. There are so many sensations happening at once. Her hand tracing my skin reverently, the emotion she sparks in me, the heat of her body against my back, her hair tickling me with every move she makes and the vibrations as she teases me, not being able to see or really touch her. It's over stimulating and not nearly enough all at once. Sweat beads on my chest as body turns into a throbbing, tingling mess of contrasting sensations.

"God — Fuck. Poppy, baby. I need..."

My words are cut off by the moan ripped from my throat when she moves the vibrator to my balls and holds it there.

"Tell me what you need, Hendrix." Her voice is husky, as she casually repeats the words I have used on her so many times. She can try to appear calm, but I can feel her rocking against me from behind, searching for friction of her own.

"You fuck — I need you." I don't care what form that comes in at this point. I reach around behind me and pull her around my body, moving her onto my lap.

Fuck yes.

This is where I need her, where I can look in her eyes and see everything I feel for her reflected back at me like a mirror.

Her hands come to my chest, and she pushes on my chest laying me flat on the bed. She's frantic as she pushes my briefs down and hovers above me to get rid of her shorts. Poppy needs me as much as I need her, fully and completely.

She shimmies up the bed, crashing her mouth against mine in a kiss. Her fingers drag through my hair tugging on the strands. When her tongue slides against mine, she grinds her slick center down on my cock. She rocks against me with a vibrator buzzing against her clit. The dual sensations of her heat enveloping me as she takes what she needs and the subtle hum of the vibrator are almost too much. I'm gone for this girl and for what she's doing to me. There's no one else on this planet that will ever stack up to her.

"Poppy — fuck, baby. Please tell me your close," I whimper holding on to her hips and guiding her over my length again. She's so wet and it does something to my ego that I do that to her.

Poppy just hums in response and gives me a wicked smile before she turns the vibrator up. The increased intensity causes my dick to twitch. Jesus — fuck, at this pace there is no way I'm going to outlast her.

Fucking finally, she takes the bullet from between us, giving me a reprieve from the added sensation. She lifts up on her knees and slides the vibrator inside her before bringing it to her clit and repeating the motion several times. My hands slide up her thighs and along the planes of her stomach to her breasts. I pluck her rosy nipples between my fingers, enraptured by her as she starts to tense above me.

"More, I need more. I need you to fuck me. Please." Her voice breaks as she pleads with me.

"Mmmm…. I love the sound of you begging but I could never deny you, Poppy. Keep that hot little toy pushed right up against your clit and use my cock."

Her mouth falls open in a silent moan as she lowers herself on to me.

A train could come through the wall of this room, and I wouldn't notice. Poppy is a masterpiece moving on top of me, her head tossed back as she moves slowly.

"I love the way you fill me up. It's like you were made just for me. Everything's better with you. Everything," Poppy chants as her breathing picks up and her hand stills holding the vibrator in place as it clamps down on me. Squeezing me so tight, it triggers my own release to thunder down my spine without warning.

I pull her close and kiss her mouth, rolling us to the side as she works through the aftershocks of her orgasm. I flip the vibrator off and set it aside. Everything in me is screaming to tell Poppy how I feel about her, but I know she's not ready yet. My beautiful girl is still dealing with the battle wounds left behind by Paul and her parents.

"Fuck. That was — you are unbelievable. A work of art. I am the luckiest bastard in the entire universe."

Her hands knit around the back of my neck and pulls my mouth to her for a kiss. The kiss is slow and deep, her tongue meets mine in languid strokes. She pulls away but just barely and whispers against my lips. Her words are quiet and her eyes vulnerable.

"Make love to me, Hendrix." I was serious when I said there was nothing I wouldn't give to her, and I don't want to deny her this either.

I roll Poppy under me, and we kiss lazily, our hands roaming everywhere before I give her exactly what she asked for because I do love her. She owns me absolutely and there's nothing on this planet that could keep me from pouring that feeling into her even though she's not ready to hear the words.

CHAPTER 31

POPPY

Hendrix's forearms rest against the hotel room wall, framing my head on both sides. He has me caged in next to the door as he looks down at me seriously, his lips drawn in a tight line. Mia is waiting in the lobby to get coffee with me before we meet Janet for our day exploring the zoo.

"I can't believe she's taking you to the zoo. You're not going to go into the snake house, right?" It's adorable how his irrational fear is so at odds with his physical presence. Especially the way he's looming over me right now, all domineering and strong.

"If it'll make you happy I'll skip the snake house." My hands run up his bare chest, tracing the outline of his tattoo. The feel of his skin beneath my fingers is distracting and my tongue darts out to wet my lips. It's all the invitation he needs.

Hendrix drops his lips to mine in a possessive kiss. Leaning forward, he covers my body with his so there's nowhere for me to go. I'm breathless when he pulls back with a sly grin on his face. "What did my grandmother whisper to you last night?"

"Aren't you nosy. Go take your nap. I'll see you at the stadium. If you play well maybe I'll tell you later tonight." I push against his chest to create some space before I skip the coffee and zoo all together and hop back into bed with him.

Mia is lounging casually on one of the lobby couches, scrolling through her phone. She looks up as I cross the lobby and her whole face lights up in a welcoming smile.

"Are you ready to talk about the book business? There's a great coffee shop down the road. It's one of my favorites when I'm here. We can grab a quiet corner and talk."

"Thank you again for taking the time to help me," I say, and Mia glares at me over her shoulder as I follow her to the door.

Stopping once we are on the sidewalk, she turns to face me. Her eyes are soft and warm, but she pops her hip out and huffs.

"Poppy, this is the last time I want to tell you this. I'm happy to help you any way I can. Even if it weren't for how head over heels my brother is for you, I love this part of my job."

The bit about her brother being head over heels for me diverts me for a moment but compartmentalize it to deal with the topic at hand.

"I know, Mia. I'm not good at accepting help like this. I didn't grow up in a home that fostered my creativity — or really anything outside of the life my parents had mapped out. Your family is so openly supportive, and aside from my friends, it's not something I'm used to. It makes me feel all squirrely."

It's never easy to verbalize the ways my parents dismissed my dreams and spirit. It always sounds whiny to my own ears. My physical needs were met. I had a safe home with food, shelter, and clothes. Emotionally, they didn't abuse me, but they didn't accept me for me. They were continually trying to smooth out my rough edges and shape me into a version of myself that better fit their expectations for what my life should look like.

Mia's lips turn into a frown and her brows knit together. She drops her hand down on my shoulder and gives it a gentle squeeze.

"I'm sorry you had to go through that. Everyone deserves to have a space where they can be their authentic selves."

I take her at face value and drop it instead of pointing out that I shouldn't complain. She was abandoned by her parents, and I'm complaining about the way I was raised.

"Head over heels? Really?" I ask, bumping her with my shoulder as we continue walking.

"Totally, but don't act like you can't tell. My brother looks at you like you are his favorite baseball glove but with boobs." Her unexpected words cause me to snort with uncontrollable laughter.

While I recover from my outburst, we grab a set of armchairs in the back corner after we order our coffee from the hipster barista. Mia jumps right in with questions about my recording setup and who I've reached out already to try to get a sense of where I'm at while we wait for our orders to be called out. I gush about the way her brother surprised me by setting up the audio booth. She beams when I talk about him and what that meant to me.

"It sounds like you have a solid plan already. There are some ways I think we can get you some additional exposure. Build up your brand and get you in front of some indie authors who are looking for narrators."

"What's the best way to do that? My strengths are going to be on the social media side. I know how to build a brand there. What else should I be doing?" I ask, working through my nerves and just focusing on receiving the help she's offering.

"I love what you are doing with your TikTok posts and reels. Don't change that at all, the weekly thirst trap Thursday is brilliant. Who would have thought reading innocuous passages from well-known books and making them sound dirty could be so entertaining?"

Mia scrolls through her phone, pulling up last week's thirst trap Thursday reel as a barista sets our order down.

"This one was my favorite," she says turning her phone so I can see a clip of myself narrating my top five favorite innuendos you didn't know were innuendos from Harry Potter books.

"I had way too much fun recording that one," I admit as she takes the phone back.

"I just shared it in my stories. Potterheads everywhere need widespread access to this goodness. Please tell me you have more planned out."

I nod and we put our heads together to work on a plan to help target indie writers. Mia gives me a list of authors to follow and connect with. She talks me through the platforms she used to find narrators when she was early in her career.

What stuck out about their bios and demos for when I create mine. I take notes on my phone like a mad woman while we talk.

By the time we leave to meet Janet, my to-do list is a mile long, which is a great thing. Our conversation left me feeling energized, which isn't something I've felt in my career for a while now.

We find Janet chatting up a distinguished looking zoo employee near the front gates when we arrive. Mia and I quickly realized that she has a full zoo itinerary planned out for us, starting with this giant rum smoothie inside a hollowed-out pineapple.

Hendrix's grandmother lives by the motto "It's five o'clock somewhere." She applies it to all areas of life. It's never too early for a drink, to pick up a guy, or to have fun. Her zest for life is impressive. Every time I see her, I end up with sore cheeks from laughing.

"I told you these were the perfect way to start our day. A little sugar, a little booze. If we would have waited until later in the day they would have melted in the heat," Nana says.

Mia rolls her eyes halfheartedly at her grandmother's justification of our day drinking. "Always looking out for us, Nana." Mia slurps on her smoothie, the umbrella in the drink hiding her smirk.

"Who's ready to see the tortoises? They're my favorite, always so frisky. Have you ever heard a tortoise when it's mating, Poppy? Once in a lifetime experience."

"Oh. My. God. Nana, you can't say things like that when someone is drinking. I almost snorted rum. Have a little decorum."

I sputter through a coughing fit, caught unprepared for the abrupt change in topic to animal mating rituals. Mia is laughing as she pats my back.

"Mia, don't be ridiculous, it's nature. That's why it's called the birds and the bees." Janet waves her hand at Mia like her chiding is absurd.

"I'm well aware. Did Hendrix tell you about my first date?" Mia gives the back of Janet's head a glacial glare as we continue to follow her through the zoo to the next exhibit. I shake my head still recovering from the pineapple smoothie up my nose.

"She took us to the zoo and chaperoned. She dragged Bennet and me from animal to animal telling us 'interesting facts' about their mating habits, birthing practices, and gestational periods."

"You didn't," I chastise Janet.

"I may be a modern woman, but I'm not stupid. I didn't need to raise a great-grandchild while I still had grandchildren in my house. Besides, it worked, didn't it?"

"It worked all right. Bennet broke up with me the next day and after the duck exhibit, I've never looked at a corkscrew the same way again."

"That boy was a tool. I did you a favor." Janet stops in front of the tortoise exhibit, pointing over at the corner excitedly. "Just in time, Poppy."

"What is that ungodly noise? Is that —"

"It's what you think it is, and I have never been happier not to be a tortoise." Mia grumbles while taking a long drink from her smoothie.

CHAPTER 32

POPPY

The flight from St. Louis to Chicago is the worst flight of my life. I'm a nervous wreck, and Hendrix has to hold my hand to keep me from fidgeting. All I can focus on is the impending dinner with my parents.

My mom and I've talked a few times since her text messages insisting Hendrix and I come to them. She went as far as to suggest that I skip the game and come by myself, insinuating that meeting Hendrix wasn't a big deal because the relationship wouldn't last. I almost canceled but after talking it over with Hendrix he convinced me not to. I know he's right — this conversation needed to happen a long time ago.

But the nerves had me considering not even going to the game. Lilah won't be there to watch with me. She flew home with Cruz after he was released from the hospital to make sure he's okay.

Hendrix would be fine if I stayed back at the hotel, but it would only make my nerves worse sitting there alone stewing. While Hendrix naps before his game, I grab my laptop and head down to the hotel bar to work on outreach to the list of contacts Mia gave me. The work calms me enough that the tension leaves my shoulders. Hendrix has been adjusting his schedule and routine to make things easier for me and though he doesn't seem to mind, I'm trying to limit the interruptions to his routine while I travel with him as much as possible.

Warm hands come down on my shoulders, I don't need to turn around to know it's Hendrix. His scent surrounds me as he leans in to kiss my temple.

"Did you get some work done?" he asks, lips moving against my skin.

"I did. Your naptime was very productive for me. When I decided to make the switch to narration, I didn't realize how much I needed it. I didn't hate my job, but it was just that, a job. The work I'm doing now makes me feel energized. I think this was always the path I was meant to take."

He turns my barstool around so I'm facing him and tips my chin up to look at him. When I look into his stunning blue eyes, they're filled to the brim with admiration.

"You are incredible. I'm proud of you for going after your dreams and can't wait to see you exceed your wildest expectations."

"Your confidence in me means everything, Ironman. Aside from Lilah or Indie, I'm not used to having people blindly believe in me." I admit, linking my fingers through his. "Do you need to get to the stadium?"

"Mhmm… but I have something to show you first." he says pulling me toward him and off the stool. Reaching around me, he grabs my laptop and leads me out of the bar to the hotel lobby without further explanation.

There sitting on one of the lobby couches is Mia. She looks pleased with herself when she sees my mouth drop open in disbelief.

"What. Why?" I stutter out. Feeling the bridge of my nose tingle with emotion. I can't believe that they would do this for me. I take a deep breath, working to keep myself from toppling over the rim of my emotions. This whole time I've been holding myself back, unwilling to let myself fall completely, but this might be the thing that breaks me.

He owned up to his mistakes and shared his pain with me. He's given up his time and sacrificed his routine to make sure I'm taken care of. Now this. Mia is here for me because he knew I needed the company today. Hendrix doesn't just give me all of himself. He has created this family around me of people who go out of their way to make sure I'm okay. It's not something I ever thought I would have.

"You've been so anxious about Chicago. With Cruz getting injured and Lilah having to go home unexpectedly, I didn't want you to be alone during the game. Mia doesn't get to enough of my games as it is, so she was excited to switch her flights around to keep you company." He brushes a loose strand of hair off my face; his voice is warm and filled with compassion. It's like the gentle caress of a feather over my skin as he talks, lighting up every cell in my body with deep unabating admiration for him.

"You continue to amaze me, Hendrix James. If you're not careful, you'll turn me into a spoiled brat with all these gestures." Looking over his shoulder, Mia stays put on the couch giving us space, but a small smile tips up her lips. "Thank you," I mouth over Hendrix's shoulder at Mia who nods subtly.

"You deserve everything I can give you. I know I screwed up early on, but I'll never stop working to make that up to you. To show you how I feel about you." His deep blue eyes bore into my soul like they see every part of me. It's intense but I don't shy away from it. I open myself up and take it in, relishing in the way his devotion makes me feel. He makes me feel whole again.

"You are a good man, Hendrix. I've always known that even when I didn't like you much." Pushing up on my toes, I weave my hands around the nape of his neck and pull him to me to push our lips together in a sweet kiss.

"I'll see you at the game." His words and his actions are at odds with his hands tight around my waist and holding me close. Even though he is saying goodbye, he's not letting go.

"Yes, you will. I'll be the one in the James jersey cheering my face off for my amazing boyfriend." My voice is infused with mirth as I try to redirect his focus to the game tonight instead of worrying about me. Having Mia here is a huge relief for me. Hendrix probably doesn't even fully grasp what a gift he's given me, opening his family up to me when mine is such a sore spot.

Hendrix releases me from his grip before wrapping his sister up in his strong arms for a hug. He whispers in her ear, and she nods, her eyes darting to me for a moment.

CHAPTER 33

POPPY

Propping myself against the cool brick wall, I scroll through my phone waiting for Hendrix to finish in the locker room. Between the fast-paced game, and Mia, I stayed preoccupied keeping my nerves under control. Now that I'm standing here alone, my stomach is churning with tension.

I had my phone notifications silenced during the game, but I saw several messages from my mom come through despite my best efforts to ignore them. My eyes roll as I read through the missed texts. None of them are necessary and all of them are biting. Without saying it, her passive aggressive texts tell me she's still not pleased with having to come into the city.

Hendrix was willing to make the two-and-half-hour drive to my hometown, but he has a doubleheader tomorrow and I didn't want to put him in that position. I groan as we aren't even at the restaurant yet and she is already disappointed with me.

The door to the locker room swings open and Hendrix strides toward me. His dark hair is still damp from his shower. Even seeing him approach me has my pulse jumping and I don't think he has a clue how deeply he affects me. He looks downright edible in a pair of dark jeans and a button down.

He stares at me intensely, eyes scanning me like he is looking for something amiss to indicate that I am falling apart.

"How are you holding up?" His rough knuckles rub over my cheekbone. His concern is written all over his face, and it causes my chest to crack open.

"I could lie and tell you I'm fine. But you wouldn't believe it anyways. Those intense blue eyes see right through me." I let out a shaky breath at the prospect of leaving this stadium. "Having Mia here was just what I needed. She got me through the afternoon without a nervous breakdown. I owe both —"

Hendrix cuts me off with a brush of his lips against mine. My eyes widen, caught off guard before I grip his shirt and pull him to me, melting into his warm embrace. We have kissed countless times, but each press of his lips on mine sends that same current of energy through my body as it did the very first time.

"You owe me nothing, Poppy." His voice is firm, leaving no room for argument, so I just nod accepting what he did for me.

"Let's get this over with."

Hendrix leads me through the stadium exit, and we walk to the restaurant. He tries to distract me with questions about my day and talking about the game, but my answers are short and unfocused. Instead of calling me out on it, he just keeps talking and doing everything he can to put me at ease.

I picked a lowkey Italian place that Hendrix recommended because it's my mom's favorite. Coming right from the game, I was careful not to pick anything too fancy, knowing that I wouldn't be able to change before dinner. I still decided to wear a black sundress under my jersey so that I could slip it off after the game and I wouldn't be too casual. I'm sure it will still be a topic of discussion tonight.

It's exhausting managing all my mom's expectations. Being around her feels like walking across broken glass, carefully trying to pick your way through while sustaining the least amount of damage.

When we get to the restaurant, the hostess directs us to a booth in the back corner. Thank God for small miracles, at least the set up provides privacy. As the hostess leads us around the partition, I see my parents beat us here.

Fuck, that means we're late.

"Mom, Dad, this is Hendrix. Hendrix, these are my parents —"

My mom's sharp voice cuts in, stopping my introduction. "Barbara and Franklin. Nice of you to join us, Poppy. Traffic was an absolute nightmare, but I knew it would be. We had to leave an hour early, and we still had to park blocks away." Her lips press into a thin line, making her typically beautiful face look severe.

My hand squeezes Hendrix's like it's my lifeline. To his credit, he doesn't even flinch — not at the way I'm squeezing his finger so hard I am sure the tips are white and not with the scathing commentary from my mom. To everyone else he looks calm as can be, but I feel him tense at her words.

"We really appreciate you making the drive to the city. My game schedule made things tricky, but I've been looking forward to meeting both of you." Hendrix says, pulling out my chair as he smiles across the table at my parents. God bless his media training and his kind heart. He's trying so hard to smooth things over, like it will make a difference.

"I'm surprised you picked this place, Poppy. Have you seen the menu? So many carbs. With that dress on it's going to show every bite," my mom says with a click of her tongue like I didn't pick this place based on her preferences. My dress flares at the waist. It's not snug at all around my stomach and if it were, I wouldn't care. I'd rather have a food baby than an empty stomach.

Out of the corner of my eye, I see Hendrix's hand grip the arm of his chair tightly. He keeps his face schooled, but I can tell he caught that dig and he's biting his tongue.

"I understand you play baseball?" my dad interjects with the change of topic. Never one to cause a scene, it's his go to method for redirecting my mother's criticisms. He's as conflict averse as they come and not willing to take sides between his daughter and his wife. I've always found him cold and detached like he doesn't know quite what to do with me.

Hendrix nods, no longer faking a big smile to smooth things over. I can see the turmoil bubbling beneath the surface, making him prickle with discomfort. I know it well. It's those same feelings my parents trigger in me.

"I do. I play outfield for the Denver Bandits. I was traded to the team this year from Los Angeles. It's how Poppy and I met. We have mutual friends associated with the team." He glances at me, granting me a warm smile.

"We don't really follow sports," my mother adds looking disinterested in the conversation as she glances over her menu. "How does that work with college? Did you just skip getting an education?"

She doesn't even try to hide her judgment, and it's wild considering she didn't go to college and put up a fuss about me going to college. She subscribes to very traditional gender roles. Man supports woman. Women raise children and serve their husband. In her mind, she has already decided that Hendrix is a jock and nothing more.

"I played three years of college ball and finished my degree in the minors. I was a double major in kinesiology and biology. Baseball can be a really uncertain career, so I wanted to have a degree to fall back on, but baseball has worked out pretty well."

The waiter comes to take our orders, and I'm relieved to have the short break from the interrogation. Hendrix pours me a glass of wine and I want to kiss him for it. I need the fortification to get through this. I still have a lot to say to my parents tonight. My mom needs to understand my boundaries, and it's going to go over like a fart in church.

When the waiter leaves, my mom launches into a story about her bible study the other day. I'm lulled into a false sense of security at the seemingly pleasant conversation.

"...Julie Barton was there, and do you know what she told me?"

No, and I don't care but I'd bet it was about her son.

"No idea, Mom." I say, dreading the direction I can feel this going. We may not even make it through appetizers if she suggests what I think is coming.

"Eddie was asking his mother about you."

My hands come down on the table hard, rattling the wine glasses and startling everyone. There is no way I'm going to let her suggest that I should be with Eddie in front of Hendrix. The disrespect to us and our relationship alone is enough to set me off, but the guy is a certified creep.

"Mom, don't. We talked about this." Hendrix's hand lands on top of mine, slowly stroking the skin. My gaze drops to where they're joined.

"Sweetie, don't be so dramatic. It's not like he's going to move to Illinois to be with you." She waves her hand toward Hendrix dismissively. His hand freezes and his brows furrow in confusion. I can feel the heat crawling up my neck in splotchy red spots as the anger boils over.

"Hendrix," I assert through gritted teeth. "Not 'he.' His name is Hendrix."

My dad looks between us nervously and clears his throat, slipping his finger under the collar of his shirt like he needs some extra room to breathe.

"And Hendrix doesn't need to move to Illinois to be with me. I have no intention of leaving Colorado to move back home. Not ever," I spit out the last words. Sick of this conversation.

"Don't be ridiculous. You can't keep playing this game. You need to start thinking about settling down and getting serious with someone you can make a life with. We've stood by as you got this phase out of your system but you're not a child anymore it's time to stop playing pretend." She levels a pitying smile at Hendrix. And I snap. Anger and hurt vibrates over my skin. I go to stand from the table, but Hendrix's grip on my hand holds me in place. My gaze darts to him and I'm met with a steely mask of barely contained rage on his face.

"What's wrong with the life Poppy has built, Barb?" His voice is cold and deadly low. I have only heard him sound like this one other time, when he thought I was cheating on him. The air changes around us, sparking with discord, but it doesn't faze my mom.

"It's Barbara, and I meant no disrespect to you. I just don't see how the two of you think this is going to work. Poppy, he's a professional athlete. Those kinds of men don't build stable family homes. Someone like —"

"Disrespect me. That's what you think this is about? That I'm offended because of your opinion of me?"

My gaze ping pongs back and forth between them. I open my mouth to speak but I'm not quick enough.

"Sorry, Barbara, but I think you are confused. Your opinion of me doesn't even register on my radar. Let me tell you a few things about your daughter that you have obviously missed over the years. She has worked hard to build her own life. She's bright and determined. For years, she has success-fully run her own company that provided her with a stable income."

My eyes widen at the topic of my career choice. I have provided the bare minimum details regarding my career choices to my parents over the years. Hendrix's eyes soften when he sees the panic written across my features.

"She's self-aware and emotionally intelligent. She launched a brand new business, recognizing that the other was no longer fulfilling her. Poppy has a kickass group of friends that love and support her. She is the funniest person I've ever met and kinder than I deserve."

My dad may as well have crawled under the table at this point for the way he's hiding behind his hands. My mom's mouth opens and closes at Hendrix's declaration, like she's at a loss for words. I have to stifle a laugh, not because it's funny, but because it's a first. I've never seen her speechless before.

"If Poppy wants to move back to Illinois and buy a house with a white picket fence to stay home and pop out my babies, all she has to do is say the word. I'll request a trade and call a moving van myself."

My head whips to Hendrix, but he's not looking at my mom anymore. His attention is on me, and his features are relaxed now as he talks to me now. I have to swallow down the emotion, not willing to let it burst free and be tainted by this dinner — by this interaction with my parents.

"But I know your daughter — better than most." The remark is cutting and directed at my parents, his fierce protectiveness renewed.

"I think that's enough," my mom says trying to regain control of the situation, but I'm not willing to let that happen.

"No, Mom. It's not even close to enough. Hendrix is right. He understands me more than you and Dad ever have. Not that either of you really tried. You just kept trying to fit me in the box you had picked out for my life and when I didn't fit, you'd just shove a little harder. But I'm done."

My dad's face falls at that and for the first time ever, I see him look at my mother and shake his head calling off her next attack.

"Stop it, Barbara. That's enough."

Those five words are the most he's ever defended me and instead of being happy that he's finally coming to my defense I'm sad. Sad that it took this long. Sad that it took Hendrix to show him how. Sad that it's only those five words. I shake my head, trying to clear the grief and focus on what I need to say.

Hendrix's hand makes soft circles on my back, encouraging me to continue with just the warmth and comfort of his touch. Letting me speak my piece, knowing that I need to do this for myself.

"You will respect my decision not to move home. You will not speak to Hendrix like that ever again, and you will respect my relationship with him and not push other men on me. Most importantly, you will treat me with respect. That means you will not make snide remarks about my career, what I eat, who I spend my time with, or anything else. If you cannot manage to learn how to be a supportive, uplifting presence in my life, then you are no longer welcome in it."

When I'm done, I inhale deeply feeling lighter than I have in years. Hendrix pulls out his wallet and drops cash on the table to cover the bill before looking at both my parents and shaking his head.

Unable to bite his tongue any longer, he narrows his eyes, giving them a look that leaves my panties damp. "The two of you need to get your heads out of your asses. Your daughter is amazing. She gave me a second chance not that long ago and I took it. I won't hurt her again. I hope the two of you do the same, but if you don't, I will love her hard enough for the both of you because she deserves to know unconditional love."

Hearing his passionate plea to my parents and the conviction in his voice when he promises to give me the love they refuse makes me swoon so hard that I can barely stand on my shaky knees. More than anything, I just want to get out of here. I want Hendrix alone. If there was any doubt before, this dinner wiped that out. I love Hendrix James with every part of who I'm. I am certain he is it for me. No one else can make me feel this complete.

CHAPTER 34

HENDRIX

Poppy leads me out of the restaurant in a haze from my fury over how her parents could treat their daughter so coldly. I have to focus on steady breaths to try to calm my rapid pulse and ticking jaw. She stops abruptly on the sidewalk when we are a few paces from the entrance to the restaurant and launches herself at me.

I catch her in my arms before she presses her lips to mine and locks her hand around my head, holding me there. I relax under her kiss. When she pulls away, she takes my hand and starts walking again without explanation.

I'm grateful for the silence. I can't bring myself to regret anything I said, including that I would love Poppy unconditionally because I meant every word of it. There was no scenario where I envisioned that I would tell her I love her for the first time in the midst of a major argument with her parents.

"Do you mind if I grab a car? We can walk if you would prefer." My offer to walk is half-hearted. After that shit-show, I just want to get Poppy alone. Check her over and make sure she's okay.

She may not have bruises from that battle, but it's hard to believe it hasn't left a mark. It had to be traumatic for her to cut her parents off until they change their behavior. It was for me, and I was abandoned by my mom as a toddler, so I'm used to fucked up family dynamics.

"Yes, I just want to get back to the hotel. I'm not really in the mood for a walk right now." Her eyes aren't filled with the sadness I expect to see there. She just looks tired, and a bit resigned to the outcome of the evening.

Taking Poppy's hand, I lead her around the corner, giving us some cover from the front door of the restaurant. The last thing she needs right now is for her parents to come out and find us standing on the sidewalk. Pulling her into my side, I order a car and hold her while we wait for the driver to pull up.

The ride back is quiet. Poppy stays tucked against me for the short ride to the hotel and up the elevator to our room. When the hotel room door slides closed with a snick behind us, I pull Poppy to my chest and bury my nose in her hair.

The scent of lavender and honey soothes my frayed nerves that are still raw from the confrontation earlier. She's been remarkably quiet since we left her parents sitting slack jawed at the table. Now that we are alone in the hotel, the quiet is unnerving. I have so much I want to say to her and if I'm not careful, it's all going to come pouring out before I can make sure she's good. The rest of it can wait. My feelings for Poppy aren't going anywhere.

Poppy's delicate hands run up the planes of my chest before her fingers find their way into the hair at the nape of my neck. Her nails scrape the base of my skull. It feels like heaven, but everything with her feels that way. Notching my knuckles under her chin, I tip her head up to look at me.

"Poppy, talk to me. Are you okay?"

Her head tilts to the side slightly as she considers me. My girl is resilient, so I don't expect her to crumble but the entire night is a lot to unpack between her parents, my declaration, and her cutting them out. She exhales a shaky breath, but doesn't falter in her response.

"I'm just really fucking glad it's over. Their expectations and judgments have been weighing on me for so long, it feels good to finally be rid of them. I wish I would've done it sooner. Maybe they'll come around, maybe they won't. I'll be fine either way. Do you know why?"

I search her bright green eyes, looking for any indication that she's burying her feelings. She pushed the baggage that is her parents down and buried it so deep for years, so I want to be certain that she's not just saying that. I don't see even a hint of lingering sadness in her eyes. They just look warm and open like the promise of spring blooming the forest.

"No, but I want you to tell me. Don't hide it from me. Whatever you're feeling, let me carry some of that burden for you."

"Hendrix, I appreciate that, but it was beyond time for that to happen. Every conversation with my mom left me emotionally drained for days afterwards. And my dad was so checked out that I don't remember what it feels like to have a relationship with him. Sure, I feel sad that it had to happen, but I feel overwhelmingly lucky."

My hands tighten around her waist, the resentment toward her parents flaring up in a physical response to her words, but I keep quiet giving her space to continue. The last thing Poppy needs is me inserting my feelings into her emotional turmoil.

"I'll be okay — No, more than okay. The life I've built for myself is beautiful and I'm thriving.. I have friends like Lilah and Indie that have stuck by me and showered me with love through it all. Because I have you. The connection we had from the beginning was intense and I think a part of me always knew that you were mine. That's why it hurt so bad when you pushed me away, but we never really gave up on each other — even when we were hurting. You came back fighting for me and you have shown me what it's like to love someone the way it's meant to be. Wholly and completely."

Fuck, she's amazing; I'm in awe of her. A situation that would have left most people in a heap of tears and anger, and Poppy is making her own silver lining. She's holding the power and refusing to hand it over to her parents, who certainly don't deserve to wield it over her any longer.

Her throat bobs up and down with emotion and I take advantage of her pause because I can't hold it back any longer. Pushing a loose hair behind her ear, I tilt my head down looking into her stunning green eyes because I don't want her to doubt a single word I'm about to say to her.

"I am so proud of you for setting boundaries with them like that. You are the strongest, most resilient person I have ever met. I'm so grateful you gave me that second chance because it changed my life forever. I can't imagine a world where I don't get that chance because it's too dark. The idea that I would have never gotten to be with you and love you causes me physical pain to even think about."

She blinks back at me, her teeth running over her bottom lip.

"I love you, Poppy. You are it for me. Every word I said to your parents was true. I'll make it my life's work to show you what unconditional love should feel like. I'll never let you question if you're enough again."

My forehead drops to hers. I've known for weeks that I was in love with Poppy and finally saying it out loud makes me feel like I could do anything. She pushes up on her toes and kisses the corner of my mouth tenderly before pulling back to look at me.

"I love you too. No one has ever gone to bat for me like that before, but I knew before you stood up for me with them that you and I were meant to be together. You own my whole heart, Hendrix James, and I wouldn't want it any other way."

My lips drop to Poppy's, and I kiss her with all the love I feel for her. I need to be close to her right now. She opens for me and our tongues slide together as my hands slide down to her ass and lift her up. She wraps her legs around me and I carry her across the room in a few fast strides to the bed.

Poppy's hands trail down her body, taking a leisurely path. One that is much too slow for my liking right now. When her hands finally grip the hem of her dress, she tugs it over her head in one smooth motion. I stare down at her reverently as she lays on the bed in front of me, letting the sight of her, and this moment sink into my bones. Committing it to memory, the way she looks, the way I feel.

"The other night at the hotel in St Louis, your grand-mother told me she knew from the moment she met me I was the right person for you. And that I could love you with the same loyalty and devotion that you loved me with. I promise to love you all in, the same wonderful way you love me. To be your partner, your equal, to push you to be better. Because that's what you do for me. You have given me so much more than a significant other. You gave me a sense of family, one that I never had at home."

My eyes roam over her, memorizing the way I feel for her, and the way she looks laying there open and vulnerable with love for me, as I work the buttons on my shirt open.

"Fuck, Poppy, I'm never going to forget this moment. You are so beautiful, so mine. I love you." I hardly recognize my voice; it comes out raspy and filled to the brim with emotion.

"Come show me."

She crooks her finger, beckoning me closer with a sly smile and a twinkle in her eyes. I want to live in this moment with her forever. I shrug off my shirt and push my pants down. Loving her might be the greatest thing I do with my life.

Poppy pushes herself up off the bed, and I mirror her movements, hovering over her as we go. Her coppery hair fans out across the stark white of the hotel pillow.

My lips drop to her neck and place soft kisses on every square inch of skin I can find. Poppy's hands roam my back like she's mapping it out through touch alone. We move together silently. The dirty talk and teasing that usually permeate the air around us in bed is gone, discarded for the moment.

Poppy pushes up on her elbows, giving me space to unclasp her bra. My lips follow the path my fingers make as I push the straps down her shoulders. I drop it off the side of the bed as I move down her body. My fingers hook into the sides of her black lace panties and slowly tug them down her toned legs. When they're free of her feet, they join the bra.

"Lose the briefs." My girl is bossy tonight. It took Poppy a little bit longer to give into her feelings, but I don't blame her not after what I put her through. So, I'll take bossy and impatient Poppy as long as she continues to let me love her. That doesn't mean I won't have a little fun with her, plus she likes it when I use my filthy mouth on her.

Poppy's gaze flows over my torso, catching on my tattoos before moving lower when my fingers slide under the waistband of my briefs.

"Don't rush me, I'm going to take my time with you tonight. I want there to be no doubts in your mind how much I love you. I'm going to worship each and every part of you."

"You're not going to get any arguments from me. I just want you naked when you do it. I love your body and I want to see all of it, now."

Her voice dances with arousal as she talks, and it only serves to feed my ego. My dick gets exponentially harder, jutting up at her praise. I lower myself over her, hovering on my forearms.

"No one has ever made me feel like this before. It's better with you because of what's in here." My hand slides up her ribs and rests right above her heart. Leaning down, I kiss her forehead. "And what's in here. Everything about you turns me on, Poppy."

Poppy's eyelids flutter closed and her back arches under me, searching for that physical connection. I lower myself, giving her what she's looking for. The hand that's resting over her heart sweeps lower, cupping her breast, and a moan slips past her lips.

My gaze drops to Poppy's soft lips parted just slightly, so pretty, and I look forward to spending every night showing her just how much I need her. I roll her nipple between my fingers. Losing myself in my slow exploration of her body, I pull her other nipple into my mouth, circling it with my tongue. Poppy writhes beneath me, brushing against me with each roll of her hips.

I grip her hips, holding her still with one hand while my other slips down between her legs, strumming her swollen clit as my fingers pump in and out.

"I need you, please. You can worship me later," Poppy pleads, her eyes dancing with emotion. "I need you inside me, right now."

Dropping down, I pull her clit into my mouth basking in her sweetness just long enough to have her tugging at my hair.

"*Hendrix*! Oh god. I love you, but I swear if you don't get up here and kiss me while you make love to me, I will never forgive you." She's desperate for me and it's a dream laid out in real life right in front of me.

"No patience tonight."

"No. None. Torture me later. Love me now." Her words are choppy, her head thrashes to the side wildly.

I pump my fingers, curling them just the way she likes two more times before I withdraw, causing her to shudder.

"Anything for you, Poppy, all you have to do is ask."

Before she can respond, I cover her mouth with mine kissing her deeply while I thrust inside her.

"Love the way you feel wrapped around me. You feel like mine. This is just the start for us, Poppy. It's you and me."

Her hands lace together behind my neck drawing me down, our foreheads touching. She moves under me, matching my pace.

"I love you, Hendrix. So much."

Then she buries her head in my shoulder and pants out my name as she comes, tensing around me and triggering my release. We stay wrapped up in each like that, kissing and caressing until I harden again, and we start all over.

Afterwards when we are spooning and Poppy's eyelids are growing heavy from the emotional toll of the night and the ensuing orgasms, I place a soft kiss on her shoulder thinking about the tattoo that decorates the delicate skin there.

"You are my Virginia bluebell. Poppy, you are strong, resilient, and so beautiful that sometimes I can't believe you're real. You are my safe haven, the place I come to recharge. I love you."

She rolls in my arms and kisses me softly before her eyes flutter closed. "I'll be your safe haven forever, Hendrix." I've never heard sweeter words.

EPILOGUE

POPPY

"Poppy, do you need any more moving boxes? I can run downstairs and grab some from Marv," Janet asks from the kitchen where she's busy packing up my cupboard.

"I could use a few more in here."

I hear her shuffling around and then the door closes. She flew in to help me pack up my apartment at her own insistence, claiming she wanted to come to another game anyways. It's been two months since the Chicago trip and Hendrix asked me to move in shortly after we got home. It wasn't even an offer I had to think about.

We had spent every night together when he was in town and sometimes I would sleep in his bed even when he was gone because I felt closer to him there. It doesn't hurt that he thought it was really hot to video chat with me from his bed on the road.

This building is in high demand, so the property manager was fine with me ending my lease early. Hendrix and I agreed that the insulation needed to be fixed, so he paid to have a contractor come in and fix it with the manager's blessing. Neither of us were excited by the prospect of hearing our new neighbors through the wall.

But the real sticking point for Hendrix was the fact that they might hear me through the wall. *"No one gets to hear the sweet sounds you make for me when you come. Those are mine and mine alone."* Then he proved just how good he was at coaxing those sounds out of me.

After the contractor finished the work, he insisted we test it out to be sure that the added insulation did its job. It might have been the highlight of my month. Hendrix came home with an app-controlled vibrator the same day.

He undressed me and laid me down on the bed in the office and teased me relentlessly before he propped my phone up and called himself on video taking the call from the comfort of our bedroom next door. He's an evil genius. Making sure he could see me, since the goal was not to hear me through the wall. Hendrix kept me on edge for what felt like hours before he finally let me come.

Both of us can confirm with confidence that the added insulation eliminated the issues with hearing the neighbors through the wall. Whoever moves in here next won't have to hear us, and we won't have to hear them.

I'm almost completely packed except for some clothes and linens. Combining our household items meant we sold or donated a lot. And Hendrix hired someone to move and reinstall the sound booth after I finished recording my first paid project.

I voiced the female main character for a why choose Christmas novella called The Men of Mistletoe Mountain. So, the help from Janet really wasn't necessary, but I suspect she has ulterior motives.

Janet keeps disappearing and finding reasons to go downstairs to grab something. She and Marv have stayed in touch since the last time she was in town. While Janet hasn't come out and admitted it, I'm pretty sure she's staying with him while she's here. Hendrix is just pretending to be ignorant of the whole situation. I can't blame him; don't ask questions you don't want the answer to.

I stretch the tape across the top of the box of towels to donate and grab a marker writing "Saving Paws Shelter" across the top. I'm recapping the marker when my phone rings, Hendrix's name flashes across the top.

"Hey, Ironman." I answer on speaker phone so I can keep working.

"Hey, Beautiful. I'm almost back. Can you come down to the garage and help me unload? It's more than I realized. I'll be there in about five minutes."

"I'll be right down," I reply, hanging up and pushing off the floor and stretching about my back. I might have gone a little crazy online shopping for some new things to tie our combined furniture and decor together.

When I enter the lobby from the stairwell, I look around for Janet to let her know where I'm going, but don't find her or Marv. I'm not sure I really even want to know what the two of them are getting up to. Hendrix is backing into the loading area when I push through the door to the garage.

After he puts the SUV in park, he opens the rear hatch and hurries around to help me. It didn't seem like this much in the online shopping cart.

"Go a little nuts? I think you bought out all of Crate & Barrel." Hendrix pulls me to him and drops a quick kiss on my lips. Even now those little touches still make me swoon. I thought I might get desensitized to it, but I'm thrilled to be wrong on that count.

"There should be a cart right around the other side of that wall," I tell him, pointing in that direction. Movement catches my eye as Hendrix turns to look.

"Oh shit." The words tumble out before I can stop them and only draw Hendrix's attention to it. There's a car rocking with steamed-up windows tucked into the corner where the garage storage area is. I don't need to look through the poorly tinted windows to know who's in there.

"Is that Marv's car?" Hendrix's face twists with realization.

"Um, I'm not sure." I lie and it's not even a good lie. I don't hide it. "I'll go grab the cart while you unload these boxes," I say, trying to pull his attention back to me, but I'm not fast enough.

A loud moan shatters the silence. "God yes, Marv. That's it." There's no question now, Janet's voice is clear as day.

"Way to go, Marv?" I say, covering my mouth to keep from laughing as I drop the bag back into the car and start loading the boxes back up. "This can wait. Give me the keys and head upstairs. I'll move the car."

Hendrix hands me the keys silently and walks away looking like he might just lose his lunch on his shoes.

Shutting the rear door, I move the SUV, parking it a few spaces down from where Marv's car has stopped rocking. After locking the doors, I turn to walk back inside when laughter and tangled limbs come pouring out of the back of the small car.

Janet straightens up, running her hands over silver her hair to smooth it down as Marv lays a kiss on her cheek. When she looks up, she freezes. Her gaze darts between the car and then me, then they land on the SUV behind me, and she pales.

"Was Hendrix out here with you?" Her voice is more timid than I've ever heard it. I almost feel bad for her, but I can't find a trace of shame on her face so I just nod and shrug. It's a struggle to contain my laughter.

"I sent him inside, but I'd give him a few minutes to gather himself before you come up. Maybe stop in the bathroom and fix your lipstick."

Her hand comes up to her mouth, fingertips brushing against her lips, and then laughter spills out of both of us.

THE END

Keep reading for a sneak peek at Delilah & Cruz's story with a excerpt from All or Nothing.

Pre-Order All or Nothing Now

ALL OR NOTHING

Prologue -DELILAH

July- Three Years Earlier

He's late...again.

I check the clock on my phone, seeing that he's now forty-five minutes late for our date. Brad's assistant called to let me know he was stuck in a meeting with an important client. There's always an important client. I remind myself that once this acquisition goes through next month, he'll have more time to prioritize us again.

I strum my polished fingernails against the bar top, debating my next move. There's no telling how much longer it will be, and I have to be up at 4:00 a.m. to open the coffee shop. My options are order something here and eat alone or walk back to the apartment, scrounge for food, and eat alone. Either way, I am eating alone tonight. I tap out a text to let Brad know I'm ordering. Then I down my wine and signal the bartender for a menu.

As I wait for the bartender to walk over, I brush my hands over the soft fabric of my dress, toying with the hem. I could be home in my leggings watching mindless tv, not being stood up in a bar by my longtime boyfriend. What's so important that he can't even be bothered to show up?

My dress is deep purple and hugs my curves. Normally it makes me feel sexy, but right now it's just a reminder that I'm not the priority tonight. I even went through the extra effort of curling my hair and shaving my freaking legs.

Being the owner of a coffee shop and bakery means I spend ninety percent of my life with my blonde hair in a bun and flour smeared across my face. After waking up at four in the morning, putting on something other than leggings and an oversized t-shirt felt like the equivalent of running a marathon. But it looks like I'll be the only one appreciating my efforts tonight.

"Do you mind if I take this seat?" someone asks as I look over the options on the menu, the bartender just slid across the bar top.

"It's all yours," I say without looking up from the menu.

"Thank you," he says in a rich voice — a voice I can't ignore. There is something warm and inviting about it. I also can't help but notice a faint accent, the southern kind, that makes women everywhere swoon.

My curiosity wins out as I turn to the man next to me. The first thing I notice when I look up is his chocolate - colored, intensely dark eyes — framed by lashes that are unfairly thick. Dark stubble covers his square jaw and when he catches me looking, he smiles, revealing the most ador- able dimples I have ever seen on a man.

It's the only thing adorable about him, everything else screams masculine sex appeal. Even seated he towers over my five-foot-three frame. His broad shoulders stretch the seams of his crisp white shirt which plays off the sliver of warm bronze skin showing where he has the top three buttons undone.

"Have you eaten here before? The crab cakes are excellent," he says, still smiling warmly at me, but I notice the smile doesn't quite reach his eyes.

"I haven't. Thanks for the recommendation. Any thoughts on desserts?"

"Don't bother, they aren't very good." He leans in closer ensuring that the bartender and other patrons can't overhear. "They had a baker on hand, but she quit, and they haven't replaced her."

"How often do you eat here?" I eye him curiously. Is he the owner or maybe just a regular?

"Too often. I just moved to Denver and live close by, it's become an easy alternative to cooking while I settle in."

Catching the bartender's eye, I ask for the crab cakes skipping the dessert. When he walks away, I turn back toward my new friend.

"This is my first time here. My apartment is right down the street too and own a coffee shop nearby, but I usually prefer someplace a little less...." Considering my words, I don't want to offend him since he is a regular, but I am honest to a fault. "I was supposed to meet my boyfriend, but he's running late. Honestly, this place really isn't my vibe. It seems kind of pretentious."

He lets out a husky laugh, and I watch the pain in his eyes fade a little. "It's very pretentious, but the food is fantastic. I always grab my food to go. I'm afraid if I stay here too long they'll convert me." He looks pointedly around the restaurant pushing his wavy dark off his forehead.

Men in suits or button-down shirts fill the table. It's like the Stepford wives, but with cufflinks and tumblers of gin.

"Oh my god... they're all clones." I can't stop the laugh that escapes me. "I don't know you, but please don't turn into one of them. We don't need more Chad in Finance clones."

The wicked smile that he gives me has a dangerous edge, and I forget about calling his dimples adorable earlier.

"Not a chance, Hermosa." His accent thickens, making every female instinct I have stand up and take notice. I might have a boyfriend, but I'm not immune to a power move like that.

The way the words roll off his tongue makes my neck prickle with heat. He's flirting with me, and I'm supposed to be here with Brad. The two of them could not be more different; Brad with his buttoned-up attitude, and his blond hair. His lean build from years of road biking, the man sitting next to me, the epitome of tall, dark, and dangerously handsome.

"Hey Dee, sorry I'm late," Brad says, startling me as he comes strolling up beside me. For a moment, I feel guilty that I was allowing this stranger to flirt with me. That thought is abruptly squashed when I realize Brad is completely absorbed in his phone as he leans against the bar.

"Should we grab a table?" He asks, wholly oblivious to the text I sent him, letting him know I wasn't waiting to order. "I was going to get the crab cakes to go. My new friend recommended them to me." He holds out his hand to Brad. "Cruz."

"Hey, thanks for keeping my girl company until I could get here." Brad gives his hand a pump as he sizes up Cruz.

"My pleasure." He returns, but his tone is clipped, like he's not at all impressed with Brad.

The bartender brings Cruz his to-go container, and he stands to leave. Before he walks away, he looks over his shoulder. "What's the name of your coffee shop? I have been drinking coffee from the corner store. It's terrible." He makes a face like he just took a sip from said coffee, causing his nose to wrinkle.

"Buns and Roses."

"Maybe I'll see you there, *Dee*, is it?"

I shake my head. Brad is the only person who has ever called me Dee. And he only gets away with it because I thought the fact he gave me a nickname was endearing when we started seeing each other in college.

"It's Delilah. Enjoy your dinner, don't let the clones get you on the way out." I tell him, waving as Brad continues tapping away at his phone.

Warm laughter rumbles free from his chest before he walks through the bar and out the door, disappearing into the crowd on the sidewalk.

"Do you mind if we eat here? One of the partners was going to stop by for a drink." Brad glance at his phone again frown at whatever lights up the screen.

As a recovering people pleaser, my first instinct is to default to what will make everyone else happy, but I am working hard to put myself first when I can. Tonight is one of those times when I need to do what's best for me, even if it still feels foreign. "I'm going to get my food to go. It's already eight and opening Buns and Roses comes early."

Even after the words leave my mouth, I have to give myself a mental pep talk, reminding myself that we were supposed to meet at seven for dinner. I am aggravated that he was late and would still ask me to stay when he knows how hard that is with my schedule.

"We need to find you some help at the coffee shop, so you aren't in there so early every morning. I need you by my side at some of these dinners."

"I'm not ready for that yet. Financially, it's a burden I don't want, and I don't want to hand the baking off to someone else. The shop is still too new to take that risk."

He pouts, but wraps his arms around my waist. "Someday, right?"

"Yes, someday." I mentally high-five myself for sticking up for my needs. Brad just wants to spend time together. I don't fault him for that, but sometimes it feels like my career becomes a bit of an afterthought in the shadow of his career goals.

"I hate that our schedules conflict so often these days. We need more time together." Brad drops a kiss on my cheek as the bartender brings my food over in a to-go container. "I'm glad I got to see you, even if it was only for a few minutes."

It's on the tip of my tongue to remind him we could have had plenty of time together if he had shown up on time for our date. I press my lips shut, resisting the urge. Reminding myself that this is all part of our plan.

We have been working toward it since our freshman year of college. I open my coffee shop and he makes partner by the time he's thirty. Providing us financial stability and the foundation to get married and start a family together. *His goals support my goals.* I repeat the mantra in my head as I push up on my toes to give him a kiss goodbye.

"You have fun schmoozing." I wipe the lipstick off his cheek with my thumb and grab my food from the bar top—my bed calling my name.

CRUZ

JULY - THREE YEARS EARLIER

Looping through the park, I run back toward downtown Denver. My lungs burn with the exertion of pushing myself hard. Just because it's the All-Star Break doesn't mean I need to be useless. My trade to Denver happened in the middle of the season. I have a lot to prove myself to a lot of people. To myself, that I'm worth the trade. To the fans, that I will deliver now when their team needs it the most. To the St. Louis Commanders, that trading me was a mistake. And to Jarett, I can live out this dream for both of us.

I slow to a walk once I hit the six-mile mark, stopping to stretch out my legs before returning to my new apartment. I'm still not used to walking in the door and not finding his shoes scattered across the mat.

Leaving behind St. Louis and the house I shared with my younger brother Jarrett was just one of the many difficult things I have had to do this year. There's nothing wrong with Denver. I just never expected to be here. This was supposed to be the year that Jarrett and I got to live out all our dreams. Instead, I moved across the country alone.

My therapist suggested I look at this trade—and move—as a fresh start after everything that happened in St. Louis. The move has helped despite feeling out of my element. Being out of the space we shared while I played baseball for the Commanders and he played for the local affiliate team, has helped me start the healing process.

Lost in my thoughts, the scent of coffee hits me when the door to the store in front of me swings open. Two women dressed for corporate jobs in the plethora of office buildings in this area step onto the sidewalk with extra tall coffees in hand. I look at the sign and see the words Buns and Roses scrawled across the windows in white script.

The memory of meeting Delilah at Tony's a few weeks ago flashes through my mind. Before I give it too much thought, I am pulling open the door to the coffee shop and step inside.

"Be with you in just a minute," Delilah says sweetly from the back. Her voice sounds lighter than it did that night, and I wonder if it's because this place makes her happy. Or because she's not stressed about her douche of boyfriend being late.

So, this is Delilah's coffee shop. I look around the space while I wait. Plants line the wide wood shelves behind the counter and there's a jukebox in the corner playing the song Peaches by the American Presidents. The décor is trendy, with white subway tile and a handwritten chalkboard menu. The details add a little quirkiness to the atmosphere.

Delilah walks backward out of the doorway carrying a tray of baked goods and her hips shimmy to the music. She's wearing her long blonde hair piled on top of her head, revealing her slender neck. Her heart-shaped ass is encased in cut-off jean shorts that elongate her toned legs. She's short. Just a couple of inches over five feet if I had to guess.

The last time I saw her she was dressed for a date and looked beautiful with her long blonde hair curling down her back. I noticed her as soon as I stepped into the bar, but I think I like this version even better. She looks comfortable here in a way she didn't at Tony's.

When she turns around her plump lips stretch into a smile. Setting the tray on the counter she wipes her hands on the folded-over apron cinched around her waist accentuating the way it nips in over her maroon shirt. A shirt that has a pair of cinnamon rolls right across her chest. As if my eyes weren't already drawn to her perfect set of breasts, now I will have to put in extra effort not to stare at them.

"Can't handle any more corner store coffee, Cruz?" She asks while she moves the scones and pastries around in the bakery case to make room for the ones on the tray.

"The smell of good coffee lured me in." Everything about her coffee shop is welcoming. It was pointless to fight the pull.

"Excellent, my evil plan is working." She wiggles her eyebrows which should make her look ridiculous but she's so carefree that it's adorable.

"Is your evil plan to lure attractive men into your clutches with a siren song of coffee aroma and then keep them here forever, feeding them baked goods? Where do you keep them all? Is there a dungeon in the basement?" I peer around the shop like I am searching out a hidden trap door.

She gasps dramatically pausing her work and standing to her full height, propping her hand on her hip as she glides her eyes over me. The shirt I'm wearing is plastered to me from my run—clinging to my upper body and consequently showing off all the work I put in to be at the top of my game as a professional athlete.

"Did one of them escape and spill my secrets?" Her voice wavers as she brings her eyes back up to my face.

"No, I'm just wildly observant. You might look sweet and innocent, but I'm on to you. Only an evil genius can make coffee and baked goods that look and smell this mouthwatering."

She steps over to the bakery case to continue refilling it. I am helpless to do anything but follow her. I lean forward to rest my elbows on the counter, watching her work. For the first time in months, the air around me feels a little less heavy. Everything is a bit easier in her presence.

Maybe because she doesn't know about my past, there's no pity when she looks at me. Unlike my teammates, she knows nothing about Jarrett or what I have been through. I noticed it that night at Tony's too—she calms the storm that's been raging inside me.

I haven't been able to get Delilah out of my mind since I saw her at Tony's. She intrigues me more than she should considering she has a boyfriend, and even if she were single, I'm not in the right headspace to date anyone. It's why I have avoided coming in here since she told me the name that night.

"The crab cakes were delightful the other night. I think that means that I owe you a recommendation as repayment. What's your guilty pleasure?"

"Pleasure never makes me feel guilty, Hermosa." Pink stains her chest and crawls up her cheeks. Leaning in further I crowd her as she works, hoping I can get another reaction out of her. I know I shouldn't, but I can't seem to help myself. Even if I am not looking for a relationship, flirting with her is fun and she makes it so damn easy.

"I have a weakness for caramel and cinnamon," I say, my eyes flicking down to her shirt before I look back up and find her eyes wide. "I'll try a sticky bun and an iced coffee."

Shaking her head, she moves quickly, grabbing the sticky bun with a tong and setting it on a plate. Our hands brush when I grab it from her. Delilah freezes for a moment before dropping her hand and getting to work on my coffee. She's flustered and I can't get enough of it.

When she finishes preparing my coffee she brings it to the counter, setting it down with a small smile. It's not the same as the ones I got earlier, Delilah is putting space between us intentionally. I pushed her too far with my flirting and now she's retreating.

I feel guilty but only because I don't want her to be uncomfortable. Maybe I should feel wrong flirting when I know she's with someone else. But in the few minutes I spent with her and Brad it was easy to see that he's not good enough for her. Who leaves their girlfriend waiting in a bar for them and then doesn't even have the decency to put away his phone long enough to say hello properly?

I bring the coffee to my lips. It's good. Just sweet enough without being too much. "This is way better than that sludge at the corner store. I hope you're ready Delilah, you just became my new best friend—I'm going to be here every day."

That earns me a laugh, her head tips back and her eyes twinkle. It's the most addictive thing I have ever heard.

That's it, Hermosa give me more of that sweet sound.

"I'll believe it when I see it. You'll be sick of me in no time." She says return to her work behind the counter.

"Mhmmm... There's still a lot you don't know about me. If I say I am going to do something I do it. I am also competitive as hell and that sounded like a challenge." Her eyes drop down to the Bandits logo across the front of my shirt.

"The same could be said for me. I can be cutthroat when the stakes are right. You never told me what brought you to Denver."

"I play for the Denver Bandits. I was traded here from St. Louis."

AUTHOR'S NOTE

Thank you so much for reading All on the Line! I hope you enjoyed reading it as much as I enjoyed bringing Hendrix and Poppy to life. If you did, it would mean everything if you write a review or rate it on Amazon, or share your love on Instagram. As a new indie author, each review and share helps to make this dream a reality.

Writing this book was a labor of love. There's no way I ever would've finished it if it hadn't been rewarding and fun. I'm grateful that I had the support system to do it because it was also really freaking hard. There were late nights and early mornings. Tears were shed, both good and bad. The thing I'm most proud of isn't the finished product but that I never gave up, but I certainly didn't do it alone. They deserve their moment in the spotlight and a little gratitude.

To my family, thank you for cheering me on every step of the way, even when it pulled me away at times. Your belief and encouragement as I chased down this dream made it possible for me to keep going when things got hard. There's nothing more motivating than your child asking every day if "the book is done yet." This is all for you! I love you.

Katie, your reaction when I told you I was planning to write my first book set the tone for the whole experience. Had you questioned me instead of openly encouraging and offering me support, I don't think I would've followed through. Thanks for being the first person to lay eyes on that very rough draft and lifting me up throughout the process. It's been fun to watch you take your own writing journey alongside me, and I couldn't be prouder of you.

Ashley S, the cover you created for All on the Line far exceeded my expectations and brought the book to life.

Jenn, your patience with me as I figure out how all things book writing and editing work has not gone unnoticed. I know this book wouldn't be what it is today if you hadn't pushed me throughout the process to make it better without ever making me feel like a moron. Thank you for all your hard work editing my baby.

Mom and Dad, you have been fearless champions of me throughout this process and have definitely seen some things on my Instagram I'd prefer you hadn't. Do me a favor and when you read the book, pretend someone else wrote it, and please, never mention any of the spicy scenes.

I was lucky enough to find the world's best beta team and I still have no idea how. Allison, Bre, Becca, Cara, Lynsey, Katelyn, and Loriana, I hope you all know how much I appreciate you. Your unending support and willingness to be my sounding board has saved me more times than I can count. I had so much fun getting to know you all throughout this process, and I hope you all keep reading my ARCs and telling it like it is.

To my readers, without you guys, my books are just words on paper. Thank you for taking a chance on this indie author and helping to make my dreams come true. Each word, page, download, and purchase, means more than I can express.

I'm not done with the Bandits. You'll get to read Delilah and Cruz's story next, and I hope you're ready because it's a slow burn. But it's worth the wait, I promise. Everyone will get their day in the sun, and there might even be a detour to small-town romance before we find out what happens to all Bandits.

Much love, Lo

Made in United States
North Haven, CT
31 December 2024

63794734R00231